The Acts of King Arthur and His Noble Knights

John Steinbeck was born in Salinas, California, in 1902.
After studying science at Stanford University he worked
successively as labourer, druggist, caretaker, fruit-picker and
surveyor. His first novel, *Cup of Gold* (1929), was about
Morgan the pirate. *The Grapes of Wrath* (1939), his most
popular book, tells of a migratory family seeking work in
California; it was awarded the Pulitzer Prize, and has been
compared in its influence to *Uncle Tom's Cabin*. His other
novels include *East of Eden*, *Of Mice and Men*, *The Pearl*,
Sweet Thursday and *Cannery Row*, all published by Pan Books.
Also available in Pan are several collections of his short stories,
and *Journal of a Novel – The 'East of Eden' Letters*. In 1962
Steinbeck was awarded the Nobel Prize for Literature.
He died in 1968.

John Steinbeck ✦ ✦ ✦ the acts of king arthur and his noble knights ✦ ✦ ✦ ✦ from the Winchester

mss of Thomas Malory and other sources ✦ ✦ ✦

edited by Chase Horton

Pan Books in association with Heinemann

First published 1976 by William Heinemann Ltd
This edition published 1979 by Pan Books Ltd,
Cavaye Place, London SW10 9PG
in association with William Heinemann Ltd
© 1976 by the Estate of John Steinbeck
Acknowledgement is made to Oxford University Press
for permission to use portions of
The Works of Sir Thomas Malory
© Eugène Vinaver 1967
ISBN 0 330 25600 9
Made and printed in Great Britain by
Cox & Wyman Ltd, London, Reading and Fakenham

contents

Whan of IX wyntre age

I toke siege wyth Kinge Arthurs felyship emonge knyghtes most orgulus and worshyppful as ony on lyve

In tho dayes grate lack was of squyres of hardynesse and noble herte to bere shylde and glayve to bockle harnyss and succoure woundid knyghtes

Than yit chaunced that squyre lyke dutyes fell to my systir of vi wyntre age that for jantyl prouesse had no felawe lyvynge

Yt haps somtymes in saddnesse and pytie that who faythful servys ys not faythful sene so my fayre and sikker systir squyre dures yet undubbed

Wherefore thys daye I mak amendys to my power and rayse hir knyghte and gyff hir loudis

And fro thys hower she shall be hyght Syr Mayrie Stynebec of the Vayle Salynis

God gyvve hir worshypp saunz jaupardye

Jehan Stynebec de Montray

Miles

When I was nine, I took siege with King Arthur's fellowship of knights most proud and worshipful as any alive. —In those days there was a great lack of hardy and noble-hearted squires to bear shield and sword, to buckle harness, and to succour wounded knights. —Then it chanced that squire-like duties fell to my sister of six years, who for gentle prowess had no peer living. —It sometimes happens in sadness and pity that faithful service is not appreciated, so my fair and loyal sister remained unrecognized as squire. —Wherefore this day I make amends within my power and raise her to knighthood and give her praise. —And from this hour she shall be called Sir Marie Steinbeck of Salinas Valley. —God give her worship without peril

John Steinbeck of Monterey

Knight

Whan of IX wyntre age

I toke siege wyth Kinge Arthures felyship emonge knyghtes
most orgulus and worshyppful as ony on lyve

In tho dayes grate lack was of squyres of hardynesse and noble
herte to bere shylde and glayve to bettle harnys and succoure
wounded knyghtes

Than yt chaunced that squyre lytle dutyes fell to my systyr of
VI wyntre age that for gentyl prouesse had no felawe lyvynge

Yt haps somtymes in saddnesse and cythe that who faythful servys
ys not successful sene so my fayre and skilfulr systyr squyre dutys
yet undubbed

Wherfore thys daye I make amendys to my power and rayse
hir knyghtste and gyff hir londis

And fro thys howre she shall be hyght syr Mayne Stynebec
of the Vayle Salynis

God gyve hir worshypp saunz jaupardye

      Jehan Stynebec de Montray
      Miles

introduction

by John Steinbeck

Some people there are who, being grown, forget the horrible task of learning to read. It is perhaps the greatest single effort that the human undertakes, and he must do it as a child. An adult is rarely successful in the undertaking – the reduction of experience to a set of symbols. For a thousand thousand years these humans have existed and they have only learned this trick – this magic – in the final ten thousand of the thousand thousand.

I do not know how usual my experience is, but I have seen in my children the appalled agony of trying to learn to read. They, at least, have my experience.

I remember that words – written or printed – were devils, and books, because they gave me pain, were my enemies.

Some literature was in the air around me. The Bible I absorbed through my skin. My uncles exuded Shakespeare, and *Pilgrim's Progress* was mixed with my mother's milk. But these things came into my ears. They were sounds, rhythms, figures. Books were printed demons – the tongs and thumbscrews of outrageous persecution. And then, one day, an aunt gave me a book and fatuously ignored my resentment. I stared at the black print with hatred, and then, gradually, the pages opened and let me in. The magic happened. The Bible and Shakespeare and *Pilgrim's Progress* belonged to everyone. But this was mine – It was a cut version of the Caxton *Morte d'Arthur* of Thomas Malory. I loved the old spelling of the words – and the words no longer used. Perhaps a passionate love for the English language opened to me from this one book. I was delighted to find out paradoxes – that *cleave* means both to stick together and to cut apart; that *host* means both an enemy and a welcoming friend; that *king* and *gens* (people) stem from the same root. For a long time, I had a secret language – *yclept* and *hyght*, *wist* – and *accord* meaning peace, and *entente* meaning purpose, and *fyaunce* meaning promise. Moving my lips, I pronounced the letter known as *thorn*, *þ*, like a 'p', which it resembles, instead of like a 'th'. But in my town, the first word of Ye Olde Pye Shoppe was pronounced 'yee', so I guess my betters were no better off than I. It was much later that I discovered that 'y' had been substituted for the lost *p*. But beyond the glorious and secret words – 'And when the chylde is borné lete it be delyvered to me at yonder privy posterne uncrystened' – oddly enough I knew the words from whispering them to myself. The very strangeness of the language dyd me enchante, and vaulted me into an ancient scene.

And in that scene were all the vices that ever were – and courage and sadness and frustration, but particularly gallantry – perhaps the only single quality of man that the West has invented. I think my sense of right and wrong, my feeling of *noblesse oblige*, and any thought I may have against the oppressor and for the oppressed, came from this secret book. It did not outrage my sensibilities as nearly all the children's books did. It did not seem strange to me that Uther Pendragon wanted the wife of his vassal and took her by trickery. I was not frightened to find that there were evil knights, as well as noble ones. In my own town there were men who wore the clothes of virtue whom I knew to be bad. In pain or sorrow or confusion, I went back to my magic book. Children are violent and cruel – and good – and I was all of these – and all of these were in the secret book. If I could not choose my way at the crossroads of love and loyalty, neither could Lancelot. I could understand the darkness of Mordred because he was in me too; and there was some Galahad in me, but perhaps not enough. The Grail feeling was there, however, deep-planted, and perhaps always will be.

Later, because the spell persisted, I went to the sources – to the *Black Book of Caermarthen*, to 'The Mabinogion and Other Welsh Tales' from the *Red Book of Hergist*, to *De Excidio Britanniae* by Gildas, to *Giraldus Cambrensis Historia Britonum*, and to many of the 'Frensshe' books Malory speaks of. And with the sources, I read the scholarly diggings and scrabblings – Chambers, Sommer, Gollancz, Saintsbury – but I always came back to Malory, or perhaps I should say to Caxton's Malory, since that was the only Malory there was until a little over thirty years ago, when it was announced that an unknown Malory manuscript had been discovered in the Fellows Library of

Winchester College. The discovery excited me but, being no scholar but only an enthusiast, I had neither the opportunity nor the qualification to inspect the find until in 1947 Eugène Vinaver, Professor of French Language and Literature at the University of Manchester, edited his great three-volume edition of the works of Sir Thomas Malory, for Oxford University, taken from the Winchester manuscript. No better man could have been chosen for the work than Professor Vinaver, with his great knowledge, not only of the 'Frensshe' books, but also of the Welsh, Irish, Scottish, Breton, and English sources. He has brought to the work, beyond his scholarly approach, the feeling of wonder and delight so often lacking in a schoolman's methodology.

For a long time I have wanted to bring to present-day usage the stories of King Arthur and the Knights of the Round Table. These stories are alive even in those of us who have not read them. And, in our day, we are perhaps impatient with the old words and the stately rhythms of Malory. My own first and continuing enchantment with these things is not generally shared. I wanted to set them down in plain present-day speech for my own young sons, and for other sons not so young – to set the stories down in meaning as they were written, leaving out nothing and adding nothing – perhaps to compete with the moving pictures, the comic-strip travesties which are the only available source for those children and others of today who are impatient with the difficulties of Malory's spelling and use of archaic words. If I can do this and keep the wonder and the magic, I shall be pleased and gratified. In no sense do I wish to rewrite Malory, or reduce him, or change him, or soften or sentimentalize him. I believe the stories are great enough to survive my tampering, which at best will make the history available to more readers, and at worst can't hurt Malory very much. At long last, I am abandoning the Caxton of my first love for the Winchester, which seems to me more knee-deep in Malory than Caxton was. I am indebted to Professor Eugène Vinaver for his making the Winchester manuscript available.

For my own part, I can only ask that my readers include me in the request of Sir Thomas Malory when he says: 'And I pray you all that redyth this tale to pray for him that this wrote that God sende hym good delyverance and sone and hastely – Amen.'

MERLIN

When Uther Pendragon was King of England his vassal, the Duke of Cornwall, was reported to have committed acts of war against the land. Then Uther ordered the duke to attend his court and to bring with him his wife, Igraine, who was famed for her wisdom and beauty.

When the duke arrived before the king, the great lords of the council made peace between them so that the king offered his friendship and his hospitality. Then Uther looked at the Lady Igraine and saw that she was as beautiful as he had heard. He loved her and desired her and begged her to lie with him, but Igraine was a faithful wife and she refused the king.

She spoke privately to the duke, her husband, saying, 'I believe that you were not sent for because of transgression. The king has planned to dishonour you through me. Therefore I beg you, my husband, that we may creep away from this danger and ride in the night to our own castle, for the king will not tolerate my refusal.'

And, as she wished, they went away so secretly that neither the king nor his council were aware of their going.

When Uther discovered their flight he was filled with rage. He called the lords together and told them of the duke's treachery. The noble council, seeing and fearing his anger, advised the king to send messengers ordering the duke and Igraine to return at once, for, they said, 'If he should refuse your summons it will be your duty and your right to make war against him and destroy him.'

And it was so done. The messengers galloped after the duke and came back with the curt reply that neither his wife nor he would return.

Then the enraged Uther sent a second message advising the duke to defend himself, because within forty days the king would drag him from his strongest castle.

Thus warned, the duke provisioned and armed his two best

fortresses. He sent Igraine to the Castle of Tintagel on the high cliffs above the sea, while he himself defended Terrabil, a thick-walled fort with many gates and secret doors.

King Uther gathered an army and marched against the duke. He pitched his tents about the Castle Terrabil and laid siege to it. In the assault and fierce defence, many good men were killed, but neither side could gain the advantage until at last Uther fell sick from anger and frustration and from longing for the fair Igraine.

Then the noble knight Sir Ulfius went to Uther's tent and asked the nature of his illness.

'I will tell you,' said the king. 'I am sick from anger and from love and there are no medicines for those.'

'My lord,' Sir Ulfius said, 'I shall go in search of Merlin the Wizard. That wise and clever man can brew a remedy to make your heart glad.' And Sir Ulfius rode out to look for Merlin.

Now Merlin was a wise and subtle man with strange and secret powers of prophecy and those deceptions of the ordinary and the obvious which are called magic. Merlin knew the winding channels of the human mind, and also he was aware that a simple open man is most receptive when he is mystified, and Merlin delighted in mystery. Therefore, as if by chance, the searching knight Sir Ulfius came upon a ragged beggar in his path who asked him whom he sought.

The knight was not accustomed to be questioned by such a one, and he did not deign to reply.

Then the ragged man laughed and said, 'There's no need to tell me. I know. You are looking for Merlin. Look no further. I am Merlin.'

'You – ? You are a beggar,' said Sir Ulfius.

Merlin chuckled at his joke. 'I am also Merlin,' he said. 'And if King Uther will promise me the reward I wish, I shall give him what his heart desires. And the gift I wish will be more to his honour and profit than to mine.'

Sir Ulfius was wonderstruck and he said, 'If this is true and if your demand is reasonable, I can promise that you shall have it.'

'Ride back to the king then; I will follow you as quickly as I can.'

Then Sir Ulfius was glad, and he turned about and put his horse to great speed until he came at last to the tent where Uther lay ill, and he told the king he had found Merlin.

'Where is he?' the king demanded.

'My lord,' said Ulfius, 'he is afoot. He will come as soon as he can,' and at that moment he saw that Merlin was already standing in the entrance of the tent, and Merlin smiled, for he took joy in causing wonder.

Uther saw him and welcomed him and Merlin said brusquely, 'Sir, I know every corner of your heart and mind. And if you will swear by your anointed kingship to grant me my wish, you shall have what I know your heart desires.'

And so great was Uther's eagerness that he swore by the four Evangelists to keep his promise.

Then Merlin said, 'Sir this is my desire. The first time you make love to Igraine she will conceive a child by you. When that child is born it must be given to me to do with as I wish. But I do promise that this will be to your honour and to the child's advantage. Do you agree?'

'It shall be as you wish,' said the king.

'Then rise and make yourself ready,' Merlin said. 'This very night you will lie with Igraine in the Castle of Tintagel by the sea.'

'How can that be?' the king asked.

And Merlin said, 'By my arts I will cause her to believe that you are the duke, her husband. Sir Ulfius and I will go with you, but we will wear the appearance of two of the duke's trusted knights. I must warn you, though, when you come to the castle, speak as little as possible or you may be discovered. Say that you are weary and ill and get quickly to bed. And, in the morning, mind you do not rise until I come for you. Now make ready, for Tintagel is ten miles from here.'

They prepared themselves and mounted and rode away. But the duke, from the walls of the Castle Terrabil, saw King Uther ride away from the siege lines, and knowing the king's forces to be leaderless, he waited until nightfall and then attacked in force from the gates of the castle, and in the fight the duke was killed, a full three hours before the king arrived at Tintagel.

When Uther and Merlin and Sir Ulfius rode through the

starlit darkness towards the sea, the fog moved restlessly over the moors like wispy ghosts in floating clothes. Half-formed mist people crept with them and the forms of riders grew changeable like figures of cloud. When they came to the guarded gates of Tintagel on its high sharp rock above the whispering sea, the sentries saluted the recognized forms of the duke, and Sir Brastias and Sir Jordanus, two of his trusted men. And in the dim passages of the castle the lady Igraine welcomed her husband and dutifully led him to her chamber. Then King Uther lay with Igraine and that night she conceived a child.

When daylight came, Merlin appeared as he had promised. And in the misty light Uther kissed the lady Igraine and hastily departed. The sleepy sentries opened the gates to their supposed lord and his retainers and the three rode away into the mist of morning.

And later, when news came to Igraine that her husband was dead, and had been dead when the form of him came to lie with her, she was troubled and filled with sad wonder. But she was alone now and afraid, and she mourned her lord in private and did not speak of it.

Now that the duke was dead, the true reason for the war was lost, and the king's barons begged him to make peace with Igraine. The king smiled secretly and let himself be persuaded. He asked Sir Ulfius to arrange a meeting and very soon the lady and the king came together.

Then Sir Ulfius spoke to the barons in the presence of the king and Igraine. 'What can be wrong here?' he said. 'Our king is a strong and lusty knight and he is wifeless. My lady Igraine is wise and beautiful'–he paused and then continued–'and free to marry. It would be a joy to all of us if the king would consent to make Igraine his queen.'

Then the barons shouted their agreement and urged the king to make it so. And, like the lusty knight he was, Uther allowed himself to be persuaded, and in all haste and with joy and mirth they were married in the morning.

Igraine had three daughters by the duke and the wedding fever spread, at Uther's wish and suggestion. King Lot of Lothian and Orkney married the eldest daughter Margawse, and King Nentres of Garlot wedded the second daughter Elaine.

Igraine's third daughter, Morgan le Fay, was too young for marriage. She was put to school in a nunnery, and there she learned so much of magic and necromancy that she became a mistress of these secret matters.

Then, within half a year, Queen Igraine grew great with her coming child. And one night, as Uther lay beside her, he tested her truthfulness and her innocence. He asked her by the faith she owed him who was the father of her child and the queen was deeply troubled to answer.

Uther said, 'Do not be dismayed. Only tell me the truth and I shall love you the more for it no matter what it is.'

'Sir,' said Igraine, 'I will indeed tell you the truth although I do not understand it. On the night when my husband was killed, and after he was dead, if the reports of his knights are true, there came to me in my Castle of Tintagel a man exactly like my husband in speech and appearance – and in other ways. And with him came two of his knights known to me: Sir Brastias and Sir Jordanus. And so I went to bed with him as I ought to with my lord. And on that night, I swear unto God, this child was conceived. I am puzzled, my lord, for it cannot have been the duke. And I do not know or understand more than this.'

Then King Uther was glad, for he found his queen truthful. He cried out, 'That is the exact truth as you tell it. For it was I myself who came to you in the likeness of your husband. It was arranged by the secret device of Merlin. Therefore, do not be puzzled or frightened any longer, for I am the father of your child.'

And the queen was easier, for she had been deeply troubled by the mystery.

Not long after this Merlin came to the king saying, 'Sir, the time draws near. We must plan for the rearing of your child when it is born.'

'I remember my promise,' said Uther. 'It shall be as you advise.'

Then Merlin said, 'I suggest then one of your lords who is a faithful and an honourable man. His name is Sir Ector and he has lands and castles in many parts of England and Wales. Send for this man to come to you. And if you are satisfied, require of him that he put his own child to nurse with another woman so that his wife may suckle yours. And when your child is born, as you promised, it must be delivered to me, unchristened and unnamed; and I will take it away secretly, to Sir Ector.'

When Sir Ector came to Uther he promised to rear the child, and because of this the king gave him great rewards of lands.

And when Queen Igraine came to be delivered, the king commanded the knights and two ladies to wrap the child in cloth of gold and to carry him through a little postern gate and give him to a poor man who would be waiting there.

Thus was the child delivered to Merlin, who carried it to Sir Ector, and his wife nursed the baby at her own breast. Then Merlin brought a holy man to christen the child and it was named Arthur.

Within two years of the birth of Arthur, a wasting sickness fell on Uther Pendragon. Then, seeing the king helpless, his enemies raided the realm and overthrew his knights and killed many of his people. And Merlin sent to the king and said gruffly, 'You do not have the right to lie here in your bed, no matter what your illness. You must go into the field to lead your men, even if you are carried there in a horse litter, for your enemies will never be defeated until you yourself are there. Only then will you win a victory.'

King Uther agreed to this, and his knights carried him out and placed him on a litter between two horses, and in this way he led his army against his enemies. At St Albans they met a great force of invaders from the north and joined battle. And on that day Sir Ulfius and Sir Brastias performed great deeds of arms, and King Uther's men took heart and attacked with fury and killed many of the enemy and put the rest to flight. When it was over the king returned to London to celebrate his victory. But his strength was gone and he fell into a coma, and for three days and nights he was paralysed and could not speak. His barons were sad and apprehensive and they asked Merlin what they should do.

Then Merlin said, 'Only God has the remedy. But if all of you will come before the king tomorrow in the morning, I shall through the help of God try to make him speak.' And in the morning the barons gathered and Merlin approached the bed where the king lay and cried aloud, 'Sir, is it your will that your son, Arthur, shall be king when you are dead?'

Then Uther Pendragon turned and struggled and at last he was able to say in the hearing of all his barons, 'I give Arthur God's blessing and mine. I ask that he pray for my soul.' Then Uther gathered his strength and he cried, 'If Arthur does not rightly and honourably claim the crown of England, he will forfeit my blessing.' And with that the king fell back and very soon died.

King Uther was interred with all the ceremony proper for a king, and his queen, the fair Igraine, and all his barons mourned for him. His court was filled with sorrow, and for a long time there was no King of England. Then danger arose everywhere, on the borders from outside enemies and within the realm from ambitious lords. The barons surrounded themselves with armed men and many of them wished to take the crown for themselves. In this anarchy no man was safe and the laws were forgotten, so that at last Merlin went to the Archbishop of Canterbury and advised him to issue a call to all the lords and all the gentlemen of arms in the kingdom to gather in London by Christmas on pain of excommunication. It was believed that since Jesus was born on Christmas Eve, He might on that holy night give some miraculous sign who should rightly be king of the realm. When the archbishop's message was sent out to the lords and knights, many of them were moved by the call and purified their lives so that their prayers might be more acceptable to God.

In the greatest church in London, perhaps St Paul's, the lords and knights gathered to pray long before dawn. And when matins and first Mass were over, there was seen in the churchyard, in a place nearest the high altar, a great block of marble and in the marble was set a steel anvil in which a sword was driven. In letters of gold was written:

WHOEVER PULLS THIS SWORD
FROM THIS STONE AND ANVIL
IS KING OF ALL ENGLAND
BY RIGHT OF BIRTH.

The people were amazed, and carried the news of the miracle to the archbishop, who said 'Go back into the church and pray to God. And let no man touch the sword until High Mass is sung.' And this they did, but when the service was over all the lords went to look at the stone and the sword and some tried to draw out the blade, but no one could move it.

'The man is not here who will draw this sword,' said the archbishop, 'but do not doubt that God will make him known. Until that happens,' he went on, 'I suggest that ten knights, men of good fame, be appointed to guard this sword.'

And it was so ordered and further proclaimed that any man who wished might try to release the sword. For New Year's Day a great tournament was planned and this was designed by the archbishop to keep the lords and knights together, for he reckoned that God would at that time make known who should win the sword.

On New Year's Day, when holy service was over, the knights and barons rode to the field where some would joust – two armoured men riding in single combat, each seeking to unhorse his opponent. Others joined the tourney, a military sport wherein chosen groups of armed and mounted men engaged in general mêlée. By these sports the knights and barons kept themselves hard and practised for war and also won honour and renown for bravery and expertness with horse, with shield, with lance and sword, for all the barons and the knights were fighting men.

It happened that Sir Ector, who was the lord of lands nearby to London, rode in for the jousting, and with him came his son Sir Kay, only made a knight at Allhallows of that year, and also young Arthur came, who had been reared in Sir Ector's house and who was Sir Kay's foster brother. As they rode towards the jousting field, Sir Kay discovered that he had forgotten his sword at his father's lodging, and he asked young Arthur to ride back for it.

'I will do it gladly,' said Arthur, and he turned his horse and galloped back to bring his foster brother's sword to him. But when he came to the lodging he found it empty and locked up, for everyone had gone out to see the jousting.

Then Arthur was angry and he said to himself, 'Very well, I will ride to the churchyard and take the sword that is sticking in the stone there. I do not want my brother, Sir Kay, to be without a sword today.'

When he came to the churchyard, Arthur dismounted and

24

tied his horse to the stile and walked to the tent, and he found no guardian knights there, for they too had gone to the jousting. Then Arthur grasped the sword by its handle and easily and fiercely drew it from the anvil and the stone, and he mounted his horse and rode quickly until he overtook Sir Kay and gave him the sword.

As soon as Sir Kay saw the sword, he knew it came from the stone and he went quickly to his father and held it out to him. 'Sir, look here! I have the sword of the stone and therefore I must be King of England.'

Sir Ector recognized the sword and he called Arthur and Sir Kay to him and all three returned quickly to church. And there Sir Ector made Sir Kay swear how he had got the sword.

'My brother, Arthur, brought it to me,' Sir Kay answered.

Then Sir Ector turned to Arthur. 'And how did you get this sword?'

Arthur said, 'When I rode back for my brother's sword, I found no one at home, so I could not get it. I did not want my brother to be without a sword and so I came here and took the sword from the stone for him.'

'Were there no knights here guarding the sword?' Sir Ector asked.

'No, sir,' said Arthur. 'There was no one here.'

Sir Ector was silent for a time and then he said, 'I understand now that you must be king of this land.'

'Why should that be?' said Arthur. 'For what reason should I be king?'

'My lord,' Sir Ector said, 'God has willed that only the man who can draw this sword from this stone shall be the rightful king of the land. Now let me see whether you can put the sword back as it was and then draw it out again.'

'That is not difficult,' said Arthur, and he drove the blade into the anvil. Then Sir Ector tried to draw it out and he could not and he told Sir Kay to try. Sir Kay pulled at the sword with all his might and he could not move it.

'Now it is your turn,' said Sir Ector to Arthur.

'I will,' said Arthur. And he drew the sword out easily.

Then Sir Ector and Sir Kay kneeled down on the earth before him.

And Arthur cried, 'What is this? My own dear father and my brother, why do you kneel to me?'

Sir Ector said, 'My lord Arthur, I am not your father nor of your blood. I believe that you are of nobler blood than I.' Then Sir Ector told Arthur how he had taken him to rear and by Uther's order. And he told him how it was Merlin's doing.

When he heard that Sir Ector was not his father, Arthur was sad and even more sad when Sir Ector said, 'Sir, will you be my good and gracious lord when you are king?'

'Why should I not be?' Arthur cried. 'I owe you more than anyone in the world, you and your wife, my good lady mother who nursed me and kept me as though I were her own. And if, as you say, it is God's will that I must be king – ask anything of me! I will not fail you.'

'My lord,' said Sir Ector, 'I shall ask only one thing of you, that you will make my son Sir Kay, your foster brother, seneschal and keeper of your lands.'

'That shall be done and more,' Arthur said. 'On my honour, no other man but Sir Kay shall have that office while I live.'

Then they three went to the archbishop and told him how the sword had been drawn from the stone, and by his order all of the barons gathered again to try to draw the sword, and all failed except Arthur.

Then many of the lords were jealous and angry and they said it was an insult and a shame that the realm should be governed by a boy who was not of royal blood. The decision was put off until Candlemas, when all the barons agreed to meet again. Ten knights were delegated to watch over the sword and the stone. A tent was put up to shelter it and five knights were on guard at all times.

At Candlemas an even greater number of lords gathered to try for the sword and no one could draw it. But Arthur, as he had done before, drew it without effort. Then the angry barons put it off until the high feast of Easter and again only Arthur could draw the sword. Some of the great lords were opposed to Arthur as king and they delayed the final test until the feast of Pentecost. Such was their anger that Arthur's life was in danger. The Archbishop of Canterbury by Merlin's advice gathered those knights whom Uther Pendragon had loved and trusted most. Such men as Sir Bawdewyn of Bretagne, Sir Kaynes, Sir Ulfius, and Sir Brastias, all these and many more stayed near to Arthur day and night to protect him until the feast of Pentecost.

When Pentecost had come, a great gathering assembled and all manner of men struggled to pull the sword from the stone and no one succeeded. Then Arthur mounted the stone with all the lords and common people watching him, and he drew the sword easily out and held it up to them. The common people were convinced and they cried with one great shout, 'We want Arthur for our king without any more delay. We see that God wills him to be king and we will kill anyone who stands in his way.'

And with that both rich and poor kneeled down and begged Arthur's pardon for having delayed so long. Arthur forgave them, and then he took the sword in his hands and placed it on the high altar. The archbishop took the sword and touched Arthur on the shoulder and made him a knight. Then Arthur swore an oath to all the lords and commons that he would be a just and true king to them all the days of his life.

He ordered the lords who held their lands and honours from the crown to fulfil the duties they owed to him. And afterwards he heard complaints and charges of wrongs and crimes committed in the land since the death of his father, Uther Pendragon – how lands and castles had been taken by force, and men murdered, and knights and ladies and gentlemen robbed and despoiled in the time when there was no king or any justice. Then Arthur caused the lands and property to be returned to their rightful owners.

When that was done, King Arthur organized his government. He appointed his faithful knights to high office. Sir Kay was made seneschal of all England and Sir Bawdewyn of Bretagne constable to keep the law and the peace. Sir Ulfius was made chamberlain and Sir Bracias became warden of the northern boundaries, for it was from the north that most of England's enemies came. In a few years Arthur overcame the north and took Scotland and Wales, and although some parts held out against him for a time, he defeated them all.

When all the land was pacified and ordered and Arthur had proved himself a true king, he moved with his knights into Wales to be formally crowned in the ancient city of Caerleon, and he proclaimed Pentecost his coronation day and prepared a great feast for all his subjects.

Many great lords with their retainers gathered at that city. King Lot of Lothian and Orkney came with five hundred knights behind him, and the King of Scotland, who was a very young man, attended with six hundred, and the King of Carados with five hundred. And finally came one who was known only as the King of a Hundred Knights, and his followers were wonderfully armed and equipped.

Arthur was pleased with the gathering, for he hoped all had come to do him honour at his coronation. In his joy he sent presents to the kings and knights who had come together. But his hopes were vain. The kings and knights refused the presents and insulted the messengers. They sent back the message that the gifts of a beardless lowborn boy were not acceptable. They told the king's messengers that the gifts they brought to Arthur were sword strokes and war, for they were ashamed that such a noble land should be ruled by an ignoble child – and that was the reason for their gathering.

When King Arthur heard the menacing reply, his hopes of early peace were crushed and he called a council of his faithful knights and by their advice he occupied a strong tower and armed and provisioned it well, and he took five hundred of his best and bravest knights into the tower with him.

Then the rebellious lords laid siege to the tower, but they could not take it, for it was well defended.

After fifteen days of seige, Merlin appeared in the city of Caerleon, and the lords welcomed him because they trusted him. They demanded to know why the boy Arthur was made King of England.

Then Merlin, who delighted in surprises, said, 'My lords, I will tell you the reason. Arthur is the son of King Uther Pendragon born of Igraine, who was once the wife of the Duke of Tintagel, and that is why he is the rightful King of England. '

And the knights cried out, 'Then Arthur is a bastard and a bastard cannot be king.'

'That is not true,' said Merlin. 'Arthur was conceived more than three hours after the death of the duke, and thirteen days later Uther married Igraine and made her his queen, and therefore Arthur was born in wedlock and is no bastard. And I tell you now that no matter who or how many may oppose him, Arthur is the king and he will defeat all his enemies and he will long reign over England and Ireland and Scotland and Wales, as well as other kingdoms I will not bother to name.'

Then some of the kings were amazed at Merlin's message and believed that what he said was true. But King Lot and others laughed in disbelief and insulted Merlin, calling him a witch and a charlatan. The most they would promise was to listen to Arthur if he would come out to speak to them.

Then Merlin went into the tower and spoke to Arthur and told him what he had done. And he said, 'Do not be afraid. Come out and speak boldly to them as their king and chief. Do not spare them, for it is ordained that you shall rule them all whether they wish it or not.'

Arthur took courage then and went out of the tower, but as a precaution against treachery he wore a shirt of double steel mail under his robe. The Archbishop of Canterbury went with him and Sir Bawdewyn of Bretagne, and Sir Kay of Sir Brastias, his best and bravest knights.

When Arthur met with the rebellious lords there were strong and angry words from either side. Arthur told them firmly that he would force them to accept his kingship. Then the kings went away in a rage and Arthur taunted them and satirically begged them to keep well, and they retorted bitterly that he should also guard his health. And then Arthur went back into the tower and armed himself and his knights and prepared to defend the place.

Now Merlin met with the angry lords. He told them, 'You would be wise to obey Arthur, for even if you were ten times as many as you are, he would still overcome you.'

King Lot answered Merlin. 'We are not the kind of men to be frightened by a trickster and a reader of dreams,' he said.

With that, Merlin vanished and appeared in the tower by the side of Arthur. He told the king to attack quickly and fiercely while the rebels were off guard and not all of one mind, and this was proved good advice, for two hundred of the best men deserted the lords and came over to Arthur, which gave him courage and comfort.

'My lord,' said Merlin, 'go now to the attack, but do not fight with the miraculous sword of the stone unless you are hard pressed and in danger. Only then may you draw it.'

Then Arthur with his best knights about him swept out of the gates of the tower and caught his enemies in their tents and bore down on them, striking to right and left. Arthur led them and fought so fiercely and so well that his knights, seeing his strength and skill, took courage and confidence from him and charged into the fight with redoubled strength.

Some of the rebels broke through the rear and circled and attacked Arthur's force from behind but Arthur turned and struck behind and before and continued in the thickest of the fighting until his horse was killed under him. As Arthur stood on the ground, King Lot struck him down. But four of his knights rushed to his rescue and brought him a fresh horse. Then only did King Arthur draw the miraculous sword of the stone, and its blade flashed with light and blinded his enemies, and he drove them back and killed many of them.

Now the common people of Caerleon rushed into the fight armed with clubs and sticks, and dragged enemy knights from their saddles and killed them. But most of the lords kept together and marshalled their remaining knights and they retreated in order, defending their rear. At this time Merlin appeared to Arthur and counselled him not to pursue them, for his men were weary with fighting and too few in number.

Then Arthur rested his knights and feasted them. And after a time, when all was in order, he marched back to London and called a general council of all his loyal barons. Merlin foretold that the six rebellious lords would continue the war with raids and forays into the realm. When the king asked his barons what he should do, they answered that they would not offer their advice but only their strength and loyalty.

Arthur thanked them for their courage and support, but he said, 'I beg all of you who love me to speak with Merlin. You will know what he has done for me. He knows many strange and secret things. When you are with him ask him for his advice about what we should do.'

The barons agreed to this, and when Merlin came to them, they begged for his help.

'Since you ask I will tell you,' Merlin said. 'I warn you all that your enemies are too strong for you and they are as good men of arms as any living. Furthermore, by this time they have drawn four more lords and a mighty duke into their league. Unless the king can find more knights than there are within his kingdom, he is lost. If he fights his enemies with what he has, he will be defeated and killed.'

'What should we do then?' cried the barons. 'What is our best course?'

'This is my advice to you,' said Merlin. 'Across the Channel in France there are two brothers, both kings and both good fighting men. One is King Ban of Benwick and the other King Bors of Gaul. These kings are at war with a king named Claudas who is so rich that he can hire as many knights as he wishes, so that he has the advantage over the two brother knights. I suggest that our king should choose two trusty knights and send them with letters to the Kings Ban and Bors, asking their help against his enemies and promising them that he will help them against King Claudas. Now what do you think of this suggestion?'

King Arthur said, 'It seems good advice to me.' He caused two letters to be written in most courteous language to King Ban and King Bors, and he called Sir Ulfius and Sir Brastias to him and charged them to deliver the letters. They rode out well armed and well horsed and they crossed the Channel and continued on towards the city of Benwick. But on the way they were intercepted in a narrow place by eight knights who tried to capture them. Sir Ulfius and Sir Brastias begged the knights to let them pass because they were messengers to the Kings Ban and Bors sent by King Arthur of England.

'You have made an error,' said the knights. 'We are King Claudas's men.'

Then two of them laid their spears in rest and bore down on King Arthur's knights, but Sir Ulfius and Sir Brastias were seasoned fighting men. They met charge with charge, with levelled spears and shields well dressed before them. The spears of Claudas's knights shattered at the impact and the men were hurled from their saddles. Without stopping or turning, Arthur's knights rode on their way. But Claudas's other six knights galloped ahead until the roadway narrowed again and two of their number levelled their lances and thundered down on the messengers. And these two met the same fate as their fellows. They were tumbled to the ground and left helpless. A third time and a fourth King Claudas's knights tried to stop the messengers and everyone was overthrown, so that all eight were hurt and bruised. The letter bearers continued on until they came to the city of Benwick. When the two kings heard that messengers had come, they sent out Sir Lyonse, lord of Payarne, and the good knight Sir Phariance to meet them. And when these knights heard that the messengers had come from King Arthur of England, they welcomed them and without delay brought them into the city. Ban and Bors gave Sir Ulfius and Sir Brastias a friendly welcome because they came from Arthur, whom they held in high honour and respect. Then the messengers kissed the letters they carried and handed them to the kings, who, when they heard the contents, were pleased. They assured the messengers that they would carry out King Arthur's request. And they invited Ulfius and Brastias to rest and to feast with them after the long journey. At the feast the messengers recounted their adventures with the eight knights of King Claudas. And Bors and Ban laughed at the tale and said, 'You see, our friends too welcomed you, our noble friends. If we had known it, they would not have got off so easily.' Then the kings gave every hospitality to the knightly messengers, and so many gifts that they could hardly carry them.

Meanwhile, they prepared their answer to King Arthur, had letters written – that they would come to Arthur's aid as quickly as they could and with as large a force of fighting men as they could gather. The messengers rode back the way they had come without hindrance and crossed the Channel to England. Then King Arthur was very glad and he asked, 'How soon do you suppose the two kings may come?'

'Sir,' said the knights, 'before Allhallows they will be here.'

Then the king sent messengers to all parts of his realm announcing a great feast on the day of Allhallows, and promising jousting and tournaments and all manner of entertainment.

And, as they had promised, the two kings crossed the sea and entered England, bringing three hundred of their best knights fully equipped with the clothing of peace and the weapons and armour of war. They were received and conducted royally and Arthur met and welcomed them ten miles from London and there was great joy in the kings and in all the people.

On Allhallows day the three kings sat together in the great hall and presided over the feast and Sir Kay the Seneschal and Sir Lucas the Butler and Sir Gryfflet saw to the service, for these three knights ruled all the servants of the king. When the feast was over and all had washed the grease of eating from their hands and mantles, the whole company moved out to the tournament ground, where seven hundred knights on horseback waited eagerly to compete. The three kings with the Archbishop of Canterbury and Sir Ector, Kay's father, took their places in a great stand, shaded and decorated with cloth of gold. They were surrounded by beautiful ladies and gentlewomen, all gathered to watch the tournament and to judge who fought best.

The three kings divided the seven hundred knights into two sides, the knights of Gaul and Benwick on one side and those of Arthur on the other. The good knights dressed their shields before them and couched their spears, preparing for the fight. Sir Gryfflet set out first and Sir Ladynas chose to meet him, and they crashed together so fiercely that their shields were torn apart and the horses fell to the ground and both the English knight and the French knight were stunned so that many thought them dead. When Sir Lucas saw Sir Gryfflet lying on the ground, he charged into the French knights and laid about him with his sword and engaged with many at one time. And with that Sir Kay, followed by five knights, rode suddenly out and struck down six of the opponents. No one fought so well as Sir Kay that afternoon, but two French knights, Sir Ladynas and Sir Grastian, earned the praise of everyone. When the good knight Sir Placidas engaged Sir Kay and struck him down, horse and man, rage rose in Gryfflet so that he toppled Sir Placidas. Then the rage entered the five knights when they saw Sir Kay fallen and each of them picked out a French knight and each unhorsed his adversary.

Now King Arthur and his allies, Ban and Bors, saw the battle rage rising on both sides and they knew that the tournament would cease to be a sport and turn to deadly war. The three leaped from the stand and mounted small hackneys and rode into the field to control the angry men. They ordered them to stop the fight and retire from the field and go to their quarters. And after a while the men cooled their anger and obeyed their kings. They went home and took off their armour and went quietly to evensong and, thus soothed, ate their suppers.

After supper, the three kings went into a garden and there awarded the prizes for the tournament to Sir Kay, Sir Lucas the Butler and to young Gryfflet. And after that they went into council and called to them Sir Ulfius and Sir Brastias and Merlin. They discussed the coming war and argued about the means of fighting it, but they were weary and retired to bed. In the morning after they had heard Mass they came back to council and there were many opinions about what was best to do, but eventually they agreed upon a plan. Merlin and Sir Grastian and Sir Placidas should return to France – the two knights to guard and protect and govern the kingdoms there and Merlin to raise an army to bring across the Channel. The royal rings of Ban and Bors were given them as tokens of their authority.

The three travelled to France and came to Benwick, where the people accepted the authority of the rings. They begged to know about the health and success of their kings and they were glad to hear good news of them.

Then Merlin, by authority of the king, called all the available fighting men together, instructing them to come armed and armoured and with provisions for the journey. Fifteen thousand men at arms answered the call, both horse and foot. They gathered on the coast with their equipment and provisions. Merlin chose ten thousand horsemen from among them and sent the rest back to help Grastian and Placidas defend the country against their enemy King Claudas.

Then Merlin collected shipping and embarked the horses and the men at arms and his fleet crossed the Channel safely and landed at Dover. And he led his army northwards by secret ways, under the cover of forests and by hidden valleys, and encamped them at Bedgrayne in a hidden valley surrounded by forest. He ordered them to remain hidden and then Merlin rode on to Arthur and the two kings and told them what he had done and how ten thousand horsemen, armed and ready, were secretly encamped in the Forest of Bedgrayne. The kings were amazed that Merlin had accomplished so much so quickly, for it seemed to them a miracle, and it was.

Then King Arthur put his army of twenty thousand in motion, and to prevent spies from knowing his movements, he sent advance guards ahead to challenge and capture anyone who could not produce the king's seal and token. His army moved day and night without resting until they came near to the Forest of Bedgrayne, where the kings went into the hidden valley and found the well-armed secret army. And they were very glad and ordered that everyone have any food and equipment that were needed.

Meanwhile, the lords of the north, raw from their defeat at Caerleon, had been preparing their revenge. The six original rebellious leaders gathered five others to their alliance, and all of them prepared for war and swore an oath that they would not rest until King Arthur was destroyed.

These were the leaders and the numbers of their forces. The Duke of Cambenet brought five thousand mounted men at arms. King Brandegoris promised five thousand. King Clarivaus of Northumberland three thousand; the young King of a Hundred Knights raised four thousand horsemen. King Uryens of Gore furnished six thousand, King Cradilment five thousand; King Nentres five thousand, King Carados five thousand, and last, King Anguyshaunce of Ireland promised to bring five thousand horsemen. This then was the army of the north – fifty thousand good men at arms on horseback and ten thousand well-armed footmen. The northern host gathered quickly and moved southward with scouts flung out ahead of them. Not far from the Forest of Bedgrayne, they came to a castle and laid siege to it, and then, leaving sufficient men to keep the siege, the main body of men moved on towards where King Arthur was encamped.

King Arthur's outriders met the scouts from the north and captured them and the scouts were forced to tell which way the northern host was moving. And men were sent out to burn and destroy the countryside ahead of the advancing army so that they could not find food or forage.

At that time the young King of a Hundred Knights had a wonderful dream and he told it to the others. He dreamed a terrible wind thundered over the land, demolishing towns and castles, and behind it came a tidal wave that carried everything away. The lords who heard the dream said it was the presage of a great and final battle.

The young knight's dream of wind and destroying wave was a symbol of what everyone sensed, that the outcome of the battle would decide whether Arthur would be King of England to rule with peace and justice the whole realm, or whether the chaos of little quarrelling ambitious kings should continue the unhappy darkness that had fallen on the land since Uther Pendragon's death.

Because they were outnumbered by their enemies, King Arthur and the allied kings from France considered how they could meet the northern host. Merlin sat with them in their planning. When the scouts reported the route of the approaching enemy and the place where they would encamp for the night, Merlin argued that they should attack at night, for a small and mobile force has the advantage over a resting army tired with travelling.

Then Arthur and Ban and Bors with their good and trusty knights moved quietly out and at midnight they launched an attack against the sleeping enemy. But the sentries gave the alarm and the northern knights strove desperately to mount and defend themselves, while Arthur's men raged in the camp, cut the tent ropes, and strove to overwhelm the camp. But the eleven lords were trained and disciplined campaigners. They quickly ordered their troops and formed a battle line and the fight continued fiercely in the darkness. That night ten thousand good men were slain, but as the dawn approached the northern lords with their numbers forced a passage through King Arthur's lines and he retired before them to rest his men and make new battle plans.

Merlin said, 'Now we can use the plan I have prepared. Ten thousand fresh, unwearied men are hidden in the forest. Let Ban and Bors command them and bring them to the edge of the woods, but keep them hidden from the enemy. Let King Arthur marshall his men in sight of the northern host. When they see you are only twenty thousand against their fifty thousand, they will be glad and will be over confident and they will enter the narrow passage where your smaller force will have an equal chance.'

The three kings agreed to the battle plan and each went to his station.

In the dawn light, when the armies could see each other, the men of the north were happy to see how small was Arthur's force. Then Ulfius and Brastias delivered the attack with three thousand men. They drove furiously into the northern host, striking right and left and causing great execution on the enemy. When the eleven lords saw how so few penetrated so deeply into their battle line, they were ashamed and mounted a fierce counter-attack.

Sir Ulfius's horse was killed under him, but he put his shield before him and continued to fight on foot. Duke Estance of Cambenet set upon Ulfius to kill him, but Sir Brastias saw his friend in danger and singled Estance out and the two ran together with such force that both of them were struck down and the horses' knees burst to the bone and both men lay stunned on the ground. Then Sir Kay with six knights drove a wedge into the enemy until they were met by the eleven lords, and Gryfflet and Sir Lucas the Butler were unhorsed. Now the battle became a confused mêlée of wheeling, charging, striking knights, and each man chose an enemy and engaged him as if in single combat.

Sir Kay saw Gryfflet fighting on fast and quickly. He struck down King Nentres and took his horse to Gryfflet and mounted him. With the same spear, Sir Kay struck King Lot and wounded him. Seeing this, the young King of a Hundred Knights ran at Sir Kay and unhorsed him and took his horse to King Lot.

Thus it went on, for it was every knight's pride and duty to help and defend his friends, and an armoured knight on foot was in double danger because of the weight of his equipment. The battle raged and neither side gave ground. Gryfflet saw his friends Sir Kay and Sir Lucas unhorsed and he returned their favour. He chose the good knight Sir Pynnel and with his great spear cast him from the saddle and gave his horse to Sir Kay. The fighting continued and many men were stripped from their saddles and their horses given to dismounted men. Then the eleven lords were filled with rage and frustration because their greater army could make no headway against Arthur and their losses in dead and wounded were very great.

Now King Arthur came into the fight with shining eager eyes and he saw Brastias and Ulfius fallen and in great peril of their lives because they were caught in the harness of their wounded horses and the threshing hoofs battered them. Arthur charged at Sir Cradilment like a lion and drove his spear into the knight's left side and he grasped the reins and led his horse to Ulfius and said with the fierce and formal gaiety of fighting men, 'My old friend, it seems to me that you could use a horse. Please use this one.'

And Ulfius replied, 'Why, so I do. Thank you, my lord.' Then King Arthur swung into the battle, striking, feinting, swerving his horse, fighting so marvellously that men watched in wonder.

The King of a Hundred Knights saw Cradilment brought to earth and he turned on Sir Ector, Arthur's foster father, and struck him down, and took his horse. When Arthur saw Cradilment, whom he had already defeated once, riding Sir Ector's horse, his fury rose and he engaged again with Cradilment and gave him such a sword stroke that the blade sliced down through helmet and shield and deep into the horse's neck, so that horse and man dropped instantly to the ground. Meanwhile, Sir Kay went to the rescue of his father, unhorsed a knight, and helped Sir Ector to mount himself again.

Sir Lucas lay unconscious under his horse and Gryfflet manfully tried to defend his friend against fourteen knights. Then Sir Brastias, newly mounted, moved in to help. He struck the first on the visor so hard that his blade went into his teeth. He caught the second at elbow with a swinging stroke and cut his arm cleanly off and it fell to the ground. He struck a third at shoulder where the armour meets gorget, and shoulder and arm were carved off. The earth was heaped with the broken killed and the struggling wounded, and mounded with dead and floundering horses, and the ground was slippery with blood. The voice of the battle echoed back from hill and forest – clash of sword on shield and crashing grunt of spearmen colliding with equal might, war cries and shouts of triumph, and yelled curses and screams of dying horses, and the sad moaning of men wounded to death.

From their hidden position in the forest, Ban and Bors watched the conflict and kept their men quiet and in line, although many of the knights shivered and shook with eagerness to be in the fight, for the fighting lust is an infectious thing to a man of arms.

Meanwhile, the deadly fight went on. King Arthur saw that he could not defeat his enemies. He raged as crazily as a wounded lion, ranging back and forth against any who stood against him, so that men were filled with wonder at him. Striking to left and right with his sword, he killed twenty knights and he wounded King Lot on the shoulder so severely that he had to leave the field. Gryfflet and Sir Kay fought on either side of their king and earned their greatness with their swords on the bodies of their enemies.

Now Ulfius and Brastias and Sir Ector rode against Duke Estance, Clarivaus, Carados, and the King of a Hundred Knights and drove them back out of the fight; behind the fighting lines they gathered to consider their position. King Lot was badly wounded and his heart was heavy at the terrible losses and discouraged that no end of the battle was in sight. He spoke to the other lords, saying, 'Unless we change our plan of driving through, we will be destroyed little by little in the pass. Let five of us take ten thousand men and retire to rest. At the same time the other six lords will hold the passage and cause as much damage as possible and wear them down. Then when they are weary, we will charge with ten thousand fresh and rested men. This is the only chance I can see of beating them.'

This was agreed to and the six lords went back to the battle-field and fought doggedly to bleed the enemy and wear him down.

Now, two knights, Sir Lyonse and Sir Phariance, were in the advance guard of the hidden army of Ban and Bors. They saw King Idres alone and weary. And against orders the two French knights broke from their concealment and rode down on him. King Anguyshaunce saw the attack and he rallied the Duke of Cambenet and a band of knights and surrounded the two so that they could not retreat to the forest, and although they defended themselves well, they finally were unhorsed.

When King Bors, watching from the forest, saw the foolish eagerness of his knights, he was grieved at their disobedience and their danger. He gathered a force and charged out so fast that he seemed to burn a black streak in the air. And King Lot saw him and knew him well from the escutcheon on his shield and Lot cried out, 'Jesus defend us now against peril of death. I see yonder one of the best knights in the whole world, with a band of fresh knights.'

'Who is he?' the young Lord of a Hundred Knights asked.

Lot said, 'He is King Bors of Gaul. How can he have come into this country without our knowledge?'

'Perhaps it was Merlin's doing,' said a knight.

But Sir Carados said, 'Great he may be, but I will encounter your King Bors of Gaul and you can send rescue if I need it.'

Then Carados and his men moved slowly forward until they came within bow shot of King Bors, and only then did they put their horses to breakneck charge. Bors saw them come and he said to his godson, Sir Bleoberis, who was his standard bearer, 'Now we shall see how these northern Britons bear their arms,' and he called the charge.

King Bors encountered a knight and drove his spear through him and out the other side, and then he drew his sword, fought savagely, and the knights with him followed his example. Sir Carados was struck down and it required the young lord and a large force to rescue him.

Then King Ban and his following broke from their concealment; the shield of Ban was striped with green and gold. When King Lot saw this shield he said, 'Now our danger is doubled. I see yonder the most valiant and renowned knight in the world, King Ban of Benwick. Two such brothers as the Kings Ban and Bors do not live. We must retreat or be killed, and unless we retreat wisely and defend ourselves we will be killed anyway.'

Ban and Bors, with their ten thousand fresh men, came on so fiercely that the northern reserves had to be thrown back into the fight although they were not rested. And King Lot wept with pity to see so many good knights go down in death.

Now King Arthur and his allies, Ban and Bors, fought shoulder to shoulder and killed and slashed on and on, and many fighting men in weariness and hopeless dread left the field and fled to save their lives.

Of the northern force King Lot and Morganoure and he of a Hundred Knights kept their men together and fought on bravely and well. The young lord saw the execution King Ban did and he tried to take him out of action. He couched his spear and rode at Ban and struck him on the helm and stunned him. But King Ban shook his head and the battle rage took him and he spurred after his opponent, who, seeing him come, put up his shield and met the charge. King Ban's great sword cut through the shield and through the coat of mail and through the steel trappings of the horse and lodged in the horse's spine, so that in falling the sword was dragged from King Ban's hand.

The young lord stepped free from his fallen horse and with his sword he stabbed King Ban's horse in the belly. Then Ban leaped for his lost sword and struck the young lord on the helm so mightily that he fell to the ground, and the weary slaughter of good knights and footmen went on and on.

Into the press King Arthur came and found King Ban on foot among dead men and dead horses, fighting like a wounded lion, so that into the circle his sword would reach no man entered without a wound.

King Arthur was fearful to see. His shield was covered with blood so that his device could not be recognized and his sword was caked and dripping with blood and brains. Arthur saw a knight nearby well mounted on a good horse, and he ran at him and drove his sword through helmet and teeth and brain, and Arthur led his good horse to King Ban and said, 'Dear brother, here is a horse for you. I am sorry for your wounds.'

'They are soon arranged,' said Ban. 'I trust in God that my hurts are not as great as some I have given.'

'That I know,' said Arthur. 'I saw your deeds from a distance, but I could not come to your aid at the time.'

The slaughter went on until at last King Arthur called a halt, and with difficulty the three kings forced their men to disengage with the enemy and to withdraw into the forest and then across a little river, where the men fell down and slept in the grass, for they had had no rest for two days and a night.

And on the bloody battlefield the eleven northern lords and their men gathered together in sadness and misery. They had not lost, but neither had they won.

King Arthur marvelled at the toughness of the northern knights and he too was angry because he also had neither lost nor won.

But the French kings advised him in courtesy, saying, 'You must not blame them. They have done only what good men ought to do.' And King Ban said, 'By my faith, they are the bravest knights and the best fighting men of great worth.' Ban continued, 'If they were your men, no king in the world could boast of such a following.'

Arthur said, 'Even so, do not expect me to love them. It is their intention to destroy me.'

'This we know well, for we have seen it,' said the kings. 'They are your mortal enemies and they have proved it. But they are such good knights, it is a pity they are against you.'

The eleven lords meanwhile assembled on the field of blood and destruction and King Lot addressed them, saying, 'My lords, we must find some new attack or the war will continue as it has. You see around you our fallen men. I believe that a large part of our failure can be blamed on our footmen. They move too slowly so that the mounted must wait for them or be killed trying to save them. I advise that we send the foot soldiers away in the night. The forests will conceal them and the noble King Arthur will not trouble himself with footmen. They may well save themselves. Meanwhile, we will keep the horses together and make a rule that anyone who tries to run away will be executed. It is better to kill a coward than through a coward to be slain. What do you say to this?' Lot said, 'Answer me – all of you.'

'You say well,' said Sir Nentres, and the other lords agreed with him. Then they swore to stick together in life and in death. After their solemn decision they mended their harnesses and cleaned and straightened their equipment. And then they mounted and set new spears upright against their thighs and they sat their horses rigid and unmoving as rocks. When Arthur and Ban and Bors saw them sitting there, they were forced to admire them for their discipline and knightly courage.

Then forty of King Arthur's best knights asked permission to ride against the enemy and break up their battle line. And these forty spurred their horses to great speed, and the lords lowered their spears and met them in full course, and the deadly wilful fight went on. Arthur and Ban and Bors rejoined the fight and killed men to the right and left of them. The field was littered with broken men and the horses slipped in blood and were reddened above their fetlocks. But slowly Arthur's men were forced back by the unyielding discipline of the northerners until they recrossed the little river over which they had come.

Now Merlin came riding in on a great black horse and he cried to King Arthur, 'Will you never stop? Haven't you done enough? Out of threescore thousand who began the battle, only fifteen thousand are left alive. It is time to call a halt to the slaughter or God will be angry with you.' And Merlin continued, 'Those rebellious lords have sworn never to leave the field alive and when men are so disposed they can take many with them to their deaths. You cannot defeat them now. You can only kill them to your loss. Therefore, my lord, retire from the field as quickly as you can and let your men rest. Reward your knights with gold and silver, for they have deserved it. There are no riches too dear for them. Never have so few knights done more in honour and bravery against a greater enemy. Today your knights have matched themselves against the best fighters in the world.'

King Ban and King Bors cried, 'He speaks the truth.'

Then Merlin bade them to go wherever they wished. 'For three years, I can promise you, this enemy will not trouble you. These eleven lords have more on their hands than they know,' Merlin said. 'More than forty thousand Saracens have landed on their coasts and they ravage the country and burn and kill. They have laid siege to the castle of Wandesborow and devastated the land. Therefore, you need not fear these rebels for a long time. They will be very busy at home.' And Merlin continued, 'When you have gathered the spoils from the battlefield, give them to King Ban and King Bors so that they may reward their knights who fought for you. The news of this gift will go out, and when you have need of men in the future they will come to you. You can reward your own knights later.'

King Arthur said, 'Your advice is good and I will follow it.'

Then the treasure of the bloody field was collected – armour and swords and jewels from the fallen men, saddles and harnesses and trappings from the war horses, the sad possessions of the dead. These valuable trophies were given to Ban and Bors, and they in turn distributed them among their knights.

After that Merlin took his leave of King Arthur and of the brother kings from across the sea and he journeyed to Northumberland to Master Blayse, who kept a chronicle. Merlin told the story of the great battle and how it ended, and gave the names and deeds of every king and every brave knight who fought there and Master Blayse wrote it in his chronicle word for word as Merlin told it. And in Arthur's days to come Merlin carried the news of battles and adventures to Master Blayse to write in his book for future men to read and to remember.

Having done this, Merlin returned to the castle of Bedgrayne in Sherwood Forest, where King Arthur was in residence. He arrived on the morning after Candlemas, disguised as was his delight. He came before Arthur wrapped in black sheepskin and dressed in a russet gown and with great boots on his feet. He carried a bow and a quiver of arrows and a brace of wild geese in his hand. He went before the king and said brusquely, 'Sire, will you give me a gift?'

Arthur was fooled by the disguise. He said angrily, 'Why should I give a gift to a man like you?'

And Merlin said, 'You would be wise to give me a gift that is not in your hand rather than to lose riches. In the place where the battle was fought there is a treasure buried in the earth.'

'Who told you so, churl?' the king demanded.

'My lord Merlin told me.'

Then Ulfius and Brastias knew him by his tricks and they laughed and said, 'My lord, he has fooled you. It is Merlin himself.'

Then the king was abashed that he had not recognized him, and so were Ban and Bors, and they all laughed at the trick he had played. Merlin was as happy as a child at the success of his game.

Now that the battle had fixed Arthur more nearly in his kingship, many great lords and ladies came to do him homage and among them the fair damsel Lyonors, daughter of Earl Sanam. When she came before the king he saw that she was beautiful and he loved her instantly and she returned his love and they were drawn together, and Lyonors conceived a child who was named Borre and years later he became a good knight of the Round Table.

Now word was brought to Arthur that King Royns of North Wales had attacked King Lodegrance of Camylarde, King

Arthur's friend, and the king decided to go to the aid of Lodegrance. But first the French knights who wished to go home were sent to Benwick to help defend that city against King Claudas.

When they had gone, Arthur and Bors and Ban with twenty thousand men marched seven days to the country of Camylarde, and they killed ten thousand of King Royns's men and put the rest to flight and rescued King Lodegrance from his enemy. Lodegrance thanked them and feasted them in his castle and gave them gifts. And at the feasting King Arthur for the first time saw the daughter of King Lodegrance. Her name was Guinevere and Arthur loved her then and always, and later he made her his queen.

Now the time had come for the French kings to depart, for word had come that King Claudas was actively at war against their lands. And Arthur offered to go with them.

But the kings replied, 'No, you must not come at this time, for you have much to do here to settle and pacify your kingdom. And we do not need your help now because, with all the gifts you have given us, we can hire good knights to help us against Claudas.' And they said, 'We promise you, by the grace of God, that if we need help we will send for you, and we also promise that if you have need, you have only to send for us and we will not be slow in coming to your aid. This we swear.'

Then Merlin, who was nearby, spoke a prophecy:

'These two kings need never return to England to fight. Nevertheless, they will not be long parted from King Arthur. Within a year or two they will need his help and he will aid against their enemies as they have against his. The eleven lords of the north will all die in one day, destroyed by two valiant knights, Balin le Savage and his brother Balan.' And Merlin fell silent.

Now when the rebel lords retreated from the battlefield they went to the city of Surhaute in King Uryens's land, and there they rested and refreshed themselves and bound up their wounds, and their hearts were heavy at the loss of so many of their followers. They had not been long there when news came to them of the forty thousand Saracens who burned and ravaged their lands and of certain lawless men who took advantage of their absence to rob and burn and pillage without mercy.

The eleven complained, saying, 'Now sorrow is laid on sorrow.

If we had not fought against Arthur he would help us now. We cannot hope for help from King Lodegrance because he is Arthur's friend, and Royns is too busy with his private war to help us.'

After consulting further, they decided to guard the borders of Cornwall and Wales and the north. King Idres with four thousand men was placed in the city of Nauntis in Bretagne to guard against attack by land or sea. King Nentres of Garlot with four thousand knights held the city of Windesan. Eight thousand manned the fortresses of Cornwall's boundaries, while others were detailed to defend the borders of Wales and Scotland. Thus they held together and mended their fortunes, drawing new men and new allies into their fellowship. King Royns came over to them after his defeat by Arthur. And all the while the northern lords built up their armies and gathered warlike implements and stored food against the future, for they were determined to revenge themselves on Arthur for their defeat at Bedgrayne.

To go back to Arthur: After the departure of Ban and Bors, he went with his followers to the city of Caerleon. Then to his court came the wife of King Lot of Orkney, pretending to bring a message, but really to spy on Arthur. She came richly dressed and royally attended by knights and ladies. This wife of King Lot was a very fair lady and Arthur desired her and made love to her and she conceived a child by him who was to be Sir Mordred. The lady remained a month in Arthur's court and then departed homewards. And Arthur did not know that she was his half-sister and that, unwitting, he had fallen into sin.

After the lady had gone from the court, and the simplicity of war was done and the mild and active fellowship of the French kings was withdrawn, there remained the realm of England, which had not really accepted Arthur as king. In war and fellowship and love he had avoided thinking of it, but now in his leisure he was troubled and uncertain. And he dreamed a dream which frightened him, because Arthur believed dreams to be important, which they are. He dreamed that dragons and serpents crawled and slithered into his land, killing the people and burning crops and harvests with their fiery breaths. And he dreamed that he fought against them with a sick futility and they stung him and burned him and wounded him, but he fought on and on, and in the end it seemed to him that he killed many and drove the rest away.

When Arthur awakened, his dream lay heavily upon him, black and foreboding. The day was darkened by his dream. To cast it out, he gathered a few knights and followers and rode out to hunt in the forest.

And soon the king started a great stag, and he set spurs to his horse and gave chase. But even the chase had the quality of his dream. A number of times he came almost near enough to cast his spear at the stag, only to see it draw away from him. In his urge to kill it, he drove his horse past exhaustion, until it stumbled and foundered and fell dead, and the stag escaped. Then the king sent a servant to fetch another horse. He went to sit beside a little spring of water, and the dream feeling was still on him and his eyes drooped towards sleep. And, as he sat, he seemed to hear the baying of hounds. Then from the forest there came a strange and unnatural beast of a kind he did not know and the sound of baying hounds came from the beast's belly. The beast came to the fountain to drink, and while it was lapping water the baying stopped, but when it moved off into the deep cover of the trees, the sound of many hounds on scent came again from its belly. And the king was astonished in the dream-darkened day and his thoughts were heavy and black, and he fell asleep.

Then it seemed to Arthur that a knight approached him on foot who said, 'Knight full of thought and sleep, tell me if you saw a strange beast pass this way.'

'That I did,' said the king. 'But he went on into the forest. But tell me, what is your interest in this beast?'

'Sir,' said the knight, 'the beast is my quest, and I have followed him for very long and killed my horse. I would to God I had another horse to follow my quest.'

Then there came a servant of Arthur's leading a horse for him and the knight begged for the horse, saying, 'I have followed my quest twelve months, and I must go on.'

'Sir Knight,' said Arthur, 'give your quest to me and I will follow it another twelve months, for I have need of such a thing to clear me of my heavy heart.'

'You ask a foolish thing,' said the knight. 'It is my quest and

cannot be given. Only my next of kin may take it from me.'
Then the knight moved quickly to the king's horse and mounted
it, and he said, 'Thank you, sir. This horse is now mine.'

The king cried out, 'Surely you can take my mount by force,
but let us decide with arms whether you deserve him more than
I.'

The knight moved away, calling over his shoulder, 'Not now,
but at any other time you may find me here at this fountain,
ready and glad to give you satisfaction.' And with that he disappeared into the forest. The king ordered his man to fetch
another horse, and then he fell into dark dreaming thought again.

It was a day with a spell cast on it; a day when reality is distorted like a reflection in disturbed water. And the day continued
so – for now a child of fourteen years approached and asked the
king why he was pensive.

'I have every reason,' said the king, 'for I have seen and felt
strange and marvellous things.'

The child said, 'I know what you have seen. I know all your
thoughts. Also I know that only a fool worries about things he
cannot cure. I know more than this. I know who you are and
that King Uther was your father and Igraine your mother.'

'That is false,' said Arthur angrily. 'How could you know
these things? You are not old enough.'

The child said, 'I know these things better than you – better
than anyone.'

'I don't believe you,' said the king, and he was so angry at the
impertinence that the child went away, and the black mood fell
again on the king.

An old man approached, a man fully fourscore years of age,
with a face full of wisdom, and Arthur was glad because he
needed help against his moody thoughts.

The old man asked, 'Why are you sad?'

And the king replied, 'I am sad and puzzled by many things
past, but just now a child came to me and told me things he
could not and should not know.'

'The child told you the truth,' said the old man. 'You must
learn to listen to children. He would have told you much more
if you had permitted. But your mind is black and closed because
you have committed a sin and God is displeased with you. You

have made love to your sister and got her with child. And that child will grow up to destroy your knights and your kingdom and you.'

'What are you telling me?' Arthur cried. 'Who are you?'

'I am Merlin the old man. But I was also Merlin the child to teach you to pay heed to everyone.'

'You are a man of marvels,' said the king. 'Always you move in mystery like a dream. As a prophecy, tell me – is it true that I must die in battle?'

'It is God's will that you be punished for your sins,' said Merlin. 'But you should be glad that you will have a clean and honourable death. I am the one who should be sad, for my death is to be shameful and ugly and ridiculous.'

A heavy cloud blotted out the sky and a quick wind rattled in the tops of the forest trees.

The king asked, 'If you know the manner of your death, perhaps you can avoid it.'

'No,' said Merlin. 'It is there as surely as if it had already happened.'

Arthur looked upwards and he said, 'It's a black day, a troubled day.'

'It is a day, simply a day. You have a black and troubled mind, my lord.'

And as they talked, retainers brought up fresh horses, and the king and Merlin mounted and made their way to Caerleon, and the dark sky fringed and steely rain fell sullenly. As soon as he could the troubled king called Sir Ector and Sir Ulfius to him and questioned them about his birth and forebears. They told him that King Uther Pendragon was his father and Igraine his mother.

'That is what Merlin told me,' Arthur said. 'I want you to send for Igraine. I must speak with her. And if she herself says she is my mother, only then can I believe it.'

Then quickly the queen was sent for and she came bringing her daughter Morgan le Fay, a strange fair lady. King Arthur received them and made them welcome.

And as they sat in the great hall with all the court and the retainers seated at the long tables, Sir Ulfius arose and spoke to Queen Igraine in a loud voice so that everyone could hear.

'You are a false lady,' he cried. 'You are a traitor to the king.'

Arthur said, 'Beware what you say. You make a serious charge – one you can't withdraw.'

And Ulfius said, 'My lord, I am well aware of what I say, and here is my glove to challenge any man who disapproves. I charge that this Queen Igraine is the cause of all your trouble, the cause of the discontent and rebellion in your kingdom, and the real cause of the terrible war. If while King Uther was alive she had admitted that she was your mother, the troubles and mortal wars would not have come. Your subjects and your barons have never been sure of your parentage or believed your clear claim to be king. But if your mother had been willing to take a little shame to herself for your sake and the sake of the country, these troubled times would not be on us. Therefore, I charge that she is false to you and to your kingdom, and I offer my body in combat against anyone who says contrary.'

Then all eyes turned to Igraine beside the king at the high table. She sat silent for a while with her eyes cast down. Then she raised her head and spoke gently, 'I am a lone woman and I cannot fight for my honour. Is there perhaps some good man here to defend me? This is my answer to the charge. Merlin knows well, and you Sir Ulfius know how King Uther by Merlin's magic contrivance came to me in the likeness of my husband, who was already three hours dead. That night I conceived a child by King Uther, and after the thirteenth day he married me and made me his queen. By Uther's command, when my child was born, it was taken from me and given to Merlin. I was never told what had become of him, never knew his name, never saw his face or knew his fate. I swear that this is true.'

Then Sir Ulfius turned on Merlin and said, 'If what she says is true, you are more to blame than she.'

And the queen cried, 'I bore a child by my lord King Uther, but I never knew what happened to him – ever.'

Then King Arthur stood up and he went to Merlin and took him by the hand and led him to Queen Igraine. He asked quietly, 'Is this my mother?'

And Merlin said, 'Yes, my lord, she is your mother.'

Then King Arthur took his mother in his arms and kissed her, and he wept and she comforted him. After a time the king threw up his head and his eyes shone and he cried out that there should be a feast of gladness – a great feast to last eight days.

It was the custom then that all of the barons and knights and retainers feasted in the great hall seated at two long tables on either side in order of their nobility and importance, while the king and great officers and ladies sat at a raised table at the end facing the assembled court. And as they feasted and drank, men came to entertain the king – singers and musicians and tellers of stories – and these stood between the long tables and faced the high seat of the king. But also to the feasts came people bringing gifts and honours or begging justice from the king's hand against malefactors. Here also stood the knights asking permission to go questing, and returning, they stood in the same place and told of their adventures. There was much more than eating and drinking at a feast.

To Arthur's feast a squire rode into the great hall on horseback and he carried before him in his arms a dead knight. He told how in the forest a knight had set up a pavilion by a well and challenged every passing knight. The squire said, 'This man has slain this good knight, Sir Miles, who was my master. I beg you, my lord, that Sir Miles may be buried honourably and that some knight may go out to revenge him.' Then there was a great noise in the court and everyone shouted his advice.

Young Gryfflet, who was only a squire, stepped before the king and asked in recognition of his service in the war that Arthur might give him knighthood.

The king protested, 'You are too young, too tender of age to take so high and stern an order on you.'

'Sir,' said Gryfflet, 'I beg you to make me a knight.'

And Merlin said, 'It would be a pity to do this and send him to his death, for he will be a good fighting man when he is of age and will be loyal to you all his life. But if he goes against the knight in the forest, you may never see him again, for that knight is one of the best and strongest and cleverest knights in the world.'

Arthur considered and he said, 'Because of your service to me, I cannot refuse you even if I wished to,' and he touched Gryfflet with his sword and made him a knight. And then Arthur said, 'Now that I have given you the gift of knighthood, I claim a gift from you.'

'Whatever you wish, I will do,' said Sir Gryfflet.

King Arthur said, 'You must promise me, on your honour, that you will run only one course against the knight in the forest, only one, and that you will then come back here without further fighting.'

'I promise this,' said Sir Gryfflet.

Then Gryfflet armed himself quickly, and mounted his horse and took shield and spear, and he rode at great speed until he came to the well near the forest path. Beside it he saw a rich pavilion, and a war horse ready saddled and bridled. On a tree nearby there hung a shield of bright colours and a spear leaned against the tree beside it. Then Gryfflet struck the shield with the butt of his spear and knocked it to the ground. And an armoured man came from the tent and asked, 'Why did you strike down my shield, sir?'

'Because I want to joust with you,' said Gryfflet.

Then the knight sighed. 'Sir,' he said, 'it is better if you do not. You are very young and inexperienced. I am much stronger than you and tempered in war. Do not force me to fight you, young sir.'

'You have no choice,' Sir Gryfflet said. 'I am a knight and I have challenged you.'

'It is not fair,' said the knight, 'but under knightly rules I must if you insist on it.' And he asked, 'Where do you come from, young sir?'

'I am a knight of King Arthur's court,' Gryfflet said, 'and I demand the joust.'

Then, reluctantly, the knight mounted and took his place, and the two couched their spears and ran together. On the impact Sir Gryfflet's spear shattered but the strong knight's spear drove through shield and armour and pierced Gryfflet's left side and then broke off, leaving the truncheon in his body. And Sir Gryfflet fell to the ground.

The knight looked sadly at the fallen young man, and he went to him and unlaced his helm and saw that he was badly wounded, and he pitied him. He lifted Gryfflet in his arms and placed him on his horse and he prayed to God for the young man. 'He has a mighty heart,' the knight said. 'And if his life can be saved he will one day prove himself.' Then he started the horse back the way he had come. The horse carried the bleeding Gryfflet to the court and there was great sorrow for him. They cleaned his wound and cared for him and it was a long time before his life came back to him.

While Arthur was sad and troubled at Sir Gryfflet's wound, twelve aged knights rode to his court. They were messengers, they said, from the Emperor of Rome. They demanded tribute in the name of the emperor and said that if it were not paid Arthur and all his kingdom would be destroyed.

Then Arthur raged and he said, 'If you did not have the safe conduct of messengers I would kill you now. But I respect your immunity. Take this answer back. I owe no tribute to the emperor, but if he demands it I shall give him his tribute with spears and swords. By my father's soul I swear this. Take this message back with you.'

The messengers departed angrily. They had arrived at an evil time.

The king was angry and vengeful because Sir Gryfflet was hurt. He felt that he was responsible, for if he had taken advice and refused the knighthood, Gryfflet would not have challenged the knight of the fountain. Therefore, feeling that he had caused the hurt, Arthur himself must take the consequence. When night had fallen he ordered a servant to take his horse and armour, his shield and spear, and convey them to a place outside the city and there to wait for him. And before dawn the king went privately out and met his man, and armed himself, and mounted, and he commanded his servant to wait where he was, and so King Arthur rode out alone to avenge Sir Gryfflet or to pay for his bad judgement, for he valued his manhood above his kingship.

The king rode softly away from the city and he entered the forest in the first light of dawn. And among the trees he saw three rough-dressed peasants running after Merlin with clubs in their hands, trying to kill him. Arthur galloped towards them, and when they saw the armed knight they turned and ran for their lives and hid themselves in the deep forest. Arthur came up to Merlin and he said, 'You see, for all your magic and your craft, they would have killed you if I had not come along.'

Merlin replied, 'It pleases you to think it, but it is not true. I could have saved myself any time I wished. You are nearer to danger than I was, for you are riding in the direction of your death and God is not your friend.'

They moved on until they came to the fountain by the path and the rich pavilion beside it with the rising sun shining on it. And in a chair beside the tent an armed knight sat quietly and Arthur addressed him.

'Sir Knight,' he said, 'why do you guard this way and challenge every knight who passes by?'

'It is my custom,' said the knight.

'Then I tell you to change your custom,' said the king.

'It is my custom,' the knight repeated, 'and I will continue it. Whoever does not approve of it is at liberty to change it if he can.'

'I shall change it,' said Arthur.

'And I shall defend it,' said the knight. And he mounted his horse and dressed his shield before him and took a great spear in his hand. The two rode together with great force and with such perfect control that the spear of each struck the centre of the shield of each and both lances shattered. Then Arthur drew his sword, but the knight called to him, 'Not that! Let us joust again with spears.'

'I have no more spears,' said Arthur.

'You shall have one of mine, I have enough,' said the knight, and his squire brought two new spears from the tent and gave one to each of them. Then again they spurred their horses and crashed together with all speed and force, and again both spears struck true and both shattered. And again Arthur laid hand to his sword. But the knight said, 'Sir, you are the best jouster I have ever met. In honour of our knighthood, let us joust again.'

'I agree,' said Arthur.

Then two more spears were brought and they ran together again, but this time Arthur's spear shattered while his opponent's held and drove both horse and man to the ground. And Arthur stepped clear of his horse and drew his sword and he said, 'I shall fight you on foot since I have lost to you on horseback.'

And the knight said mockingly, 'I am still mounted.'

Then the king was furious and he put his shield before him and advanced towards the mounted knight.

When the knight saw this fierce bravery he quickly dismounted, for he was an honourable man and took no pleasure in unfair advantage. He drew his sword and the two fought fiercely, striking and slashing and parrying, and the swords cut through shields and carved through armour, and blood dripped and flowed, and their hands were slippery with blood. After a time they rested, panting with weariness and weak from loss of blood. Then in renewed fury they rushed together again like two rams. Their sword blades collided in mid-stroke and Arthur's sword broke in two pieces, and he backed away and lowered his hand and stood sad and silent.

Then the knight said courteously, 'So I have won and I have the choice either to kill you or let you live. Yield to me and admit that you are beaten or you must die.'

Then Arthur said, 'Death is welcome when it comes. But defeat is not welcome. I will not yield.' And with that, unarmed, he leaped at the knight and grasped him around the middle and threw him down and ripped off his helmet. But the knight was powerful. He wrestled and twisted until he rolled free and tore Arthur's helmet off and raised his sword to kill him.

Then Merlin intervened, saying, 'Knight, hold your hand. This one is much more than you know. If you kill him you give a dreadful wound to the whole kingdom.'

'What do you mean?'

'This is King Arthur,' said Merlin.

Then panic, fear of the wrath of the king, came over the knight and again he raised his sword to kill him. But Merlin looked in his eyes and made an enchantment, and the knight's sword dropped and he fell into a deep sleep.

Then Arthur cried, 'Merlin, what have you done? Have you killed this good knight with your magic? He was one of the best knights in the world. I would give anything if he were alive.'

Merlin said, 'Do not worry about him, my lord. He is not as badly hurt as you are. He is asleep and will waken within the hour.' And Merlin said, 'I warned you this morning what a knight he was. He would surely have killed you if I had not been here. There is no knight living better than he. In the future he will render you good service.'

'Who is he?' asked Arthur.

'He is called King Pellinore. And I foresee that he will have two sons named Percival and Lamorake, who will grow up to be great knights.'

The king was weak and wounded and Merlin took him to a hermitage nearby where the hermit cleaned his wounds and stopped the blood with bandages and healing balms. For three days the king rested there before he was able to mount his horse and go on his way. And as he rode with Merlin by his side, the king said bitterly, 'You must be proud to serve me, Merlin, a defeated king, a great and worthy knight who does not even have a sword, disarmed, wounded, and helpless. What is a knight without a sword? A nothing – even less than a nothing.'

'It is a child speaking,' said Merlin, 'not a king and not a knight, but a hurt and angry child, or you would know, my lord, that there is more to a king than a crown, and far more to a knight than a sword. You were a knight when you grappled Pellinore unarmed.'

'And he defeated me.'

'You were a knight,' said Merlin. 'Somewhere in the world there is defeat for everyone. Some are destroyed by defeat and some made small and mean by victory. Greatness lives in one who triumphs equally over defeat and victory. But you want a sword. Very well, you shall have one. There is a sword nearby that shall be yours if I can get it for you.'

They rode on until they came to a broad lake of clear and lovely water. And in the middle of the lake Arthur saw an arm with a sleeve of rich white silk, and the hand held up a sword by its scabbard.

Merlin said, 'There is the sword I spoke of.'

Then they saw a damsel who walked lightly on the surface of the lake.

'This is a wonder,' said the king. 'Who is that damsel?'

'She is the Lady of the Lake,' said Merlin, 'and there are other wonders. Under a great rock deep in the lake is a palace as rich and beautiful as any on earth where the lady lives. She will come to you now, and if you are courteous and ask her nicely, she may give you the sword.'

Then the lady drew near and saluted Arthur, and he greeted her and asked, 'Lady, please tell me what is that sword that I see in the lake. I wish I might have it, for I have no sword.'

The damsel said, 'The sword is mine, my lord, but if you will give me a gift when I ask it, you shall have the sword.'

'On my honour, I will give you anything you ask for,' said the king.

The lady said, 'Then it is yours. Go to the little boat you see there and row out to the arm and take both sword and the scabbard. I will ask for my gift when the time comes.'

Then Arthur and Merlin dismounted and tied their horses to trees, and they went to the little boat and rowed to the arm. And Arthur gently took the sword, and the hand released it and hand and arm disappeared under the water. And the two rowed back to the shore and mounted and rode on their way.

Near the pathside they came to a rich tent and Arthur asked about it.

'Don't you remember?' Merlin said. 'That is the pavilion of your late enemy King Pellinore. But he is not here. He fought with one of your knights, Sir Egglame, who finally turned and fled to save his life. And Pellinore gave chase and followed him as far as Caerleon. We will meet him soon returning.'

'Good,' said Arthur. 'Now that I have a sword I will fight him again, and this time I will not lose.'

'That is not well spoken, sir,' Merlin said, 'Sir Pellinore is weary with fighting and chasing. There will be little honour in beating him now. I advise you to let him pass, for he will give you good service soon and his sons will serve you after his death. In a short time you will be so pleased with him that you will give him your sister for his wife. Therefore, do not challenge him when he passes.'

'I will do as you advise,' said the king, and he looked at his new sword and admired its beauty.

Merlin asked, 'Which do you like better, the sword or the scabbard?'

'The sword of course,' said Arthur.

'The scabbard is far more precious,' said Merlin. 'While you wear the scabbard you can lose no blood no matter how deeply you are wounded. It is a magic scabbard. You will do well to keep it always near you.'

As they came near to Caerleon they met King Pellinore, but

Merlin did not trust the temper of either of the knights and he cast a spell so that Pellinore did not see them.

'It is strange that he did not speak,' Arthur said.

'He did not see you,' Merlin explained. 'If he had, there would have been a fight.'

And so they came to Caerleon and Arthur's knights were glad when they heard the story of his adventures. They were amazed that the king would endanger himself alone, and the bravest men were filled with happiness to serve under a chieftain who rode to his adventure as any poor knight would. They gave King Arthur honour and love, but also fellowship.

But Arthur could not taste the full flower of the fellowship because his mind went brooding back to Merlin's words about the king's sin with his sister and the bitter prophecy that his own son would destroy him.

Meanwhile, King Royns of North Wales, so lately defeated by Arthur, had been raging continuously in the north and had taken Ireland and the Isles. Now he sent messengers to King Arthur with a savage and arrogant demand. King Royns, the message said, had overcome the eleven lords of the north, and as wild tribute he had skinned off their beards to trim his cloak. Eleven beards Royns had and he demanded the twelfth – King Arthur's beard. Unless Arthur sent his beard Royns promised to invade the land and put it to burning ruin and take King Arthur's beard and his head also.

Arthur heard the messengers and he responded almost with joy, for it took him for a moment from his foreboding.

'Say to your master that his boastful, shameful demand has been received. Tell him my beard is not well grown enough to line his cloak. And as for giving him homage, I promise to bring him to his knees crawling for my mercy. If he had ever associated with honourable men, he could not have sent so shameful a message. Now take those words with you.' And he sent the messengers away.

Then Arthur asked his assembled men, 'Does anyone here know this King Royns ?'

And one of the knights, Sir Naram, answered, 'I know him well, my lord. He is a wild, proud, passionate man. But do not hold him lightly because of his arrogance, for he is one of the best fighting men alive. And do not doubt that he will try with all his force to carry out this threat.'

'I will take care of him,' said the king. 'When I have time I will deal with him as he deserves.'

And his brooding fell on him again. He called Merlin and questioned him. 'Is the child you spoke of born?'

'Yes, my lord.'

'When?'

'On May Day, my lord,' said Merlin. Arthur sent him away and sat thinking with narrowed eyes, and his inward thoughts were dark and mean. He could not bear to have his incestuous shame known, and at the same time he was frightened at the prophecy. He sought a way to escape from ill fame and his fate. Then a cruel and cowardly plan grew in his mind with which to save his honour and his life. He was ashamed to tell his plan to Merlin before he put it into action. To conceal his incestuous sin, couriers went out to all his barons and his knights, ordering that any male child born on May Day must be sent to the king on pain of death. The barons were angry and afraid and many put the blame on Merlin more than on Arthur, but they did not dare refuse and many children born on May Day were taken to the king, and they were only four weeks old. Then the king conveyed the babies to the coast, for he could not bring himself to slaughter them. He placed the month-old babies in a little ship and set the sail to an offshore wind and it moved out to sea unattended. King Arthur with shamed and evil eyes, watched the little ship carry its evidence of his fate away, shrinking in the distance. And the king turned and rode heavily away.

The wind arose, shouting, and veered about and drove the ship back on the land. Below a castle it struck a sunken rock and spilled its wailing cargo into the waves. On the shore a good man sitting in his hut heard a cry above the whining wind and lash of surf. He walked to the beach and in the soil he found a baby wedged in a bit of wreckage. He took it up and warmed it under his cloak and carried it home with him, and his wife took Mordred to her breast and suckled him.

the knight with
the two swords

In the long and lawless time after Uther Pendragon's death and before his son Arthur became king, in England and Wales, in Cornwall and Scotland and the Outer Isles, many lords took lawless power to themselves, and some of them refused to give it up, so that Arthur's first kingly years were given to restoring his realm by law, by order, and by force of arms.

One of his most persistent enemies was the Lord Royns of Wales whose growing strength in the west and north was a constant threat to the kingdom.

When Arthur held court at London, a faithful knight rode in with the news that Royns in his arrogance had raised a large army and invaded the land, burning crops and houses and killing Arthur's subjects as he came.

'If this is true, I must protect my people,' Arthur said.

'It is true enough,' said the knight. 'I myself saw the invaders and their destructive work.'

'Then I must fight this Royns and destroy him,' said the king. And he sent out an order to all loyal lords and knights and gentlemen of arms to meet in general council at Camelot, where plans would be made to defend the kingdom.

And when the barons and the knights had gathered and sat in the great hall below the king, a damsel came before them saying she was sent by the great lady Lyle of Avalon.

'What message do you bring?' asked Arthur.

Then the damsel opened her richly furred cloak and it was seen that from her belt there hung a noble sword.

The king said, 'It is not seemly for a maiden to go armed. Why do you wear a sword?'

'I wear it because I have no choice,' the damsel said. 'And I must wear it until it is taken from me by a knight who is brave and honourable, of good repute and without stain. Only such a knight may draw this sword from its scabbard. I have been to the camp of Lord Royns where I was told were good knights, but neither he nor any of his followers could draw the blade.'

Arthur said, 'Here are good men, and I myself will try to draw it, not that I am the best, but because if I try first my barons and knights will feel free to follow me.'

Then Arthur grasped sheath and girdle and pulled eagerly at the sword, but it did not move.

'Sir,' said the damsel, 'you need not use strength. It will come out easily in the hands of the knight for whom it is destined.'

Arthur turned to his men and said, 'Now all of you try it one by one.'

The damsel said, 'Be sure, you who try, that you have no shame or guile or treachery before you try. Only a clean and unstained knight may draw it and he must be of noble blood on both his mother's and his father's side.'

Then most of the gathered knights attempted to draw the sword and none succeeded. Then the maiden said sadly, 'I believed that here I would find blameless men and the best knights in the world.'

Arthur was displeased and he said, 'These are as good or better knights than you will find anywhere. I am unhappy that it is not their fortune to help you.'

A knight named Sir Balin of Northumberland had remained apart. It had been his misfortune in fair fight to kill a cousin of the king, and the quarrel being misrepresented, he had been a prisoner for half a year. Only recently had some of his friends explained the matter and had him released. He watched the trial anxiously, but because he had been in prison and because he was poor and his clothing worn and dirty, he did not come forward until all had tried and the damsel was ready to depart. Only then did Sir Balin call to her, saying, 'Lady, I beg you out of your courtesy to let me try. I know I am poorly dressed, but I feel in my heart that I may succeed.'

The damsel looked at his ragged cloak and she could not believe him a man of honour and of noble blood. She said, 'Sir, why do you wish to put me to more pain when all of these noble knights have failed?'

Sir Balin said, 'Fair lady, a man's worth is not in his clothing. Manhood and honour are hidden inside. And sometimes virtues are not known to everyone.'

'That is the truth,' said the damsel, 'and I thank you for reminding me. Here, grasp the sword and see what you can do.'

Then Balin went to her and drew the sword easily, and he looked at the shining blade and it pleased him very much. Then the king and many others applauded Sir Balin, but some of the knights were filled with jealous spite.

The damsel said, 'You must be the best and most blameless knight I have found or you could not have done it. Now gentle and courteous knight, please give me the sword again.'

'No,' said Balin. 'I like this sword, and I will keep it until someone is able to take it from me by force.'

'Do not keep it,' the damsel cried. 'It is not wise to keep it. If you do, you will use it to kill the best friend and the man you love best in the world. That sword will destroy you.'

Balin said, 'I will accept any adventure God sends me, lady, but I will not return the sword to you.'

'Then in a short time you will be sorry for it,' the lady said. 'I do not want the sword for myself. If you take it, the sword will destroy you and I pity you.'

Then Sir Balin sent for his horse and armour and he begged the king's permission to depart.

Arthur said, 'Do not leave us now. I know you are angered by your unjust imprisonment, but false evidence was brought against you. If I had known your honour and your bravery, I would have acted differently. Now, if you will stay in my court and in this fellowship, I will advance you and make amends.'

'I thank Your Highness,' said Balin. 'Your bounty is well known. I have no resentment towards you, but I must go away and I beg that your grace may go with me.'

'I am not glad of your departure,' said the king. 'I ask you, good sir, not to be long away from us. We shall welcome your return and I will repay you for the injustice done against you.'

'God thank your good grace,' replied the knight, and he made ready to depart. And there were some jealous men in the court who whispered that witchcraft rather than knightly virtue was responsible for his good fortune.

While Balin armed himself and his horse, the Lady of the Lake rode into Arthur's court, and she was richly dressed and well mounted. She saluted the king and then reminded him of the gift he had promised her when she gave him the sword of the lake.

'I remember my promise,' said Arthur, 'but I have forgotten the name of the sword, if you ever told it to me.'

'It is called Excalibur,' the lady said, 'and that means Cut Steel.'

'Thank you, lady,' said the king. 'And now, what gift do you ask ? I will give you anything in my power.'

Then the lady said savagely, 'I want two heads – that of the knight who drew the sword and the head of the damsel who brought it here. I will not be content until I have both heads. That knight killed my brother and the damsel caused my father's death. This is my demand.'

The king was taken aback at the ferocity. He said, 'I cannot in honour kill these two for your vengeance. Ask for anything else and I will give it.'

'I ask for nothing else,' said the lady.

Now Balin was ready to depart and he saw the Lady of the Lake and knew her for the one who by secret craft had brought death to his mother three years before. And when he was told that she had demanded his head, he strode near to her and cried, 'You are an evil thing. You want my head ? I shall have yours.' And he drew his sword and slashed her head from her body with one stroke.

'What have you done ?' Arthur cried. 'You have brought shame to me and to my court. I was in this lady's debt, and moreover she was under my protection. I can never forgive this outrage.'

'My lord,' said Balin, 'I am sorry for your displeasure, but not for my deed. This was an evil witch. By enchantment and sorcery she killed many good knights, and by craft and falsehood she caused my mother to be burned to death.'

The king said, 'No matter what your reason, you had no right to do this and in my presence. It was an ugly deed and an insult to me. Now leave my court. You are no longer welcome here.'

Then Balin took up the head of the Lady of the Lake by the hair and carried it to his lodging, where his squire awaited him, and they mounted their horses and rode out of the town.

And Balin said, 'I want you to take this head to my friends and relatives in Northumberland. Tell them my most dangerous enemy is dead. Tell them that I am free from prison and how I got this second sword.'

'I am sad that you have done this,' said the squire. 'You are greatly to blame for losing the friendship of the king. No one doubts your courage, but you are a headstrong knight and when you choose a way you cannot change your course even if it lead to your destruction. This is your fault and your destiny.'

Then Balin said, 'I have thought of a way to win the king's affection. I will ride to the camp of his enemy Lord Royns and I will kill him or be killed. If it should happen that I win, King Arthur will be my friend again.'

The squire shook his head at such a desperate plan, but he said, 'Sir, where shall I meet you?'

'In King Arthur's court,' said Balin confidently, and he sent his squire away.

Meanwhile, the king and all his followers were sad and shamed at Balin's deed and they buried the Lady of the Lake richly and with all ceremony.

In the court at that time there was a knight who was most jealous of Balin for his success in drawing the magic sword. He was Sir Launceor, son of the King of Ireland, a proud and ambitious man who believed himself to be one of the best knights in the world. He asked the king's permission to ride after Sir Balin to avenge the insult to Arthur's dignity.

The king said, 'Go – and do your best. I am angry with Balin. Wipe out the outrage to my court.'

And when Sir Launceor had gone to his quarters, to make ready for the field, Merlin came before King Arthur, and he heard how the sword was drawn and how the Lady of the Lake was slaughtered.

Then Merlin looked at the damsel of the sword who had remained in the court. And Merlin said, 'Look at this damsel standing here. She is a false and evil woman and she cannot deny it. She has a brother, a brave knight and a good and true man. This damsel loved a knight and became his paramour. And her brother, to wipe away the shame, challenged her lover and killed him in fair fight. Then in her rage, this damsel took his sword to the lady Lyle of Avalon and asked help to be revenged on her own brother.'

And Merlin said, 'The lady Lyle took the sword and cast a spell on it and laid a curse on it. Only the best and bravest of knights would be able to draw it from its sheath, and he who drew it would kill his brother with it.' And Merlin turned again on the damsel. 'This was your spiteful reason for coming here,' he said. 'Don't deny it. I know it as well as you do. I wish to God you had not come, for wherever you go you carry harm and death.

'The knight who drew the sword is the best and bravest, and the sword he drew will destroy him. For everything he does will turn to bitterness and death through no fault of his own. The curse of the sword has become his fate. My lord,' Merlin said to the king, 'that good knight has little time to live, but before he dies he will do you a service you will long remember.' And King Arthur listened in sad wonder.

By now Sir Launceor of Ireland had armed himself at all points. He dressed his shield on his shoulder and took a spear in his hand and he urged his horse at utmost speed along the path Sir Balin had taken. It was not long before he overtook his enemy on top of a mountain. And Sir Launceor shouted, 'Stop where you are or I will make you stop. Your shield will not protect you now.'

Balin answered lightly, 'You might better have remained at home. A man who threatens his enemy often finds his promise turns back on himself. From what court do you come ?'

'From King Arthur's court,' said the Irish knight. 'And I come to avenge the insult you have put on the king this day.'

Sir Balin said, 'If I must fight you, I must. But believe me, sir, I am grieved that I have injured the king or any of his court. I know your duty is plain, but before we fight, know that I had no choice. The Lady of the Lake not only did me mortal injury but demanded my life as well.'

Sir Launceor said, 'Enough of talking. Make ready, for only one of us will leave this field.'

Then they couched their spears and thundered together, and Launceor's spear splintered, but Balin's lanced through shield and armour and chest and the Irish knight went crashing to the ground. When Balin had turned his horse and drawn his sword, he saw his enemy lying dead on the grass. And then he heard galloping hoofs and he saw a damsel ride towards them as fast as she could. When she drew up and saw Sir Launceor dead, she burst into wild sorrow.

'Balin!' she cried. 'Two bodies you have killed in one heart and two hearts in one body and two souls you have released.' Then she dismounted and took up her lover's sword and fell fainting to the ground. And when her senses returned she screamed her sorrow and Balin was filled with pain. He went to her and tried to take the sword from her, but she clung to it so desperately that for fear he might hurt her he released his hold. Then suddenly she reversed the sword and placed the pommel on the ground and drove her body on the point, and the blade pierced her and she died.

Balin stood with heavy heart and he was ashamed that he had caused her death. And he cried aloud, 'What love there must have been between these two, and I have destroyed them!' He could not bear the sight of them, and he mounted and rode sadly away towards the forest.

In the distance he saw a knight approaching, and when he could see the device on the shield, Balin knew it was his brother Balan. And when they met they tore off their helmets and kissed each other and wept for joy.

Balan said, 'My brother, I could not have hoped to meet you so soon. I came upon a man at the castle of the four catapults and he told me that you were released from prison and that he had seen you in King Arthur's court. And I rode from Northumberland to look for you.'

Then Balin told his brother about the damsel and the sword and how he had killed the Lady of the Lake and so angered the king, and he said, 'Yonder a knight lies dead who was sent after me, and beside him his love who destroyed herself, and I am heavy-hearted and grieved.'

'It is a sad thing,' Balan said, 'but you are a knight and you know you must accept whatever God ordains for you.'

'I know that,' said Balin, 'but I am sorrowful that King Arthur is displeased with me. He is the best and greatest king who reigns on earth. And I will get back his love or leave my life.'

'How will you do that, my brother?'

'I will tell you,' said Balin. 'King Arthur's enemy Lord Royns, has laid siege to the Castle Terrabil in Cornwall. I will ride there and prove my honour and courage against him.'

'I hope it may be,' Balan said. 'I will go with you and venture my life with yours as a brother should.'

'How good it is that you are here, dear brother,' Balin said. 'Let us ride on together.'

As they talked a dwarf came riding from the direction of Camelot, and when he saw the bodies of the knight and his beloved damsel he tore his hair and cried out to the brothers, 'Which of you has done this deed?'

'What right have you to ask?' said Balan.

'Because I want to know.'

And Balin answered him, 'It was I. I killed the knight in fair combat in self-defence and the damsel destroyed herself in sorrow, and I am grieved. For her sake I will serve all women while I live.'

The dwarf said, 'You have done great damage to yourself. This dead knight was the son of the King of Ireland. His kin will take vengeance on you. They will follow you all over the world until they have killed you.'

'That does not frighten me,' said Balin. 'My pain is that I have doubly displeased my lord King Arthur by killing his knight.'

Then King Mark of Cornwall came riding by and saw the bodies, and when he was told the story of their death, he said, 'They must have loved each other truly. And I will see that they have a tomb in their memory.' Then he ordered his men to pitch their tents and he searched the country for a place to bury the lovers. In a church nearby he had a great stone raised from the floor in front of the high altar and he buried the knight and his damsel together, and when the stone was lowered back, King Mark had words carved on it saying, 'Here lies Sir Launceor, son of Ireland's king, slain in combat with Sir Balin and beside him his love the lady Colombe, who in sorrow slew herself with her lover's sword.'

Merlin entered the church and he said to Balin, 'Why did you not save this lady's life?'

'I swear I could not,' said Balin. 'I tried to save her but she was too quick.'

'I am sorry for you,' Merlin said. 'In punishment for the

death you are destined to strike the saddest blow since the lance pierced the side of our Lord Jesus Christ. With your stroke you will wound the best knight living and you will bring poverty and misery and despair to three kingdoms.'

And Balin cried out, 'This can't be true. If I believed it I would kill myself now and make you a liar.'

'But you will not,' said Merlin.

'What is my sin?' Balin demanded.

'Ill fortune,' said Merlin. 'Some call it fate.' And suddenly he vanished.

And after a time the brothers took leave of King Mark.

'First, tell me your names,' he asked.

And Balan answered, 'You see that he wears two swords. Call him the Knight with the Two Swords.'

Then the two brothers took their way towards the camp of Royns. And on a broad and windswept moor they came upon a stranger muffled in a cloak who asked them where they were going.

'Why should we tell you?' they replied, and Balin said, 'Tell us your name, stranger.'

'Why should I, when you are secret?' said the man.

'It's an evil sign when a man will not tell his name,' said Balan.

'Think what you wish,' the stranger said. 'What would you think if I told you that you ride to find Lord Royns and that you will fail without my help?'

'I would think that you are Merlin, and if you are, I would ask your help.'

'You must be brave, for you will need courage,' said Merlin.

Sir Balin said, 'Don't worry about courage. We will do what we can.'

They came to the edge of a forest and dismounted in a dim and leafy hollow, and they unsaddled their horses and put them to graze. And the knights lay under the sheltering branches of the trees and fell asleep.

When it was near midnight Merlin awakened them quietly. 'Make ready quickly,' he said. 'Your chance is coming. Royns has stolen from his camp with only a bodyguard to pay a midnight visit of love to Lady de Vance.'

From cover of the trees they saw horsemen coming.

'Which is Royns?' Balin asked.

'The tall one in the middle,' Merlin said. 'Hold back until they come abreast.'

And when the cavalcade was passing in the starlit dark, the brothers charged out from their concealment and struck Royns from his saddle, and they turned on his startled men, striking right and left with their swords, and some went down and the rest turned tail and fled.

Then the brothers returned to the felled Royns to kill him, but he yielded and asked mercy. 'Brave knights, do not murder me,' he said. 'My life is valuable to you and my death worth nothing.'

'That is true,' the brothers said, and they raised up the wounded Royns and helped him to his horse. And when they looked for Merlin he was gone, for he by his magic arts had flown ahead to Camelot. And he told Arthur that his worst enemy, Lord Royns, was overthrown and captured.

'By whom?' the king demanded.

'By two knights who wish your friendship and your grace more than anything in the world. They will be here in the morning and you will see who they are,' Merlin said and he would not speak further.

Very early the two brothers brought their wounded prisoner, Royns, to the gates of Camelot and delivered him into the safe-keeping of the warders and they rode away into the dawning day.

When it was reported, King Arthur went to his wounded enemy and he said, 'Sir, you are a welcome sight to me. By what adventure have you come?'

'By a bitter adventure, my lord.'

'Who took you?' the king asked.

'One who is called the Knight with the Two Swords and his brother. They overturned me and swept away my bodyguard.'

Merlin broke in, 'Now I can tell you sir. It was that Balin who drew the cursed sword and his brother Balan. Two better knights you will never find. The pity is that their fate is closing in and they have not long to live.'

'He has put me in debt to him,' said the king. 'And I do not deserve kindness from Balin.'

'He will do much more for you than this, my lord,' said

Merlin. 'But I bring you news. You must prepare your knights for battle. Tomorrow before noon the forces of Royns's brother, Nero, will attack you. You have much to do now and I will leave you.'

Then King Arthur mustered his knights quickly and rode toward the Castle Terrabil. Nero was ready for him in the field with forces that outnumbered those of the king. Nero led the vanguard and he waited only for the arrival of King Lot with his army. But he waited in vain, for Merlin had gone to King Lot and held him enthralled with tales of wonder and of prophecy, while Arthur launched his attack on Nero. Sir Kay fought so well that day that the memory of his deeds has lived forever. And Sir Hervis de Revel of the line of Sir Thomas Malory distinguished himself, as did Sir Tobinus Streat de Montroy. Into the battle Sir Balin and his brother raged so fiercely that it was said of them that they were either angels from heaven or devils from hell, depending on which side you held. And Arthur in the vanguard saw the brothers' actions and praised them above all his knights. And the king's forces prevailed and drove the enemy from the field and destroyed Nero's power.

A messenger rode to King Lot and reported the battle lost and Nero killed whilst Lot had listened to Merlin's tales. King Lot said, 'I have been bewitched by this Merlin. If I had been there Arthur could not have won the day. This magician has fooled me and held me like a child listening to stories.'

Merlin said, 'I know that today one king must die, and much as I regret it, I would rather it were you than King Arthur,' and Merlin vanished in the air.

Then King Lot gathered his leaders. 'What should I do?' he asked. 'Is it better to sue for peace or to fight? If Nero is defeated, half our army is gone.'

A knight said, 'King Arthur's men are weary with battle and their horses exhausted, while we are fresh. If we attack him now we have the advantage.'

'If you all agree, we will fight,' said King Lot. 'I hope that you will do as well as I will try to do.'

Then King Lot galloped to the field and charged Arthur's men, but they held firm and did not give ground.

King Lot, out of shame for his failure, held the forefront of his knights and fought like a devil raging, for he hated Arthur above all men. Once he had been the king's friend wedded to Arthur's half-sister. But when Arthur in ignorance seduced his friend's wife and got her with the child Mordred, King Lot's loyalty turned to hatred and he strove desperately to overcome his once friend.

As Merlin had foretold, Sir Pellinore, who once overthrew Arthur at the Fountain in the Forest, had become the king's loyal friend and fought in the first line of his knights. Sir Pellinore forced his horse through the press around King Lot and aimed a great swinging sword stroke at him. The blade glanced off and killed Lot's horse, and as he went down Pellinore struck him on the helm and drove him to the ground.

When King Lot's men saw him fallen, they gave up the fight and tried to flee, and many were taken and more were killed in flight.

When the bodies of the dead were gathered together, twelve great lords were found who had died serving Nero and King Lot. These were carried to St Stephen's Church in Camelot for burial, while the lesser knights were interred nearby under a huge stone.

King Arthur buried Lot in a rich tomb separately, but the twelve great lords he placed together and raised a triumphal monument over them. Merlin by his arts made figures of the twelve lords in gilded copper and brass, in attitudes of defeat, and each figure held a candle which burned night and day. Above these effigies, Merlin placed a statue of King Arthur with a drawn sword held over his enemies' heads. And Merlin prophesied that the candles would burn until Arthur's death and at that moment would go out; and he made other prophecies that day of things to come.

Soon after this, Arthur, wearied with campaigns and governing and sick of the dark, deep-walled rooms of castles, ordered his pavilion set up in a green meadow outside the walls where he might rest and recover his strength in the quiet and the sweet air. He laid himself down on a camp bed to sleep, but he had not closed his eyes when he heard a horse approaching and saw a knight riding near who spoke words of complaint and sorrow to himself.

As he passed the pavilion, the king called out to him, saying, 'Come to me, good knight, and tell me the reason for your sadness.'

The knight answered, 'What good could that do? You cannot help me.' And he rode on towards the castle of Meliot.

Then the king tried to sleep again, but his curiosity had risen to keep him awake, and as he pondered, Sir Balin rode near, and when he saw King Arthur he dismounted and saluted his lord.

'You are always welcome,' said the king. 'But particularly now. A short time ago a knight went past and he was crying out in sorrow, and he would not answer when I asked the cause. If you wish to serve me, ride after this knight and bring him to me whether he wishes to come or not, for I am curious.'

'I will bring him to you, my lord,' Sir Balin said, 'or else he will be more sad than he is.'

And Balin mounted and cantered after the knight, and after a time he found him sitting under a tree with a damsel beside him. Sir Balin said, 'Sir Knight, you must come with me to King Arthur and tell him the cause of your sorrow.'

'That I will not do,' said the knight. 'I would be in great danger if I did and you would gain nothing.'

'Please come with me, sir,' said Balin. 'If you refuse I must fight you, and I don't want to.'

'I have told you my life is in danger. Will you promise to protect me?'

'I will protect you or die in the attempt,' said Balin. And with that the knight mounted his horse and they rode away, leaving the damsel under the tree. As they came to King Arthur's tent, they heard the sound of a charging war horse but saw nothing, and suddenly the knight was hurled from his saddle by an invisible force, and he lay dying on the ground with a great spear through his body. And he gasped, 'That was my danger – a knight named Garlon who has the art of invisibility. I was under your protection and you have failed me. Take my horse. He is better than yours. And go back to the damsel – she will lead you to my enemy and perhaps you may avenge me.'

Balin cried, 'On my honour and my knighthood I will. I swear it before God.'

And with that the knight, Sir Harleus le Berbeus, died, and

Balin pulled the truncheon of the spear from his body and rode sadly away, for he was grieved that he had not protected the knight as he had promised, and he understood at last why Arthur had been enraged at the death of the Lady of the Lake under his protection. And Balin felt a darkness of misfortune hanging over him. He found the damsel in the forest and gave her the truncheon of the spear that had killed her lover, and she carried it always as a sign and a remembrance. She led Sir Balin on the quest he had accepted from the dying knight.

In the forest they came upon a knight fresh from hunting, who, seeing Balin's sorrow-clouded face, asked the reason for his pain and Balin curtly answered that he did not wish to speak of it.

The knight resented the discourtesy, saying, 'If I were armed against men instead of stags, you would answer me.'

Balin answered wearily, 'I have no reason not to tell you,' and he recounted his strange and fatal history. The knight was so moved by the tale he begged leave to join him in the quest of vengeance. His name was Sir Peryne de Monte Belyarde, and he went to his house nearby and armed himself and joined them on their way. And as they rode past a little lonely hermitage and chapel in the forest, there came again the sound of charging hoofs and Sir Peryne fell with a spear through his body.

'Your story was true,' he said. 'The invisible enemy has slain me. You are a man fated to cause the destruction of your loved friends.' And Sir Peryne died of his wounds.

Balin said in sorrow, 'My enemy is something I cannot see. How can I challenge the invisible?'

Then the hermit helped him to carry the dead into the chapel and they buried him in pity and honour.

And afterwards Balin and the damsel rode on until they came to a castle with strong defences. Balin crossed the drawbridge and entered first, and as he did the portcullis rattled down and held him prisoner, with the damsel outside, where many men attacked her with knives to kill her. Then Balin ran up to the top of the wall and he leaped into the moat far below, and the water broke his fall and saved him from injury. He crawled from the moat and drew his sword, but the attackers drew away and told him that they only followed the custom of the castle. They explained that the lady of the castle had long suffered a dreadful wasting sickness and the only cure for it was a silver dish of blood from the virgin daughter of a king and so it was their custom to take blood from every damsel who passed that way.

Balin said, 'I am sure she will give you some of her blood, but you need not kill her to get it.' Then he helped to lance her vein and they caught it in a silver dish, but it did not cure the lady, wherefore it was thought that the damsel did not fulfil one or the other or both of the requirements. But because of the offering they were made welcome and given good cheer, and they rested for the night and in the morning took their way again. Four days they continued without adventure, and at last lodged in the house of a gentleman. And as they sat at their supper, they heard moans of pain from a chamber nearby and Balin asked about it.

'I will tell you about it,' the gentleman said. 'Recently at a jousting I rode against the brother of King Pelham. Twice I struck him from his horse and he was angry and threatened revenge against someone near to me. Then he made himself invisible and wounded my son, whom you hear crying out in pain. He will not be well until I have killed that evil knight and taken his blood.'

'I know him well, but I have never seen him,' Balin said. 'He has killed two of my knights in the same way, and I would rather meet him in combat than have all the gold in the realm.'

'I will tell you how to meet him,' said the host. 'His brother, King Pelham, has proclaimed a great feast within twenty days. And no knight may attend unless he brings his wife or his mistress. The king's brother, Garlon, is sure to be there.'

'Then I will be there also,' Balin said.

And in the morning the three started their journey and they rode for fifteen days until they came to Pelham's country, and they came to his castle on the day the feast began, and they stabled their horses and went to the great hall, but Balin's host was refused because he had brought neither wife nor paramour. But Balin was welcomed and taken to a chamber where he unarmed and bathed himself and servants brought him a rich robe to wear to the feasting. But then they asked him to leave his sword with his armour; Balin refused. He said, 'In my country a knight must keep his sword with him always. If I cannot take it, I may not feast.' Reluctantly they let him take his weapon, and he went into the great hall and sat among the knights, with his lady beside him.

Then Balin asked, 'Is there a knight in this court named Garlon, brother of the king?'

'There he is now,' said a man nearby. 'Look, he is the one with the dark skin. He is a strange man and he has killed many knights because he has the secret of invisibility.'

Balin stared at Garlon and considered what he should do, and he thought, 'If I kill him now, I will not be able to escape, but if I do not I may never see him again, because he will not be visible.'

Garlon had noticed Balin staring at him and it angered him. He arose from his place and came to Balin and slapped him in the face with the back of his hand and said, 'I do not like you staring at me. Eat your meat, or do anything else you came to do.'

'I will do what I came to do,' Balin said and he drew his sword and cut off Garlon's head. Then he said to his lady, 'Give me the truncheon that killed your love,' and he took it from her and drove it through Garlon's body, crying, 'You killed a good knight with that. Now it sticks in you,' and he called to his friend outside the hall, 'Here is blood enough to cure your son.'

The assembled knights had sat astonished, but now they leaped to their feet to set on Balin. King Pelham stood up from the high table, saying, 'You have killed my brother. You must die.'

And Balin taunted him, 'Very well – do it yourself if you are brave enough.'

'You are right,' Pelham said. 'Stand back, you knights. I will kill him myself for my brother's sake.'

Pelham took a huge battle axe from the wall and advanced and aimed a blow and Balin parried with his sword, but the heavy axe broke his sword in two so that he was weaponless. Then Balin ran from the hall with Pelham following. He went from chamber to chamber looking for a weapon but he could not find one and always he could hear King Pelham following.

At last Balin came to a chamber and saw a wonder. The room was hung with cloth of gold figured with mystic holy symbols and a bed was curtained with marvellous curtains. On the bed under a cover woven of golden thread lay the perfect body of an ancient and venerable man, while on a golden table beside the bed there stood a strangely wrought spear, a haft of wood, a lean iron shank, and a small pointed head.

Balin heard Pelham's pursuing steps and he seized the spear and drove it into the side of his enemy. And at that moment an earthquake rumbled and the walls of the castle cracked outwards and the roof fell in and Balin and King Pelham rolled in the tumbling rubble to the ground and they lay unconscious, pinned under stones and pieces of timber. Inside the castle most of the gathered knights were killed by the falling roof.

After a time Merlin appeared and cleared the stones from Balin and brought him to his senses. And he brought him a horse and told him to leave the country as quickly as he could.

But Balin said, 'Where is my damsel?'

'She lies dead under the fallen castle,' Merlin said.

'What caused this ruin?' Balin asked.

'You have fallen on a mystery,' Merlin said. 'Not long after Jesus Christ was crucified, Joseph, a merchant of Arimathea who gave our Lord his sepulchre, came sailing to this land bringing the sacred cup of the Last Supper filled with the holy blood and also that spear with which Longinus the Roman pierced the side of Jesus on the Cross. And Joseph brought these holy things to the Island of Glass in Avalon and there he built a church, the first in all this land. That was Joseph's body on the bed and that Longinus's spear, and with it you wounded Pelham, Joseph's descendant, and it was the dolorous stroke I spoke of long ago. And because you have done this, a blight of sickness and hunger and despair will spread over the land.'

Balin cried, 'It is not fair. It is not just.'

'Misfortune is not fair, fate is not just, but they exist just the same,' said Merlin, and he bade Balin farewell. 'For,' he said, 'we will not meet again in this world.'

Then Balin rode away through the blighted land and he saw people dead and dying on every side, and the living cried after him, 'Balin, you are the cause of this destruction. You will be punished for it.' And Balin in anguish pushed his horse to leave the destroyed country. He rode eight days, fleeing from the evil, and he was glad when he passed out of the blighted land and into a fair, untroubled forest. His spirit awakened and threw off its gloomy garments. Above the tops of the trees in a fair valley he saw the battlements of a slender tower and turned his horse towards it. Beside the tower a great horse was tied to a tree and on the ground a handsome, well-made knight sat mourning aloud to himself.

And because he had given death and suffering to so many, Balin wished to make amends. He said to the knight, 'God save you. Why are you sad? Tell me and I will try my best to help you.'

The knight said, 'Telling you would give me more pain than I have already.'

Then Balin walked a little apart and looked at the tethered horse and its equipment, and he heard the knight say, 'Oh, my lady, why have you broken your promise to meet me here at noon. You gave me my sword, a deadly gift, for I may kill myself with it for love of you.' And the knight drew his shining sword from its sheath.

Then Balin moved quickly and grasped his wrist.

'Let me go or I will kill you,' cried the knight.

'There is no good in that. I know now about your lady and I promise to bring her to you if you will tell me where she is.'

'Who are you?' the knight demanded.

'Sir Balin.'

'I know your fame,' said the knight. 'You are the Knight with the Two Swords, and you are said to be one of the bravest of knights.'

'What is your name?'

'I am Sir Garnish of the Mountain. I am a poor man's son, but because I served well in battle, Duke Harmel took me under his protection and knighted me and gave me lands. It is his daughter I love and I thought she loved me.'

'How far away is she?' Balin asked.

'Only six miles.'

'Then why do you sit here mourning? Let us go to her and find the reason for her failure.'

Then they rode together until they came to a well-built castle with high walls and a moat. And Balin said, 'Remain here and wait for me. I will go into the castle and try to find her.'

Balin went into the castle and found no one about. He searched through the halls and the rooms and at last came to a lady's chamber, but her bed was empty. He looked from her window to a lovely little garden within the walls and on the grass under a laurel tree he saw the lady and a knight lying on a green silken cloth, and they had fallen asleep in a close embrace, their heads on a pillow of grass and sweet herbs. The lady was fair but her lover was an ugly man, hairy and heavy and uncouth.

Then Balin went quietly out through chambers and halls and at the castle gate he told Sir Garnish what he had seen and led him softly to the garden. And when the knight saw his lady in the arms of another, his heart drummed with passion and his veins burst and blood streamed from his nose and mouth. In his blinding rage he drew his sword and cut off the heads of the sleeping lovers. And suddenly the rage was gone and he was sick and weak. And he blamed Balin bitterly, saying, 'You have brought sorrow to me on sorrow. If you had not brought me here I would not have known.'

Balin replied angrily, 'Was it not better to know her for what she was and so be cured of loving her? I only did what I would want done for me.'

'You have doubled my pain,' Sir Garnish said. 'You have caused me to kill what I loved most in the world and I cannot live,' and suddenly he plunged his own bloody sword through his heart and fell dead beside the headless lovers.

The castle was quiet, and Balin knew that if he were found there he would be charged with murdering all three. He went quickly out of the castle and rode away among the forest trees and the thick darkness of his fate was on him and he felt the curtains of his life closing in on him so that he seemed to be riding in a mist of hopelessness.

After a time he came to a stone cross in the path and on it in letters of gold was written, LET NO KNIGHT RIDE ALONE ON THIS WAY. An old and white-haired man approached him as he read the words and he said, 'Sir Balin, this is the boundary of your life. Turn back and you may save yourself.' And the old man vanished.

Then Balin heard a hunting horn blowing the call that announces the death of a stag. And Balin said sombrely, 'That death call is for me. I am the quarry and I am not dead yet.'

And suddenly a crowd of people clustered around him, a

hundred lovely ladies and many knights in rich and glinting armour, and they welcomed him sweetly and petted and soothed him and led him to a castle nearby where they unarmed him and gave him a rich soft robe and led him to sit in the great hall where there was music and dancing and gaiety and brittle joy.

And when Balin was comforted the Lady of the Castle came to him and said, 'Sir Knight with the Two Swords, it is the custom here that any passing stranger must joust with a knight who guards an island nearby.'

Balin said, 'It is an unhappy custom to force a knight to joust whether he wants to or not.'

'It is only one knight. Is the great Balin afraid of one knight?'

'I don't think I am afraid, my lady,' Balin said. 'But a man who has travelled far can be weary and his horse worn out. My body is weary but my heart is fresh.' And he said hopelessly, 'If I must, I must, and I would be glad to find here my death and rest and peace.'

Then a knight who stood nearby said, 'I have looked at your armour. Your shield is small and the handles are loose. Take my shield. It is large and well made.' And when Balin protested, the knight insisted, saying, 'I beg you to take it for your safety.'

Then Balin wearily armed himself and the knight brought his new and well-painted shield and forced it on him, and Balin was too weary and confused to argue, and he thought how his squire had said he was a headstrong knight and therein lay his trouble, and so he accepted the shield and mounted and rode slowly to a lake, in which there was a small island so near to the castle that it was overlooked by the battlements. And ladies and knights were gathered on the walls to see the combat.

A boat big enough for horse and man was waiting at the waterside and Balin entered it and was rowed to the island, where a damsel stood waiting for him, and she said, 'Sir Balin, why have you left your shield with your own device?'

'I don't know why,' said Balin. 'I am ground down with misfortune and my judgement all askew. I am sorry I ever came to this place, but since I am here I may as well go on. I would be ashamed to turn back. No. I will accept what comes to me, my death or my life.'

Then from long habit in the field he tested his weapons and

tightened the girth of his saddle. Then he mounted and said a prayer for himself and closed the visor of his helmet and rode towards a little habitation on the island, and the knights and ladies watched him from the tower.

Then a knight in red armour and red horse trappings rode towards him. It was Sir Balan, and when he saw that his opponent wore two swords, he thought it was his brother, but when he saw the device on the shield, he knew it could not be.

In dreadful silence the two knights couched their spears and crashed together, and both spears struck true and did not shatter, and both knights were flung to the ground and lay stunned. Balin was sorely bruised by the fall and his body ached with weariness. And Balan was the first to recover. He rose to his feet and came towards Balin and Balin staggered up to face him.

Balan aimed the first stroke but Balin raised his shield and warded it, and striking underneath he pierced helmet, and he struck again with that unhappy sword and staggered Balan, and then they drew apart and fought warily, cutting and parrying until they were breathless.

Balin looked up at the towers and saw the ladies in bright dresses looking down on them and he closed with his opponent again. Then both drew new strength from battle rage and they slashed and cut ferociously and blades chopped through armour and blood poured from each one. A moment they rested and then returned to the deadly fight, each trying to kill quickly before their strength bled away; each cut mortal wounds in the body of the other until Balan staggered away and lay down, too weak to raise his hand.

Then Balin, leaning on his sword, said, 'Who are you? I have never found anywhere a knight who could stand up to me.'

And the fallen man said, 'My name is Balan, and I am a brother of the famous knight Sir Balin.'

When Balin heard this his head whirled and he fainted and fell to the ground. And when he came to his senses he crawled on hands and knees and took off Balan's helmet and saw his face so cut to pieces and covered with blood that he did not know that face. And Balin laid his head on his brother's breast and wept, and he cried, 'Oh, my brother, my dear, dear brother. I have killed you and you have wounded me to death.'

Balan said weakly, 'I saw the two swords, but your shield had a device unknown to me.'

'It was a knight of that castle who made me take his shield because he knew you would have recognized mine. If I could live I would destroy that castle and its evil customs.'

'I wish that might be done,' Balan said. 'They made me fight here on the island, and when I killed the defender they forced me to be the champion and would not let me go. If you should live, my brother, they would keep you here to fight for their pleasure, and you could not escape over the water.'

Then the boat brought the Lady of the Castle and her retainers to the island, and the brothers begged her to bury them together. 'We came out of one womb,' they said, 'and we go to one grave.'

And the lady promised that it would be done.

'Now send for a priest,' Balin said. 'We want the sacrament and to receive the blessed body of our Lord Jesus Christ.' And it was done, and Balin said, 'Write on our tomb how through ill fortune two brothers killed each other so that passing knights may pray for us.'

Then Balan died, but Balin's life lingered with him till midnight, and in the darkness the brothers were buried together.

In the morning Merlin appeared and by his arts he raised a tomb over the brothers and on it in letters of gold he wrote their story.

And then Merlin prophesied many things that were to come: how Lancelot would come, and Galahad. And he foretold tragic matters: how Lancelot would kill his best friend Gawain.

And after Merlin had done many strange prophetic things, he went to King Arthur and told him the story of the brothers, and the king was saddened. 'In all the world,' he said, 'I never knew two such knights.'

Thus endeth the tale of Balin and Balan,
two Brethirne that were borne in Northumbirlonde,
that were two passynge good knyghtes
as ever were in those dayes.
Explicit

the wedding of
king arthur

Because Merlin's counsel had so often proved valuable, it was King Arthur's habit to consult him in matters of war and of government, as well as in personal plans. So it was that he called Merlin to him one day and said, 'You know that some of my barons are still rebellious. Perhaps it would be well if I took a wife to assure the succession to my crown.'

'That is well reasoned,' Merlin said.

'But I do not want to choose a queen without your advice.'

Merlin said, 'Thank you, my lord. One in your position should not be without a wife. Does any lady please you above all others?'

'Yes,' said Arthur. 'I love Guinevere, the daughter of King Lodegrance of Camylarde. She is the fairest and noblest damsel I have seen. And did you not tell me that my father King Uther once gave a great round table to King Lodegrance?'

'That is true,' said Merlin. 'And surely Guinevere is as lovely as you say, but if you do not deeply love her I could find another good and beautiful enough to please you. But if your heart is set on Guinevere, you will not look at anyone else.'

'That is the truth,' said the king.

'If I should advise you that Guinevere is an unfortunate choice, would that change you?'

'No.'

'Well then, if I should tell you that Guinevere will be unfaithful to you with your dearest and most trusted friend—'

'I would not believe you.'

'Of course not,' said Merlin sadly. 'Every man who has ever lived holds tight to the belief that for him alone the laws of probability are cancelled out by love. Even I, who know beyond doubt that my death will be caused by a silly girl, will not hesitate when that girl passes by. Therefore, you will marry Guinevere. You do not want advice – only agreement.' Merlin sighed and said, 'Very well then, give me an honourable retinue and I will make formal request of King Lodegrance and Guinevere.'

And Merlin, properly attended, rode to Camylarde and asked that king for his daughter to be Arthur's queen.

Lodegrance said, 'That so noble and brave and powerful a king as Arthur wishes my daughter for his wife is the best news I have ever heard. If we wished her dowered with lands, I would offer them, but he has lands enough. I shall send him a gift that will please him more than anything – the Table Round that Uther Pendragon gave to me. The table seats a hundred and fifty and I will send a hundred knights to serve him. I cannot furnish the full number because so many of my knights have been killed in the wars.'

Then Lodegrance brought Guinevere to Merlin and also the Table Round, and a hundred knights richly armed and dressed, and the whole company took their way to London.

King Arthur was overjoyed and he said, 'This fair lady is more than welcome to me, for I have loved her since I first saw her. And the hundred knights and the Table Round please me more than any riches.'

And Arthur married Guinevere and crowned her his queen with all possible dignity, and there was feasting and joy in his court.

And after the ceremony Arthur stood by the great Round Table and he said to Merlin, 'Search through all my kingdom and find fifty honourable, brave and perfect knights to fill the fellowship of the Table Round.'

And Merlin combed the country, but he found only twenty-eight and he brought them to the court. Then the Archbishop of Canterbury blessed the seats about the table. Merlin then said to the knights, 'Go now to King Arthur and swear allegiance and do him homage.' When they returned to the table each man found his name in letters of gold inscribed on his seat but two places had no names. As they sat at the Round Table young Gawain came into the court and asked a gift in honour of the marriage of Arthur and Guinevere.

'Ask it,' said the king.

'I ask that you make me a knight,' said Gawain.

'I will gladly,' said Arthur. 'You are my sister's son and I owe you every honour.'

Then a poor man came into the court and with him a fair

young man riding a skinny mare and the poor man said, 'Where shall I find King Arthur?'

'There he is yonder,' said a knight. 'Do you want something of him?'

'Yes, I do. That is why I am here,' and he approached the king and saluted him, saying, 'Best of kings, I pray that Jesus may bless you. I have been told that now at the time of your marriage you will grant reasonable requests.'

'That is so,' said the king. 'I have promised this and I will keep it, if your request does no harm to my dignity or my kingdom. What is your wish?'

'I thank you, my lord,' the poor man said. 'I ask that you may make my son here a knight.'

'You ask a great thing,' said Arthur. 'What is your name?'

'Sir, my name is Aryes and I am a cowherd.'

'Did you think of this?'

'No, sir,' said Aryes, 'I must tell you how it is. I have thirteen sons and all of the rest of them work as I tell them good sons should. But this boy will not do labourers' work. He is always shooting arrows and throwing spears and running to tournaments to look at knights and fighting, and day and night he gives me no rest, for he thinks only of knighthood.'

The king turned to the young man. 'What is your name?' he asked.

'Sir, my name is Torre.'

The king looked at the boy and saw that he was handsome and tall and well made, and he said to Aryes, 'Bring in your other sons.'

When the brothers stood before Arthur he saw that they were labourers like Aryes and not like Torre in face and carriage. Then the king said to the cowherd, 'Where is the sword with which to make him knight?'

Torre threw back his mantle and displayed his sword.

Arthur said, 'Knighthood may not be granted unless it is requested. Draw your sword and ask.'

Then Torre dismounted from his lean mare and drew his sword, and kneeling before the king, he begged to be knighted and to be joined to the fellowship of the Round Table.

'A knight I will make you,' the king said, and he took the

sword and struck Torre symbolically on the neck with the flat of the blade, saying, 'Be a good knight. I pray to God that you may be. And if you prove brave and honourable you will be of the Round Table.' And then the king addressed Merlin. 'You know the future,' he said. 'Tell us whether Sir Torre will be a good man.'

'Sir,' said Merlin, 'he should be. He comes of royal blood.'

'How so?' the king asked.

'I will tell you,' said the wizard. 'Aryes the cowherd is not his father or any kin to him. King Pellinore is his father.'

'That is not so,' said Aryes angrily, and Merlin commanded, 'Bring your wife here.'

And when she came into the court she was a fair and well-made housewife and she spoke with dignity. She told the king and Merlin that when she was a young maiden she went out to milk the cows one evening, and she said, 'A stern knight saw me and half by force took my virginity, and I conceived my son Torre. I had a greyhound with me and that knight took it away, saying he would keep my greyhound for love of me.'

The cowherd said, 'I wish this were not true, but I believe it now, for Torre has never been like me or like my other sons.'

Sir Torre said angrily to Merlin, 'You dishonour my mother, sir.'

'No,' Merlin said, 'it is more honour than insult, for your true father is a good knight and a king. And he will advance both you and your mother. You were conceived before she was married to Aryes.'

'That is the truth,' said the wife.

And the cowherd said, 'I will not grieve about it then if it happened before I knew her.'

The next morning Sir Pellinore came to the court and Arthur told him the story and how he had made Sir Torre a knight. And when Pellinore looked at his son he was greatly pleased with him and he rejoiced.

Then Arthur made Gawain his nephew a knight, but Sir Torre was the first to be knighted at the feast when the fellowship of the Round Table was created.

Arthur looked at the great table and he asked Merlin, 'How does it happen that there are vacant places with no names?'

And Merlin said, 'Two of the seats may be held only by most honourable knights, but the last is the Siege Perilous. Only one knight shall sit there and he will be the most perfect ever to live. And if any other knight shall dare to take that place, he will be destroyed.' Then Merlin took Sir Pellinore by the hand and led him to one of the vacant seats, and he said, 'This is your place, sir. No one deserves it more.'

Then Sir Gawain was filled with envy and with anger and he said softly to his brother Gaheris, 'That knight who is so honoured killed our father, King Lot. My sword is sharpened for him. I will kill him now.'

'Be patient, brother,' Gaheris advised. 'This is not the time. I am only your squire now, but when I am knighted we will kill him and later take our vengeance away from the court. We would suffer for it if we brought violence to this feast.'

'Perhaps you are right,' Gawain said. 'We will wait our chance.'

At last the preparations for the marriage of King Arthur and Queen Guinevere were completed, and the best and bravest and most beautiful of the realm poured into the royal city of Camelot. The knights and barons and their ladies gathered in St Stephen's Church and there the wedding was celebrated with regal ceremony and religious solemnity. That being done, the feast was called, and in the court the guests and retainers were seated each in the place proper to his position in the world.

Then Merlin said, 'Let everyone sit quietly and do not move, for now begins an age of marvels, and you will see strange happenings.'

Then all sat motionless in their places as though frozen and the great hall was silent and waiting. The preparing was over, Arthur was king, the Table Round existed, and its fellowship of courage and courtesy and honour sat each in his place – the king above, rigid and still, and Merlin beside him listening. They might have been asleep as they have been and will be many times over, sleeping but listening for the need, the fear, the distress, or the pure and golden venture that can call them awake. King Arthur and his knights quiet and waiting in the great hall at Camelot.

Then came the sharp quick beat of pointed hoofs on the flagstones and a white stag bounded into the hall pursued by a pure white hound bitch and followed by a pack of black hounds baying on the scent. The stag leaped past the Round Table with the bitch on his flank, and as he raced by a sideboard the white hound fastened on his flank and tore out a piece of flesh. In pain the white stag leaped in the air and overturned a seated knight. And with that the knight caught the bitch and carried her from the hall in his arms, and he mounted his horse and rode away, carrying the brachet with him, while the white stag bounded away and disappeared with the black pack baying after him.

Then as the hall stirred alive a lady rode into the court mounted on a white palfrey and she called loudly to the king, 'Sir, that knight has taken my white brachet. Do not permit this insult, my lord.'

'I have nothing to do with it,' said the king. And with that an armed knight on a great war horse galloped in and grasped the reins of the palfrey and pulled the lady by force from the hall, while she cried and screamed with anger and complaint. And when she was gone, the king was glad, for she made a great noise, but Merlin reproached him.

'You cannot know a venture from its beginning,' Merlin said. 'Greatness is born little. Do not dishonour your feast by ignoring what comes to it. Such is the law of quest.'

'Very well,' said Arthur. 'I will follow the law.' And he instructed Sir Gawain to hunt down the white stag and bring it to the feast. And he sent Sir Torre to find the knight who took the white brachet. Sir Pellinore was given the order to search out the lady and the forceful knight and return them to the court. 'Those are the quests,' said Arthur, 'and may you have marvellous adventures to tell about when you return.'

The three knights accepted their quests and armed themselves and rode away. And we will tell of each one separately.

Here begynnith the fyrst batayle
that ever Sir Gawayne ded after he was made knyght.

Sir Gawain, with his brother, Gaheris, as squire, rode through the green countryside until they came upon two knights on horseback fighting fiercely. The brothers separated them and asked the reason for the quarrel.

'It is a simple and a private matter,' said one of the knights. 'We are brothers.'

'It is not good for brothers to fight each other,' Gawain said.

'That is your opinion,' said the knight. 'We were riding towards the feast at King Arthur's court when a white stag ran by, chased by a white brachet and a pack of black hounds. We understood that this was a strange adventure fit for telling in the court and I prepared to give chase to win fame before the king. But my brother said he should go because he was a better knight than I. For a time we argued about who was better and then decided that the only proof lay in combat.'

'This is a silly reason,' Gawain said. 'You should prove your worth on strangers, not on brothers. You must go to Arthur's court and beg his mercy for this foolishness or I will have to fight you both and take you there.'

'Sir Knight,' said the brothers, 'through our wilfulness we are exhausted and we have lost much blood. We could not fight with you.'

'Then do as I say – go to the king.'

'We will, but who shall we say sent us?'

Sir Gawain said, 'You must say you were sent by the knight who follows the Quest of the White Stag. What are your names?'

'Sorlus of the Forest and Brian of the Forest,' they said, and they departed towards the court, and Sir Gawain continued on his quest.

And as they rode near to a deep forested valley the wind brought to them the full baying of hounds in chase, and they urged their horses to speed and followed the pack down the slope and to a swollen stream, where they saw the white stag swimming across it. And as Gawain prepared to follow, a knight stepped out on the other bank and called to him, 'Sir Knight, if you follow this chase you must first joust with me.'

Gawain answered, 'I am on quest. I will take any adventure that falls to me,' and he urged his horse to swim the deep swift water to the other side, where the knight awaited him with closed visor and couched spear. Then they rode together, and Sir Gawain unhorsed his opponent and called on him to yield.

'No,' said the knight. 'You have beaten me on horseback, but I pray you, gallant knight, to dismount and prove if you can do as well with your sword.'

'Willingly,' said Gawain. 'What is your name?'

'I am Sir Alardine of the Outer Isles.'

Then Sir Gawain left his horse and dressed his shield before him, and with his first blow he cut through the helm and into the brain and the knight fell dead before him, and without pausing Gawain and his brother took up the chase again, and after a long run the exhausted stag ran into the gates of a castle and the brothers pursued it into the great hall and killed it there. Then a knight came from a side chamber with a sword in his hand and he killed two of the milling hounds and drove the rest of the pack from the hall, and when he returned he kneeled by the beautiful deer and said sadly, 'My dear white pet, they have killed you. The sovereign lady of my heart gave you to me and I did not take care of you.' And he raised his head in anger. 'It was an evil deed,' he said. 'I will revenge you, my beauty.' He ran to his chamber and armed himself and came out fiercely.

Sir Gawain stepped out to meet him, saying, 'Why have you taken your anger out on the hounds? They did only what they were trained to do. I killed the stag; vent your rage on me, not on a dumb beast.'

The knight cried, 'That is true. I have vengeance on the hounds and I will have vengeance on you also.'

Sir Gawain engaged him with sword and shield, and they slashed and cut and parried, and each wounded the other so that blood spattered the floor, but gradually Sir Gawain's greater strength began to tell on the failing knight and one last heavy blow drove him to the ground, and he yielded and begged for his life.

'You shall die for killing my hounds,' said Gawain.

'I will do anything to make amends,' said the fallen knight, but Sir Gawain was merciless and he unlaced the helmet to strike off his head. As he raised his sword a lady came running from the chamber, tripped on the helpless knight, and fell full length on him. The descending sword struck her on the neck and cut through her spine, and she lay dead on the fallen knight.

Then Gaheris said bitterly, 'That was a foul deed, my brother, a shameful deed that will stick to your memory. He asked for mercy and you gave him none. A knight without mercy is without honour.'

Gawain was stunned by the accident to the fair lady. He said to the knight, 'Arise. I will give you mercy.'

But the knight replied, 'How can I believe you when I saw the cowardly blow that killed my dear and beloved lady.'

'I am sorry for it,' Gawain said. 'I did not strike at her. The cut was meant for you. I release you now on condition that you go to King Arthur and tell him the whole story and tell him you are sent by the knight of the Quest of the White Stag.'

'Why should I care for your conditions,' said the knight, 'when I do not care whether I live or die now?'

But when Sir Gawain prepared to kill him, he changed his mind and prepared to obey, and Gawain made him carry one dead hound before him on his horse and the other behind to prove his story. 'What is your name, before you go?' Sir Gawain asked.

'I am Sir Blamoure of the Marys,' said the knight, and he rode away towards Camelot.

When he had gone, Gawain went back into the castle and in a chamber he started to remove his armour, for he was weary and wished to sleep. Gaheris followed him and said, 'What are you doing? You cannot disarm in this place. News of your deed will make enemies spring up everywhere.'

And he had no sooner spoken than four well-armed knights came in with shields and drawn swords and they cursed Gawain, saying, 'You are a new-made knight and already you have shamed your knighthood, for a merciless knight is dishonoured. Also, you have slain a fair lady and your name will carry that burden for all time. You who would not give mercy will need mercy now.' And one of the knights aimed a great stroke at Gawain and staggered him, but Gaheris leaped to his brother's aid and the two defended themselves against the four, who attacked them all at once. Then one knight stepped back and took up a bow and shot a steel-tipped arrow into Gawain's arm so that he could not defend himself, and the brothers would have fallen soon, but four ladies came into the hall and pleaded for their lives. And at the request of the fair ladies, the knights granted the brothers mercy and made them prisoners.

Early in the morning, when Gawain lay moaning in his bed, one of the ladies heard him and went to him. 'How do you feel?' she asked.

'Not good,' said Gawain. 'I am in pain and I think I may be maimed for life.'

'It is your own fault,' the lady said. 'It was a foul thing to kill the lady of the castle. Are you not one of King Arthur's knights?'

'Yes, I am.'

'What is your name?'

'Fair lady, I am Sir Gawain, son of King Lot of Orkney. My mother is King Arthur's sister.'

'You are a nephew of the king,' the lady said. 'Well, I will plead for your release.'

And when she told the knights who he was they gave him leave to go, because they were loyal to King Arthur. And they gave him the white stag's head to prove that the quest was completed. But in punishment they hung the dead lady's head from his neck and made him carry her headless body before him on his horse.

And when at last Sir Gawain came to Camelot and stood before the king and the fellowship, he humbly and truthfully told the whole story.

The king and queen were displeased with him for killing the lady. Then Guinevere set an eternal quest on Gawain that during his whole life he would defend all ladies and fight in their cause. And she further commanded that he should be courteous always and he should grant mercy when it was asked.

And Sir Gawain swore by the four Evangelists to keep this quest.

And thus endith the adventure of Sir Gawayne
that he did at the mariage of Arthure.

Now go we to the questing of Sir Torre.

When he was armed and ready, he went in pursuit of the knight who had taken away the white hunting brachet, and on his way he came upon a dwarf who barred his way, and when Sir Torre tried to pass, the dwarf struck his horse on the head with his staff so that it reared and nearly fell backwards.

'Why did you do that?' Torre demanded.

'You may not pass this way unless you joust with the two knights yonder,' said the dwarf.

Then Sir Torre saw among the trees two pavilions and two spears leaning against two trees and two shields hanging from the branches. 'I cannot stop now,' Torre said. 'I am on a quest and I must go on.'

'You may not pass,' the dwarf replied, and he blew a shrill blast on his horn.

An armed knight came from behind the tents, took spear and shield, and bore down on Sir Torre, but the young knight met him midway and unhorsed him.

Then the felled knight yielded and begged mercy and it was granted. 'But, sir,' he said, 'my companion will demand a joust with you.'

'He will be welcome,' said Torre.

The second knight came on at great speed, and at the shock of meeting his spear splintered, but Torre's spear drove below the shield and entered the knight's side but did not kill him. And as he struggled to his feet, Torre quickly dismounted and struck him a great blow on the helm, and he fell to the ground and begged for his life.

'I give you your life,' Torre said, 'but both of you must go to King Arthur and yield to him as my prisoners.'

'Who shall we say defeated us ?' they asked.

'Say you were sent by the one who went in quest of the knight with the white brachet – Now be on your way, and God speed you, and me.'

Then the dwarf approached him and begged a favour.

'What do you wish ?' Torre asked.

'Only to serve you,' said the dwarf.

'Very well, take a horse and come with me.'

The dwarf said, 'If you are searching for the knight with the white brachet, I can bring you to where he is.'

'Then lead me to him,' said Sir Torre, and they went forward into the forest for a time until they came to a priory, and beside it two tents were set up and in front of one hung a red shield and on the other a white shield.

Then Sir Torre dismounted and handed his spear to the dwarf and he went to the pavilion of the white shield and inside he saw three damsels sleeping. He looked in the other tent and there a lady slept and beside her was the white hound bitch of his quest and it barked furiously at him. Sir Torre grabbed the dog and took it howling to the dwarf. And the noise awakened the lady and she came from the tent and the damsels followed from their tent. And the lady cried out, 'Why do you take my brachet?'

'I came in quest of this brachet all the way from King Arthur's court,' said Torre.

'Sir Knight,' said the lady, 'you will not get far with her before you will be met with force.'

'By God's grace, I will accept what comes, my lady,' he said, and he mounted and turned back on the way to Camelot, but night began to fall as he rode and he asked the dwarf if he knew of any lodging nearby.

'There is nothing near but a hermitage,' the dwarf said. 'We must take what we can find,' and he led the way to a dark stone cell beside a chapel and they fed their horses, and the hermit gave them what he had, a little coarse bread for their supper, and they slept on the cold stone floor of the cell. In the morning they heard Mass in the chapel and afterwards Sir Torre begged the hermit's blessing and his prayers and then he rode on towards Camelot.

They had not gone far before a knight came galloping after them, and he called out, 'Knight, give back the brachet you took from my lady.'

Sir Torre turned about and saw that the knight was a handsome man, well mounted and well armed at all points. Then he took his spear from the dwarf and set his shield and he met the knight in full career and the shock of meeting drove both horses to the ground. Then both knights stepped clear and drew their swords, and they fought like lions. Their swords cut through shields and armour and each wounded the other severely and thick hot blood poured from the cloven mail and a great weariness fell on both. But Sir Torre felt that his opponent weakened more than he, and he drew on his young strength and redoubled his attack, until at last, under a heavy blow, the knight toppled to the ground, and Sir Torre demanded his surrender.

'I will never yield while I have life and soul, unless you give me the white brachet.'

'That I cannot do,' said Torre. 'It is my quest to bring you and the white hound to King Arthur.'

Then a damsel on a palfrey galloped to them and pulled up short and said, 'I beg a gift from you, gentle knight. And if you love King Arthur you will grant it.'

And Torre without thinking, said, 'Ask anything you wish. I will grant it.'

'Thank you, noble sir,' she said. 'This fallen knight is Sir Arbellus and he is a murderer and a false knight. I demand his head.'

'Now I am sorry for my promise,' said Torre. 'If he has injured you, perhaps he can make amends to your satisfaction.'

'Only his death can make amends,' the damsel said. 'He fought my brother and overcame him and my brother begged mercy. And I kneeled in the mud and begged for my brother's life, but he refused and killed my brother before my eyes. He is a treacherous man and has wounded many good knights. Now keep your promise to me or I will shame you in King Arthur's court as a breaker of oaths.'

When Arbellus heard this he was filled with dread and he yielded to Sir Torre and asked mercy of him.

And Torre was puzzled. He said, 'A moment ago I offered you mercy and you refused to yield unless I gave the brachet of my quest. But now that I have made a sad promise, you yield and ask the mercy you refused.'

Then in his fear Arbellus turned about and fled among the trees, and Sir Torre pursued him and struck him down and killed him, and stood wearily over his body.

The damsel came to him and said, 'That was well done. He was a murderer. Night is coming and you are weary. Come to my house nearby and take your rest.'

'That I will,' said Torre. 'My horse and I have had little rest and less food since we left Camelot on this quest.' Then he went with her and at her lodging her husband, an old and honourable knight, welcomed him and gave him good food and drink and a pleasant bed, and he fell into the bed and slept soundly. And in the morning after they heard Mass he prepared to leave the old knight and his young wife and they asked his name.

'I am Sir Torre,' he said. 'I have only just now been made a knight and this was my first quest, to bring Arbellus and the white brachet to King Arthur's court.'

'Truly you have fulfilled the quest,' said the lady. 'And when in the future you are nearby, this is your lodging and we will always serve you and give you welcome.'

And then Sir Torre rode on towards Camelot and he came there on the third day at noon when the king and queen and all the fellowship sat in the great hall and they were glad of his coming. And as the custom was, he told his deeds and proved them with the white hound and the body of Arbellus – and the king and queen were pleased with him.

Merlin said, 'He went on his quest with no help and no retainer. Pellinore, his father, gave him an old horse and Arthur worn-out armour and a sword. But this is nothing to what he will do, my lord. He will be a brave and noble knight, gentle and courteous and truthful, and he will never shame his knighthood.'

And when Merlin had spoken, King Arthur gave Sir Torre an earldom of lands and a place of honour in the court.

And here endith the queste of Sir Torre,
Kynge Pellynors sonne.

Go we now to Sir Pellinore's Quest of the Lady taken by force from the court.

While King Arthur and his noble fellowship sat in the great dim-lighted hall, feasting and hearing causes and minstrelsy, Sir Pellinore went to his lodging and armed himself, and saw his horse well equipped and housed, and then he mounted and rode at a fast mile-covering trot after the lady who had been led away unwilling by an unknown knight. And he entered the forest and came to a little tree-shaded valley where, beside a gushing spring, he saw a damsel sitting on the moss-carpeted earth holding a wounded knight in her arms. And when she saw Pellinore she called out to him, 'Help me, Sir Knight, for Jesus's sake.'

But Pellinore was eager for his quest and he would not stop there. And the damsel called after him piteously, but when she saw that he would not pause she cried aloud a prayer to God that Pellinore might someday know a need as great as hers and find no help anywhere. It is said that soon afterwards the hurt knight died in the damsel's arms and that she slew herself in her despair.

But Pellinore proceeded down the path through the valley until he came to a poor labouring man in the trail, and the knight asked whether he had seen a knight leading an unwilling lady.

'That I did,' said the man. 'I saw them both and the lady complained so loudly that her voice rang through the valley. A little below here,' the poor man said, 'you will see two pavilions, and one of the knights there challenged the lady's companion and said she was his cousin. Then one said the lady was his by right of force and the other that she was his by right of kinship, and when they had argued and insulted and challenged, they fell to fighting. It is not wise for a poor man to be near when knights are battle-minded and so I came away to avoid trouble. But if you will hurry you may find them still fighting. The lady is guarded by two squires in the pavilion awaiting the decision of the combat.'

'I thank you,' said Pellinore, and he put his horse to a gallop and came soon to the pavilions, where sure enough they were still fighting while the lady watched them from the shelter of the tent.

Pellinore came near to her and he said, 'Fair lady, you must come with me to King Arthur's court. It is my quest to return you there.'

But the squires stood before her and one said, 'Sir, you see for yourself two knights fighting for this lady. Go and part them, and if they agree you may have the lady to do with as you please. Otherwise we cannot let her go.'

'I can see that you are obeying orders,' said Pellinore, and he rode out and put his horse between the fighting men and courteously asked them why they fought.

One said, 'Sir Knight, she is my cousin, and when I heard the cry that she was taken against her wish, I challenged this man who abducted her.'

The other said rudely, 'My name is Sir Ontelake of Wenteland. I took this lady by my own bravery and by force of arms as is my right.'

'That is not true,' said Pellinore. 'I was there and I saw it. You came in armed to King Arthur's marriage feast, where weapons and violence were forbidden, and you took this lady before any of the company could run for a sword to stop you. And because you broke the law of the court of the king, it is my quest to bring her back and you also, if you are alive to go. For believe me, sir, I have promised King Arthur to bring her back. Therefore, stop your fighting, because neither of you will have the lady. Of course, if either of you wish to fight with me for her, I am quite willing to accommodate you.'

Then the two knights who had been painfully trying to kill each other joined forces, and they cried, 'You must fight both of us before you can take her.'

As Sir Pellinore tried to move his mount from between them, Sir Ontelake drove his sword into the horse's side and killed it and shouted, 'Now you will be afoot as we are.'

Sir Pellinore stepped lightly from his fallen beast and drew his sword, and he said bitterly, 'That was a cowardly thing to do. Guard your health, my friend, for I have something here for a man who stabs a horse,' and with that Pellinore loosed a swinging sword cut that sliced through Ontelake's helm and split his head down to the chin and he fell dead.

Then Pellinore turned on the other, but that knight had seen the terrible strength of Pellinore's stroke and he kneeled on the ground and said, 'Take my cousin and fulfil your quest, but I require you as a true knight to put no shame on her.'

'Will you not fight for her?'

'No, not with such a knight as you after what I have seen.'

'Well,' Pellinore said, 'it is not my custom to dishonour my knighthood. The lady will not be molested – that I promise you. Now I need a horse. I will take Ontelake's horse.'

'No,' said the knight, 'come dine with me and lodge with me and I will give you a much better horse than that.'

'I will,' said Pellinore. And that night he had good cheer and good wine and slept softly, and in the morning after Mass he breakfasted.

'I should know your name,' said his host. 'You are taking my cousin as your quest.'

'That is reasonable. My name is Sir Pellinore, King of the Isles and knight of the Round Table.'

'I am honoured that such a famous knight conducts my cousin. My name, sir, is Meliot of Logurs and my lady cousin is named Nyneve. The knight in the other pavilion and my sworn brother in arms is Sir Bryan of the Isles, a man of purity. He will not fight any man unless he is forced to.'

'I wondered why he did not come out to fight with me,' said Pellinore. 'Bring him to the court one day. You will be welcomed there.'

'We will come together,' said Sir Meliot.

And then Pellinore mounted and the lady accompanied him and they rode towards Camelot. But as they went through a stony valley, the lady's horse stumbled and then fell and the lady was badly bruised by the fall. 'My arm is hurt. I cannot go on for a while.'

'Very well, we will rest here,' said Pellinore, and he helped her to a pleasant grassy place under a spreading tree and lay down beside her and soon he fell asleep and did not waken until after dark. When he awakened, Pellinore was anxious to go on, but the lady said, 'It is too dark. We could not find our way. Take off your armour and rest until dawn.'

A little before midnight they heard the sound of a trotting horse. 'Be quiet,' said Pellinore. 'Some strange thing is happening. Men do not ride at night.' And quietly he slipped on his armour and buckled it and the two sat silent. Then in the near darkness, in the path beside their retreat, they dimly saw two knights meet, one from the direction of Camelot and the other from the north, and they spoke quietly. One said, 'What is the news from Camelot?' and the other replied, 'I have been in the court, and they did not know I came as a spy. And I tell you that King Arthur has gathered such a fellowship of knights as you will not find anywhere. And the fame of these knights of the Round Table is travelling throughout the world. I am riding north to tell our chieftains how strong King Arthur has become.'

'I have with me a remedy for his strength,' said the other, 'a little powder that will melt his power. We have a man trusted and near to the king who for a price has promised to put this poison in the king's cup – then we will see this power disappear.'

The first knight warned, 'Beware of Merlin then. He can detect such things.'

'I will be careful, but I am not afraid,' said the other and they separated and rode each his way.

When they had gone, Pellinore quickly made ready and they picked their way along the path until dawn. It was light when they came to the spring where Pellinore had refused help to the lady and the wounded knight. Wild beasts had torn them to pieces and eaten them all save their heads.

Pellinore wept when he saw them. 'I might have saved her life,' he said. 'But I was hot on my quest and I would not listen to her pleading.'

'It was not your quest. Why are you so sad?' she asked with the detachment of ladies for other ladies.

'I don't know,' said Pellinore, 'but my heart is torn to see this damsel, so fair and so young, destroyed when I could have helped her.'

'Then I advise you to bury what is left of the knight and take the lady's head to King Arthur, and let him judge what you should have done.'

'She called a frightful curse after me,' said Pellinore.

'Anyone may curse. You were sworn to a quest,' Nyneve said primly. 'I was your quest.'

Then Pellinore found a Holy Hermit nearby and asked him to bury the knight's bones in blessed ground and to pray for his soul. And he gave the knight's armour to the hermit for his trouble. Afterwards Sir Pellinore took up the head of the damsel with golden hair and he grieved when he looked at the young and lovely face.

By noon they came to Camelot, where Arthur and Guinevere and the noble fellowship sat at their noonday feast. And Pellinore told his quest to the company and swore by the four Evangelists that every word was true.

Then Queen Guinevere said, 'Sir Pellinore, you were greatly to blame that you did not save the lady's life.'

And the knight replied, 'Madame, you would be to blame if you would not save your own life if you could. My sorrow is greater than your displeasure, for I was so intent on my quest that I would not wait, and that will be a weight on my conscience all the days of my life.'

Then all eyes turned to Merlin where he sat at the high table, for this tale had the sound of fate.

Merlin's eyes were sad when he spoke. 'You have every reason to repent your thoughtless haste,' Merlin said. 'This damsel was Alyne, your own daughter, born of your love for the Lady of Rule. And the knight was Sir Myles of the Lands, her affianced and a good man. They were coming to the court to be wedded when a cowardly knight, Loraine le Sauvage, attacked Sir Myles from behind and drove a spear through his back. When you refused your help, Alyne, in despair, killed herself with her lover's sword.' Merlin paused and then he said, 'You will remember that she cursed you. Well – that curse will be your fate. Your best friend will fail you in your greatest need as you failed your daughter. The man you trust most will leave you to be killed.'

'I am grieved at what you tell me,' said Pellinore, 'but I believe that God can change destiny. I must have faith in that.'

And thus was ended the quests of the Wedding of King Arthur, but at the last the laws of the Round Table were laid down and every knight of the fellowship swore to keep the laws. They swore never to use violence without good purpose, never to fall to murder or treason. They swore on their honour to be merciful when mercy was asked and to protect damsels, ladies, gentlewomen and widows, to enforce their rights and never enforce lust on them. And they promised never to fight in an unjust cause or to fight for personal gain. All the knights of the Round Table took this oath. And every year at the high feast of Pentecost they renewed the oath.

Explicit the Weddyng of Kyng Arthur

the death of
merlin

When Merlin saw the damsel Nyneve, whom Sir Pellinore brought to court, he knew that his fate was on him, for his heart swelled like a boy's heart in his aged breast and his desire overcame his years and his knowledge. Merlin wanted Nyneve more than his life, as he had foreseen. He pursued her with his wishes and would not let her rest. And Nyneve used her power over the besotted old Merlin and traded her company for his magic arts, for she was one of the damsels of the Lady of the Lake and schooled in wonders.

Merlin knew what was happening to him and knew its fatal end, and still he could not help himself, for his heart doted on the Damsel of the Lake.

He went to King Arthur and told him that the time he once spoke of had come and that his end was not far off. He spoke to the king about things to come and instructed him in what he should do to meet his future. And particularly he warned him to guard well the sword Excalibur and even more its scabbard. 'It will be stolen from you by one you trust,' Merlin said. 'You have enemies you do not know.' And Merlin said, 'You will miss me and wish for my advice. The time will come when you would give up your kingdom to have me with you again.'

'This is beyond understanding,' said the king. 'You are the wisest man alive. You know what is preparing. Why do you not make a plan to save yourself?'

And Merlin said quietly, 'Because I am wise. In the combat between wisdom and feeling, wisdom never wins. I have told you your certain future, my lord, but knowing will not change it by a hair. When the time comes, your feeling will conduct you to your fate.' And Merlin bade farewell to the king he had created.

And he rode with Nyneve from the court, and whatever path she took he took also. Knowing her power over him, she refused him the favour of her person, so that in his yearning he invoked his magic craft to overcome her reluctance. But Nyneve knew he would try his secret arts and she told him that if he wanted to possess her, he must swear to use no necromancy to that end. And Merlin, burning with the desire of his dotage, took that oath and sealed his fate.

The mismatched two went restlessly. They crossed the Channel to France and came to Benwick, where Ban was king and the war with King Claudas still continued.

Queen Elaine was King Ban's wife, a good and fair lady, and she begged Merlin's help to end the war. And as they spoke, Elaine's young son came in, and Merlin looked at him.

'Do not worry,' Merlin said. 'This boy here within twenty years will settle Claudas and, more than that, this child is destined to be the greatest knight in all the world, and his memory and fame will sweeten and strengthen the ages to come. I know you first called him Galahad, but at his christening you named him Lancelot.'

'Why, that is true,' said Queen Elaine. 'I did first call him Galahad. But tell me, Merlin, will I live to see his greatness?'

'You will see it, I swear to you, and you will live many years after.'

Nyneve was bored and restless and she left Ban's court with Merlin panting after her, begging her to lie with him and stanch his yearning, but she was weary of him, and impatient with an old man as a damsel must be, and also she was afraid of him because he was said to be the Devil's son, but she could not be rid of him, for he followed her, pleading and whimpering, wherever she went.

Then Nyneve, with the inborn craft of maidens, began to question Merlin about his magic arts, half promising to trade her favours for his knowledge. And Merlin, with the inborn helplessness of men, even though he foresaw her purpose, could not forbear to teach her. And as they crossed back to England and rode slowly from the coast towards Cornwall, Merlin showed her many wonders, and when at last he found that he interested her, he showed her how the magic was accomplished and put in her hands the tools of enchantment, gave her the antidotes of magic against magic, and finally, in his aged folly, taught her those spells which cannot be broken by any means. And when she clapped her hands in maidenly joy, the old man, to please her, created a room of unbelievable wonders under a great rock cliff, and with his crafts he furnished it with comfort and richness and beauty to be the glorious apartment for the consummation of their love. And they two went through a passage in the rock to the room of wonders, hung with gold and lighted with many candles. Merlin stepped in to show it to her, but Nyneve leaped back and cast the awful spell that cannot be broken by any means, and the passage closed and Merlin was trapped inside for all time to come. She could hear his voice faintly through the rock, pleading for release. And Nyneve mounted her horse and rode away. And Merlin remains there to this day, as he knew he would be.

Not long after his great marriage feast, King Arthur moved his court to Cardolle, and there he received bitter news. Five kings – he of Denmark and his brother, King of Ireland, together with the Kings of the Vale, of Sorleyse, and of the Isle of Longtaynse, had joined forces and with a large army invaded England, destroying everything in their path; castles, towns, cattle, and killing the people who could not flee.

When he heard this report Arthur said wearily, 'Since I have been king I have not had one month of rest from trouble. And now I cannot rest until I have met and destroyed these invaders. I cannot permit my people to be destroyed. All you who will come with me, make ready.'

Then some of the barons were secretly angry because they wished to live in comfort. But Arthur sent a message to Sir Pellinore asking him to gather what forces of men at arms he could and to hurry to join him. And also he sent letters to all of his barons who were not at court to join him as quickly as they could. Finally, he went to Guinevere and told her to make ready to go with him. 'I cannot bear to be away from you,' he said. 'Your presence with me will make me braver in the field, but I do not want to endanger you, my lady.'

The queen replied, 'Sir, I will obey your desires. I am ready when you wish.'

The next morning the king and queen started on their way with all the fellowship who were at the court, and they made their way rapidly northwards by forced marches until they came to the Humber River on the border, and there they encamped.

A spy carried word to the five kings that Arthur was already in the north, and the brother of one of the kings spoke in council. 'You must know,' he said, 'this Arthur has the flower of knight-hood with him, as he proved when he fought the eleven rebel lords. At present he has not great numbers with him, but his men will flock to him. Therefore, we must meet him soon, for the longer we wait, the stronger he will be and we weaker. I tell you that he is so brave a king that he will accept battle even against a larger force. Let us attack him before daylight and cut down his knights before the reinforcements arrive.'

The five kings agreed and they moved quickly through North Wales and fell upon King Arthur in the night when his retainers slept in their tents. King Arthur lay with Queen Guinevere in his tent. When the attack came he started up, crying, 'To arms! We are betrayed!' And he hurried to buckle his armour while the noise and shouting and clash of arms sounded in the darkness.

Then a wounded knight came to his tent and cried, 'My lord, save yourself and your queen. We are overwhelmed and many of our fellowship are killed.'

Then Arthur mounted with Guinevere beside him, and with only three knights, Sir Kay, Sir Gawain, and Sir Gryfflet, he rode to the Humber to try to cross to the other side for safety, but the water was so rough that they could not get across. And Arthur said, 'We must choose either to defend ourselves or risk the crossing. Be sure our enemies will kill us if they can.'

The queen said, 'I would rather die in the water than be captured and killed by our enemies.'

As they spoke, Sir Kay saw the five kings riding alone without retainers. 'Look,' he said, 'there are the leaders. Let us attack them.'

'That would be foolish,' Sir Gawain said. 'They are five and we only four.'

But Sir Kay said, 'I will fight two if you will each engage one of them.' And with that he couched his spear and thundered against them, and his point found its mark and pierced the body of a king and dropped him dead on the ground. Then Sir Gawain engaged a second king and killed him with his lance. Sir Gryfflet unhorsed a third with such a stroke that he broke his neck in falling. King Arthur toppled and killed the fourth, and then, as he had promised, Sir Kay engaged the fifth and with a sword stroke cut through his helmet and beheaded him.

'That was well done,' said Arthur. 'You have kept your promise and I shall see you rewarded.'

Then they found on the shore a barge to take the queen to safety, and she said to Sir Kay, 'If you love any lady and she does not return your love, she is a fool. You made a great promise and fulfilled it greatly, and I shall see that your fame is spread over the land.' Then the barge was launched and carried the queen across the Humber.

Then Arthur and his three knights rode into the forest to look for any of their men who had escaped the sudden attack, and they found a large number and told them that the five kings were dead. And Arthur said, 'Let us remain hidden here until full daylight comes. When the enemy find their leaders dead, the heart will go out of them.'

It happened as Arthur had supposed. When the dead kings were discovered, the invaders were filled with panic and many of them dismounted and stood wondering what to do. And then Arthur launched his attack on the dispirited men and killed them right and left, and with his few he overcame many and many fled in terror. And when the battle was over, King Arthur knelt upon the ground and gave thanks to God for the victory. Then he sent for the queen, and when she arrived, he greeted her joyfully. Then word was brought that Sir Pellinore approached with a large force and greeted the king and saw with wonder what had been done there. When they counted their dead they found two hundred men dead and eight knights of the Round Table slain in their tents before they could arm themselves.

Then Arthur ordered that an abbey should be built on the battlefield as an offering of thanks and he endowed it with lands for its support. And when news of the victory travelled to the lands beyond the border, the enemies were afraid and any who had planned to attack Arthur gave up their intention.

Arthur returned to Camelot, and he said to Pellinore, 'Now there are eight vacant seats at our Round Table. Eight of our best knights are dead. We will find it hard to fill their places.'

'Sir,' said Pellinore, 'there are good men in this court, both young and old. My advice is that you choose four of the older knights and four of the younger.'

"Very well,' the king said. 'Which of the older do you suggest?'

'The husband of your sister Morgan le Fay, Sir Uryens, for one; then the knight known as King of the Lake; for the third the noble knight Sir Hervis de Revel; and last Sir Galagars.'

'Those are well chosen,' said Arthur. 'Who among the younger do you prefer?'

'First your nephew Sir Gawain, my lord. He is as good a knight as any in the land. Second, Sir Gryfflet, who has served you well in two wars, and third, Sir Kay the Seneschal, your foster brother, whose fame is growing.'

'You are right,' said the king. 'Sir Kay is worthy of the Round Table if he never fought again, but who for the fourth young knight? There remains a vacant seat.'

'I suggest two names, sir, but you must choose between them – Sir Bagdemagus and my son, Sir Torre. Because he is my son I cannot praise him, but if he were not my son I could say that for his age there is no better knight anywhere.'

Then King Arthur smiled at Pellinore. 'You are right not to praise him,' he said. 'But because he is not my son, I can say that he is as good a candidate as any you have mentioned. I have seen him proved. He says little and does much. He is wellborn and very like his father in courage and courtesy. Therefore, I choose him and leave Sir Bagdemagus for another time.'

And Pellinore said, 'Thank you, my lord.'

Then the eight knights were proposed to the fellowship and accepted by acclaim, and in their places their names were found in letters of gold, and the new knights took their seats at the Round Table.

But Sir Bagdemagus was hurt and angry that Sir Torre was chosen over him. He armed himself and left the court followed by his squire, and the two rode far into the forest until they came to a cross set up in the branching path. There Bagdemagus dismounted and said his prayers devoutly, but his squire found writing on the cross which said that Sir Bagdemagus would never return to court until he could defeat a knight of the Round Table in single combat.

'Look,' said the squire, 'this writing concerns you. You must return and challenge one of the king's knights.'

'I shall never return until men speak of me with honour and say that I am worthy to be a knight of the Table Round.' And he remounted and rode doggedly on and in a little glade he found a plant which is the symbol of the Holy Grail, and his heart was lighter then, because it was known that no knight found such a token unless he was virtuous and brave.

Many adventures came to Sir Bagdemagus and he acquitted himself well. One day he came to the great rock where Merlin was imprisoned and he could hear Merlin's voice through the stone. He tried his best to force an entrance, but Merlin called to him that it was not possible. No one could free him save she who had put him there. Reluctantly, the knight passed on, and in many lands he proved his worth and his knightliness so that his fame spread abroad, and when finally he returned to Arthur's court, he was accepted for a newly vacant seat and took his place at the Round Table by right of worth.

Explicit

morgan le fay

Morgan le Fay, King Arthur's half-sister, was a dark, handsome, passionate woman, and cruel and ambitious. In a nunnery she studied necromancy and became proficient in the dark and destructive magic which is the weapon of the jealous. She joyed in bending and warping men to her will through beauty and enchantment, and when these failed she used the blacker arts of treason and murder. It was her pleasure to use men against men, fashioning from their weaknesses weapons for their strength. Having Sir Uryens for her husband, she made promises to Sir Accolon of Gaul and so enmeshed him in dreams and enchantments that his will was slack and his honour drugged, and he became the implement of her deepest wish. For Morgan hated her brother, Arthur, hated his nobility and was jealous of his crown. Morgan le Fay planned her brother's murder with intricate care. She would give the crown to Uryens but keep its power for herself, and the entangled Accolon would be the murder weapon.

By her arts Morgan the Witch made a sword and sheath exactly like Excalibur in appearance, and secretly she substituted it for Arthur's sword. Then she beguiled Accolon with promises, cancelled his conscience with his lust, and instructed him in the part he was to play, and when he agreed he thought her eyes lighted with love when they were fired with triumph, for Morgan le Fay loved no one. Hatred was her passion and destruction her pleasure.

Then Accolon by instruction took his place near Arthur and never left his side.

When there were no wars or tournaments it was the custom of knights and fighting men to hunt in the great forests which covered so much of England. In the breakneck chase of deer through forest and swamp and over rutted and rock-strewn hills, they tempered their horsemanship, and meeting the savage charge of wild boars, they kept their courage high and their dexterity keen. And also their mild enterprise loaded the turning spits in the kitchens with succulent meat for the long tables of the great hall.

On a day when King Arthur and many of his knights quartered the forest in search of quarry, the king and Sir Uryens and Sir Accolon of Gaul started a fine stag and gave chase. They were well horsed, so that before they knew it they were ten miles from the rest of the fellowship. The proud, high-antlered stag drew them on, and with whip and spur they pushed their foaming horses through tangled undergrowth and treacherous bogs, leaped streams and fallen trees until they overdrove their mounts and the foundered horses fell heaving to the ground, with bloody bits and rowel stripes on their sides.

The three knights, now footbound, watched the stag move wearily away. 'This is a pretty thing,' said Arthur. 'We are miles from help.'

Sir Uryens said, 'We haven't any choice but to go on foot and look for some place to lodge and wait for help.' They walked heavily through the oak forest until they came to the bank of a deep, wide river, and on the bank lay the exhausted stag, ringed with hounds, a brachet tearing at his throat. King Arthur scattered the hounds and killed the stag, and he raised his hunting horn and sounded the death call of a prize taken.

And only then did the knights look about them. On the smooth dark water they saw a little ship covered with silken cloth that hung over the sides and dipped into the water, and the boat moved silently towards the bank and grounded itself in the sandy shallows nearby. Arthur waded to the boat and looked under the silken hangings and saw no one there. He called to his friends to come, and the three boarded the little vessel and found it laden with luxury, with soft cushions and rich hangings, but they could see no occupants. The three men sat tiredly down on the soft cushions and rested while the evening came and the forest darkened around them. Night birds called in the forest and wild ducks came coasting in and the black wall of the forest reared over them.

As the companions nodded sleepily, a ring of torches flared up around them, and from the cabin of the ship twelve lovely damsels emerged, dressed in flowing silken gowns. The ladies curtsied to the king and saluted him by his name and welcomed him, and Arthur thanked them for their courtesy. Then they led the king and his fellows to a cabin hung with tapestry, and at a rich table they served wine and meats of many kinds, and such delicacies that all sat in wonder at the variety and profusion of the supper. And after they had supped long and pleasantly, and their eyes were heavy with good wine, the damsels led each to separate cabins richly hung with beds deep and soft. Then the three sank into the beds and instantly they fell into a deep, drugged sleep.

In the dawn Sir Uryens opened his wine-swollen eyes and saw that he lay in his own bed in his own lodgings in Camelot and Morgan le Fay seemingly asleep beside him. He had gone to sleep two days' journey away, and he could remember nothing else. He studied his wife through slitted lids, for there were many things he did not know about her and many other things he did not want to know. And so he held his peace and concealed his wonder.

King Arthur came to his senses on the cold stones of a dungeon floor. Dusky light from a high slit in the wall showed him the restless figures of many other prisoners. The king sat up, asking, 'Where am I, and who are you?'

'We are captive knights,' they told him. 'There are twenty of us here and some of us have been kept in this dark cell for as much as eight years.'

'For what reason?' asked the king. 'Is it for ransom?'

'No,' said one of the knights. 'I will tell you the cause. The lord of this castle is Sir Damas, a mean and recreant man, and also a coward. His younger brother is Sir Outlake, a good, brave, honourable knight. Sir Damas has refused to share the inherited lands with his brother, except for a small manor house and lands Sir Outlake holds by force and guards against his brother. The people of the countryside love Sir Outlake for his kindness and justice, but they hate Sir Damas, because he is cruel and vengeful, as most cowards are. For many years there has been war and contention between the brothers, and Sir Outlake has issued a challenge to fight in single combat for his rights against his brother or any knight Sir Damas may appoint. But Sir Damas has not the courage to fight, and moreover he is so hated that no knight will enter the field for him. And so he with a gang of hired fighting men has laid traps for good knights venturing alone, and fallen on them and brought them captive to this place. He offers freedom if we will fight for him, but everyone has refused and some he has tortured and some starved to death. All of us are faint from hunger and the cramping prison so that we could not fight even if we wished to.'

And Arthur said, 'May God in his mercy deliver you.'

Now a damsel looked through the iron grille of the dungeon door and beckoned to Arthur, and she said softly, 'How do you like it here?'

'Am I supposed to like a prison?' said Arthur. 'Why do you ask?'

'Because you have a choice,' the damsel said. 'If you will fight for my lord you will be released, but if you refuse, as these other fools have, you will spend your life here.'

'It is a strange way to get a champion,' said the king, 'but for myself I would rather combat with a knight than live in a dungeon. If I agree to fight, will you release these other prisoners?'

'Yes,' said the damsel.

'Then I am ready,' the king said, 'but I have neither horse nor armour.'

'You shall have everything you need, sir.'

The king looked closely at her and he said, 'It seems to me that I have seen you at King Arthur's court.'

'No,' she said. 'I have never been there. I am the daughter of the lord of this castle.'

While the girl went to make arrangements, Arthur searched his memory, and he was quite sure he had seen her attending his sister Morgan le Fay.

Sir Damas accepted Arthur's offer and he took an oath to deliver the prisoners and the king swore to fight his utmost against Sir Damas's enemy. Then the twenty weak and starving knights were brought out of the dungeon and given food, and they all remained to see the combat.

Now we must go to Sir Accolon, the third knight, who had slept the enchanted sleep. He awakened close beside a deep well where a movement in his sleep would have cast him down. From the well there issued a silver pipe spouting water into a marble fountain. Morgan's magic had weakened with her absence, so that Accolon blessed himself, and he said aloud, 'Jesus save my lord King Arthur and Sir Uryens. Those were not ladies in the ship but fiends from hell. If I can come clear of this misadventure I will destroy them and all others who practise evil magic.'

And at that moment an ugly dwarf with thick lips and a flat nose came out of the forest and saluted Sir Accolon. 'I come from Morgan le Fay,' said the dwarf, and the spell settled back on the knight. 'She greets you and bids you be strong-hearted, because tomorrow in the morning you are to fight with a knight. Because she loves you, she sends you this sword Excalibur and its scabbard. And she says if you love her you will fight without mercy, as you promised her in private. She will also expect the king's head as proof that you have fulfilled your oath.'

Sir Accolon was deep enchanted now. He said, 'I understand. I shall keep my promise and I can, now that I have Excalibur. When did you see my lady?'

'A little time ago,' said the dwarf.

Then Accolon in his rapture embraced the ugly dwarf and kissed him and said, 'Greet my lady for me and tell her I will keep my promise or die in the attempt. Now I understand the little ship and the sleep. My lady has arranged all of it, isn't that true?'

'You may well believe it, sir,' said the dwarf and he slipped away into the forest and left Accolon dreaming beside the silver fountain.

And soon there came a knight accompanied by a lady and six squires, and he begged Accolon to come to a manor nearby to dine and rest, and Accolon accepted. All this was planned by Morgan le Fay, for the lord of the manor was Sir Outlake, who lay wounded by a spear thrust in the thigh. And as Sir Accolon sat with him, word was brought that Sir Damas had a champion to fight against his brother in the morning.

Then Sir Outlake was furious with his wound, for he had wanted this test of arms for a long time, but his legs were so hurt that he could not sit a horse.

Sir Accolon was confident because he had the protection of

the sword Excalibur, and he offered to fight as Sir Outlake's champion.

Then Sir Outlake was glad and he thanked Sir Accolon with all his heart for his offer, and he sent Sir Damas a message saying that his champion would fight for him.

This combat had the blessing of custom and the authority of religion. It was an appeal to God to decide which of two men was right and to show His decision in the victor. The outcome had the force of law. And because of the hatred men felt for Sir Damas and the esteem in which Sir Outlake was held, the whole countryside assembled to see the trial by arms, knights and free men, and on the fringes of the gathering bondsmen and serfs. Twelve honourable men of the country were chosen to wait upon the champions where they sat with their horses, shields dressed, visors down, and spears booted, waiting for the signal to begin. The morning sun slanted through the leaves of great oaks which surrounded the jousting ground. Mass had been sung and each champion had prayed for the decision, and now they waited.

Then a damsel rode on to the field and from under her riding cloak she drew a sword and scabbard – the counterfeit Excalibur. The damsel said, 'Because of her great love for you, your sister Morgan le Fay sends you Excalibur, my lord, the sheath to protect your life and the sword to give you victory.'

'How kind my sister is,' said Arthur. 'Give her my thanks and love.' And he took the false sword and belted it to his side.

Now the horn blew its savage signal, and both knights couched their spears and hurtled together, and both spears struck true and held, and both men were hurled to the ground, and they sprang up and drew their swords and faced each other. They circled and feinted, each testing the other and looking for a weakness or an opening.

And as they opened the fight, Nyneve of the Lake rode up, driving her horse fast, the same damsel who had beguiled Merlin and sealed him in the rock. The necromantic art she had wrung from the adoring old man had given her power, but also it aroused rivalry and suspicion in Morgan le Fay. Nyneve loved the king and hated his evil sister. She knew the plot against Arthur's life and she had come at speed to save him before the combat joined and the laws against interference were applied.

But she arrived late and had to watch the unequal contest, for although each knight delivered strokes and cuts, Excalibur bit deep and ripped its wounding way through Arthur's armour, while the false sword of the king glanced harmlessly from the shield and helm of Accolon.

When Arthur felt his blood pouring from his wounds and felt the blunt uselessness of his sword, he was dismayed, and suspicion grew in him that he had been tricked. Then he was afraid, for every stroke of Accolon bit deep while Arthur's strongest blows were impotent. The counterfeit sword in his hand was forged of base metal, soft and useless.

Now Accolon felt his advantage and pressed on, and the king struck such a furious stroke that the very weight of it staggered Accolon, who stepped away to get his breath and clear his head, but in a moment he came on again, and without art or skill the two rained strokes until Arthur bled from a hundred wounds, while Accolon was unhurt, protected by the sheath of the true Excalibur.

Then a murmur of wonder went through the circle of watchers. They saw that Arthur fought well and yet could not wound his enemy, and they were amazed that he could continue with such loss of blood. Then Arthur drew back to rest and gather his strength, but Accolon cried out in triumph, 'Come! Fight. This is no time to let you rest,' and he charged forward and forced the battle so that Arthur in despair leaped in and swung a great stroke to the helm, and his sword blade broke and left only the pommel in his hand. Helpless, he covered himself with his shield while Accolon showered cuts upon him, trying to finish him. And as he attacked Sir Accolon said, 'You are finished, helpless and lost. I don't want to kill you. Surrender and give up the cause.'

The king said weakly, 'I can't. I promised to fight as long as I had life. I would rather die with honour than live in shame. If you kill an unarmed man you will never live down the shame.'

'It is not your affair to worry about my shame,' said Accolon. 'You are a dead man.' And he pressed home his attack, careless of defence.

Arthur took the only possible opening. He pressed close and thrust his shield against Accolon's sword arm and swung at his exposed helmet with the broken pommel of his sword with such force that Accolon reeled back three steps and stood swaying dizzily.

Nyneve had watched the combat hoping for the decision of God against the treason of Morgan le Fay, but when she saw Arthur's last despairing stroke with the broken sword and Accolon recover his strength and advance on the weak and disarmed king, she knew that he was lost without her help. Then she searched her memory for Merlin's teaching and she forged a spell and flung it with her eyes at the advancing traitor. Sir Accolon raised Excalibur, measured his distance, and aimed a deadly finishing stroke, but as the blade touched the shield, the hand that held it lost its grip and the fingers went lax. The sword fell to the ground and Accolon watched with helpless horror as Arthur picked it up. The pommel felt good in his hand and he knew it was the true Excalibur and he said, 'My dear sword, you have been too long out of my hand and you have wounded me. Now, be my friend again, Excalibur.' He looked at Accolon and saw the scabbard, and leaped forward and tore it free and flung it as far as he could over the heads of the circled people.

'Now, Sir Knight,' he said to Accolon, 'you have had your turn and I my wounds. Now we change places and you shall have what you have given me.' He rushed on Accolon, shield forward to raise his guard, but Accolon fell to the ground rigid with paralysing fear. Arthur dashed off his helm and struck him on the head with the flat of Excalibur so that blood started from his nose and ears. 'Now I will kill you,' said Arthur.

'That is your right,' said Sir Accolon. 'I see now that God is on your side and your cause is right. But as you promised to fight to the end, so did I, and I cannot beg for mercy. Do what you will.'

Arthur looked at the unvisored face, distorted and dirtied with dust and blood, and he said, 'I know your face. Who are you?'

'Sir Knight, I am of the royal court of King Arthur. My name is Accolon of Gaul.'

Then Arthur thought of the enchantment of the ship and the treachery whereby Excalibur came into his enemy's hand, and he asked softly, 'Tell me, Sir Knight, who gave you this sword?'

'The sword is my misfortune. It has brought death to me,' said Accolon.

'Whatever it has brought, where did you get it?'

Sir Accolon sighed, for the power of his promised mistress had failed and disappeared. 'I see no reason now to conceal anything,' he said hopelessly. 'The king's sister hates him with a death hate because he has the crown and because he is loved and honoured above her. She loves me and I love her to the point of treason. She has betrayed Sir Uryens, her husband, and been my paramour. She promised me that if I would kill Arthur with her help, she would rid herself of her husband and make me king, and she would be my queen, and we would reign in England and live in happiness.' He fell silent, remembering, and then he said, 'It is all over now. My plans have invited my death.'

Arthur spoke through his closed visor. 'If you had won this fight, do you know you would have been king? But how could you have contained the sin of treason against your anointed king?'

'I don't know, Sir Knight,' said Accolon. 'My mind and soul have been under a spell so that even treason seemed a nothing. But that is gone now like a dream. Tell me who you are, before I die.'

'I am your king,' said Arthur.

Then Accolon cried out in sorrow and in pain. 'My lord, I did not know. I thought I fought a champion. I have been tricked as you have. Can you grant mercy to a man who has been cheated and beguiled even to plotting your death?'

The king thought long and then he said, 'I can grant mercy because I believe you did not know me. I have honoured Morgan le Fay, my sister, given in to her, and loved her better than my other kin. And I have trusted her more even than my wife, even though I knew her jealousy and lust of flesh and hunger for power, and even though I knew she practised the black arts. If she could do this to me, I can believe and forgive what she has done to you. But I will not have mercy on her. My vengeance on my evil sister will be the talk of Christendom. Now rise, Sir Accolon. I have granted mercy.' Then Arthur helped him to his feet and he called to the people clustered about the field, 'Come closer.' And when they had gathered around him he said, 'We have fought and wounded each other sorely, but if we had known each other there would have been no combat.'

Accolon cried out, 'This is the best and bravest knight in the world, but he is more than that. He is our lord and sovereign, King Arthur. By mischance I have fought against my king. He can grant mercy, but I cannot forgive myself, for there is no sin or crime worse than treason against the king.'

Then all the people kneeled down and begged for mercy.

'Mercy you shall have,' said Arthur.' You did not know. Only remember from this what strange and fatal adventures and accidents may come to errant knights. Now I am weak and wounded and I must rest, but first here is my judgement of the test of right by combat.

'Sir Damas, as your champion I have fought and won. But because you are proud and cowardly and full of villainy, hear my decision. You will give this whole manor to your brother, Sir Outlake, with all its equipment of farms and houses. He in payment will send you a palfrey every year, for you are better fit to ride a lady's hackney than a war horse. I charge you on pain of death never to distress or injure knights errant who ride through your lands. As for the twenty knights in prison, you will return their armour and any other things you have taken from them. And if any of them comes to my court to complain of you, you shall die. That is my judgement.'

Then Arthur, weak from loss of blood, turned to Sir Outlake. 'Because you are a good knight, brave and true and courteous, I charge you to come to my court to be my knight, and I shall so favour you that you will live in comfort and in honour.'

'Thank you, my lord,' said Sir Outlake. 'I am at your command. Only be sure, sir, that if I had not been wounded I would have fought my own combat.'

'I wish it had been so,' said Arthur, 'for then I would not have been so hurt, and hurt by treachery and enchantment by one near to me.'

Sir Outlake said, 'I can't imagine anyone plotting against you, my lord.'

'I will deal with that person,' said the king. 'Now, how far am I from Camelot?'

'Two days' journey,' said Outlake. 'Too far to travel with your wounds. Three miles from here there is an abbey with nuns to care for you, and learned men to heal your wounds.'

'I will go there to rest,' said the king, and he called farewell to the people and helped Sir Accolon to his horse, and mounted and rode slowly away.

At the abbey their wounds were cleansed and cared for with the best-known salves and unguents, but within four days Sir Accolon died of the terrible last wound on his unshielded head.

Then Arthur ordered his body to be taken to Camelot by six knights and delivered to Morgan le Fay. He said, 'Tell my dear sister I send him to her as a present in payment for her kindness to me.'

Meanwhile, Morgan believed her plan had been carried out and the king killed with his own sword. The time had come, she thought, to rid herself of her husband Sir Uryens. In the night she waited until he was asleep and then called a maiden who attended her. 'Fetch me my lord's sword,' she said. 'There will never be a better time to kill him.'

The maid cried out in terror, 'If you kill your husband, you will never escape.'

'That is not your worry,' Morgan said. 'Go quickly and bring the sword.'

Then in fear the damsel crept to the bed of Sir Ewain, Morgan's son, and she awakened him. 'Get up,' she whispered. 'Your mother is going to kill your father in his sleep. She has sent me for a sword.'

Ewain started awake and rubbed his eyes, and then he said quietly, 'Obey her orders. Get the sword. I will take care of it,' and he slipped from his bed and armed himself and crept along dark corridors and hid himself in his father's room.

The damsel brought the sword with shaking hands, and Morgan le Fay took it from her and boldly she stood over her sleeping husband, coldly judging the proper place to drive in the blade. When she raised the sword to strike, Sir Ewain leaped from his hiding place and caught her wrist and held her, struggling. 'What are you doing?' he demanded. 'It is said that Merlin was sired by a fiend. You must be an earthly fiend. If you were not my mother, I would kill you.'

But Morgan trapped was doubly dangerous, She stared wildly about as though awakened suddenly. 'What is this?' she cried. 'Where am I? What is this sword? – Oh, my son, protect me!

Some evil spirit has entered while I slept. Have mercy on me, my son. Do not tell of this. Protect my honour. It is your honour, too.'

Sir Ewain said reluctantly, 'I will forgive you if you promise to give up your magic crafts.'

'I promise,' said Morgan. 'I will swear it. You are my good son, my dear son.' Then Ewain, half-believing, released her and took the sword away.

In the morning one of her secret people brought news to Morgan le Fay that her plan had failed. Sir Accolon was dead and Arthur, alive, had Excalibur again. Inwardly she raged against her brother and mourned the death of Accolon, but her face was cold and composed and she showed no anger or fear or shed any open tears for her lover. She well knew that if she stayed for the king's return her life was forfeit, for there could be no clemency for her unmentionable crime against her brother and her king.

Morgan went sweetly to Queen Guinevere and asked permission to leave the court.

'Can you not wait until your brother, the king, comes home?' asked Guinevere.

'I wish I might, but I cannot,' said Morgan. 'Bad news has come of revolt on my estates and I must go.'

'In that case you may go,' said the queen.

Then in the dark, before morning, Morgan le Fay assembled forty trusted followers and she rode out and gave no rest to horse or man for a day and a night. And early on the second morning she came to the abbey where she knew King Arthur lay.

She entered boldly and demanded to see her brother, and a nun replied, 'He is sleeping now at last. For three nights his wounds have given him little rest.'

'Do not awaken him,' said Morgan. 'I will go quietly to see my brother's dear face.' And she dismounted and went inside with such authority that no one dared stop the sister of the king.

She found his room and saw by a small rush light that the king lay on his bed asleep, but his hand gripped the handle of Excalibur and its naked blade lay beside him on the bed. Morgan did not dare to take the sword for fear he might awaken, for he slept restlessly. But on a chest nearby she saw the scabbard and slipped it under her cloak and went out thanking the nuns, and she mounted and rode away with speed.

When the king awakened, he missed his scabbard. 'Who has taken it?' he demanded angrily. 'Who has been here?'

'Only your sister Morgan le Fay, and she has gone.'

'You have not guarded me,' he cried. 'She has taken my scabbard.'

'Sir,' said the nuns, 'we could not disobey your sister.'

Then Arthur struggled from his bed and ordered the best horse to be found, and he asked Sir Outlake to arm and come with him, and the two galloped after Morgan.

At a wayside cross they asked a cowherd if he had seen a lady pass.

'Aye, that I did,' he said. 'A little time ago she went riding by and forty horsemen with her. They rode towards yonder forest.'

Then Arthur and Sir Outlake gave chase, and in a short time they sighted her and whipped up their horses.

Morgan saw them coming and she drove her horse through the forest and out on an open plain beyond it, and when she saw the pursuers gaining on her, she spurred her horse into a little lake. 'Whatever happens to me, he shall not have this sheath to protect him,' she said, and she threw the scabbard as far out as she could in the water. It was heavy with gold and cut jewels and sank quickly out of sight.

Then she rejoined her men and galloped on into a valley where there were rings of great standing stones. And Morgan cast enchantment so that her men and she became tall stones like the others. When Arthur entered the valley and saw the stones, he said, 'She has drawn the vengeance of God on her. My vengeance is not needed.' He looked about on the ground for his scabbard and could not find it, for it was in the lake. And after a time he rode slowly back towards the abbey.

As soon as he had gone, Morgan le Fay resumed her form and freed her men from the skins of stone. 'Now you are free,' she said, 'but did you see the king's face?'

'We did, and it was icy rage. If we had not been turned to stone we would have run away.'

'I believe you would,' said she.

They took up their march again, and on their way they met a knight leading a prisoner bound and blindfolded.

'What are you doing with that knight?' Morgan asked.

'I am going to drown him. I found him with my wife. And I will drown her too.'

Morgan asked the prisoner, 'Is this true what he says?'

'No, madame, it is not true.'

'Where do you come from? What is your name?' she asked.

'I am of King Arthur's court,' he said. 'My name is Manessen. I am Sir Accolon's cousin.'

Morgan le Fay said, 'I loved Sir Accolon. In his memory I shall deliver you to do to this man what he would have done to you.'

Her men unbound him and tied the other with the same cords. Sir Manessen put on the armour and weapons of his captor and took him to a deep spring and threw him in. Then he returned to Morgan. 'I will return to Arthur's court. Have you any message for him?'

She smiled bitterly. 'I have,' she said. 'Tell my dear brother that I rescued you not for love of him but for love of Accolon. And tell him I have no fear of him, for I can turn myself and my followers into stones. Lastly, tell him I can do much more than that and I will prove it to him when the time comes.'

She went to her lands in the country of Gore, and she strengthened her castles and towns, and armed and provisioned them, because in spite of her brave message she lived in fear of King Arthur.

Gawain, Ewain, and Marhalt

King Arthur brought gloom and anger back to Camelot, for there is no defence against treachery, and only rage and suspicion follow to measure the depth of the wound.

The knights of the court caught the king's anger and enlarged it. Treachery against the king's person is treason, since every subject feels the blow. Morgan le Fay should be burned, they said. That she was the king's half-sister made her crime more horrible. When Sir Manessen brought Morgan's message of defiance, the fellowship growled and looked to Arthur to order them to their arms – but the king said bitterly, 'You see now what it is to have a dear and loving sister. I will take my own way with this and I promise you that the whole world will speak of my revenge.' And by this the knights knew that their king was confused and had made no plan.

Like many cruel and evil women, Morgan le Fay knew men's weaknesses and discounted their strengths. And she knew also that most improbable actions may be successful so long as they are undertaken boldly and without hesitation, for men believe beyond proof to the contrary that blood is thicker than water and that a beautiful woman cannot be evil. Thus, Morgan played a deadly game with Arthur's honesty and innocence. She prepared a present for her brother, a cloak of such beauty that she knew his eyes would sparkle. Flowers and curling leaves patterned in jewels covered the cloak with preciousness and flashing colour, and Morgan le Fay sent this gift to Arthur by one of her damsels and she rehearsed her in her message.

The girl stood before the king, and she shuddered at his cold anger.

'Sir,' said the damsel, 'your sister now knows her terrible crime and that she cannot be forgiven. She is resigned to her fate, but she wishes you to know that it was not her act but the work of an evil spirit which trapped and controlled her.' She saw the king's eyes waver with uncertainty and pressed on. 'Your sister

Morgan sends this present, my lord, a gift befitting your fame for justice and wisdom and mercy. She begs you to wear her gift when you sit in judgement on her and perhaps remember not the foul spirit which controlled her but the beloved sister you have warmed with your kindness.'

The damsel unrolled the shining cloak and spread it before the king and she watched his face, hardly daring to breathe. She saw the quick light of pleasure at the beauty come into his eyes.

'Well – there are evil spirits,' he said. 'Everyone knows there are.'

'Your sister made this cloak with her own white fingers, my lord. She stitched every jewel to it and would not allow any help.'

Arthur looked at the cloak. 'She was always clever,' he said. 'I remember once when she was a girl—' He stretched his hand towards the shining beauty.

Then a shrill voice cried out, 'My lord, do not touch it.' And Nyneve of the Lake came forward and said, 'Sir, I saved you against treachery before.'

The king's eyes went back to the shining cloak. But Nyneve said, 'Sir, even if I am wrong it will do no harm to test it. Let Morgan's messenger wear it first.'

Arthur turned to the trembling damsel. 'No harm in that if it is harmless,' he said. 'Put it on!'

'I must not,' the damsel said. 'It would not be seemly to wear the king's cloak. My mistress would be angry.'

'I will forgive the fault. Put it on!'

Then, as the girl shrank back, Nyneve took the cloak by its edge with her fingertips and cast it over the damsel's shoulders, and her skin reddened and then turned black and she fell to the floor in convulsions while the corrosive ate through her flesh and shrivelled her.

Arthur looked at the twitching horror robed in jewels and he was filled with the wonder and pain of treachery. 'My sister made this death for me with her own hands,' he said. 'My own sister.' Then he glanced suspiciously at everyone around him and he called to Sir Uryens, Morgan's husband, to come to him privately.

When they were alone he said, 'Sir, treachery is the saddest crime of all. Even if it fails, the poison spreads. Before his death

Sir Accolon confessed his guilt and swore that you were innocent – you, my friend and my brother. But innocence is no antidote. I know that you refused to plot against me, but how can I forget that you knew there was a plot. I can easily excuse you because I know that my sister tried to kill you as well as me. I will try to trust you – but can cracked trust be mended? I don't know. As for your son and my nephew, Sir Ewain – all I can remember is that he suckled at a poisoned breast. The hands that fashioned his youth sewed jewels on my death. What a sickening mould suspicion is. Ewain must leave the court. I haven't time to watch and to suspect even innocent acts.'

'I understand,' Sir Uryens said. 'If you can conceive a way to prove my loyalty – I am ready.'

'Send your son away,' said Arthur.

Ewain accepted his banishment and he said, 'There is only one way to prove myself. I will ride on quest and let my actions speak for me. Words can be traitors but deeds have no advocate.'

His friend and cousin, Sir Gawain, was not so patient. 'Who banishes you banishes me,' he said. 'I will go with you. This is injustice.'

And Arthur, watching the two young good knights preparing a long journey, said musingly, 'When I had Merlin I suspected no one. He always knew and saved me from uncertainty. I wish I had Merlin back again.' And then he remembered Merlin's prophecies concerning Guinevere and he was not so sure he wished to know. 'With knowledge there is no hope,' he said. 'Without hope I would sit motionless, rusting like unused armour.'

In the morning before day the young knights heard Mass and confessed and were shriven so that their souls were as clean and shining as their swords, and they rode away from Camelot and eagerly entered a new world of wonders. They looked back at the old walls of Camelot high against the dawn on the impregnable hill, and at the four deep ditches that protected the walls. They were glad and proud and humble to be men in a world where men were valuable. They passed through valleys among surrounding heights and they saw the turf-crusted ramparts of hill forts that had crumbled before the world was born. On a great level meadow they saw rings of giant stones set up possibly by ancient peoples but more likely by present goblins, and since these things were outside the quest, they looked away and circled widely.

Then, within sight of a forest, they drew near to a small conical hill crowned with dark pines, and their horses stopped and trembled with ears laid back and eyes showing white with fear. Sir Ewain and Sir Gawain recognized the signs and turned aside to avoid the barrow. It was not their business or their world. Their own was full enough of wonders.

It was with relief that they entered a covering forest of great oaks and left the haunted ground behind. The tree trunks, thick as horses, rose darkly up and blotted out the sky with a cover of tumbling leaves, and only a dimpsy green light strained through. The hoofbeat was muffled on the mossy ground and no birds sang in the upper branches. Only the tap of shield cantle against breastplate, the gritty whisper of straining leather, and the clink of spur rowels marked their passage through the wood. The horses found their way, for, as everyone knows, horses with free rein will travel where others have been before. High overhead the oak leaves stirred and rustled under a wind which did not reach the ground. The dimness and the quiet entered the young knights and they did not speak, and they were glad when they topped a hill and saw below them a grassy meadow and, on its far forested edge, a dark stone tower with castellations and thin arrow slits, for here must be something they understood, if even it was filled with danger.

Gawain and his cousin straightened in their saddles, moved their shields a little forward, and their right hands moved to their sword hilts. From the meadow came the sound of women's voices, shrill and vindictive. The knights tested their buckles, and gently lowered their visors before they moved on down towards the tower.

On the meadow's edge they drew up, for they saw twelve ladies running back and forth near a small tree from which a white shield hung. And as each lady passed the shield she threw mud on it and screamed a curse and moved away to gather more mud. From the top of the tower nearby two armed knights looked down on the strange scene.

The young cousins rode to the ladies and Sir Ewain asked sternly, 'Why do you dirty and insult an undefended shield?'

The ladies squealed with laughter and one said, 'I will tell you, since you ask. The knight who owns the shield hates ladies. That is an insult to us and so we insult his shield in return. That's a fair exchange.' And her companions shrieked with ugly laughter.

Sir Gawain said, 'It is not seemly in a knight to despise ladies, I agree, but if he does, perhaps he has some cause. Or he may love some other lady. Do you know his name?'

'Certainly we know. He is Sir Marhalt and he is a son of the King of Ireland.'

'I know him well,' Sir Ewain said. 'He is as good a knight as any living and I have seen him prove it in a tournament where he won the prize above everyone.'

Sir Gawain said sternly, 'I think you are to blame. It is not a lady's part to dishonour a man's shield. He will return to defend his shield and he will not love ladies more when he finds what you have done. It is not my quarrel, but I will not stand by and see a knight's shield dishonoured— Come, cousin, let us ride on. I find I myself do not love such ladies as these.'

As they neared the edge of the forest, Sir Marhalt appeared on a huge charger and he galloped towards the ladies, who screamed with fright and ran falling and stumbling towards the safety of the tower.

Sir Marhalt looked at his muddy shield and slung it on his shoulder, and at that moment one of the knights of the tower rode out crying, 'Defend yourself.'

'With joy,' said Marhalt, and he leaned fiercely over his couched spear, and under the shock of the meeting both horse and man went tumbling in a welter of harness and flying hoofs. Before Sir Marhalt could turn, the other knight of the tower began his charge, but Marhalt, turning in his saddle, glanced the spear point off and struck down his opponent.

Then Marhalt turned his shield and scraped the filth from its white surface, and he held up the shield towards the tower where the damsels lay shaking with fear. He shouted, 'Part of the insult is avenged. A lady gave me this white shield. And I shall wear it as it is. Even dirty it is cleaner than you.' Then he saw the cousins on the edge of the forest and he approached them guardedly and asked them their pleasure.

Sir Gawain said, 'We are from King Arthur's court and we ride for adventure. Have you anything to suggest?'

'No,' said Marhalt, 'but if you call a small do with spears adventure, I would not refuse, if you would ask nicely.' And he wheeled and took his battle position in the centre of the meadow.

'Let it go,' said Ewain. 'He is a good man. What is to be gained? We have no quarrel with him.'

Sir Gawain looked up at the sun. 'It is not yet midday,' he said. 'Mine is morning strength, as you know, and it wanes with afternoon. It would be a shame not to fight him, but it must be soon or not at all.'

'Perhaps we could ride away,' said Ewain.

'Not after his challenge. We would be laughed at and scorned.'

'Very well then, cousin,' said Ewain. 'I am not as strong or as experienced as you are. Let me make the first run. If I go down I leave you to avenge me.'

'Very well,' Gawain agreed, 'but if you will suffer me to say so, yours is an unfortunate attitude to take into battle.'

Sir Ewain charged, and Marhalt unhorsed him and gashed his side. Sir Marhalt trotted back to his battle station, and he sat his horse, stern and motionless, waiting to meet his next opponent.

Sir Gawain made sure his cousin was not badly hurt and then he looked at the sun and saw that there was time. Child of the morning he was, his strength and courage waxing with the sun, and waning with it. His heart pounded with joy. He laid his spear in rest and lifted his horse to trot, to canter, and to wild flying charges. Sir Marhalt met him in mid-course. Each spear struck true in centre shield and bent under the plunging might, while ashen staff fought ashen staff, and Gawain's spear flew to splinters and he and his horse were thrust to the ground.

When Marhalt checked his mount and wheeled to return, he saw Sir Gawain standing by his fallen horse, shield dressed and sword dancing in his hand. He called out, 'Sir Knight, dismount and fight on foot or I will kill your horse and you will have no honourable choice.'

Sir Marhalt drew rein. 'I thank you for the lesson,' he said. 'You put teeth in the laws of courtesy.' And he rode to a small tree and leaned his spear against it and slowly dismounted, tied his horse to a branch, and loosened the girth. Then he deliberately tested his shield strap, tightened his sword belt, drew his sword and inspected its edge, while Gawain impatiently waited and the sun crawled nearer to noon.

Now Sir Marhalt moved ponderously near, his sword at parry and his shield held forward and lightly swaying. Gawain leaped towards him, striking, forcing, pushing frantically, trying to get in a killing blow while his strength increased. But Marhalt was long trained in war. He kept his helm down, covered with his hovering shield, feinted to draw the charge, and let it spend itself on his retreating weight. 'Why do you hurry?' Marhalt asked. 'We have the whole day to fight.'

The question maddened Gawain. He flickered past Marhalt's shield and drew blood from his side and too late felt the countering sword point enter his thigh. He danced about the defending knight and rained blows on the close-held shield and forward-tilted helm.

'You are a strong man,' Marhalt said softly. 'You get stronger every moment. Save your strength and your breath for the long fight. Come – let us rest a moment.'

But Gawain saw his shadow creeping under him and he drove in again and his swinging sword shone like a wheel. He wounded Marhalt and got short quick counterwounds and his breath grew short as he tried to break through the defence of his practised and deliberate foe. He dashed in like a shining ram, clawed at the covering shield, and saw his shadow disappear beneath him and fell back under the weight of the thrusting shield. Then Gawain felt his strength begin to ebb, and his lungs rattled with exhaustion. The joy of combat drained away and a little pain took its place. He backed away and circled warily.

Marhalt had saved his strength for such a time. Now he moved forward slowly and without warning lashed out, cut into the cantle of Gawain's shield, and saw it fly sideways in his faltering grip. And now Marhalt moved in to blind Gawain with his shield and stab him in the belly, and he saw the young knight exposed and open to the blow. He hesitated, waiting for the shield to cover, and it did not. It hung to the side useless and weakly held.

Sir Marhalt moved back cautiously in case it was a ruse, and when he was fifteen feet away and safe from a lunge, he rested his sword point on the ground and he said, 'Young sir, a little time ago you were as good a knight as ever fought with me. But now you are fought out and your strength is gone. If I killed you now it would be murder and I am not a murderer. I can let you rest until you recover, and then you might kill me or I might kill you. You have no quarrel with me great enough for one or both of us to die or be shamed. It is only adventure. Will you be satisfied to make peace with neither of us claiming victory?'

Sir Gawain shook with emotion. 'Gentle knight, you are the noblest man I have ever met. I could not say that because I am weakened. But you, strong and fresh, can say it and that is knightly courtesy. I accept the peace, Sir Knight, and I thank you.'

Then, to prove his faith, Gawain laid down his sword and unlaced his helm and took it off. Then Marhalt did the same and they two embraced like brothers and swore that they would live like brothers. Now Ewain came near, holding his wounded side, and they helped him to disarm, and then Marhalt led them to his manor, which was not far distant, where his servants bathed their wounds and made them comfortable. And those three knights grew close in friendship and loyalty so that soon after as they sat at ease in the great hall, with the gnawed bones of their supper around them and wine cups in their hands, Sir Gawain said, 'One thing troubles me, sir. You are a valiant man, as I know, and a courteous gentle knight, as you have proved to me. How does it happen that you hate ladies?'

'I? Hate ladies?' Marhalt asked.

'Those ladies who threw filth on your shield said you did.'

Then Marhalt laughed. 'Have you not found,' he said, 'that if you do not like a certain damsel she will spread the word that you dislike all ladies? In this way she saves her vanity and proves you are not a man.'

'But those who dishonoured your white shield?' asked Gawain.

'They were right to say I hated them,' said Marhalt. 'But they should not have included all ladies. There is a kind of woman who deeply hates men and is jealous of real men. She it is who preys on weaknesses and tries to tear down men's strength by arts and tricks. Such ladies I dislike and such were those at the tower. But to all good ladies and gentlewomen I owe my service as a good knight should. Such ladies would not befoul a man's shield when he is absent or speak curses behind his back and then flee like frightened chickens when he returns. No – there are ladies living who can tell you differently about me.'

Then they spoke of knighthood and adventuring, and Sir Ewain said, 'I must continue on as soon as I can. My name is clouded with the king through no fault of my own and I must prove my honour and my knighthood before all the world so that the king will hear of it.'

Gawain said, 'I have no cloud except that I feel injustice has been put on my cousin and I will not leave his side in his quest for honour.'

Marhalt became gloomy. 'I shall not like to see you go away,' he said. 'We make good companions. Will you not stay here with me?'

'I may not, sir,' said Ewain. 'I have been banished and that is a shame that must be wiped out with brave deeds and honourable actions.'

'Well,' said Sir Marhalt, 'I may tell you that nearby begins a great and mysterious wood called the Forest of Arroy. No one has ever passed through it without finding wonders and dangers and more adventures than he can handle. Your talk has fired my blood. If you will permit, I will ride through the forest and share the excitement of your quest. I had forgotten how good questing can be.'

'We will be glad of your company, sir,' said Gawain. 'And even gladder of your strong arm.' And they continued to speak of adventuring far into the night, and they spoke of battles and rescues of fair ladies, and they dreamed at last of fame well gained and honour in the world.

Ewain said, 'Sir, tell us about your lady who gave you the white shield so spitefully befouled.'

Sir Marhalt was silent and Sir Gawain said, 'Cousin, your question is unmannerly. What a worthy knight does not tell of his own accord he does not wish to tell. Perhaps there was an oath, perhaps a jealous husband. You are wrong. You must learn.'

'It was an oath,' said Marhalt hastily.

'Forgive me, sir,' said Ewain. 'And thank you, cousin.'

In the morning the three companions prepared themselves for adventure – polished their armour, saw to the sharpness of their swords, and chose their spears with care that the grain of the ash was straight and balanced, for on these things life and victory depend. And when they mounted and rode towards the Forest of Arroy, which stood up darkly in the distance, Sir Gawain asked, 'Sir, do you know the forest ? What adventures may we hope to find ?'

'I do not know it,' said Marhalt. 'If I did, it would not be adventure. But knights who have passed by have told that it shelters wonders.'

It was a forest of oak and beech, laced with may and white thorn, tangled and guarded with briars. No opening showed on its dark frontier, so that they had to hack an entrance with their swords, but in a short time they came upon a path opened through the undergrowth by red deer and they followed the passage knowing it would lead to water and to pasturage, for deer must drink and graze. After a time they came to a valley of stones, square cut and tumbled about as though some ancient city had been pillaged and destroyed. Among the stones they saw a few hovels of piled stones like sheepcotes roofed with branches. A little stream of turbulent water gabbled down from the farther hill, and after they had refreshed their horses and themselves they followed the watercourse up the slope to the source, where it bubbled from a spring that opened from the mossy mountainside. Above the spring on a ferny shelf three ladies sat under a cluster of birch trees. When the knights were close enough to see, they drew up and regarded the strange trio. One lady was past middle age, and with the lean memory of beauty, and she wore a heavy chaplet of gold on her white hair. Beside her sat one of thirty years, full-blown and handsome, a golden circlet on her auburn hair, and the third a lovely child of fifteen but lately come to be a woman and she had woven flowers in her golden hair, and all three wore the clothing of gentlewomen, embroidered in gold and silver thread, and their furred cloaks lay on the ground behind them.

The knights approached slowly and removed their helmets in courtesy and saluted the seated three.

Sir Marhalt spoke. 'Ladies,' he said, 'we are errant knights ready for any adventure God may send. You are safe with us because we honour our knighthood, by which you are to understand we honour ladies.'

'You are welcome,' said the oldest of the three.

Sir Gawain said, 'If you have made no contrary oath, tell us why you sit here as though waiting.'

And the second lady replied, 'It is no mystery. We sit here waiting for knights errant such as you. It is our custom, just as questing is yours. If you agree we can lead you to adventures if you will follow our custom; each of you must choose one of us as his guide. When you have done so, we will conduct you to a place where three paths meet. There each of you will choose a path. Thus you have two unknown choices towards your fates, and only God can direct which course you take. Then each of us will ride with one of you towards whatever may be in store. But you must swear that twelve months hence, if you live, you will meet here again, and may God save your lives and send you luck.'

'Now that is well said,' Sir Marhalt cried. 'That is the way adventuring should be. But how shall we choose our ladies?'

'As your hearts and minds direct,' said the damsel, and she glanced at the young Sir Ewain and dropped her eyes and blushed.

But Sir Ewain said, 'I am the youngest of the three and not so strong and experienced; therefore, let me have the oldest lady. She has seen much and she can best help me when I have need, for I shall need help more than the others.'

The youngest damsel flushed with anger.

Sir Marhalt said, 'Very well, if there is no opposing wish, I will choose the lady of maturity and grace. We too will have much in common, being neither very old nor very young but eased of vanities and not too demanding of each other.'

Sir Gawain crowed, 'I thank you, gentle companions. The one remaining is the one I would have chosen at the risk of offending, for she is the youngest and fairest of all and I like her best.'

Sir Marhalt said, 'Either we are fortunate by accident or God has chosen for us so that there is no dissension or anger. Now, ladies, lead us to our starting place.'

The ladies rose and each took the bridle of her knight, and where the path split into three they promised to return to this spot in twelve months' time and then they embraced and each knight set his lady on his horse behind him and gaily they set out on the triple quest, Sir Ewain to the west, Sir Marhalt south, and Gawain on the path that led northwards.

And first we will follow Sir Gawain as he rode gaily through the green forest with his lovely damsel panting behind him. Gawain chattered merrily to his companion.

'How fortunate that you fell to me,' he said. 'If it had not been so, I would have contended for you. You do not answer. That is easily explained. You are very young and you had never the company of a gallant knight from the great world. You are blushing, I know, although I cannot see your face. Well, that is proper in so young a damsel. Perhaps your tongue is tied with confusion at the honour you have been paid – or maybe you were taught to keep silence when a knight speaks. That is the good old-fashioned way. Too seldom practised now. You must not be afraid or too impressed with me. You will see that beneath my royal position and the aura of my knighthood I am as human as you are, a man, in fact, in spite of appearance. You are dazzled, my dear, and I can easily understand that.'

The damsel sat scowling behind him and she kicked her heels into the horse's flank so that he shied.

'Perhaps some animal, or snake,' said Gawain. 'If you are frightened, put your arm about me. I will protect you from falling. You know, I like a girl who does not chatter all the time.'

'Is Sir Ewain your brother?' the damsel asked.

'No, my cousin, and a very good boy. I can see that you would feel him too young and inexperienced to be interesting – and it is true that he is barely out of childhood, but when he has seen as much of the world as I have he will be a good knight. He comes of a noble line. But of course girls like an older man.' The horse shied again. 'I don't understand this,' said Gawain. 'He is a very steady mount. If you are fond of music I could sing to you. While I don't agree, I am said to have a fine voice. What song would you like to hear?'

'I don't like singing,' said the damsel. 'Look, there is a pretty manor house ahead. I am thirsty, sir.'

'How like a girl,' said Gawain. 'Thirsty, hungry, cold, overheated, sad, happy, loving, hating – always something to draw attention. Well, perhaps that is why girls are attractive.'

An old knight sat near the path before the manor house and Gawain drew up.

'Sir,' he said, 'God give you good fortune. Do you know of any adventures hereabouts, for a noble knight on quest ?'

'God grant you first if there is shortage,' said the old knight courteously. 'Adventures ? Yes, more than you can shake a spear at, but the day is waning. What is adventure in the light is quite different at night. Alight, young sir, and stay the night. In the morning I will lead you to adventure.'

'We should go on,' said Gawain. 'It is proper that we should take our rest under the spreading branches of a tree.'

'Nonsense,' said the damsel. 'I am tired and thirsty.'

'She is very young,' Gawain explained. 'Very well, my dear. If you must.'

The damsel went into a little room and supped alone, and locked the door and did not answer Gawain's gentle knocking. And he returned to sit beside the fire with the old knight, to talk of horses and armour and whether a shield should be flat or duck-breasted to glance a spear aside. Thus they talked of their trade until sleep came.

In the morning when they were mounted and armed, Sir Gawain said, 'Now, sir. What adventure have you saved for me ?'

The old knight said, 'Nearby there is a place which you will see – a cleared field in the forest, a stone cross, and turf level and firm, and on its verge a fountain of clear cold water. This place draws adventures as meat draws flies. I don't know what we will find, but if any wonder is about to happen, it will happen there.'

When they came to the clearing with its green velvet lawn, it was deserted, and the three dismounted and sat beside the ancient stone cross. And very soon they heard a voice crying out against outrageous fate and into the meadow rode a strong fair knight of noble stature, well armed and handsome. When he saw Sir Gawain he ceased his wailing and offered his salute and prayed God to send honour and repute to him.

'Thank you,' said Gawain. 'And may he give you honour and fame also.'

'I must put such things aside, sir,' said the knight. 'For me there is nothing but sorrow and shame, as you will see.' And he rode on to the farther side of the glade and sat his horse and waited. And he had not to wait long, for ten knights filed from the forest in a line. The first knight couched his spear and the sad knight met him mid-field and toppled him. Then one after another he met the other nine and with his one spear he unhorsed every one. When that was done he sat his horse with downcast eyes and the ten knights approached on foot and pulled him unresisting from his horse. They roped him hand and foot and slung him under his horse's belly and led the horse away with the sad knight swaying like a sack.

Gawain watched in wonder. 'What is this?' he asked. 'He beat them all and then permitted them to take him.'

'That is true,' said the old knight. 'If he had wished he could have beaten them on foot as he did mounted.'

The damsel said shrilly, 'It seems to me that you could help him if you are as great as you say. He is one of the best and handsomest knights I ever saw.'

'I would have helped if he wished. But it seemed to me he wanted what he got. It is not wise or courteous to interfere in other people's business unless you are asked.'

'I think you didn't want to help him,' said the girl. 'Perhaps you are jealous of him. It is possible that you are afraid.'

'You are a silly country girl,' said Gawain. 'I afraid? Let me tell you I am never afraid.'

And as they argued the old knight said, 'Hush! The day is young, and more adventures are thronging. See, on the right hand of the meadow a knight all armed except his head.'

'I see him,' the damsel said. 'A handsome head, a manly face.'

As she spoke, another horseman entered the glade from the left, a dwarf in armour, and he too with bare head, a monster with shoulders wide as a door, a wide, thick frog's mouth, flat broad nose like an ape, and glittering eyes that sparkled like jet, an ugliness so perfect as to be beautiful. The dwarf called out to the waiting knight, 'Where is the lady?'

A handsome damsel stepped from the shelter of the trees, crying, 'I am here.'

The knight said, 'It is silly to argue and strive for her. Come, dwarf, and arm yourself to fight for her.'

The dwarf replied, 'Gladly, if there were no other way. But there a good knight sits by the cross. Let him decide which of us shall have her.'

'I agree,' said the knight. 'If you will swear to abide by his decision.'

When they consulted Gawain he said, 'There doesn't seem to be much choice. If you put it to me, I say let the lady decide who shall have her, and I will defend her choice.'

The lady did not hesitate. She went to the frog-faced dwarf and raised her arms to him, and he leaned from his saddle and plucked her from the ground and set her in front of him, and she embraced him and kissed him. The dwarf smiled wisely and bowed satirically to the company and rode away into the forest with the lady in his arms.

The defeated knight came disconsolately and sat by the stone cross and all of them were unable to believe what they had seen. The old knight in disgust mounted his horse and rode away towards his manor.

Now a strange knight, full armed, rode into the glade and he shouted, 'Sir Gawain, I know you by your shield. Come joust with me for the honour of your knighthood.' And when Gawain hesitated, his damsel said, 'You had a reason to avoid the ten knights, what reason will you give to avoid this one who challenges you?'

Gawain stood up angrily. 'No reason. I accept.' And he mounted and rode against the challenger, and both went down. Then ponderously they drew their swords and engaged on foot in slow, heavy combat, striking a few blows and then resting as though their hearts were not in it.

Meanwhile, at the cross, the disappointed knight said to the damsel, 'I cannot understand why she went with that dreadful dwarf.'

'Who knows what draws a maiden's heart?' she said. 'A woman is not misled by the features of a man. She looks more deeply for her love.'

'You have no need,' he replied. 'Your love is as handsome as any I have seen.' And he watched the two knights feinting and parrying on the lawn-like glade.

'That proves what I said,' the damsel remarked shyly. 'He is not my love. I do not even like him. Your face may not have his arrogant perfection but to me it is more manly.'

'Do you mean that if you had a choice you would choose me?'

'What have I said?' And the damsel blushed. 'He is a boaster. He thinks he is better than anyone else. He believes a lady has only to look at him to love him. Such a man needs a lesson.'

The knight said eagerly, 'While they are fighting, come ride away with me.'

'It would not be seemly,' she said.

'But you say you have no love for him.'

'That is true. I much prefer you.'

'I will care for you and give you all my heart.'

'He thinks of no one but himself.'

'Do you think he would follow us?'

'I don't think he would dare. He is a fool.'

The two knights fought for a long time and the sun shone hotly down on their armour so that they dripped more sweat than blood, and at last the challenger stepped away and leaned on his sword and said, 'For my part I think everything has been properly done and both of us have behaved worthily. If you have no particular savagery towards me, let us make peace. Understand, I do not beg for peace.'

'I understand,' said Gawain. 'There's no dishonour in mutual accord, and both of us have increased our honour. Agreed?'

'Agreed,' said the knight, and they removed their helmets and formally embraced, and they moved to the fountain and drank deeply and washed the stinging salt sweat from their eyes. Then Gawain looked about and asked, 'Where is my damsel? I left her sitting by the cross.'

'Was she yours?' the other asked. 'I saw her ride away behind that other knight. I thought she was his damsel.'

Now Gawain scowled a moment and then he laughed uneasily. 'It may sound ungallant, but I'm glad she is gone. I drew her by lot, a silly country girl, pretty now, but the kind that runs to fat.'

'I didn't see her close up.'

'You didn't miss much,' Gawain said. 'She nearly drove me crazy with her rattling talk. I like a lady more mature, with some experience of the great world, not a stupid little country girl.'

'A chatterbox was she? I know the kind.'

'Never stopped,' said Gawain. 'And that poor fellow probably thinks he stole her from me. He will find out.'

'Well, I'm glad for you,' said the knight. 'I have a pleasant little estate and houses not far from here. Come lodge with me. Perhaps some farm girl will take your mind off your chatterbox.'

'Gladly,' said Gawain. And as they rode towards the lodging he said, 'If you live hereabouts, perhaps you can tell me what knight it is who could strike down ten men with a spear and then permit them to take him and bind him without a struggle.'

'I know him well,' said the host. 'And I know his story. Do you wish to hear it?'

'I do,' said Gawain. 'My heart went out to him.'

'His name is Sir Pelleas,' said the host. 'He is one of the best knights in the world, I guess.'

'I could see that from his jousting – ten knights went down before one spear.'

'Oh, he has done more than that. When the lady Ettarde, who has great holdings and a castle near here, announced a three-day tournament, Sir Pelleas entered the fight, and although five hundred knights tried for the prize, he overturned everyone who came against him. The prize was a fine sword and a golden chaplet to give to the lady of his heart. There was no question who should have the prize, but when Sir Pelleas saw the lady Ettarde, he fell in love with her and he gave the chaplet to her and proclaimed her the fairest lady in the land, although there is some question about that, and he challenged anyone who should deny it to mortal combat. But this Ettarde is a curious vain and proud thing. She would have none of him. I will never understand women.'

'Nor I,' said Gawain. 'Only today a lady chose a dwarf with the face of a toad.'

'There you are,' said the other. 'In the castle there are many ladies much more beautiful than Ettarde and not one of them would have refused so handsome and well-made a knight as Pelleas, particularly after he demonstrated his prowess against five hundred knights for three days. But Sir Pelleas would not look at any other lady. He followed Ettarde moaning like a puppy, and the more he pleaded with her the more she disliked him and insulted him and tried to drive him away. I can't understand what he saw in her to love.'

'Who knows the mysteries of a man's heart?' said Gawain. 'He must love her very deeply.'

'Well may you say so, sir. He has said that he will follow her to the end of the earth and give her no peace until she returns his love.'

'Sometimes that is the worst possible way,' said Gawain. 'It might be better to blow a kiss and ride away. Some ladies do not prize what they can have.'

'There is no doubt that she means it. She has tried every way to be rid of him. But he has taken up his quarters in a priory nearby her castle and rides back and forth under her window crying out his pain and pleading for her mercy until Ettarde, driven out of her mind, sends knights against him. Then he defeats them all on horse and afterwards allows them to take him.'

'That's what he did today. Why is that?'

'It is the only way he can see her. And though she insults him and dishonours him in every way, he only loves her more and begs to be her prisoner so he may see her. And so she has him thrown from the castle and again he rides under her window baying like a lovesick hound.'

'It is a shame to see a man sink so low,' said Gawain.

'Well,' his host said, 'he has worked it out that if he keeps at it long enough he will wear her down, but the only result is that her dislike for him has turned to bitter hatred. He has caused her so much trouble that she would adore the man who killed him – but she can find no knight able to defeat him on the field and none will kill him.'

'It is a pity,' Gawain said. 'Tomorrow I will search him out and try to help him.'

'You will fail,' said the host. 'He will not listen to reason.'

'Nonetheless you have given me an idea,' said Gawain.

In the morning Gawain asked his way to the priory where Sir Pelleas had his residence and he found that knight bruised and beaten.

'How can you allow this without defending yourself?' asked Gawain.

Sir Pelleas began, 'I love a lady and she—'

'I know the story,' said Gawain. 'But I do not understand why you allow her to trample on you.'

'Because I hope she will have pity on me at last. Love causes many a good knight to suffer before he is accepted. But, alas, I am unfortunate.'

Gawain said, 'Among the ornaments of ladies, pity is a rarity.'

'If I can prove the depth of my love, she will relent.'

'Stop your mooning,' Gawain said. 'Your method is painful, insulting, and ineffective. If you will give me leave, I have a plan to deliver the lady's heart into your hands.'

'Who are you?'

'I am Sir Gawain of King Arthur's court, his sister's son. King Lot of Orkney was my father.'

'I am Sir Pelleas, Lord of the Isles. And I have never loved a lady or a damsel until now.'

'That is apparent,' said Gawain. 'You need the help of some good friend.'

'I will die if I do not see her. She insults me and curses me, but I can wish no more than to see her, even though she wishes me gone or dead.'

'If you can stop your moaning long enough to listen, I have a plan. She wishes you dead. Give me your armour. I will go to her and tell her I have killed you. This will bring sharply to her what she has lost, and when she mourns for you I will bring her to you and you will know her love.'

'Is that the way of it?' Pelleas asked.

'I believe that ladies love best what they do not have,' said Gawain.

'You will be faithful to me? You will not act against me?'

'Why should I?' said Sir Gawain. 'I will return here within a day and a night. If I do not, you will know that something has gone amiss.'

On this agreement the two exchanged armour and shields, and they embraced, and then Gawain mounted and rode towards the castle of the lady Ettarde.

Ladies' pavilions were set up in the grassy meadow without the gate, and Ettarde and her damsels played and danced and sang in the sweetness of field flowers.

153

When Gawain, bearing Sir Pelleas's device on his shield, came in view, the ladies sprang up and fled towards the castle gate in fright and dismay. But Gawain called out that he was not Pelleas. 'I am another knight,' he cried. 'I have killed Pelleas and taken his armour.'

Ettarde stopped warily. 'Take off your helmet,' she said. 'Let me see your face.'

And when she saw that it was not Pelleas she begged him to dismount. 'Have you really slain Pelleas?'

'I have,' said Gawain. 'He was the best knight I ever met, but in the end I defeated him, and when he would not yield, I killed him. How else do you think I could have got his armour?'

'That is true,' Ettarde said. 'He was a wonderful fighting man – but I hated him because I could not be rid of him. He cried and wept and moaned like a sick calf until I wished him dead. I like a man of decision. Since you have slain him for me, I shall grant you anything you wish.' And Ettarde blushed when she said it.

Now Gawain looked at her and saw that she was fair, and he remembered his faithless little damsel with loathing, and his vanity cried out for conquest. He smiled with confidence. 'I will hold you to your promise, my lady,' he said and he was pleased to see her cheeks turn rosy with excitement. She led him to her castle and set a bath for him with scented water, and when he was clad in a loose robe of purple cloth, she gave him food and wine and sat beside him so that her shoulder touched him. 'Now tell me what you wish of me?' she said softly. 'You will find I pay my debts.'

Gawain took her hand. 'Very well,' he said. 'I love a lady, but she does not love me.'

'Oh!' Ettarde exclaimed in confusion and jealousy. 'Then she is a fool. You are a king's son and a king's nephew, young, handsome, brave. What ails your love? No lady in the world is too good for you. She must be a fool.' She looked into Gawain's smiling eyes.

'As my reward,' he said, 'I want your promise that you will do anything in your power to get me the love of my lady.'

Ettarde controlled her face to conceal her disappointment. 'I don't know what I could do,' she said.

'Do I have your promise, on your faith?'

'Well – yes – yes. I promise, since I promised. Who is the lady and what can I do?'

Gawain looked long at her before he replied, 'You are the lady, you are my love. You know what you can do. I hold you to your promise.'

'Oh!' she cried. 'You are a trickster. No lady is safe with you. You have laid a trap for me.'

'Your promise!'

'I suppose I cannot help myself,' said the lady Ettarde. 'If I should not give you what you ask I would be false to my oath, and I hold my honour above my life, my love.'

It was the month of May and the fields were green and gold, sweet with flowers and soft and warm in the afternoon sun. Gawain and Ettarde strolled out of the dark castle and walked in the meadow hand in hand to the bright pavilions set up on the grass. They had their supper sitting on the grass, and when the evening came a trouvère from across the sea sang songs of love and chivalry, and Ettarde's knights and damsels strolled in the evening listening and slipped away to other pavilions set at a little distance.

And when the night chill shivered them, Gawain and Ettarde entered their house of silk and dropped the door cloth. In a soft bed with coverlets of down they lay together in love and languor and then in love again, and time passed over them unnoticed. In the golden morning they broke their fast and loved and dined and loved and suppered and loved and slept to awaken loving – and three days passed as though an hour had moved.

In his priory Sir Pelleas waited nervously through the promised day and night, and Gawain did not return. 'Something has delayed him,' Pelleas told himself, and he waited sleepless another day and night. Then, hollow-cheeked and frantic, he paced his cell saying, 'Perhaps he is injured, perhaps ill. And yet if I go now I might spoil his subtle plan. But suppose she has taken him prisoner.' Before daylight of the third night he could stand it no longer. He armed himself and rode towards the silent castle standing dark and unguarded, and he saw the pavilions in the meadow, their striped sides moving gently in the morning breeze. Silently he tethered his horse and moved to the first pavilion, and looking in saw three knights sleeping. And in the second he found four damsels sleeping tousled and content. Then he opened the door cloth of the third pavilion and saw his lady and Gawain clasped in each other's arms, sleeping in the deep, contented weariness of love.

Pelleas's heart broke. 'So – he was false,' he thought. 'Did he plan this treachery or was he enchanted into it?' In agony he crept away and mounted his horse. When he had gone half a mile with the picture of the lovers behind in his eyes, anger arose in him. 'He is not my friend. He is my enemy. I will go back and kill him as a traitor to his promise. I should kill them both.' He turned about and started back the way he had come. And many years of honour and innocence assailed him. 'I cannot kill an unarmed sleeping knight,' he thought. 'That would be treason worse than his, treason against my knighthood and the whole order of knighthood.' And he turned back again towards the priory. And as he went rage clamoured shouting in his breast, and he cried, 'Damn knighthood, damn honour! Have they been honourable? I will kill them both for the foul things they are and rid the world of infamy.' And he whirled his horse and galloped towards the castle. He tied his horse and crept towards the pavilion in growing dawn and he eased his sword silently from his sheath and his nostrils flared and his breath whistled from the pressure in his chest. In the tent he stood over the sleeping lovers. Ettarde turned in her sleep and her lips whispered some quiet dream and Gawain, sleeping, drew her close again. Sir Pelleas had never done a cruel or unjust thing in his life, and though he tried to raise his sword, he could not. Silently he leaned over them and laid his naked sword blade across their throats and he went silently away and he rode back to the priory weeping helplessly. He found his squires looking anxiously about for him, and when they gathered about him, Pelleas said, 'You have been faithful and true to me in a faithless world. I give you all my goods, my armour and everything I have. My life is over. I will go now to my bed and I will never rise again. I shall die soon now, for my heart is broken. When I am dead you must promise to take my heart out of my body and lay it in my covered silver dish and deliver it with your own hands to the lady Ettarde, and tell her that I saw her sleeping with my false friend Sir Gawain.'

The squires protested, but he quieted them and went to his bed and fell down in a faint and lay for many hours under the dulling shock of his sorrow.

When Ettarde awakened and felt the sword blade on her throat she started up and by its handle knew it for the sword of Pelleas, and she was frightened and angry. She shook Gawain awake and she said, 'So you have lied. You did not kill Pelleas. Here is his sword. He is alive and he has been here and he has not slain us. You have betrayed both of us. If he had done to you what you have done to him you would be dead now, for you would not forgive another what you have done yourself. Now I know you and I shall warn all ladies against your love and all good knights against your friendship.'

When Gawain tried to answer, she stopped him. 'Do not excuse yourself. You will only make it worse.'

And Sir Gawain smiled darkly at her and turned from her and walked to the castle for his armour. And when he had armed himself he rode away, saying to himself, 'She was far from the prettiest. And as for Pelleas – this is my reward for revenging him on that woman who had made him miserable. Well – there it is. There is no gratefulness in the world any more. A man must look after himself. And I will from now on. It is a lesson to me.'

In the Forest of Adventure Nyneve of the Lake journeyed restlessly. She had much changed since as an impatient girl she had robbed Merlin of his secrets and then his life. Then she had wanted power and eminence without control. But in the years since, her power had made its own control. She could do things ordinary people could not do, and rather than making her free, she was a slave to the helpless. With the gift of healing she was the servant of the sick, her power over fortune tied her to the unfortunate, while her knowledge, which made evil apparent to her no matter what its mask, enlisted her in constant war against the ambitious plots of greed and treason. And, more than this, she sadly realized that while her strength bound her to the weak and troubled, it did not bind them to her, for they could not offer friendship as payment of a debt. Thus she found herself alone and lonely, praised but desolate, and often she longed for the old time when love and kindliness were cast equally in a coffer by all, for there is no loneliness like that of one who can only give and no anger like that of those who only receive and hate the weight of debt. She stayed little in one place, for always gladness for her services changed to uneasiness towards her power.

As she travelled through the forest she passed a young squire and he was weeping, and when she asked his sorrow he told her how his beloved master had been betrayed by his lady and a knight, and how his heart was broken and he lay with arms open for death.

'Take me to your lord,' Nyneve said. 'He shall not die for love of an unworthy woman. If she is merciless in love the proper punishment is to love and be unloved.'

Then the squire was glad and he conducted her to the bed where Sir Pelleas lay with lean cheeks and fevered, staring eyes, and Nyneve thought she had never seen so goodly and handsome a knight. 'Why does good throw itself under the feet of evil?' she said. And she put her cool hand on his brow and felt the hot blood throbbing in his temples. Then she crooned softly to him, and soothed him until her repeated magic brought peace to him and the enchantment of dreamless sleep. Then she charged his squires to watch over him and not to awaken him until she returned. Then she went quickly to the lady Ettarde and overcame her will and brought her to the bedside of the sleeping Pelleas.

'How do you dare bring death to such a man?' she said. 'What are you that you could not be kind? I offer you the pain you have inflicted on another. Already you feel my spell and you love this man. You love him more than anything in the world. You love him. You would die for him, you love him.'

And Ettarde repeated after her, 'I love him. Oh, God! I love him. How can I love what I so hated?'

'It is a little parcel of the hell you were wont to offer others,' Nyneve said. 'And now you will see the other side.'

She whispered a long time in the ear of the sleeping knight and then she awakened him and stepped aside to watch and to listen.

Sir Pelleas glanced wildly about him and his eyes fell on Ettarde, and as he looked at her he was filled with loathing for her, and when her loving hand moved towards him he shrank away in disgust. He said, 'Go away. I cannot stand the sight of you. You are ugly and horrible, leave me and never let me see you again.'

And Ettarde sank to the ground weeping. Then Nyneve raised her up and conducted her from the cell, saying, 'Now you know the pain. This is what he felt for you.'

'I love him,' Ettarde screamed.

'You will always while you live,' Nyneve said. 'And you will die with your love unwanted and that's a dry, shrivelling death. Go now. Your work is finished here. Go to your dusty death.'

Then Nyneve went back to Pelleas and said, 'Rise up and begin to live again. You will find your true love and she will find you.'

'I have worn out my capacity to love,' he said. 'That is over.'

'Not so,' said Nyneve of the Lake. 'Take my hand. I will help you find your love.'

'Will you stay with me until I do?' he asked.

'Yes,' she said, 'I promise to stay beside you until you find your love.'

And they lived happily together all of their lives.

Now we must return to the three-forked crossroads and start southwards with Sir Marhalt and his damsel of thirty years of age. She sat sideways behind him on his horse with one plump arm about his waist. And Marhalt said, 'How glad I am that you fell to me. You appear to be a competent and comfortable woman. When one reaches a certain age it is hard enough to concentrate on questing without the heat and cold of young tempestuous love further to complicate an already confused way of life.'

'Questing is a curious business,' she said. 'One can make it what one will.'

'You have gone adventuring before, my lady?'

'Many times, sir.' She laughed nobly. 'The wonders of the quest are all a day's work to me. It is not a bad life when one rides with a good companion.'

'I hope I may prove to be,' said Marhalt. 'I can remember but vaguely how once I would have contended for the pretty little sullen face, the golden hair, the mind as unformed as the breasts – yes, I remember.'

'But now you find me more attractive?'

'I find you comfortable. But I wonder why a comfortable woman goes on quest. The cold nights, the hard damp ground to sleep on, the bad food or no food.'

'There are ways to make it comfortable, sir. You saw that each of us had a bag. Mine is here tied to your saddle string. Does it interfere with you?'

'Not at all,' he said. 'It has of course the thousand little things a woman needs.'

'It has,' she said. 'But different women, different needs. The little damsel has a bag also and in it scents, kerchiefs, gloves, a mirror, red earth for lips and cheeks, and most important a white physic powder to clear the body of cold greasy food and keep the complexion clear.'

'And what has your bag, ma'am?'

'I am like you. A little comfort does no harm. I have a little kettle to boil water, herbs and smoked meat for emergency, lye to mix with ashes and fat for soap, for one does get very dirty, a good unguent for wounds and insect bites, and a light, tight-woven cloth to cover us against the rain. And of course that same white powdered physic.'

'And for your woman's vanity, my dear?'

'A change of clothes for my skin's health, a comb, and a small sharp knife in case—in case—'

'In case of me?'

'I do not think I will need the knife, except perhaps to chop wild onions for the little pot.'

'How glad I am to have you for my guide,' he said. 'You are not only wise but also good company.'

'I, like others, am only as good as my companion.'

'You have a graceful tongue, my dear.'

'And you. Tell me,' she said, 'are you a great champion, a good fighting man?'

'I have been fortunate,' said Sir Marhalt. 'I have in recent years won more often than I have lost. But then I have the advantage of a thousand days of practice. It is possible that I fight well because I have fought often.'

'You are not boastful, sir.'

'I have seen too many good men go down, and I never permit myself to forget that one day, through accident or under the charge of a younger, stronger knight, I too will go down.'

'Why then do you go adventuring? You must have lands, you could settle down with a good comfortable wife.'

'Oh, no!' he said, 'I have tried that. I was born noble, trained nobly, aimed like a well-directed spear at the life I lead. One might as easily reverse a charging horse as change a knight born to his knighthood. Do hind dogs hunt deer or hounds sniff after hinds? We kill them if they do.'

'Hark!' she said. 'I hear running water, a spring or a little stream. If you will find dry wood for a fire I will boil water, and I have a little box of dried camomile flowers to make a tea. And I have a small meat pie and a bit of cheese.'

'You are a comfortable woman, my lady,' Marhalt said.

And after they had eaten and warmed themselves with tea, she said, 'It seems a pleasant time to sleep a little.'

'Shouldn't we get on with our questing?'

'We have a year,' she said. 'I think we might take the time to sleep a little. Here, my lord, I will fold my cloak for your pillow.'

He rested on his elbow and looked at her. 'Why, you have lovely eyes,' he said. 'Hazel, I think, and warm.'

'Lie back, my lord,' she said. 'When I was young as the little damsel yonder I fished in muddy waters for a quick compliment. But I have learned. If you had seen my young eyes once, you would never have seen them again, but now – well, it is different, isn't it?'

'Yes,' he said, and yawning, 'yes, very different, my lady.'

When they awakened and rode on, the forest thinned and the afternoon was greenly gold and warm and windless, and the creeping ground thyme released its perfume under the horse's hoofs. The lady said, 'My lord, if I do not speak, it is because I will sleep a little. I will lay my head against your back if you don't mind.'

'Did you not sleep?'

'No, I watched. But now you will watch for me.'

'Can you sleep on a horse? Won't you fall?'

'In some of my adventuring I slept only on a horse,' she said.

But Marhalt said, 'I am afraid the horse might stumble. Put your scarf around your waist and pass me the ends.' And he knotted the scarf in front of him so that they were bound together. 'Now sleep, my dear. You cannot fall.'

As the evening approached the forest thickened also and seemed to crowd closer, and it was no longer friendly, for enemies crept in on the edge of darkness. The lady shivered and awakened and sneezed. 'I slept long,' she said. 'You can untie me now. Will we stop soon?'

'I hope to find some house to stop in even if we travel in the dark. Are you fearful of the dark, ma'am?'

'No,' she said. 'I once was, and then I thought, I can see as well in the dark as they can.'

'They?'

'Whatever is in the dark.'

'Dragons can see in the dark, like cats,' he said.

'Yes, I guess they can. I myself have not seen a dragon. My sister did many times, but she saw everything. Cats do not bother me, and until I see a dragon I will not go out of my way to trouble them. It is dark, sir. Could you see a house if we passed by one?'

'I smell wood smoke,' Marhalt said. 'Where there is a fire there may be shelter.'

And sure enough they saw a black bulk against the inhospitable darkness and a clink of light shining around the door cracks. And the dogs rushed out barking around the weary horseman. The door flung open and a black figure holding a boar spear peered out, calling, 'Who is there?'

'A venturing knight and a lady,' Marhalt said. 'Call your dogs, sir. We wish to shelter from the dark.'

'You can't stay here.'

'That is not courteous,' Marhalt said.

'Courtesy and darkness are not friends.'

'You do not speak like a gentleman.'

'What I am not is not as pertinent as that my two feet are planted in my own doorway and my spear will keep them so.'

'Save your pig spear for your children,' Marhalt said angrily. 'And tell us, if you know, where a knight and lady may find shelter.'

'A knight venturing.' The dark man laughed. 'I know your kind, a childish dream world resting on the shoulders of less fortunate men. Yes, I can direct you if you will trade adventure for a night's lodging.'

'What kind of adventure?'

'That you will find out when you get there. Ride on towards the red star until you see a bridge, if you don't miss it in the dark and drown yourself.'

'Look, my ugly friend, I am weary and my lady is weary and my horse is weary. I will pay you to guide us.'

'Pay first.'

'I will, but if you do not lead us truly I will return and burn your treasured house.'

'I know you would. Gentlemen always do,' said the man, but he brought a little lantern with windows of horn and walked ahead of them, lighting the way. And in an hour's time he brought them to a fair castle of white stone standing against the blackness of the wood. He pulled a bell cord, and when the porter opened a little postern in the castle gate, the guide said, 'Simon, I've brought a knight errant to lodge.'

Both men chuckled and the porter said, 'He may repent it.'

'He has paid me, Simon. It's none of my business. Come, Sir Knight – here is your lodging. Sleep well.' And he went away, laughing unpleasantly.

The porter led him by torchlight, and in the courtyard a number of well-dressed men helped him down and his lady and took his horse to stabling.

In the great hall a mighty duke sat high at table above many seated retainers.

'What have we here?' the duke asked coldly.

'Sir, I am a knight of King Arthur's Round Table. My name is Marhalt, and I was born in Ireland.'

'This is good news for me and bad for you,' the duke said. 'Rest the night. You will have need. I do not like your king or your fellowship. In the morning you will fight me and my six sons.'

'This is not a happy thing for the most errant of knights,' Marhalt said. 'Is there no way to avoid fighting seven men at once?'

'No,' said the duke, 'there is no remedy. When Sir Gawain killed my second son in battle I made a vow that any knight of Arthur's court who passed this way must fight with us until my son is avenged.'

'Will it please you to tell me your name, my lord?'

'I am the Duke of the South Border.'

'I have heard of you,' Marhalt said. 'You have been King Arthur's enemy a long time.'

'If you live through tomorrow morning you will know how much an enemy.'

'Must I fight, sir?'

'Yes, you have no choice unless you wish to stretch your throat for the cook's slaughtering knife.' And the duke said to his retainers, 'Take him and his lady to a chamber. Give them what they wish and mount guard over the door.'

In the cold, inhospitable chamber, Marhalt and the lady ate the bread that was given them and she brought the remains of cheese from her bag to piece out the unfriendly repast.

Marhalt said gloomily, 'Knowing that knights errant are rarely married to their ladies, he might at least have given us separate chambers for appearance.'

The lady smiled. 'In the forest, sir, I would have had my private tree. I am more worried about the morning. Seven men against one. How will you manage that? The odds are savage.'

Marhalt said, 'I am an old hand. If he had said he alone would fight me I would be more afraid. If he needs six sons to back him up, he is not confident in himself or in them. This is a precise and a skilled profession and numbers do not make up for incompetence. Sleep as well as you may, my dear. If we come safely out of this we will look for lodgings after this before darkness falls.'

She sighed contentedly. 'I am pleased with a man who neither overrates his powers nor disparages his skill. Sleep you well, my dear lord.'

Early in the morning the trumpets sounded and the castle came rumbling to life. Sir Marhalt looked from the window and saw his host and sons preparing for the fight. He noted how they sat their horses, watched them swing their swords to loosen their sleepy muscles, saw how they practised at the ring, how this horse faltered and that knight fumbled his reins, and in a few moments he was whistling happily.

'You are gay, my lord. Don't look around. I am changing to my spare underclothing.'

'Tell me when you are done,' he said. 'I think it will be all right,' he continued. 'If you will not think it boastful, I believe the thing I have to fear most is a bad breakfast.'

But he controlled his smile, and found the breakfast excellent. He kneeled with the others and heard Mass and was shriven, and then with all the form and ceremony of trumpeters and flying pennons, and stiff-standing retainers and ladies fluttering their kerchiefs from the wall, the fight began.

The fierce duke and his six sons mounted in single file. The duke bore down and at the impact Marhalt raised his spear and took the shock on his shield and the duke's spear shattered. Behind him came the sons one after another. The first lost his reins and his horse swerved off and had to be stopped at the postern gate. The third aimed his spear at the centre of Marhalt's shield and missed. The fourth came charging in and his horse stumbled and pitched on his head with his spear buried in the earth. The fifth made mighty contact and his spear was driven backwards from his hand, tearing the leather from his saddle. The sixth struck true and his spear shattered, and at every charge Sir Marhalt raised his spear insultingly and did not strike at them. And Marhalt looked to the wall where his lady stood watching and saw that she had covered her face with her scarf and her shoulders shook.

The seven were ready again, and now Sir Marhalt brought down his spear and with seeming laziness he stripped them from their saddles one by one. But now his anger rose and he rode to the fallen duke and dismounted. 'Sir Duke,' he said, 'you forced this fight. Now yield or die.'

Two of the less bruised sons came forward with drawn swords, but the duke cried out, 'Go back, you fools! Would you have your father killed?'

Then the duke got to his knees and offered his sword pommel first, and his sons crept up and kneeled beside him.

'You have my grace,' Sir Marhalt said. 'But at next Whitsuntide you must all go to King Arthur and beg his forgiveness.'

Then the lady came to him, and Sir Marhalt mounted and pulled her lightly up behind him. And the silent retainers watched them as they rode out of the castle and took their way to the south through the forest.

As they went, the lady said, 'I have not seen you tested yet.'

'You are right,' Marhalt said. 'That great frowning duke and his six sons. When will men learn that there is more to knighthood than a horse and armour?'

'You must be one of the best knights in the world to raise your spear as you did and take the blow.'

'Are you testing my self-love, my dear? Here is what I think of myself. I am a good knight, well trained and skilful, and although I have many faults, I think I also have some virtues. But do not think, because I played tricks with those clumsy men, that I take jousting lightly. There are many knights whom I could name, who, if I saw them ride at me over my levelled spear, would turn my blood to water.'

'You are an honest gentleman,' she said. 'It is a joy to go adventuring with you.'

'Thank you, my lady. What have we now? You must lead me.'

She said, 'Ladies who go on quest must be informed. This is about the time when Lady de Vawse holds her tournament. She lives in a lonely castle two days' ride from here. And every year she offers a fine prize and good cheer to draw good company to her. It is an honourable and pleasant meeting. It is my custom to conduct my venturing knights to her tournament. I think you may find worthy competitors there. Then after that and farther south the young Earl Fergus has his seat. And I have heard that he is troubled by a giant. Are you a good hand with giants?'

'I have had some experience with them, lady. Let us see how we feel about it when we get there. Meanwhile, let us go to Lady de Vawse. The angry duke's accommodation was more dangerous than his fighting. I am ready for good champions, and good quarters.'

'It will be pleasant to wash my hair. You have not seen me, my lord, as I could wish. I have a gown of fine silk and gold thread in the bottom of my bag, and thin little shoes.'

'I find you charming as you are,' he said, 'but I yield to no one in my joy of pretty ladies.'

She sighed. 'I wish all errant knights were as you,' she said.

They came to the castle of Lady de Vawse before the tournament, and being early they had their choice of pleasant chambers overlooking the gardens of the inner court. Lady de Vawse made them welcome and carried the damsel away to baths and unguents and the nimble fingers of serving women. Sir Marhalt found a squire to polish and repair his gear, and a groom to condition his steed, and even a craftsman to paint his device brightly on his shield, while he dawdled with other visiting knights, discussing other days, recalling great fights, boasting a little by understatement, testing the nature of the turf of the tournament ground, and looking often at the sky, and making little prayers for noble weather. And in the afternoon in the great hall they feasted, heard and told tales, and listened to the sweet voices of fair young troubadours, singing of brave deeds and wonders, of dragons, and giants, of ladies beautiful as air and pure, and loving knights whose right arms carried lightning, singing what everyone would like and hope to believe. And they inspected the prize for the winner of the tournament, a golden circlet wonderfully wrought and estimated to be worth a thousand besants.

Sir Marhalt's lady dazzled him with glowing hair and skin like a rose petal. She moved with the slow dignity of music in her gown of blue and gold, and she wore a tall blue cone and a flowing wimple of sheer white satin. And when she saw the golden prize her eyes shone so that Sir Marhalt said, 'My lady, if fortune and my knighthood can equal my wish, you will wear the prize.'

She smiled at him and blushed, and her hands, which could tighten a girth and cook a forest stew, fluttered like pale butterflies, so that Sir Marhalt was aware that being a good lady is as much a skill as being a good knight.

In the morning of the tournament, when lovely ladies took their places on the stand and the competing knights prepared their mounts and chose their spears with care, a page boy brought a parcel to Sir Marhalt in the tiltyard. Unwrapping it he found a blue silken sleeve embroidered with threads of gold, and he fastened it to the crown of his helmet so that it would float like a pennon when he rode. And when the knights marshalled to choose sides, the lady saw her blue sleeve streaming from Marhalt's helm and she was glad, and even gladder when he raised his great spear in salute to her.

The fight was long and glorious, for there were good men engaged, and the judges and the ladies in the stands under the coloured canopy leaned forward, seeing the subtleties, noting the scores, for they were expert in the sport and knew flamboyance from good solid knightly skill. And as the day progressed one single quiet knight, without fuss and feathers, met everyone who came against him and unhorsed each one, and such was his ability that what he did seemed easy, almost casual. The watchers made marks for points on scraps of wood, and when the trumpet called cessation, there was no argument. The golden circlet was brought to Marhalt where he kneeled bareheaded before Lady de Vawse. It glittered on his short cropped greying hair, and then Sir Marhalt thanked his hostess and strode to his lady errant and publicly offered the prize to her. She swept her headdress off with one motion and, blushing, leaned forward, and Sir Marhalt placed the circlet on her brow, and the company applauded the skilful knight and the equally skilful lady.

Then followed three days of feasting and music and love, and speechmaking and boasting and a few angry quarrels and very little sleep, all in all the best tournament and feast anyone could remember.

On the fourth day, when the sun was well up, Sir Marhalt, with his lady behind him, rode wearily out of the castle gate and took his way southwards through the green countryside. The lady wore her travelling clothes and her bag of domestic wonders was tied to the saddle stirrup.

'It's good to be gone,' Marhalt said. 'Feasting is harder than jousting. My bones ache.'

'A few nights in the open, my lord, a quiet time and peace. Yes, I admit I am glad. It was good, but it is also good to be alone. We need not hurry. At the end is a tomb. Do we need to rush towards it? It will wait.'

'I agree,' Sir Marhalt said. 'When we have gone a little we will look out for a quiet place near water and I will cut bracken for our rest, and maybe even build a little bower where we can recover from the rounds of pleasure.'

'I have a roasted chicken and a good wheat loaf in my bag, my lord.'

'I have a treasure riding pillion,' he replied.

In a little glade beside a spring of cold bubbling water he built a cunning little house of boughs hacked off with a sword, and bedded it deep with dried sweet-smelling ferns. Nearby he fitted stones in a structure to hold the little pot, and gathered a heap of dry wood cloven from the underside of a fallen tree, and he tethered his horse in nearby grass. His armour hung on the oak beside the bower and his shield and lance beside it. The damsel was not still. When he had robed himself she washed his underthings and hung them on a gooseberry bush to dry. She filled her little pot with gooseberries and watching and listening followed the flight of bees and brought wild honey from a hollow tree for sweetening. And in the bower she busied herself spreading wild thyme to perfume the couch, rolling sweet grasses in her tight-woven cloth to make a rich soft pillow, arranging her little store of needments in domestic order, and with her small strong knife she cut and notched saplings from which to hang her clothing. Her knight begged the golden pin that held her hair, and he pulled tail hair from his horse and braided a line, and he went towards the sound of water falling in a pool and gathered mayflies as he went. And shortly he returned with four fine speckled trout, straightened her hairpin, and gave it her. And then he wrapped the trout in a blanket of green fern and laid them by to place in hot ashes in the evening.

'No, rest, my lord,' she said. 'Your work is done. Please do not rob me of my contribution. See, I have made a soft seat of bracken. Rest, sir, against the tree and see a lady strive to please her lord.'

He smiled and took his seat and smelled the gooseberries bubbling in honey at the fire. He stretched his limbs and raised his arms over his head. 'Contentment requires so little and so much,' he said. 'See the clear blue summer sky pink with afterglow and the evening star. It's no small work to bring all that about for one content. Let us speak about the future, my dear.'

'I would prefer to be silently happy about the now, my lord.'

'Yes, yes,' he said. 'I did not mean the far future rolled up and waiting. We are adventuring. I have adventured much but never so happily. But certain things are required. We must do what is required. We have defeated the king's enemies and fought in tournament. We have a year from the beginning and there is no need for hurry. Now – we can take adventure slowly and spread it out, or we can get it done with and find a pleasant seat and let the time pass softly over us.'

She stirred the gooseberries with a twig, smiling with contentment and good humour. 'As a damsel errant I am an old hand,' she said. 'One adventure is a reasonable score. Two are better, three worth recording, and four – no one will raise a question about four. We have two prime ones already. There are some would include the ugly householder but we will not. Ahead of us we have the giant I spoke of. How are you with giants, my lord?'

'I've had a go with a giant or so,' he said. 'I've always felt sorry for them. No one will have them about, and in their loneliness they turn angry and sometimes dangerous.'

'But how are you at fighting them?'

'Don't worry about that,' Sir Marhalt said. 'Of course I don't know the coming giant, but those I've met before were stupid in relation to their size, the larger the more stupid. There is a way of fighting giants which is usually successful.'

'It is true that they kill and capture many knights, my lord.'

'I know, and that is no compliment to the knights. Knights have a way of using the same weapons for all enemies. They do not like to change. Heavy armour and a shield against a giant is the sheerest folly.'

A scream came from the darkening hill above them, and he reassured her. 'It is a hare,' he said. 'I have laid a snare. We will have meat for morning. If you have done with the fire I will lay the trout in the hot ash.'

'I will do it, sir. You must not take away my pride in serving you.'

When the sweet steam rose lazily from the ferns and baking trout, he said, 'Come sit beside me, my dear.' And when she rested her back against the tree he brushed her dark hair away from her little ear and with his finger he traced the outline of the lobe and he saw the evening stars reflected in her eyes. 'So little needed for contentment,' he said, 'and so much.'

And she sighed deeply and stretched with ecstasy like a kitten in the grass. 'My lord,' she said. 'My dear lord.'

The young Earl Fergus welcomed them at his drawbridge and led them through double portcullis and gate into the inner court-yard of his castle, and signalled the bridge to be raised, the port-cullis dropped, and the gate closed.

'You can never tell,' he said uneasily. 'Welcome, Sir Knight. I hope you've come about the giant. Why, my lady, welcome. At first I didn't recognize you. You are more beautiful. I do hope you have more luck than the last time. Your knight still lies prisoner in the giant's keep, if he hasn't died.'

'You have the wrong knight, my lord,' she said. 'My last knight errant rode full armed at your giant, and the monster grabbed his spear and swatted him like an insect from his horse, and picked him up and threw him in the top branches of a tree.'

'I remember,' Fergus said. 'We had to wait till night and take a ladder to get him down.'

'He was not very good company afterwards,' the lady said. 'He sulked and talked about honour and made me promise never to tell. And I have not until now. Lord Fergus, my lord here, Sir Marhalt, is a different kettle of man. He is a giant fighter with experience.'

'My dear,' said Marhalt, 'it isn't seemly. Besides, it's bad luck to ruin a victory before the fight.'

'I hope you will kill him,' Fergus said. 'At first he was an attraction and brought good company every year. But against this he makes the country dangerous. His keep is full of prisoners and he holds up and robs commercial traffic until it is impossible to get a piece of cloth or a new sword. His tower must be filled with goods and jewels and gold and captured arms. I do hope you can make away with him, sir, I am tired of him.'

'I will do what I can,' Marhalt said. 'Does he fight on horse?'

'Oh no. He is much too big. No horse could bear him. In fact he can take a horse like a puppy in his arms.'

'What is his name?'

'He is called Taulurd.'

'I have heard of him, sir. He has a brother in Cornwall named

Taulas. I've had a do with him and came off second best, but then I was young. He taught me something.'

Fergus said, 'I wouldn't mind if he simply took what he needed. But what he can't use Taulurd destroys like a sullen child.'

'Ah well,' Marhalt said, 'I suppose that's what he is, for all his size. Does he wear armour?'

'No, only the skins of animals, and for weapons he has clubs. Tree trunks and bars of iron, anything he can come by.'

'Well, we'll see,' Marhalt said. 'I suppose I could go to find him now, but I would rather wait until the morning. May I use a grindstone on my sword, sir?'

'I'll call a servant to sharpen for you.'

'No,' said Marhalt. 'I would prefer to do it myself. I want a very special edge. And now, my lord, are we free to disarm and make ourselves comfortable?'

'A thousand pardons,' Fergus said. 'Please come into my hall – or better, let us sup in my little room before the fire. There is no company here. Taulurd is making this whole area unpopular. Come, my lady. Come, sir. I hope you don't mind country fare. The beds are comfortable though. I'll have hot stones placed in them to dry and warm them. It's been a rainy spring.'

Earl Fergus's little castle was a pleasant place near the edge of the River Cam. The castle formed an island, moated by the fresh flowing water of the Cam. And because the moat was deep the walls could be low. It was a light and airy place where the sun could penetrate, as it did in the morning when Sir Marhalt prepared to fight the giant. He dressed himself in a soft leather jacket and pants, which ordinarily he wore under his armour, but this day he wore no metal to cover his body or his head. His feet he clad in deerskin stockings, wrapped to the knee with bands.

Fergus protested, 'Are you insane? Taulurd will mince you with his club.'

But Marhalt smiled at him. 'I will not carry my own trap,' he said. 'Would armour save me from the battering?'

'No, I guess not.'

Marhalt said, 'His brother taught me this. He nearly killed me. The only weapons against strength and size are smallness and speed. Give me my shield, my dear,' he said to his lady, and he took his sword, sharpened to cut a single hair, and balanced it in his hand.

'I will belt on your scabbard,' the lady said.

'No, my lady. I will not take it. I want nothing to stick out, nothing to get in my way. Now, my lord Fergus, will you guide me to this giant?'

'I don't think I could bear the sight of you out against an elephant. I will send a man with you.'

'I will go,' the damsel said.

'No, my dear. Wait here for me.'

'Why should I not go?'

'For the same reason I do not take the scabbard, my lady.'

The guide conducted Marhalt along an ill-marked pathway on the sward and over stony ground with a growth of thorny yellow gorse, and on the riverbank he pointed to a large dark lump on a pile of rocks. 'There he is, sir, the monster thing, and here you be and, if you permit, sir, I will be hence.'

'Take my horse,' Sir Marhalt said. 'Ride back a pace and wait for me.'

'You'll fight afoot?'

'I want no horse to bother with. If he should clobber me, try to save a little piece of me for my lady. She treasures keepsakes.'

Marhalt walked quietly in his light soft shoes towards the giant sitting on the rock pile. His great unclipped head was sunk on his breast and his shoulders moved, and he sang a tuneless song like a rebellious child. His skin was caked with dirt and the breeze brought the filthy smell of him to Marhalt's nose. About him on the ground lay oaken clubs and battle maces with fluted crowns, and knobkerries of heavy thorn and a huge iron bar with a lump of lead set with nails on its end. The giant, intent on his baby son, did not hear Marhalt approaching.

'Good morning, Taulurd,' the knight said quietly. 'I bring you greetings from your brother, Taulas.'

The huge head snapped up. Red eyes glared from the thicket of dirty hair and the wide mouth bubbled foam like a burped infant.

'Hub,' said Taulurd. 'Ho.'

'I'm sorry to have to tell you this, Taulurd, but you will have to go away, far away. You don't know how to get along with people. You hurt people and you haven't learned to respect other people's property. Why, Taulurd, you haven't learned to clean yourself. Shame. You smell like a combination of a charnel house and a privy. You can't stay around here.'

Taulurd's eyes watered and he seemed about to weep and then his little eyes went wild with rage and his singsong turned into an animal howl. His great hand felt stealthily on the ground, crept to the long iron club, and suddenly he leaped up – twelve feet high he was and his haystack head was against the sky and his drooling lips opened to show black-painted teeth. He shambled forward, swinging his hips like a gorilla, and he beat his chest with his left fist and made a high-pitched scream of menace. The muscles of his arms and chest were like serpents.

Sir Marhalt stood his ground quietly until the giant towered over him and he could smell the fetid breath. The iron club rose and started down, and only then the knight slipped under the blow and stood behind the giant and the bad knob thudded to the ground.

'It's no use,' Marhalt said. 'You're just a big strong baby. I don't want to hurt you; if you go away we could be friends.'

He saw a crafty look come to the giant's eyes as he turned slowly, and he saw the club rise a little, and from the muscle tension he knew a quick sideswipe was coming. Instantly he plotted its swing and knew where he should dodge. The club swung like a scythe and Marhalt tried to leap away, but a stone rolled under his foot and he staggered, and the club struck his shield and the iron studs sank in and tore it from his hand and nearly tore his left arm off in the process. He rolled and scampered away on hands and knees, and when he stood the pain in his left shoulder was dreadful.

Taulurd jumped up and down, landing on his heels, crowing and giggling. 'Ho!' he cried. 'Ha! Ha-ha!'

'You're a bad boy,' Marhalt said. 'I don't want to hurt you, but if you act like a bad animal I'm afraid I'll have to kill you, and it seems a shame.'

Now the giant came at him with a shambling run, raising his club as he came and roaring with delighted rage. Marhalt looked quickly at the ground for rolling stones. He waited until the giant was six feet away, then ducked down and jumped left under the tree trunk of a right arm, and as he went his razor sword leaped upright and sliced the tendon of the arm, and the arm bent backwards and the club fell to the ground.

Taulurd looked astonished at his ruined arm, with blood pumping in spurts from the severed artery, and suddenly the giant burst into tears and cried like a hurt and frightened child. He shambled towards the river and waded in and continued until only his head showed above the surface, and there he stood out of reach, gibbering and moaning, and the water reddened about him from his pumping blood.

Marhalt stood on the bank. He could not go to the giant because of the water's depth. 'Poor thing,' he said. 'I have killed many things and many men and never so sadly as now. I'm sorry, Taulurd, but perhaps the quicker the better.'

He picked up a round stone from the water's edge and cast it at the huge head. The giant dodged and the stone splashed under his ear. Marhalt cast again, and missed, but his third stone struck the forehead above and between the staring red eyes, and Taulurd sank quickly with open mouth, and a burst of bubbles rose to the bloody surface of the river.

Marhalt stood waiting and in a moment the monster floated, rolling a little like a felled timber. Then the current took control and urged the great carrion downstream towards the sea.

Now the retainer galloped near, crying, 'Victory, my lord. It was beautiful.'

'Let us go quickly to his castle. He has prisoners and treasure.'

'Yes, let us go!'

The castle was a rude structure of piled stones like a huge sheepcote roofed with branches and sod. And in the darkness knights and ladies and sheep and pigs lay bound hand and foot, rolling in filth and misery.

'Tear off the roof,' Marhalt said. 'Let some light into this sty.' And when he could see, he cut the bonds of animals and people with his sharp sword, and they struggled to get up and fell back in pain until the blood should circulate.

In a corner lay the giant's hoard. Gold and silver, jewels and bright cloth, crucifixes of precious things and chalices set with rubies and emeralds, and along with these coloured stones and pieces of broken glass from church windows and quartz and knobby crystal and shards of blue and yellow pottery – a mighty mixture of great wealth and great nonsense. And Sir Marhalt, looking at the heap, said sadly, 'Poor thing. He didn't know the difference. He couldn't learn to steal only valuable things as civilized men and women do.'

'There's still enough,' the retainer said. 'You will be rich all your days though you live two hundred years.'

'Have it carried to Earl Fergus's castle, my friend,' said Marhalt. 'And see you don't steal broken glass.' He mounted his horse and rode away, and his triumph was a sad and ugly feeling in his throat. 'And yet it had to be,' he told himself. 'He was a danger, poor thing.' And in his memory he saw the frightened eyes of the monster child and he knew that fear is the most ghastly wound of all.

Earl Fergus was pleased and grateful. He said, 'You can't imagine the damage that giant did – whole hides of land unploughed because he ate the horses, no traders or tinkers or gypsies coming through, no singers or storytellers from France to tell us our own history. Now it is changed and due to you, my friend. I would give you lands if you wanted them. But you have treasure enough to satisfy four men. Why don't you rest here as my guest? This is your house for as long as you can keep your restless heart in leash.'

In the evening, walking in the meadow by the moat, Marhalt said to the lady, 'Why not? I am old enough not to have to collect adventures for themselves. It is many months before we meet my friends at the three-way cross. I will be governed by you, my lady, but if in your judgement we could stay a while, I would not say no. A good bed and regular meals appeal to me. Perhaps it is my age.'

'It sounds pleasant,' she said. 'If I could get some good Flanders cloth I would engage my needle. There are idle damsels here. Earl Fergus has asked me to teach their fingers.'

Sir Marhalt said, 'I could send a party to the southern coast. The Tuscan ships bring Prato cloth woven from English wool but dyed and finished as only Florentines can do it. Expensive stuff, but don't forget I have a treasure, ma'am.'

'Would you do that for me? You are a good friend. Buy a great piece of royal red and I will make a royal robe for you, my king, and on it I will embroider the adventures of this year, a record of our questing written in bright-coloured silk.'

It was a sweet domestic time. The lady set her allotted sewing to order, kept servants busy, cobwebs swept, and clean linen drying and bleaching on the meadow grass. And Marhalt caught salmon in the river, ran greyhounds after buckling leverets, and hardly a day passed that he did not bring back hawk-caught birds. Fergus happily improved his lands, and in the long summer evenings they gossiped of crops and recipes and people; told stories they remembered, drank mead made of fermented honey and sometimes the strong spiced mead called metheglin, which set their heads to reeling and tuned their voices to laughter.

More and more the lady cared for her questing lord, trimmed his hair and clipped his nails, and picked up after him. 'Why don't you wear the blue and yellow robe tonight?' she said. 'You are handsome in it. It brings out the colour of your eyes.'

'I hadn't thought to change, my dear.'

'Oh, but you must! Fergus does. Everybody does.'

'I am not Fergus. I am not everybody.'

'I don't see why you mind. It's very little trouble and it is much more comfortable to be clean. Here – smell your blue robe. I put it in the chest with lavender.'

And towards the summer end she said, 'I don't see why you drop your clothes. It's just as easy to pick them up. Someone has to, have you thought of that?'

And in September, 'My lord, if you are looking for that smelly hawk's hood and jesses, you will find them in the box at the end of the passage. You left them lying on the window ledge. They blooded my drying handkerchiefs.'

'Can I not have a window ledge for my things, my dear?'

'Such things belong in the box at the end of the corridor. Put them there and you will always be able to find them.'

'I know where to find them on the window ledge.'

'I hate things lying around.'

'Except your things.'

'You are quarrelsome, sir.'

When the November frost sparkled on the grass, she said, 'You are never at home. Are horses such good company, or is there a gallant stable maid with straw in her hair?'

177

And when the squalls of winter returned and whined against the walls and felt their way behind the hangings, she complained, 'You should get out and take some exercise. You are gaining weight.'

'No, I am not.'

'You may tell lies to yourself, sir, but they don't convince the buttons I must sew back when they have snapped off. No, don't get up and leave the room. That is insulting.'

In February she said, 'You are restless, sir, and I know why. It is not pleasant to be a guest. Fergus is a fine man and I am the first to say so always. But don't you think he might like our room?'

'He says not. I asked him.'

'Nonsense. A woman can tell. I wish you would stop pacing. It's because you have no responsibility. You have lands, my lord. Why don't we go to them? Then you would have your work as Fergus has and you wouldn't be so restless. It would be pleasant to build a little castle of our own. Why do you stare at me, my lord? Are you going to have a temper again?'

He came to her and stood, mouth open, breathing heavily. 'Madame,' he said, 'you have changed since you rode pillion. Madame – enough.'

'If I have changed, so have you. You are not gay or thoughtful any more. You pick and complain. Changed! Look in the mirror if you want to see a change! Don't roll your eyes and scowl. You do not frighten me as you did that poor giant.'

He turned and strode quickly out, and she went back to her needlework, humming a little to herself. She heard him come clanking along the corridor and the door burst open. He wore armour polished and oiled, and under his arm he carried his helmet.

'What is this?' she asked. 'Another tantrum?'

'Damsel,' he began. 'And remember I said "Damsel". Pack the necessities in your little bag. Take a warm cloak. We go. I have ordered my war horse readied.'

'In the winter? Are you mad? I would not think of it.'

'Damsel, farewell,' he said, and the clashing of his metalled footsteps echoed in the corridors. She sprang up. 'My lord,' she cried, 'wait! Wait for me, sir. I am coming. Wait for me, my lord.' She threw open a chest, dug out her questing bag, and threw things into it. She seized a cloak and ran out after him.

In the afternoon, riding north with a thin hail rattling against his shield, and the wind whining over his visor, he came upon three knights of Arthur's court. He set his damsel in the lee of an oak out of the wind and Sir Marhalt ran four courses and left fair knights sprawling on the ground. Then he went back and handed his lady lightly up behind him. 'Wrap up well, my dear,' he said. 'We may not find a place to shelter tonight.'

'Yes, my lord,' she said, and she drew the hood of her travelling cloak over her head and laid her head against his broad iron back.

When the sweet showers of April had pierced the roots of March, they came near to the trysting place where the path tripled to stamp the oath of quest.

'What a good year,' he said. 'And the returning here is not to be ashamed of.'

'Good my lord, what will you do now? Will you go to your holding, will you go to Arthur's court? Don't tell me, sir. I know. Either way a shaft of spring will find its way to you, and you will pace and fret, and one day, without warning, you will mount and ride away.'

'Perhaps so,' he said. 'That is not what worries me. What will you do? Would you come to my manor? We could perhaps build a little castle.'

She laughed and slipped to the ground and untied her little bag from his saddle string. 'Farewell, my lord,' she said. She climbed the slope to the mossy place where the fountain of clear water bubbled, and she spread her cloak on the ground and seated herself gracefully upon it. Then she dug in her bag and brought out a chaplet of gold and placed it on her head. She looked down where Marhalt sat his horse; she smiled at him and waved her hand.

A young knight rode by. 'Is that a damsel seated there, sir?' he asked.

'It is, young sir.'

'What does she there?'

'Why don't you ask her?'

'What is her name, sir?'

'I never thought to ask,' Marhalt said, and he reined his horse about and rode to the triple cross to wait.

Now must we flip back the pages of the year and follow Sir Ewain riding with the lady of threescore years, and his road was to the westward towards Wales.

Young Ewain could not have told why, taking the first choice, he had picked his companion. Her hair was white and her years were written boldly on her face in lines and little wrinkles, and her cheeks had known cold, and heat and wind had made a leathery accommodation. Her nose was bold and high-bridged like a bald eagle's beak and her eyes were aquiline, yellow, and far-seeing and fierce, hot with tragic humour, or, when her lids squinted, sharp with inspection. When Ewain had surprised himself with his choice, she stood quickly and took his reins and led him away from the others as though to prevent a change of mind, for she had seen the glance of the young damsel. The lady was lithe as a willow but short-coupled and ready as a drawn bow. She did not wait for the young knight's hand but grasped his saddle by the high cantle and flung herself lightly on the horse's rump. And when the oaths were taken, she urged him away as quickly as she could.

'Let us go on, young sir,' she said. 'We have much to do. There take the westward road – quickly – quickly.' And she looked back at the others still standing at the triple cross.

'Lady – there must be adventures nearby,' Ewain said.

'Adventures? Oh, yes, adventures. We will see. I want to get out of sight of the others. I was afraid you might not choose me. I willed you to choose me, and you did – you did.' Her voice was shrilly gay.

'Did you love me so quickly, lady?'

'My name is Lyne,' she said. 'You are Ewain, son of Morgan le Fay, nephew of the king. Love you?' She laughed. 'No, I judged you among the others. Marhalt, a good, dependable knight, a superb fighter, and might be great except that he is more good than great. But Marhalt is fixed. Nothing will change in him. Gawain? A temperament, a handsome ugly bachelor who feeds upon himself like those lizards who consume their tails. Gawain has up days when the moon is an easy jump, and down days when an earthworm makes a high arc over his head.'

'These are tried knights, my lady Lyne. Why did you choose me?'

'For that very reason. You are not tried and therefore are not fixed. Your knighthood came to you through being the nephew to the king, not as a prize for battle. Tell me, my son, are you a good fighter?'

'No, my lady, I am young and not experienced and my strength is not great. I have won a few rounds in the tiltyard against young men, and lost more. Today against a seasoned knight I went down like a rabbit under a blunt arrow. But Gawain couldn't beat him either.'

'Good,' she said. 'Very good.'

'Why good, my lady?'

'Because you have not perfected your faults, young sir. You are well made but not hardened. I watched you move – and you use your whole body well as a natural endowment. I have long waited for such material as you. Look – at the branching path take the right hand. Do you find it unseemly for a lady of my age to go adventuring?'

'I find it unusual, ma'am.' He glanced over his shoulder and saw her face, her mouth tight with pleasure and fierce intention in her yellow eyes.

'I will tell you,' she said, 'and then you must not wonder more or ever ask me again. A little girl, hating embroidery, I watched the young boys practising and I hated the hobbles of a gown. I was a better rider than they, a better hunter, as I proved, and alone with quintain I proved myself with spear. Only the accident of girlness prevented me from being more than equal to the boys. Hating my limiting sex, I sometimes dressed in boys' clothes, masked myself against shame, and waited in a forest glade like a child errant for boys and young men. I beat them wrestling and with quarter stave, stood against them with sword and shield, until one time I killed a young knight in a fair fight. Then I was afraid. I buried his body, hid his armour, and crept back to the protection of my needlework. You know that burning is the punishment for a lady's treason against a knight.'

'What are you telling me?' Sir Ewain cried. 'This is a tale of terror and unnatural.'

'Perhaps it is,' she said. 'I wonder how unnatural? Then I knew I must forgo knighthood. And bitterly I watched jousting and tournaments. I saw where men made mistakes and were too stupid to correct them. My mind was tuned to fighting, but good fighting; not the clumsy ceremony of carving up bodies like lumps of meat. I saw great knights compete and noted that their greatness was no accident. Perhaps they did not think of it, but they knew their weapons and their opponents; I recognized superiority and studied it and saw errors and remembered them until I knew possibly more than any knight living about the art of war. And there I sat, loaded with lore and no way to use it until – when the juices of my vanity dried up and the poison of my anger sweetened – in a word, when middle age came to me, I found an outlet for my knowledge. Have you known a young and untried knight to ride away and in a year return as tempered as a sword, as sure and deadly as an ashen spear?'

'Why yes, I have. Last year Sir Eglan, whom even I could best, returned to win the prize at a tournament.'

She laughed with pleasure. 'Did he now? A good boy. One of the best I have handled.'

'He never mentioned you.'

'Well, how could he? What man in this man's world would admit he got his manners from a woman? I did not need an oath from any of my knights.'

'You mean you lesson them?'

'Lesson them, train them, teach them, harden them, sharpen them, and test them, and only then release a perfect fighting instrument on the world. It is my revenge and my triumph.'

'Where do we go now, ma'am? Will we have adventures?'

'We go to my manor, hidden in the Welsh hills. Adventure you will have when you are ready, not before.'

'But I am supposed to be on quest.'

'Is it a bad quest to search for perfect knighthood? Say the word and I will slip down and go back to wait for another young candidate, and you can topple like a rabbit all your life.'

'Oh no!' said Ewain. 'No, madame.'

'Then will you resign yourself to my law and my regimen?'

'Yes, madame.'

'Good boy,' she said. 'It won't be easy, but you will be glad.'

'But what will I say when I return without adventures?'

'For ten months you will train and learn,' she said. 'And then, I promise you, you will have more adventures and more profitable ones than the others in twelve months. Ride on, the school begins, the school of arms.' And then her voice took on the compelling timbre of command. 'You ride your stirrups short. We will lengthen them. Your feet must be as low as possible so that when you stand upright in your stirrups you clear the saddle just a hair. Short stirrups make an armoured man top-heavy. Sit loosely, shoulders back. Take up the motion in your thighs and back. Now, let your feet hang free.'

'Madame,' he said, 'I've ridden all my life.'

'Men have been known to ride badly all their lives. Most men do. That's why a horseman so stands out among men.'

'But, madame, my instructor says—'

'Silence. I am your instructor. The more loosely you ride, not sloppily but easy, offering no counter to the horse, the easier it is for your horse. And when you trot, rise to one shoulder for a while and then rise to the other. It rests the shoulders of your animal. Oh, I know there are many who, having many horses, wear them out, founder them, and with one day of hunting leave them heaving ruins. You will not do that. You will train two horses only, but train them as you train yourself, and you will comfort them and treasure them. I tell you, a good horse is better than good armour. A horseman is one thing, one single unit, not a man roosting on top of an animal. You will comfort and pleasure your horse before yourself, feed him before you eat, search his wounds before your own. Then when you have need, you will have both an instrument and a friend. Do you understand?'

'I am listening, ma'am.'

'You will do more than listen. Now, your armour. We will sell it to some unsuspecting fool.'

'It's the best armour, ma'am. Made by a great artist in the mountains of Germany. It cost a fortune.'

'I can well imagine. On parade it draws all eyes. Ladies roll their eyes and coo at it as though the clothing wore the man, as it often does, but for fighting it's no damned good.'

'What's wrong with it? It comes from Innsbruck.'

'I'll tell you what's wrong. It is too thick and heavy. Metal never takes the place of skill. It protects areas that need no protection. It is full of lumps and hollows to catch spear point or offer cutting surface to a sword. You can't bend your right arm to deliver a stroke on the near side, and when you raise your arm, the little metal rose slips aside and exposes three inches of your pretty little armpit. Do I make myself plain? In a word, it is no damned good. You move in it like a jackass with loaded panniers. I myself in a long skirt could beat you with a sword, and you armoured. It's armour to see, not to use.'

Ewain said with a touch of anger, 'You are critical, madame.'

'You think so? I am cooing like a dove. Wait until you hear me truly critical. And if you resent it, let me down and go your way.'

'Madame, I did not mean—'

'Then be silent until you mean something. You'll not only clear out this foolish fruit dish you are wearing but also a mass of collected rubbish from your mind. You are starting fresh, my boy, fresh as a baby held by the heels and newly spanked. Where was I? Oh! Yes, armour. Open your darling ears and listen, and remember. You might even repeat after me. The purpose of armour is to protect only what skill and speed and accuracy cannot. It should be as light as possible, and offer only angles to glance a blow. It should never have to be tested with direct impact. Its purpose is to deflect. The helmet should be so shaped as to slip a blade, not resist it. Your visor is so cunning that you cannot see. How can you fight if you can't see? An angled helm is better than thick plate, because even with a cast-iron pot on your head one solid blow with battle mace will stun you like a rabbit. Now, let us go to gauntlets – and then gorget – and then – we'll take up saddles later. Now – I will lay down the law and you will learn it word by word, and every word must be edged with fire. This is the law. The purpose of fighting is to win. There is no possible victory in defence. The sword is more important than the shield, and skill is more important than either. The final weapon is the brain, all else is supplementary.' And suddenly she was silent. And then she said, 'I've drenched you, haven't I, my son? But if you could learn only what I have told you so far, few men in the world could meet you and fewer beat you. The night is coming. Pull into that copse on the hillside. While you wipe down your horse I'll dig out some supper for you.'

When Ewain returned from staking out his horse, she asked, 'Did you wipe him dry?'

'Yes, madame.'

'And hang your saddle cloth to dry?'

'Yes, madame.'

'Very well, here's your supper.' And she tossed him a slab of oaten bread, hard and tasteless as a roof tile. And as he gnawed at it uncomplaining, the lady Lyne squatted on the ground and wrapped her great cloak around her like a tent. 'The night air brings out pains in my joints. I suppose age is whittling away at me. Oh, well, the world will not remember me, but I will leave men behind me. My tiltyard is the womb of knights. Tell me, young sir, what is your mother like? Some odd stories have gone out about Morgan le Fay.'

'She has been very good to me,' he said. 'Of course, with her holdings and all her special duties, perhaps I have not been with her as much as she wished, but – yes, she has always been kind and even thoughtful. And when she is in good temper and all goes well, there's no one who can be more gay. She sings like an angel then and dances and makes jokes so funny that you crack your sides laughing.'

'When she is not gay, what then?' the lady Lyne asked.

'Well, then we have learned to slip away. She is a person of very strong character.'

'I hope she hasn't given you instructions in her kind of fighting?'

'What do you mean, ma'am?'

'Don't avoid the question boy. I mean magic, and you know I mean magic.'

'Oh! She never uses magic. She has warned me about that.'

'She has? Well, good.' The lady lay back on the ground and tucked her cloak carefully about her feet, and hunched her shoulders under it. 'You must see Arthur often. Tell me about the king. What is he like when he is off the throne?'

'No different, ma'am. He is always on the throne except—'

'Except what?'

'I shouldn't say it.'

'You must judge that. Is it disparaging?'

'No – only puzzling – because you see, ma'am, he is the king.'

'And you saw something human.'

'You could call it that, I guess. On a night when my lady mother was very gay and we were all laughing fit to kill, a messenger came to her and she went black. And of course I slipped away as I have learned and went to the battlements to look at the stars and feel the wind.'

'As you always do.'

'Yes – how did you know? And I heard a sound like a puppy's hungry whine or like pain held in by tight fingers and squeezing through. I went towards it quietly and in the shadow of the tower I saw the king – and he was weeping with his hands over his mouth to hold it in.'

'And you slipped away without speaking?'

'Yes, madame.'

'Good!' she said. 'That was the seemly thing.'

'It puzzled me, ma'am – and – it broke my heart. The king can't weep – he is the king.'

'I understand. Don't ever tell it again. And I will not repeat it. But it's not a bad thing to think about if ever you should dream of being a king. Go to sleep now, son. We ride early.'

And by early she meant the first paling of the misty stars. Lyne stirred Sir Ewain from his soggy sleep. 'Up here,' she said. 'Say your prayers.' She dropped a tile of bread on his chest. And as they made ready to ride she made a sullen litany. 'Rust on the balls and sockets of my bones,' she said. 'It's not night weariness that reports age. It's the little gritty pains of the morning.' Young Ewain stumbled blindly in half-sleep to saddle his reluctant mount. And when he armed, the buckles and straps resisted his fingers. They were well on their way when the thin grey morning light picked out the path and set the trees up about them.

They forded a broad, shallow river when the sun rose against their backs and came into an open country that climbed gorsy hills and then more hills to hills beyond, a rocky country that seemed to hold the night's darkness to itself. Sheep raised their heads and watched them, chewing, and then dropped their heads to graze again, and on every ridgetop a dark shepherd watched jealously, with a tousled dog asking his master's wishes, whining softly in anticipation.

'Are those men or not men ?' Ewain asked.

'Sometimes one, sometimes the other, sometimes both. Do not approach them. They have stingers.' The lady was silent in the morning, but when the horse slowed his steps on the hillside she showed her impatience. 'Pick up your mount, lad,' she said irritably. 'The hills won't come to us.' And she permitted no rest at midday, only a watering at a freshet that tumbled downhill.

It was mid-afternoon when they climbed a last long slope and came to a pocket under the top, a cup hidden from everyone but birds, and in it low stone buildings crouching from the wind, roofed with split stone shingles, with low doors for short broad men, and lighted by arrow slits. These cotes were ranged on three sides of a tiltyard from which the stones were raked, and there Ewain saw a quintain on which was mounted a bag of sand the size of a man, and a hanging tilting ring, a wooden man with a club set on a pivot who automatically punished a spearman's clumsiness. It was a poor establishment. Some of the buildings sheltered sheep, some pigs, and some, not very different, were for men, and there was little to choose between them.

The lady screamed an order as she slipped to the ground, and short dark men emerged truculently from the houses and came to take the horse. They touched their brows to the lady and looked at Ewain with appraising, baleful eyes, and spoke among themselves in an unknown language that seemed like a song.

Lyne said, 'Welcome, lad, to a lady's bower. If you can find any comfort here, it's something I have overlooked.' She glanced at the sky—'Look at your quarters, son. Gaze at the sweet hospitality of these hills, consult the smiling faces of my men. You have three hours until dark. You may go before the sun sets and the road will be clear before you. But if you are here in the morning you may not leave, and if you do these little men will track you if you leave no more trace than last week's west wind, and crows will feast on young tender meat.'

In the morning Ewain was still there and his training began –

hour upon weary hour with a lance, while the lady stood and watched and caustically described the errors and found little good. And after a time, when the spearhead could find the mark, she set the target dancing on a rope, and crowed with triumph when the spearhead missed. And after lance work, hours with a sword weighted with lead to tear and mould the muscles, and not against an opponent but chopping work on an upright log, with every angle of cut inspected and criticized. The feeding was as rough as the work – porridge boiled with mutton and cold, bracken-flavoured water – and struck the dark, Ewain stumbled bleary-eyed to his sleep skin in a corner and sometimes pushed a goose aside to make room for himself. Heavy sleep fell, until a rough boot stirred in the dark for a new day.

In two months' time his eye and arm responded without thought or intention, and his motion and balance had become one thing. The lady watched every move and compared it with the day before, and at last she saw she had the material of a fighting man. And only then did she begin to talk to him with something beyond carping criticism.

'You do fairly well, boy,' she said. 'I've seen better. I've watched your pride flare into anger again and again. "I am a knight," you said in your mind. "How shall I live like a pig?" Do you know what "knight" means? It is an old, old word. It means a servant, and that is well thought out, because who would be master must learn his trade by being mastered. It's an old saw, I know, but like others it only becomes true when you have done it. I'm going to give you an opponent soon.'

Then two months of riding at a tricky dodging Welshman who drifted from his poised spear point like unstable smoke. And now the lady talked to him not as to a pig but more as to an intelligent dog or a backward child.

'I suppose it is natural to close your eyes just before the moment of impact,' she said. 'Therefore, you must learn to keep them open, for in that moment of blindness anything may be done.'

And two more months and two more. Ewain was gaunt and lean and as muscled as a yew tree. He did not long for death in the evening any more or dread the toe in his ribs that awakened him if he did not rise first. Now he found his own errors and tried to correct them, and no longer did he slink away to sleep on the heels of his dismissal.

'You will never be one of those rocklike men who stand against the waves. Not having the weight, you must make other men's weight fight for you. See that your spear is long. Lean forward in the saddle, as far forward as you can. You present a smaller target then, and more than that, if your point strikes first, it steals the force of a counterblow. Never, never present a flat surface. Never match force with force, but study your opponent before you fight, learn his strengths as well as his weaknesses, so that you may avoid the first and utilize the second. There are some foolish knights who think to disguise themselves with new devices or armour of a different colour. If I have ever seen a man fight I will know him though he wear a beer barrel for armour and come to the lists riding on a goose.'

In the ninth month with the year well turned, the lady Lyne conducted Ewain over the brow of the hill where he had never been, and in a sheltered vale they came upon a dozen of the broad dark truculent men of the country, who had there set up butts under the river trees, and where they practised with bows as tall as themselves and arrows that drew back to the ear. The arrows flew with angry whispers; the butts were small and far away, but the shafts found them.

'Here is the future,' the lady said, 'Here is the death of knighthood.'

'Why, what do you mean, my lady? This is a pleasant sport.'

'True,' she said. 'But give me twenty of these peasant sportsmen and I will stop twenty knights.'

'This is insane,' he cried. 'These toys are insects to an armed knight.'

'You think so? Give me your shield and breastplate.' And when he had disarmed she had the armour hung on a stake a hundred paces distant. 'Now, Daffyd,' she said, 'shoot eight and rapidly.'

The arrows flew as though threaded together, and when the armour was fetched it was a flattened pincushion, and inside where a man would have been, four of the iron-headed shafts had driven.

'So much for knights,' the lady said. 'If I wanted war I would take these.'

'They wouldn't dare. Everyone knows no peasant will stand up to a noble knight, a man born to arms.'

'They may learn. I know that it is as paralysing to put war in the hands of a soldier as to place religion under the marshalling of priests. But one day a leader who puts victory before ceremony will lead these men – and then – no more knights.'

'What a dreadful thought,' Sir Ewain said. 'If lowborn men could stand up to those born to rule, religion, government, the whole world would fall to pieces.'

'So it would,' she said. 'So it will.'

'I don't believe you,' Ewain said. 'But for the sake of the discussion, what then, my lady?'

'Why then – then the pieces would have to be put together again.'

'By such as these—?'

'Who else? Who indeed else?'

'If this should be true, my lady, I pray I am not alive to see it.'

'If it should be true, and you, my lord, charged into a flight of shafts, you wouldn't be. Come now, we will go back. In one more month you will be ready for your trial, a good knight, one of the best, but before that I wanted you to see the future of the best knights in the world.' She spoke unknown words to the men with the long bows and the yard-long shafts, and they laughed and touched their brows.

'What did they say?' the young knight asked uneasily.

'What should they say? They said, "Go in peace."'

The last month fled under the demands put upon it. Never had the lady been so critical, so caustic, so insulting. An action which in the past had drawn a little praise brought shrill attack. With blazing eyes she raked him and her thin mouth dripped poison as she tried to squeeze into him all of her knowledge, her observation and invention. And then one evening of a day that had been soaked and shrivelled with invective and despair, her voice dropped. She stepped back and looked at him, dirty, sweaty, weary, and insulted.

'There,' she said. 'That's all I can give you. If you aren't ready now, you never will be.'

It took him a little time to know that the training was over. 'Am I a good knight?' he asked at last.

'You aren't a knight at all until you are tested. But at least you are the earth out of which a good knight may grow.' And she asked anxiously, 'Have I been a hard taskmistress?'

'I can't imagine worse, my lady.'

'I hope so,' she said. 'I truly hope so. Tomorrow you will clean yourself and the next day we will start.'

'Start where?'

'Adventuring,' she said. 'I have made a tool. Now let us see whether it is a good tool.'

In the morning he started up in the dark to avoid the kick in the ribs and remembered it would not come. He tried to sleep again as he had prayed one day he might, but sleep was gone. That day he was bathed and scrubbed and scraped and clipped. The retainers laughed to see the colour of his skin show up under the layers of dirt and grease and ashes. And when he was dressed in a new jacket and pants of sheepskin, soft and supple as suede, the lady Lyne had brought to him his gifts.

'Here is magic armour,' she said. 'The magic resides in the surfaces. There is no place where blade or point can find a resting place. Lift it. You see it weighs little. Now here is a pot of clean mutton fat. See that you rub the armour with it every day to keep rust away, and to guide strokes helplessly away. Your shield, you see, is smooth and angled and the cantle lies flush with the surface. If you should dent it, see you take the depression out. Here is your helm – a pretty thing, isn't it? Simple, light, and very strong. Here in this hole you may put feathers, but nothing else. Now your magic sword. Take it in your hand.'

Sir Ewain lifted it. 'It weighs nothing, ma'am. Isn't it too light?'

'Your arm finds it light because you have been using a lead-weighted sword. No, it has weight enough, but the magic is in the balance. It is not point-heavy, because the handle is weighted – and its curious shape is designed to confuse the eye about its length.'

'It looks too short.'

'Compare it with another. You see, it is really the longer of the two. Now last, your spear, and he is magic also, made by these good fairies here. Keep him well.'

'But when he shatters ?'

'He will not shatter. He is not what he seems. His heart is a long rod of steel wrapped in rawhide nearly as hard as his heart. No, he will not shatter. And notice, he has two grips, one a foot behind the other. With a heavy opponent, extend him and make contact first. Now I have taught you what I can. If I have informed your head as well, I am content. Go to your rest. We ride tomorrow, but not too early. We have time to enjoy a little.'

When Ewain crept to his bed he found it dressed in clean linen smelling of dried lavender and at its head a cushion of the softest goose down. And before he slept he tried to remember every lesson of the weary months.

In the morning after prayers and breakfast he armed himself, marvelling at the lightness of his armour and the ease of movement in it.

And when the lady Lyne came out to him he was startled at the change in her, for she was a woman, almost damsel. Her hair was dressed craftily and her eyes soft gold instead of eagle yellow, and she walked with the graceful, secure gait of a lady. Her gown was violet edged in golden braid and over it was flung a travelling robe of purple, lined and collared with miniver, and on her head she wore a little golden crown like a demi-queen. She rode a palfrey with a coat like pale gold; two leathered retainers followed her on shaggy ponies. Their unstrung bows were long staffs in their hands, and sheaves of shafts showed their feathers over their left shoulders.

'Lead on!' the lady said.

'Which way, ma'am ?'

'The way we came,' she said.

They moved through a wet mist blown like ragged shreds of cloth over the open hills. The shepherds saw them pass and called melodic greetings to their countrymen.

At the mountain's foot they crossed the shallow of the river and entered the forest, grim and darkly gaunt in the pre-spring, oaks and beeches with bare spars like rigging close-hauled against a storm, a desolate way in a desolate month.

Sir Ewain said, 'Not an auspicious day for adventures, madame.'

She had ridden silently the long slipping way down from the

hills, but now she laughed gently. 'Adventures come or do not as they wish,' she said. 'When the singers tell of guests, a day clusters with mysteries like grapes. But I have ridden weeks at a time with no more wonder than a swollen joint after a wet night.'

'Do we go to some adventure known to you, my lady?'

'Not far from here a tournament is called, and early in the year to attract good men. Later in the year when the juices of errantry begin to flow, the great knights go to greater places. I hope you will have occasion to try your arms before the tourney.'

And as she spoke a knight came jingling behind them and called to them. 'Come have a do with me,' he cried.

Sir Ewain looked at his mended armour, rust-covered and poor, and at his sprained horse, and he saw how the knight sat his mount uneasily as though there were needles in his saddle. For a moment he was undetermined and his hand caressed his spear lovingly, but then he said, 'Fair knight, I beg you of your courtesy to permit me to withdraw with honour when I tell you I am oath bound towards one certain enemy. I have sworn to draw no weapons until I find him.'

The newcomer said, 'Why certainly, young sir, I respect your oath and release you from the challenge as I honour my knighthood.'

'That is gently said, sir, and I thank you.'

The meandering knight touched his visor in salute to the lady and jingled on, swaying uneasily, while his aged horse fought at the bit like a cantankerous colt. When he had gone, the lady said, 'That was well done, sir.'

'I had to tell a lie, my lady.'

'A courteous and kindly lie,' she said. 'Why should you hurt his pride as well as his body.'

'Still,' said Ewain, 'I hope to test my arms before I go to tourney.'

'Patience also is a knightly virtue,' she said.

Soon afterwards in a glade they came upon the rusty knight seated on the ground holding his broken shield over torn armour, while over him on horseback a tall knight speared at him like a gardener picking up leaves on a spike.

Then Ewain's heart was light. 'Hold, sir,' he called.

'What have we here?' the tall knight said. 'I see a little boy in toy armour. This is my evil day. A rusty midden heap and a little boy.'

Now Ewain looked anxiously to the lady Lyne for instruction, but she had moved to the side of the glade and she would not look at him or help him. And in his first fight since his training Ewain wished to do well. He brought out all his lessons like a swarm of bees, and one bee left the cluster and buzzed, 'I am your opponent before you fight him.' And suddenly young Ewain was calm. He tested his girth quickly and loosened his sword in its scabbard, and saw to his shield's strap, and then he moved out very slowly and deliberately towards the farther side of the open space, watching the tall knight as he went.

The knights lowered their spears to feauter and started the charge, but halfway there Ewain turned his horse and circled back to his start, while the tall knight fought his snorting, plunging horse.

'I am sorry, sir,' Ewain called. 'My girth is loose.' And he pretended to pull tight the straps, but he had seen what he wished to see, the tall knight's seat and the quality of his mount and how he handled himself. Ewain looked for a second at the lady and saw her eyes gleaming yellow and a little smile of understanding on her thin lips.

'That's how it is with children,' the tall knight shouted. 'Look to yourself!' He brought his angry but shy horse to a lumbering gallop. Ewain could see the spear point rise and fall. He charged far to the off-side and made his enemy rein towards him, and at the last moment he swerved surely in and almost tenderly placed his point against the ribbed breastplate and stripped the tall knight from his saddle and sent him clattering to the ground, while his furious mount went galloping away into the forest.

Ewain turned and trotted back and said, 'Yield, Sir Knight?'

The other lay moodily on the ground, looking up at the young man and seeing him for the first time, and he said, 'If that stroke was luck, I am unlucky; if it was not luck, I am unluckier still. I can't fight you on foot. I think my hip is broken. Tell me, sir, was your girth really loose?'

Ewain said, 'Yield!'

'Oh! I yield readily enough. I have no choice. And here I sit who was going to the tournament and all because I fought that bag of bones.'

'You are the prisoner of that gentleman,' said Ewain. He moved to where the rusty knight rose unsteadily to his feet. 'I deliver him into your hands, sir,' he said. 'I know you will use him courteously as you did me. His armour is your prize. Look to his hurt.'

'What is your name, sir?'

'It is an unproven name,' said Ewain. 'Do you go to the tournament, I hope to prove it there.'

'Yes, I am going there, and I beg the honour of fighting at your side.'

As they went on their way the lady Lyne said caustically, 'Don't try that with a seasoned knight. It was too obvious.'

'I felt it necessary to win my first fight.'

'It was well enough done,' she replied. 'But it reeked of technique. Next time try to make it seem more casual. I think you could have met him stroke for stroke, instead of that. Another course and he would have fallen with no help from you.' And as she saw Ewain slump forward under her criticism, she continued, 'It was all right for a first time. Perhaps you did well to be overcautious. But don't be proud until you have met a good opponent.'

Three times during the afternoon they overtook knights moving towards the first tournament of spring, and each time Ewain jousted and each time he unhorsed his men and on instructions refused to fight on foot, saying, 'Let us save that for the tournament.'

The lady was grimly satisfied but she said, 'I am a little worried. I distrust your excellence. Perhaps I distrust myself.' For a little time she withdrew into herself, answered him shortly and ill-temperedly, but at last she said, 'It's no use. It never has been. Have you noticed, young sir, that today I have been a lady?'

'Yes, my lady.'

'How did you like it?'

'It seemed strange, ma'am. Strange and unfriendly.'

She sighed with relief. 'Always has been strange, like a chicken with fur. At heart I'm a fighting man and a teacher of fighting men. Oh, I've tried, tried manfully to be womanly. You didn't like it?'

'Not as well, my lady.'

'My name is Lyne,' she said. 'Now – I don't think men are very good at fighting. The average, that is. Too softhearted, too fair, too vain. A woman with a man's body would be a champion. You will be a reasonably good knight, but your very manness will limit you. Can you imagine what a warrior your mother would have been? Think of the great champions – not one of them really liked women, whatever reason they may have given. It is true that women invented chivalry, but for their own ends. If women had been the knights, they would have punished chivalry as a crime and a danger.

'Now,' she said, 'there's no choice. We must use what we have. I have a fighting thought. Understand, it will never be accepted. It's too reasonable and men are creatures of fashion. I suppose in jousting leg armour is required. A clumsy or a deflected point has injured a man's legs. But on foot – how many leg wounds have you seen? And yet,' she said, 'men wear the heavy greaves just the same. And when the strength of a man goes, it is not his arms that tire. It is his legs. And when a fighting man shows age, it is his legs that give first evidence against him. If leg armour could be built into the saddle, that might work. Or if not, a simple hook so that the weight could be dropped. A man unarmoured below the groin would be a faster, longer-lasting man on foot.'

'But it would look ridiculous', Sir Ewain said.

'There you have it. And they say women are vain.'

So they travelled, and as the evening fell two more knights were challenged and unhorsed. The lady Lyne was in a merry mood when they arrived at the castle of the tournament on the border of Wales.

It was a small and ugly castle of great age and semi-ruinous, uncomfortable as a caul. The walls of the inner rooms sweated with moisture, and the smell of death and, worse, of living, hung in the chambers, while in the moat the fish had died of emptied filth. The gathered knighthood of the countryside were seated in the great hall, trying to engorge enough weak beer to warm their blood.

The lady Lyne did not complain about the castle, but when she saw the gathered chivalry she grew restive and anxious to be gone. She spoke quietly to Ewain sitting beside her at the long table littered with the grisly corpses of half roasted sheep.

'I don't like it,' she said. 'I'm afraid. There isn't a knight here who could hold a bridge against a rabbit. And yet it is in meetings such as this that good knights are destroyed by accident. I don't mind losing a man in a famous and well-matched fight, but accidents – look, my boy, and listen carefully. Take no chances, none at all. You'll have no trouble with the men you fight. What I fear is a clumsy blow aimed at someone else. Last year in a gathering like this I had a pupil, Sir Reginus, who would have astonished the world of fighting men. Then a lout aimed a great blow at another man, and lost his grip. His sword flew through the air and the point slipped through the bars of Reginus's visor, sneaked through his right eye into his brain, and he fell slowly like a timbered pine tree. No, I don't like this. The feast is more dangerous than the fighting.'

In the morning in the rain the sad and slippery tournament took place, and even caked with mud and blinded by splashed manure, Ewain still unseated thirty knights and won the prize, a shimmering gyrfalcon and a white horse housed in yellow cloth called cloth of gold to make it noble. Ewain wiped his eyes and carried his prizes to the lady Lyne.

'I thank your gentle courtesy, fair knight,' she said, and under her breath, 'If you had not won, I would have drowned you in the moat, except that the moat is the only dry place in the country.'

'I pledge my duty and my service to you, my lady,' Ewain proclaimed.

'Let us go away quickly,' she said. 'I'll sleep better and drier under a forest tree.' She approached her noble host and thanked him prettily. 'My lord,' she said, 'my champion has just received news of a revolt in his domain. If you will grant permission, he must go to put it down.'

'Of course he must. Where is his domain, my lady?'

She waved a vague hand to the east, 'Far,' she said. 'On the very edge of the world. He must go at once.'

'That must be Muscony, my lady.'

'Yes, Muscony,' said the lady Lyne.

At night, in a good shelter under a rock, lined and floored with rich clothes from the retainers' saddle bags, the lady leaned back against her couch of fur and sighed contentedly. 'Poor things,' she said. 'They can learn only one thing at a time. Only now have I taught them not to steal from me. Now, tomorrow is a different thing. Tomorrow we travel to the Castle of the Lady of the Rock.'

The cold March rain continued as they travelled on. The horses ducked their heads against it and tucked their tails tight.

'I hope you rubbed fat on your armour,' the lady said. 'If not you'll shortly look like a rusty nail. Fortunately, the Castle of the Rock is not far away. Now here you will have an adventure worth the telling. I believe when you were dubbed knight you swore to succour ladies and to protect widows and orphans, particularly if they were gentle people.'

'That is so,' said Ewain. 'And I will keep my oath.'

'You are fortunate,' she said. 'The Lady of the Rock is all these – a widow and an orphan and a gentlewoman. Furthermore, she needs succouring as much as anyone I know. When the lady's lord departed from this world, he left his lady in possession of fair lands, forest and pasture, cottages and serfs, and two well-made and well-defended fortresses, one called the Castle of the Rock and the other the Red Castle. Seeing the lady bereaved of her lord and protector, two brothers named Edward and Hugh took the Red Castle and the great part of her lands, leaving her only the Castle of the Rock, and even that they hope to take in their good time, and the lady also, for she is fair and courteous and wellborn. Meanwhile, these brothers call themselves Sir Edward and Sir Hugh of the Red Castle, collect rents, dues, fees, and socage, and lord it on the land with hireling men at arms behind them.'

Ewain said, 'My lady, this is clearly a case for succouring. I will do battle with these knights for the lady's heritage.'

'I must tell you, young sir, that these are not errant knights to venture life for honour at a crossroads. These are good, honest, hard-working, conscientious thieves. They will not fight unless they are sure to win.'

'I will challenge them on their honour,' Ewain said.

'I think you will find them more interested in their property,' said Lyne. 'Perhaps their grandsons may have a go at honour when they come to be born. Now, hear me well.' She pointed to a fallen oak which, lifting its roots, had made a little cavern later occupied by foxes, boars, badgers, bears, and perhaps dragons before men ousted the lot. 'Let us get under cover from this rascal rain,' she said.

A little firepit in the cavern showed recent occupation, and on this hearth one of the bowmen prepared to build a fire, but the lady stopped him. 'We can't have smoke,' she said. 'We are near to the Castle of the Rock, from the top of this next hill it will be seen and all the country round about. If I were such as Edward and Hugh and had their wish to live and increase, I would post men on the hill to guard the path in case some young knight should feel the urge to succour a lady in distress.'

'I will ride up and clear them from the way, my lady.'

'You will sit here and wait, my lord.' She called her men and spoke to them in the old Celtic tongue, and they nodded and smiled and touched their shaggy forelocks. Then from their pouches they took well-waxed bowstrings and bent their long-bows. Each man chose eight arrows, whetted their iron tips, and sighted along the shafts for warp. Then they moved silently up the hill, not on the path, but through the dripping thickets, and no sound gave news of their passing.

Lyne said, 'We must think of some way to bring the two knights to combat. If you could make some concession, appear to fall into a trap – well, we will see. Did you hear that?'

'What, my lady?'

'I thought I heard a cry – Hark! There's another.'

'I heard that. It sounded like a death scream.'

'It was,' the lady said.

For a long time they heard only the drip of rain and the gurgling of freshet water. And then the men came back and each carried armour strung on a thong and slung on their backs, and their belts were weighted down with heavy swords. They dumped the clattering metal in the cavern's entrance and smiled slightly as they spoke.

'There were only two,' Lyne explained. 'They think the way

is open now, but when we move they will go ahead to make sure.'

The Lady of the Rock greeted them with pleasure and relief. She was a fair and noble lady worn with anxiety. 'No help has come,' she said. 'They have taken all my lands, all my villeins. We have a little stock of salted herrings, a little salted pork, and nothing more. My men at arms are gaunt. What can one young knight do?'

Ewain said, 'I will challenge them to combat to let God show whose cause is right.'

The two ladies exchanged a commiserating glance. 'I thank you, gentle knight,' said the Lady of the Rock.

The brother knights came quickly to the summons, and they were followed by a hundred men at arms, for they had discovered their two guardians of the path stripped and dead of strange wounds.

The Lady of the Rock would not allow Ewain to go out and parley with them. 'For,' she said, 'they are not men to respect the sacred conventions.' The gates were closed and the drawbridge raised. The lady Lyne, by permission of Sir Ewain, spoke to the brothers from the wall. She called, 'We have a champion to fight one of you for the lands you have stolen from my Lady of the Rock.'

The brothers laughed at her. 'Why should we fight for something we have already?' they asked.

She had anticipated this reply and now she moved cautiously, for there are some men, she knew, who can be taken only in traps of their own devising. 'Our champion is a young man newly knighted and hot after fame. You know how young men are. Well, if you will not help to gild his spurs, you will not. I wish I might speak privately with you.'

The brothers consulted together and then one of them said, 'Come down to us then.'

'What surety do you offer, sir?' she asked.

'Lady,' he said, 'consult your reason for your surety. What is our gain in making war against a landless lady? If we are treacherous, what have we but a bag of bones?'

The lady smiled to herself. 'What joy it is to speak with lords who take advice from thought rather than from passion. I will come down to you alone. I am not afraid, but those of this castle might be timid. Withdraw your men the distance from you that you are from the wall.'

She brushed aside the warnings of her friends, but before she descended to the gate her two bowmen were disposed behind arrowslits, unseen from without but with shafts ready notched on bowstrings and a clear distance to the mark.

She took her position by the moat and let the brothers come to her at a place where she knew that two arrows would cut them down if she raised her hand.

'My lords, we are not children. Now that we are out of earshot of sweet chivalry, let us discuss the position. You have the lady's lands as well as the Red Castle. Why should you fight for them?'

'You speak truth. You are indeed a lady of experience.'

'However, you do not have the Castle of the Rock and I don't think you can take it by assault. It is well made and well defended.'

'We have no need,' Sir Edward said. 'When its food is gone, it will fall into our hands. Nothing can enter. We control the countryside.'

'You have a formidable argument,' said Lyne. 'Or you did until recently. Have you inspected the pass to the west, my lords?'

They looked quickly at each other.

'You found the path open, my lords. But do you know what came in through the unguarded way? I will tell you. Fifty Welsh bowmen, silent and secret as cats, and you have inspected the work of only two. I need not tell you what your nights will be. Every shadow may be your death, a little breeze the whisper of dark wings.' And she paused to let uncertainty take control. And after a moment she went on, 'I agree it would be stupid to fight for what you already have. But would you fight for what you have not? The Castle of the Rock and with it the certainty that you will continue to have everything? You are reasonable men.'

'What do you suggest, madame?' Sir Hugh demanded.

'If you have the courage to play for a high stake, I suggest you fight the lady's champion. It isn't as though he were a great and far-famed knight. He is little more than a boy.'

'What is your interest, my lady?' they asked suspiciously.

'My position is a happy one,' she said. 'If I bring about the fight, my Lady of the Rock will reward me. And if you should win, I can perhaps hope that you will not be ungrateful.'

The brothers went a little apart to confer and after some difference they returned. 'Lady,' Sir Edward said, 'we are two brothers born at the same time of one womb. One of us does nothing without the other or ever has since our babyhood. We fight together and only together. Do you think your champion will fight both of us at once?'

'I don't know. He is very young and headstrong. You know what ambitious boys are. I can ask him. But if he agrees to fight you in the morning, you must leave your men two hundred paces distant.'

'Is this a trick, lady?'

'No,' she said. 'It is the distance of a bowshot. If the wild bowmen should grow excited or your men should move to interfere, many men would die.'

'That is sensible,' they said. 'Try if your champion will fight with us two for one.'

'I will do my best, my lords. And if God should give you victory, I hope you will remember me.' She smiled at them and went back into the Castle of the Rock, and the drawbridge rose and the huge gate closed after her.

When they had supped, the Lady of the Rock retired to the chapel to enlist aid from Heaven, but Lyne drew Sir Ewain to the gate tower where they could look down on the drawbridge and the fair meadow beyond.

'You must not be concerned that I made you out a fool,' she said. 'The problem was to get them to fight at all. They really had no reason, but now they think they have. Did you observe them closely while I spoke with them?'

'Yes, madame.'

'And what did you see?'

'They are well made, fair in body, taller than I, and of equal weight. The one to the right—'

'That is Sir Hugh, remember it.'

'He has been wounded in the right knee or leg. He drags his foot a little. I would think they are men who can contend worthily.'

'What else? Consult your memory.'

Ewain closed his eyes and formed the picture. 'Yes, there's something, something strange. I know, they wear their swords opposite. That's it. One is right-handed and one left.'

She put out her hand and touched him on the shoulder – a little accolade. 'Good, my lord,' she said. 'How did they stand?'

Again he closed his eyes. 'The scabbards were together as they stood – therefore, the one on the right facing me, Sir Hugh, is left-handed.'

'And they will fight that way,' she said. 'Their sword arms on the outside, shields together, it is a deadly way. You must be sure that they will edge apart and try to take you from behind. You must give ground and put the slightly raised drawbridge at your back. Now, there's a trick I have seen only once—'

'Perhaps I know, ma'am, or can imagine. How could I swing them opposite?'

The lady's eagle eye shone with pride. 'That's it,' she cried. 'I chose you well or good fortune was with me. If you can bring their sword arms together they will interfere and the advantage will be yours. But wait, my boy, and when they are a little weary—' She drew with her finger in the dust of the tower's stone floor. 'A feint here would draw this one. Then if you back around quickly and make him follow you to here. Then charge in here, retreat, then rush – rush quickly. Do you see? You will have reordered their front. But you must do it quickly, you will not have two chances. I think these men have fought this way for many years. Now, let us talk about the courses. I do not worry about that. You are a good spear man against any. And it is difficult for two knights to run at one and the same time. You have a good mount and you can avoid and receive them as you wish. But there is another advantage. Did you see it?'

'I don't know,' said Ewain. 'The greatest knights fight equally well with either hand. I've seen them switch from right to left and back.'

'I think you will find these are not the best knights,' she said. 'These are two robbers who hope to beat a boy. Let them believe it until the last moment. Now go to your rest. And have no fear. I do not intend to lose a good knight of my training to a pair of rascals.'

The morning was kind to battle. The first blackbirds of spring responded to the sun and warmed their song in the bushes that edged the moat, and the meadow grass was golden green. On every sunny verge rabbits dried their fur and licked down their breasts. A school of new-hatched pollywogs cavorted on the surface of the moat like miniature whales, while a heron, stately on one shafted leg, let them come to him, then picked them one by one like ripe cherries with his tweezer beak.

Young Ewain was early awake, edging his sword, grinding the head of his black spear to an immaculate point, and last, he anointed his armour with clarified fat and rubbed it gently into every moving piece with his fingertips. He was excited and gay, and when his lady Lyne stood over him clucking like a broody hen, he said, 'Madam, have you not a favour for my helm?'

'Go along,' she said. 'Would you have a strand of grey hair or a damp glove?' But she moved restlessly away, and when he had put his helm aside and entered chapel to hear Mass, she brought a single eagle feather, brown, black, and tufted with white at the quill, and she fastened it securely to his visor hinge.

At the hour of prime the brothers appeared with scraped-up dignity, with raucous trumpets and retainers armed by conquest in every manner of equipment. They arranged their followers on a line a bowshot away, and then the two came forward with only a trumpeter blowing brassily ahead of them.

Ewain seized his shield to go to them, but his lady restrained him. 'Let them blow awhile,' she said. 'The longer you keep them waiting, the better.

'Go down to the courtyard and mount your horse, but do not go out until I give the word.' She spoke in detail to her two outlandish bowmen, and placed them on the gate tower beside her, concealed by the battlements and each with a wealth of arrows at his side, two small forests of bustling grey goose feathers. The bowmen watched her face like hunting dogs.

Lyne looked down to the courtyard and saw Ewain sitting his armed horse, his great black spear erect and the eagle feather curved over his helmet. And still she waited until the trumpeter in the meadow was out of breath and all the grandeur of the approach was lost in restlessness.

Sir Hugh shouted at the silent castle, 'Come down, recreant knight, if you are not afraid.'

Still she waited until the brothers had drawn together, suspecting treachery, and looking up with suspicion and the beginning of fear. Only then she raised her hand. The drawbridge crashed down, the gates flew open, and Ewain galloped bravely out, went past the brothers, and, turning, took his position facing the castle, and then waited silent and still.

The brothers lowered their spears and charged together, but in the course Sir Edward's horse was faster and Ewain, holding his horse in check, angled across the line of Edward's charge, then cut back and took Sir Hugh on the side of his disadvantage and tumbled him from his saddle. In a rage, Sir Edward charged again, watching for a trick of horsemanship. High on the tower Ewain saw the lady Lyne looking down on him. He raised his spear in salute to her, then fettered it and drove clearly through, took Edward's point and set his own and saw his enemy's spear shatter and Sir Edward go flying, taking his saddle with him. The lady clapped her hand and an eagle scream of triumph floated down from the battlements.

The brothers got up from the earth and drew together, sword arms opposite, shields side by side as a result.

Sir Ewain rode near and he said, 'Since you are two against one, it is my right to fight from horseback.'

'You are a coward and a traitor,' Sir Edward shouted.

And Ewain heard Lyne's harsh voice in his ears saying, 'Deeds are the only proper answer to words. Save your breath.'

He saw the drawbridge open a little to give him haven for retreat. He rode as near as he could and still have time to dismount and prepare himself. Then he dismounted, dressed his shield, drew his sword, and moved towards the drawbridge. The brothers saw his object, and as a unit they moved at a heavy run to cut him off. They caught him before he could turn and they moved in, striking like a broad man with a sword in each hand. Ewain fell under a blow, and on the tower two heads appeared and two shafts were drawn back feathers to ears. Then Ewain rolled and stood, and he ran painfully from the brothers, blessing the lightness of his arms, and with the bridge at his back he turned to face them.

They were old at this game. They separated a little, and when Ewain struck at one he opened his defence to the attack of the other. They wounded Ewain in the side and then, while one aimed high to raise his shield, the other cut low and ripped at his legs. Ewain felt his blood flowing hotly down his side and the earth grew slippery under him. He tried to remember the drawing in the dust of the tower, but a little dizziness kept the picture from him. A quick blow on his helm shocked him and cleared his eyes. He saw his feather zigzag to the ground, and at the same time he heard the eagle screaming from the tower and the dust drawing came clear to his mind. He leaped from his sheltering place to the right and circled close, and Sir Edward turned to meet his attack. And then he lunged towards Hugh and drew him whirling to defence. And as the eagle screamed again he moved in between them and they closed to meet him. Both swords rose and their blades clashed together. Ewain stepped left and forced Sir Hugh's shield aside, and with a short backhand cut he drove him against his brother's arm. Then, without pause, he moved left and low and close and his sword chopped through Edward's shoulder and cut down into his chest, and Edward fell dying to the ground. Now Ewain turned on Hugh, but that knight without his brother was half a man and his courage dropped from him. Sir Hugh kneeled on the ground and raised his helm and begged for mercy.

Sir Ewain of his gentleness received his sword and took him by the hand and led him to the castle gate, and there Sir Ewain fell into a swoon, for he had lost much blood in the fighting.

The ladies put him to bed and cleaned his wounds and waited on him tenderly. He was a young man and his hurts healed quickly.

The Lady of the Rock was passing glad, and when he was recovered she thanked him prettily and she said, blushingly, 'You, Sir Knight, have won through the deeds of your hands any gift in my power to offer. Do not speak now but think of it.'

He thanked her gently and fell asleep, and when he awakened the lady Lyne sat beside his bed. 'Sir,' she said, 'I have counselled you in many things, but here I will not enter. You may well believe the Lady of the Rock will keep her promise. I saw her face and felt the heat of her generosity. You, so young, have achieved what nearly every man desires. The lady has lands and castles, and now you have given her her own again, she has wealth. I think you know the gift she had in mind and she is free to offer it. You must consider carefully. It is a princely holding and the lady has charms not to be denied. The life she offers you is what most men dream of and cannot have. Think of what it will be. You may hunt in the forests, collect the rents, fight with the neighbours, eat well, drink deep, sleep softly with a gentle wife who is not yet past her prime. Don't think it would be an idle life. There are fields to drain and crops to oversee. The government of a manor is no small matter. You have manorial right to sit in court and offer judgement over who is at fault when A's hen scratches in B's garden plot. And if Jack o' Woods is taken with a hare in his pot it will be your duty as well as your right to cut a hind foot from Jack's dog, to turn his scurvy children from their hearth, and on a sunny morning after Mass to hang Jack kicking from a tree before you go to noonday meal, and sleep afterwards with a sense of duty done. And don't think for a moment you will lead a lonely life. Once a year – sometimes as much as twice – an errant knight will ride in and over good sour beer he will tell you all the news of tournaments and wars – what Arthur says and does, and how he looks, and what new fashions have come to the court ladies from France.' She saw that he was laughing gently.

'You are an evil woman,' Ewain said.

'I only kept my promise to the lady. I engaged to plead her cause and you can swear that I have done it.'

'Ask her to come in, and do you stay also.'

And when the Lady of the Rock stood beside his bed, he said solemnly, 'My lady, I am conscious of your high gifts and proud that you have found me worthy. But since you have used me with all gently courtesy, I would be recreant if I did not tell you the truth of it. To accept your gift would make me unworthy to receive it. For I have taken an oath on the four Evangelists and on my knightly honour to complete a quest. I think you will agree that a knight who flouts one oath is not to be trusted to keep another. Therefore, my lady, I ask you to withdraw your noble gift and in its stead to give me the little ring from your finger, so that in dreadful and dubious combat I may look at it and relight my courage at the steady fire of your memory.'

And afterwards Lyne said to him, 'I taught you only use of sword and spear. You must have had that other from your mother. With that weapon you will go far.'

Anon they rode back towards the trysting place, and as they neared the triple fork, Sir Ewain said, 'Madame, you have given me gifts beyond price. Will you then ask of me whatever is in my power to give?'

'That I will,' she said slowly. 'As a boon I will ask you to keep my memory green.'

'That is no boon, my lady. I could not do otherwise even if I wished.'

'Peace,' she said, 'I know promises and I know memory. But there is a way. As Holy Church makes every year a new Birth and Death and Resurrection through re-enactment, so might you do regarding me.'

'What do you mean, my lady?'

'Without disrespect, I mean an act is better than a thought. When you fetter your black spear, remember to ride low and forward. When you fight, fight to win, and, having won, be generous. And at night, before you rest, rub your armour well with fat – with this boon I will be content.'

'Will you go back to find another knight?' he asked with jealousy.

'Yes, I suppose I will. But I will be critical. It will not be easy. Oh, God! how dreadful it must be to have a son!'

He greeted Gawain and Marhalt at the cross and conducted the lady to her seat beside the fountain where the damsel of thirty winters sat wearing her chaplet. Lady Lyne seated herself and placed her chaplet on her hair. And Ewain asked, 'Where is the youngest damsel?'

'She will come,' they said. 'She is always late.'

'Then farewell, my lady,' Sir Ewain said. And as he rode away he thought he heard her say, 'Farewell, my son.'

At the cross the three companions came together and each one knew that there was much to tell and more they would not tell. And as they sorted the year, a king's messenger rode up. 'You are Sir Gawain and Sir Ewain!' he said. 'I have searched for you. King Arthur asks you to return to court.'

'Is he angry still?'

'No,' said the messenger. 'The king repents his hastiness. You will be welcomed.'

Now the cousins were joyful, and they said to Marhalt, 'You must come with us to court.'

'I should be returning to my manor.'

'But that would be a defect in a perfect quest, the only one.'

Marhalt laughed. 'As I honour my knighthood I cannot be guilty of such a thing,' he said.

And the three rode happily towards Camelot. And each prepared his tale as he would have it told and repeated down the ages.

the noble tale of sir lancelot of the lake

(And noble it is. JS)

After a long and turbulent time King Arthur, through fortune and force of arms, destroyed or made peace with his enemies inside his realm and out, and established in men's minds his right to rule. To accomplish this, the king had drawn to his person and his court the best knights and the hardiest fighting men in the world.

Having made peace through war, King Arthur found the dilemma of all soldiers in tranquillity. He could not disband his knights in a world where violence slept uneasily. And, on the other hand, it is difficult, if not impossible, to keep the strength and temper of fighting men without fighting, for nothing rusts so quickly as an unused sword or an idle soldier.

Arthur, knowing this, took the way of all generals in all time. He set up games which imitated war to keep his knights hard and hardy – jousts, tournaments, hunting, and endless warlike images. By these deadly games the fellowship of the Round Table sought to keep skill and courage high by venturing their lives in return for fame. In these games of simulated battle some knights increased in honour, while others were thrust down through misfortunate encounters with spear and sword on the tourney ground.

And while the older war-bred knights kept their arms bright, perhaps in memory of real battle, the young men, whose knighthood knew only the games of combat, did not love them.

Then Arthur learned, as all leaders are astonished to learn, that peace, not war, is the destroyer of men; tranquillity rather than danger is the mother of cowardice, and not need but plenty brings apprehension and unease. Finally he found that the longed-for peace, so bitterly achieved, created more bitterness than ever did the anguish of achieving it. King Arthur watched in apprehension while the young knights, who should have filled the fighting ranks, dissipated their strength in the mires of complaint, confusion, and self-pity, condemning the old time without having created a new one.

Among the battlewise fellowship of the Round Table, Sir Lancelot stood above all others. He proved himself and increased in honour and worship until he was known as the best knight in the world. No one defeated him in battle, joust, or tournament except by enchantment or treachery. This was that same Lancelot, who, when he was a child, heard Merlin prophesy for him preeminence above the knighthood of the world. During his boyhood and young manhood he had set himself to fulfil the prophesy, forsaking all else save his knighthood until he towered over the knights of the Round Table as they towered over all others. He was the victor in all contests and won the prize in every tournament until the older knights were reluctant to engage with him and the younger found contemptuous reasons not to fight at all.

King Arthur loved Sir Lancelot, and Queen Guinevere took kindly notice of him. And in return Sir Lancelot loved both the king and queen and swore to devote his knighthood to the queen's service all the days of his life.

It came about that the best knight in the world was without opponent in the court, and he felt his fighting skill rusting, and he grew despondent, for he could find no opposing sword to keep his sword sharp, no competing arm to muscle and advise his arm. And since the exclusive pathway of his life had led to what he had become, the world's best knight, Lancelot could find no crossroads to lead him to love or ambition, no obstructions to drive him to envy or to treachery or to greed, neither sorrow nor frustration to suggest religion beyond habit. His long-conditioned body found no interest in or understanding of comfort and appetites. He was a hound without a deer, a landbound fish, a stringless bow, and, like all unused men, Lancelot grew restless and then irritable, and then angry. He found pains in his body and flaws in his disposition which were not there before.

Then Guinevere, who loved Lancelot and understood men, sorrowed to see the disintegration of a perfect instrument. She held long council with the king and heard from him his worry about the young knights.

'I wish I could understand it,' Arthur said. 'They eat well, sleep in comfort, make love when and to whom they wish. They feed appetites only half awakened and reject all the pain and hunger, weariness and discipline, which give pleasure the stature – and still they are not content. They complain that the times are against them.'

'And so the times are,' said Guinevere.

'What do you mean?'

'They are idle, my lord. The times make no demand on them. The fiercest hound, the fastest horse, the best of women, the bravest knight, none can resist the smothering of idleness. Even Sir Lancelot grumbles like a Sunday child in sedentary discontent.'

'What can I do?' King Arthur cried. 'I see the noblest fellowship in the world crumbling – eroding like a windblown dune. In the hard dark days I prayed and worked and fought for peace. Now I have it and peace is too difficult. Do you know, I find myself wishing for war to solve my difficulties?'

'You are not the first or the last,' said Guinevere. 'Consider, my lord. We have general peace, it is true, but as a healthy man has little pains, so is peace a composite of small wars.'

'Explain this, madame.'

'It isn't new. A recreant knight mounts guard on a ford and exacts tribute or a life. A thief in armour desolates a district. A giant batters down the walls of a sheepcote and dragons burn fields of ripening corn with their fiery snortings – tiny wars everywhere and always too small for an army, too big for the neighbours to set aright.'

'The quest?'

'I was thinking...'

'But the young knights laugh at old-fashioned questing and the old knights have seen real wars.'

'It is one thing to make oneself great but quite another to try to be not small. I think that every man wants to be larger than himself and that he can be only if he is part of something immeasurably larger than himself. The best knight in the world, if he is unchallenged, finds himself shrinking. We must seek a way to declare a great war on little things. We must find a word, a thought, a standard, under which small evils may enlist in a great wrong. Against this we could raise a fighting army.'

'Justice?' Arthur asked.

'Too vague – too meaningless – too cold. But the "King's Justice" – that's better. Yes, that's *it*. Every knight the personal agent and keeper of the King's Justice, responsible for it. That might do – for a time. Then every knight would be an instrument of something larger than himself. And when that runs out we may think of something else. Merlin made prophecies about everything, on both sides of everything. We should call Merlin. Men do like to be the children of light, even if they work in darkness. A young knight who spends his waking hours trying to deflower a demoiselle will rush to the defence of damsels.'

'I wonder how I could declare this war,' King Arthur said.

'Start with the best knight in the world.'

'Lancelot?'

'Yes, and let him take the worst.'

'That is harder to choose, my dear, but now I think of it, his nephew Lyonel is a likely candidate as the least, the laziest, the most worthless.'

'My lord,' said Guinevere, 'if I can make Lancelot the first guardian of the King's Justice, would you try to make him guardian and teacher of Sir Lyonel?'

'It is a good thought. I will try. You are a good counsellor, my dear.'

'Then let me counsel you a little more, my lord. Sir Lancelot is only different from other men in degree. If you can find a way to allow him to think of it himself, it will be easier. Let me prepare him for questing and then turn him over to you.'

'The worst and the best,' King Arthur said, and he smiled. 'It is a powerful combination. Such an alliance would be unbeatable.'

'It is only through such alliances that wars can be fought at all, my lord.'

At this time Queen Guinevere loved Lancelot for his bravery, for his courtesy, for his fame, and for his lack of cleverness. She did not as yet want to change him, push back his untamed lock of hair, whip him with doubt and confusion and jealousy to keep her image glowing in his brain. She did not yet love him enough to be cruel to him. Her affection was warmly self-contained, the quality of love with which a woman can be kind, and friendly, and very wise – too wise to instruct him openly.

She confided her restlessness to the restless knight, her feeling of uselessness to the unused knight. 'How fortunate men are,' she said. 'Without notice or warning or permission, you can creep away from boredom into the great green world of wonders, of adventures in desert places. You can search out and correct injustices, punish evils, overcome traitors to the King's Peace. For all I know, you may be preparing now to leave this sapless stronghold of the useless and unused to go where men are needed, where courage and knightly honour are prayed for and rewarded.'

'My lady—'

'Don't tell me. If you are making secret plans, I would rather not know them. That would make me darkly miserable. Sometimes I wish above everything to be a man, sir. But I must wait. My only adventures are in the pictures in coloured thread of the great gallant world. My little needle is my sword. That's not a very satisfying conflict.'

'But you must be happy in the knowledge that men wear your image in their hearts, my queen; yes, and in their prayers commend themselves to you and silently beseech your blessing as though you were a goddess.'

'I'm afraid I do not hear silent prayers, Sir Knight. I don't deny that they are so, but I do not hear them, not being a goddess. Only one kind of devotion is self-evident.'

'What is that, my lady?'

'I can only give you an example. A brave knight on lonely quest came upon a viper's nest of tyranny. Two evil brothers far in the north made existence unbearable, life unliveable, and spread their arrogance on the countryside until my questing knight met them and overthrew them. Then, instead of killing them, he sent them to me to sue for pardon and forgiveness. Through them he prayed my blessing. There was a prayer I could hear – and more – for in their telling I could participate in a world I cannot visit.'

'Who was that knight?' Lancelot demanded.

'No— No! He prayed that I keep his name secret, and his prayer binds me as surely as my oath.'

'I will inquire, my lady. It should not be hard to—'

She stopped him in mid-ramble. 'Sir Lancelot – are you my knight?'

'I am, my lady – sworn.'

'And has my wish currency with you?'

'It is my law.'

'Then you will not inquire.'

'I will not inquire, my queen. But did this act of his give you such pleasure?'

'More than I can say. It seemed to me that through that knight I became valuable in the world. I feel myself to be a little precious because of him.'

She smiled to see him walk away in thought, his coarse, rebellious hair rioting on his forehead.

The king saw Lancelot pacing darkly on the wall and laid a trap for him. For Arthur, studying to be a king, had learned that a sovereign's request for advice and help chains a subject helplessly to the throne.

Thus Lancelot found his lord with elbows on a battlement staring moodily down at a squadron of cygnets manoeuvring on the moat. 'Pardon, sire, I did not know you were here.'

'Oh, yes. It is you. I was deep in thought.'

'Should you be here, sire, alone, without some bodyguard?'

'I am not alone,' said Arthur. 'I am surrounded by perplexities. Strange that you should pass. I was about to search for you. Do you believe that a man in need can call soundlessly to another?'

'Perhaps, my lord. It has happened to me that thinking of a friend and meeting him are connected. But does thinking draw him or his coming draw the thought?'

'That's very interesting,' said Arthur. 'We will discuss it sometime. What was drawing me to you was need for your help.'

'My help, sire?'

'May I *not* turn to you for help?'

'Always, my lord. Only I can't think how I can carry water to the fountain.'

'What a pretty speech.'

'It's in a song, my lord. I heard a jongleur singing.'

'Sir,' said the king. 'I come to you as a man of arms, a soldier and an old comrade. I know you have observed and surely worried over what we see around us. It is not long since we had a force second to none in the world, as we did prove to the world. And now – so soon – it is evaporating. The older knights are losing their edge. The young ones refuse the temper. Soon, without a stroke, we will have lost an army.'

'Perhaps we need the stroke, sire.'

'I know, I know. But where do we strike ? There is no enemy. By the time one appears we will be helpless. I do not worry so about the older men. They deserve their rest and their decay. But the young men – if they earn their spurs in dancing, find their only opponent in a reluctant petticoat, we are lost. Help me, my friend. I need your help.'

'They must be forced to learn the profession of arms, sire.'

'But how ? They will not enter the tournament, and in jousting they demand the claw instead of the spear point, to save themselves from injury.'

'That isn't the way we earned the accolade, is it, sire ? If I remember, you fought to the death unknown beside a certain fountain.'

'Let us not refight old duels, much as I like to. If the young, mincing gallants were a few medium, wellborn sluggards, it would be different, but the best are the worst. Your own nephew has more ribbons than wounds and his only scars he got from picking roses.'

'Sir Lyonel, my lord ?'

'Sir Lyonel. I don't single him out to insult you. He is only one of the many giggling in the dark, engaging with battalions of words. The most dangerous weapon in this court is the lute. They challenge each other with deadly banquets.'

Lancelot said harshly, 'I'll take the young pup out and drown him in the moat.'

'You'd have to take a pack of pups. They would fill up the moat. Wait – you have said it! I knew I could depend on you. Maybe that is the way.'

Lancelot was not capable of pretending. 'What have I said ?' he asked. 'I don't remember offering—'

'You said, "I'll take the young pup out—" '

'—and drown him,' Lancelot finished.

'Go back to the first part – take him out. You suggested it

yourself. Suppose we sent them out – a battlewise old knight and a young pup – sent them with something to perform, some mission difficult and dangerous. Why – that might be the best way to train and season them. Thank you, my friend. And the older knights might love to get their harness dented in memory of old times.'

'What kind of missions, sire?'

'Wherever there is need. The kingdom is infested with little wrongs to be righted. We could call them – let's see – Protectors of the King's Peace. They could wear the royal authority as a device. What do you think of it?'

'I must consider it, sire. But one thing does occur to me. It should be started slowly. If you sent out a hundred pairs of authority, the King's Peace would be hopelessly at war with the King's Peace before sundown.'

'That might not be a bad solution,' Arthur said. 'Well – let us think about it. I will not forget it was your suggestion, my friend.' And the king went away satisfied, for he had seen an ill-concealed flame spring to life behind Sir Lancelot's eyes.

The flower of the young knights met regularly at the well beside the keep. There, seated on the broad coping, they could watch the girls drawing water, evaluate their bosoms when they stooped to draw the bucket, and sometimes a windy gust careened their skirts and drew squeals of appreciative laughter from the budding knights, who spoke mysteriously of their conquests of receptive noble damsels and meanwhile tried to arouse receptiveness in water-bearing kitchen wenches. When the bucket swung idly the young lords compared the colours of their hose and measured the length of their pointed toes one against another. When an old knight passed by, they whispered behind their hands and looked at the sky with elaborate innocence, until his distance made it safe for tongue-sticking and eye-crossing, which forms of silent satire they had invented.

The evening gathering counted heads and asked, 'Where's Lyonel? He's usually here before now. Gets here before the *men* in Amen at evensong.'

'You remember – he had an assignation with a lovely dream. Did he tell anyone her name?'

'No – but he made it easy enough to guess.'

'If it's who I think you mean, I don't believe it. Why she's twenty-three if she's a day.'

'Well – I think he had an assignation with his uncle. I saw them together – Sir Lance what's-his-name.'

They rolled and rocked with laughter and repeated the riposte: 'Lance what's-his-name. You know, we might make that stick.'

'You'd better not let him hear it. Your cheeks would burn and not on your face.'

Sir Lyonel sauntered near and sat silently on the coping while they inspected his pouting mouth.

'What's the matter ? Cat got your tongue ?'

That set them off. They howled with laughter, slapped backs, or doubled over, rolling their chests against their stomachs.

'Cat got your tongue ? Ohee. He's better than a trouvère. Why, that's funnier than a dwarf.'

'I'll buy him a bladder and bells myself.'

And then their laughter collapsed, as it so often did without prodding.

'What is wrong with you ?' they asked Sir Lyonel.

'I can't tell you.'

'Is it about your uncle, Sir Lance what's-his-name ?' The flavour was not there any more. 'We saw you with him.'

'If it's an oath – solve it to absolve.'

'It's not an oath.'

'Then tell.'

'He wants me to go on a quest with him.'

'What kind of a quest ?'

'What other kind is there – damsels and dragons and damn all.'

'And ?'

'And I don't want to go.'

'I can see that. You might get slapped by a giant.'

'No – wait – listen to me. Listen to me, Lyonel. If you don't go, you're crazy. Why, you'd dine on it for years. I can just hear you. "Uncle – is that a dragon ?" or "Then I jewtered my ashen spear and crashed into Sir Junkpile and brast his breastbone." You've got to go, Lyonel. We can't stand it if you don't.'

'Well, it might be amusing. Only he means it. No bed if he can help it, even alone. He'll sleep on the ground by preference.'

'Well, that's reputation anyway.'

'No – look, Lyonel. You could pretend to go along with it. Sir Lyonel, knight errant. You could ask him old-fashioned questions and get his opinion about everything. It would be better than a juggler.'

'Well – I—'

'Lyonel, think of it this way. Of course we want to hear you tell it afterwards, but just think who would roll his little fat bottom all over a bed laughing.'

'We'll make up lots of innocent questions to ask him.'

'If you don't go I won't ever speak to you – none of us will.'

'I have thought long as you suggested, sir. I want to go out into the world of marvels and adventures.'

'I am glad,' said Lancelot. 'You will not regret it. It is not well to stay too long in courts and halls.'

'When shall we go, uncle?'

'We must walk carefully. If we proclaim our purpose there will be sadness in the court. It is even possible that the king and queen might forbid our going. Let us prepare quietly and depart in secrecy. If there is sorrow or anger at our going, it will disappear when word of our adventures drifts back.'

Lyonel controlled his laughter, and later at the well he said, 'And then I said, "That is well considered, sir. I will be secret as a sobbet."'

'What's a sobbet?'

'He didn't ask. Why should you? And then I said, "I agree. We will leave like smoke. But it would be amusing to see their faces when they find us vanished."'

They prepared for their journey with such mystery, with guarded words and fingers raised to lips, with whispered conferences in corners, that the hounds in the halls and the pigeons in the towers knew something unusual was in progress. Sir Lancelot and his nephew drew up their plans in secret places so that some of the less intelligent knights reported treason to the king, for they said, 'Why would they whisper together in the rain-swept shadow of the barbican if they are loyal?' To which the queen replied, 'I would be more afraid if they spoke quietly in the great hall.'

In great cloaks, disguised by the folds of the hoods, wind whipping about their ankles, they conferred. 'You must instruct me, sir,' said Lyonel. 'I have never fought or even seen a dragon.'

'Be at ease, my child,' said Lancelot. 'In France I have met dragons and giants. You will see when the time comes. Have you arranged to have the horses taken outside the walls ?'

'I have, sir.'

'And are the squires instructed about secrecy ?'

'They are, sir.'

'We must confess our sins and be shriven,' Lancelot said. 'A knight must be as ready and prepared for his death as for an enemy.'

'I would have forgotten that,' said Lyonel.

The squires imposed secrecy on their damsels, who in turn had the promise of their sisters, who told their lovers only after oaths had sealed their lips, until at last the king said, 'I wish they would be on their way, my dear. They are disturbing the whole city.'

'It will be soon,' said Guinevere. 'Sir Lancelot begged my little blue veil today. He said he wanted to match the colour on his device.'

And when the two errant knights finally crept out of the city in the night, a hundred eyes watched them go and the battlements concealed an audience. Outside the walls, the squires disengaged themselves from their damsels' arms.

They were far away from discovery before the dawn broke, disclosing the world of errantry – a forest deep and green picked out in tapestry against the morning. It was a day which arranged itself for the colour and form of chivalry. A great stag raised his antlered head and watched them pass, fearless in the knowledge that they were not hunting. A peacock in a sunshafted glade spread his great fan and glittered like a jewel, while the arching blue iridescence of his neck and throat screamed like a giant cat. The unfrightened rabbits rose on their haunches, ears erect and front paws tight against their breasts. And the forest rang with carillons of birds. The squires chattered of affairs until Lancelot turned and stilled them with his eyes.

Sir Lyonel choked. 'It seems a proper day for questing, sir.'

'It is a perfect day,' said Lancelot.

'Should I speak or must I keep silence, uncle?'

'That depends. If your words reflect the quest as the day reflects it, if your speech is proud as the stag, noble as the peacock, humble and unafraid as the coneys there, then speak.'

'Are questions fit, sir?'

'If they are fit questions.'

'I am new at questing, sir. But I have heard in the great hall a hundred recountings by returning knights sworn by holy things to tell the truth.'

'If they honour their knighthood, they honour their oaths.'

'How does it happen then that a knight, attended by his squire, sometimes by a retinue, finds himself suddenly alone?'

'I can only tell you that it happens. What more do you wish to know?'

'I love a lady, sir.'

'That is good. Your knighthood requires that you honour all ladies and love one.'

'She did not want me to go away, sir. She asked what was the good of loving if the lovers were parted.'

Sir Lancelot turned quickly and his grey eyes were cold. 'I submit to you that she is not a lady. I hope you have sworn no embarrassing oaths. You must not think of her again.'

'But she is a king's daughter, sir.'

'Silence! Were she the daughter of the Emperor of Africa, were she the golden princess of Tartary, it would make no difference if she did not acknowledge a knight's love, and understand that knightly love is not a coupling of dog and bitch.'

'Yes, sir, yes, my uncle. Don't be angry. It is the question of a young man. You love a lady, sir, a lady who—'

'It is well known, and no secret,' said Lancelot. 'I love the queen. And I will serve her all my days, and I have permanently challenged any qualified knight who may say she is not the fairest and most virtuous lady in all the world. And may she have only honour and joy from my love, as I have sworn.'

'Sir, I meant no disrespect.'

'See you do not then, or you will find your death in it, nephew or not.'

'Yes, my lord. I ask only to be instructed. You, sir, are the greatest knight now living and it is said the most perfect knight in any time past or in years to come. Give me the benefit of your knighthood, sir, for I am young and ignorant.'

'Nephew, perhaps I was overquick, but learn from that. You cannot be too sensitive where your lady is concerned.'

'I thank you for your courtesy, my lord. You are famed throughout the world as perfect knight and perfect lover. Many young knights, such as I am, wish to pattern themselves on you. Must perfect knight, by which is understood perfect lover, never sigh, yearn, suffer, burn, desire, to touch his love?'

Sir Lancelot turned slowly in his saddle and saw that the squires had sidled close to listen. Under his glance they drifted back out of hearing and then out of sight, and they were not seen again until they were wanted.

When the two knights were alone, Sir Lancelot said, 'When I was a child, great Merlin prophesied my greatness. But greatness must be earned. And I have spent my life in helping his prophecy to be true. Now I will answer your question. To sigh for my lady's favour, yes. To yearn for her grace, again yes; to suffer when she is displeased, triply yes; but to burn, to desire, that is not knighthood. Animals drool, serfs sniff and grin after females. No. You have it wrong. You have it very wrong. Could I love my queen, who is wife to my liege king, and desire her without dishonouring all three of us? I hope you find your question answered.'

'Then it is better, sir, to love whom one cannot have?'

'Probably better,' Lancelot said. 'Certainly safer.'

'So many things I want to ask,' said Lyonel. 'Who is so fortunate as I? To ride a-questing with great Lancelot. Do you know, sir, the young knights of my acquaintance, when they are aware I rode with you, will gather like wine flies at a bunghole. They will demand of me, "What did he say?" "How did he look?" "Did you ask him thus and so?" "What did he answer?"'

Sir Lancelot smiled kindly at his nephew. 'Is it so?' he asked.

'More than so, sir. You are the perfect knight of now and then and of a thousand unhatched years. Men will know your deeds written with your sword, but they will ask, "What was he like?" "What did he say?" "Was he gay or sad?" "What did he think about this and that?"'

Sir Lancelot looked to the forest's edge, which bore ahead,

and he said uneasily, 'Why should they ask these things? Aren't deeds enough? Can you tell me? Aren't deeds enough?'

'It's not that, sir. The young men will be looking for greatness in themselves, and they will find parcels and packages not so great, and spoils and tangles of darkness. They will wonder whether you ever had doubts.'

'I had no reason to doubt. Merlin foretold it all. Why should men look for weakness in me? What is their advantage?'

'I can only speak for myself, Sir Uncle. I have many sad faults leaping around my knees like hungry hounds. If I could claim kinship with you, then this greatness would not be out of reach. Perhaps it is so with everyone, that he looks for weakness in the strong to find promise of strength in his weakness.'

Lancelot said angrily, 'I will not throw that bone. If weariness and cold, and hunger, yes, and fear, have found a roosting place in me, do you imagine I will open the gates to doubt and so lose the whole castle? No, the gates are closed and the drawbridge up. Let your young knights stumble in their own darkness. If I were weak they would not find strength but only excuses for their weakness.'

'But, sir, if you close the gates you recognize the enemy.'

'My weapons are sword and lance, not words.'

'That must be how it is,' said Lyonel. 'I shall tell them you have neither fear nor doubt.'

'You do not know that much, young sir. In truthfulness you can only say you saw no evidence, if you do not.'

For a time they rode in silence, and then Sir Lyonel said, 'I must ask it even risking your displeasure, sir.'

'Questions have bored me more often than angered me. Very well, what is your question? Let it be the last.'

'Sir, there is no place in the world where your name is not known.'

'I am told that this is true.'

'And you are known as the world's perfect knight.'

'I have tried to make it so.'

'You are alone in your perfection.'

'Until a better comes along. Anyone may challenge it. But these are statements or opinions. What is the question?'

'Is it enough?'

'What?'

'Are you content with it?'

A black rage shook Sir Lancelot, drew his lips from his teeth. His right hand struck like a snake at his sword hilt and half the silver blade slipped from the scabbard. Lyonel felt the wind of his death blow on his cheek.

Then, in one man he saw a combat more savage than ever he had seen between two, saw wounds given and received and a heart riven to bursting. And he saw victory, too, the death of rage and the sick triumph of Sir Lancelot, the sweat-ringed, fevered eyes hooded like a hawk's, the right arm leashed and muzzled while the blade crept back to its kennel.

'Here is the end of the forest,' said Sir Lancelot. 'I've heard it said the forest stops where the chalk begins. How golden the sun is on the golden grass. Not far from here there is a figure of a giant with a club on a hillside. And in another place I know of a monster white horse. And no one knows who made them or when.'

'Sir—' Lyonel began.

And the greatest knight in the whole world turned to him, smiling. 'Tell them that I was sleepy,' he said. 'Tell them that I was sleepier than I have been in seven years. And tell your young friends that I looked for a little piece of shade to comfort me against the sun.'

'On my left hand, sir, I see an apple tree.'

'So you do. Let us go there, for my eyes are heavy.'

And Lyonel knew how hard the fight had been and how tired the victory, but the prize – the prize was sleep.

Sir Lancelot lay in the grass under the apple tree, his helmet for a pillow, and he fell into the darkest of all the caverns of forgetfulness. Sir Lyonel sat beside his uncle and knew that he had seen greatness beyond reason and courage that made words seem craven and peace that must be earned with agony. And Lyonel felt small and mean and treacherous as a dungfly while Sir Lancelot slept like carven alabaster.

Watching over the sleeping knight, Sir Lyonel thought of the endless talking of young knights gathered to celebrate death without having lived, critics of combat by those whose hands had never held a sword, losers who had laid no wager. He remembered how they said this sleeping knight was too stupid to know he was ridiculous, too innocent to see the life around him, convinced of perfectibility in a heap of evil, romantic and sentimental in a world where reality is overlord, an anachronism before the earth was born. And in his ears he could hear the words of smug failure, weakness, and poverty sneering that strength and richness are illusions, cowardice in the armour of wisdom.

Sir Lyonel knew that this sleeping knight would charge to his known defeat with neither hesitation nor despair and finally would accept his death with courtesy and grace as though it were a prize. And suddenly Sir Lyonel knew why Lancelot would gallop down the centuries, spear in rest, gathering men's hearts on his lance head like tilting rings. He chose his side and it was Lancelot's. He brushed a dungfly from the sleeping face.

The sky was clear and the noonday sun drove a pocket of shade under the lone apple tree. The heat cut a small apple free and Lyonel caught it in the air over Lancelot's face. He bit it and it was green and sour, and malformed with worm, so that he cast it away and spat the bitter pulp on the ground. The rolling plain stretched away to the southward, where it was bounded by a hill ramparted with turf and defended by eight monstrous ditches, an ancient mouldering fortress of the dead gods or a forgotten giant people near enough to gods. The heat shook the distance and put a dream on the fortress and the plain. The growling wings of a bumblebee brought Lyonel's eyes back to the sleeping knight, and he waved the honey-heavy brute away. And Lancelot slept so deeply that his breathing could not be seen. His face was sweet with dignity and innocence and his mouth was hooked upwards in a little smile. Sir Lyonel thought he seemed one under marble enchantment cast by a kindly witch, or a perfect husk from which the soul had sped after a fulfilled life and a peaceful death. The young knight loved this uncle and wanted to protect him from the mould of the little evil which is disappointed meanness of small men who dress their poverty and nakedness in cynicism. He felt lapped by outmoving rings of serene greatness, and he wished to be related to this man by more than blood – perhaps by a deed of high courage, performed by Lyonel and dedicated to Sir Lancelot.

The grass and the summer flowers of gold and blue sang under a chair of bees – and in the distance three heat-warped figures appeared, and after them a fourth, and all of them insubstantial and changing, but now Lyonel felt the beat of flying hoofs on the earth and knew that these were not figures of enchantment that sometimes haunt the earth. As they emerged from the quaking mirage, he saw that they were three mail-clad knights who drove their horses with the desperation of fear, and behind them came a towering armoured man on a foam-flecked stallion, gaining on the fleeing knights. As Sir Lyonel watched, the tall knight closed in like a cloud and swept the last knight from his saddle, and without pause he struck like a falcon and poised and struck again, and the other two went rolling. Then the pursuer swooped back and dismounted and tied the fallen men with their own reins, and he lifted them like bound sheep and flung them face down over their saddles.

Sir Lyonel looked quickly at Sir Lancelot and marvelled that the noise had not awakened him from his tranced sleep. And Lyonel had caught the calm courage, and he thought how glad and proud he would be awakening to find his nephew victorious over so great a knight. He slipped quietly away to do this deed for his uncle. Quickly he mounted and rode out and called the victor to combat. The huge man leaped lightly to his saddle, but Sir Lyonel charged him so savagely that he drove knight and horse clear around, but did not unseat him. When he returned to run again, the big man was sitting quietly looking at him.

'Now that was well struck,' he said. 'And now I see you I am amazed. You are hardly more than a boy in size and still you rocked me more than any man has in my memory. Let us make peace, sir. You are too good a man to tether like these cattle.'

Lyonel looked towards the apple tree where his uncle still slept and he said proudly, 'I will gladly make peace when you have surrendered to me and released your prisoners and begged for mercy. I promise you mercy.'

The big knight regarded him with wonder. 'If you had not given me such a stroke, I would think you insane,' he said. 'Why you are less than half of me. First a man-sized stroke and then man-sized words. Come, let us be friends. It would plague my conscience to hurt such a good little man as you.'

'Yield,' said Sir Lyonel. 'Yield or fight.'

'I won't do either,' said the knight.

Lyonel spurred his horse and plunged in with levelled spear.

In mid-course the big knight dropped his spear and cast off his shield and, as Sir Lyonel's point wavered uncertainly, ducked under the spear, and his right arm, thick as a hawser, circled the young knight's waist and tore him from his saddle. Lyonel fought helplessly against the embrace that tightened about his chest and crushed him until the blood pounded to bursting behind his eyes and he spiralled off into a swoon.

And when his aching senses returned he was face down and bound, bumping along on his own horse bunched with the other three prisoners. After a time they came to a lowering house, moated and walled, and on its oaken gate Lyonel saw many shields nailed up. He knew many of the devices and some were the signs of the fellowship of the Round Table and among them the shield of his older brother Sir Ector de Marys.

Lyonel was thrown on the stone floor of a dim room and his captor stood over him, saying, 'The others have gone to the dungeon, but you I have spared for your bravery and because you nearly unseated me. Come now, yield to me, and give me your promise of loyalty and I will release you.'

Sir Lyonel rolled painfully and looked up. 'Who are you and why have you taken those knights whose shields I saw?'

'My name is Sir Tarquin.'

'That name has a sound of tyranny, sir.'

'You will judge how properly. I have a hatred too big for most men, so heavy that even I am weighed down by it. I hate a knight who killed my brother. In honour of my hatred I have killed a hundred knights and captured more, and all preparing to meet my enemy. But you I love and I will make peace with you if you will gain me.'

'Whom do you hate?'

'Sir Lancelot. He slew my brother Sir Carados.'

'It was a fair fight?'

'What matter? He killed my brother and I will kill him. Will you give me your parole?'

'No,' said Lyonel.

Then rage darkened Sir Tarquin and he stripped armour and underclothing from the young knight and he beat his naked body with thorns until the blood flew and he shouted, 'Yield!'

'No,' said Lyonel, and the thorns tore at his flesh again until for loss of blood he paled and fainted, and then Sir Tarquin, raging and foaming, threw him down the dark stairs to the dungeon floor among his other prisoners. His brother, Sir Ector, was there, and many others who knew him. And when they had wiped his wounds and brought his senses back, he told them weakly how he had left Lancelot sleeping. And the prisoners cried out, 'No one else may beat Sir Tarquin. You did wrong not to waken him. If Lancelot does not find us we are doomed.' And the prisoners moaned in the darkness of the dungeon and wept in helpless misery. But Lyonel remembered the calm, sleeping face and he said softly to himself, 'I must be patient. He will come, Sir Lancelot will come.'

Now leve we thes knyghtes presoners,
and speke we of sir Lancelot de Lake that lyeth
undir the appil-tre slepynge.

The afternoon was thick with heat, the blue sky milky from damp. The high white crowns of thunderheads looked over the hills to the northeast and muttered in the distance. The still, hot, humid air brought flies, sticky and sluggish. A congress of rooks barrelled over, rolling and playing – cawing one another to new flying exploits, and when they saw the horse tied to the apple tree they circled low and inspected the sleeping knight, but a jackdaw tried to gain them and they flew away in disgust. The deserted daw alighted and cautiously inspected the horse and the sleeping man; then reassured, he strode forward like a heavy-shouldered fighter. A great sword lying beside the knight drew the attention of the bird. He tried to remove a red jewel from the pommel, but a rushing black cloud of wings and beak whirled in and drove the thief away. A huge and ancient raven regarded the scene, hopped sideways with wings half spread, then, reassured, approached the sleeping figure with hopscotch jumps, croaking softly to himself. His purple-black feathers were crusty with age. Hopping close, he turned his noble head sideways, inspected the face with one eye and then the other. The feathers under his throat ruffled out and vibrated. 'Hahg,' he croaked softly. 'Dead—Curse!—Dog!—Rat!—A page Christas, alack. Morgan – Morgan!' The great bird sprang aside and the wings of power jerked him into the air, and he flapped powerfully towards a cavalcade, iridescent, warm, in the distance, where four queens rode in slow and unreal pageantry, four queens robed in velvet and crowned, and four armed knights supported a green silken canopy on their spear tips to protect the ladies from the sun. The Queen of the Outer Isles came first, golden of hair as well as of crown, eyes blue as slate when the sea changes, high-coloured cheeks of fast warm blood, her cloak sea-blue lined with sea-grey, her palfrey dappled as a spume-flecked rock. Next came the Queen of North Galys, red of hair, green-eyed, green-robed, with purple under colour in her face, and her horse was red-roan as her hair was roan. The Queen of Eastland followed her – ashen-haired but warm as ashes of roses, eyes of hazel, clothed in a robe of pale lavender. Her horse was white as milk.

Last came Morgan le Fay, Queen of the land of Gore, sister of King Arthur. Black of hair, of eye, of robe, and a horse as black and shining as Satan's heart. Her cheeks were white, the living white of white rose, and her midnight cloak was blacker for its points of ermine.

Before and following the queens under their canopy rode armoured men, rigid and with visors closed. The pageant moved silently without beat of hoof or clink of mail. It took its way against the thunderheads and towards a ditched and ramparted hill called Maiden's Castle, and shunned by daylight folks as a place of ghosts and a cover for witches whereon a turreted castle might rise in a night and be gone by morning. Only those schooled and proved in necromancy foregathered there.

The great raven dropped from the sky and lighted on the black trappings of Morgan's black steed and he croaked softly to his mistress, and cocked his head when she questioned him.

'Croak,' he said. 'Dog!—Pig!—Death!—Pretty—Pretty—Lady!'

Then Morgan shrilled laughter. 'A titbit, sisters,' she cried.

'A honeyed plum.' She threw the raven into the air and he led the way towards the apple tree where Lancelot slept.

The wind of afternoon printed its invisible shape on the grass and flowers of the plain where the four unearthly queens dismounted and moved cautiously towards the apple tree. Lancelot's tethered war horse snorted and stamped, laid back his ears, and showed the whites of his eyes, for horses are particularly sensitive to cracks and breaches in normality. And still the knight slept, although his face twitched and his right hand opened and slowly closed.

'It cannot be a natural sleep,' said Morgan quietly. 'I wonder whether some other has control of him.' She stood over him, looking down. 'No,' she said. 'No enchantment here – only weariness, month weariness, year weariness.' She raised her black eyes and saw her lovely sister queens licking their lips like wolves about a bleeding slaughter.

'You know him then ?'

'Of course,' said she of the Outer Isles. 'It is Lancelot.'

'I told you it was a sweetmeat. But sisters of the earth should not bite sisters. I know that we will strive for him. But let it not be with tooth and claw. Also, I know you well enough, my dears, to be sure you will not share.'

The Queen of North Galys asked sweetly, 'What do you propose ?'

Now Lancelot's body shuddered, his head turned back and forth like a man in fever, and he licked his lips and groaned.

From under her cloak Morgan brought out a small, long-necked bottle of lactucarium, iridescent with age. She unstoppered it and, leaning down, poured a few thick black drops on Lancelot's lips, and as he licked his lips and grimaced at the bitterness, Morgan le Fay spread a soft-spoken hood of magic words over him and he drew a deep, shuddering breath and sank into a sable sleep. Morgan did not speak softly now, for there was no chance of his awakening. 'This I propose,' she said. 'That we carry this prize with us to Maiden's Castle and then compete for him, but with such silken subtlety that when the winner grasps the prize the dove will think he has chosen the falcon's talons. Is it a bargain, sisters ?'

The others laughingly agreed, for each one thought that in this kind of tournament she had no peer. Then Lancelot was laid upon his shield and two knights carried him between them. The stately progress moved like figures painted on a wall towards the prodigious prehistoric fortress on the hill. The sun went down as they entered the narrow approach between a steep wall of earth and stars flickered to life as they crossed narrow causeways over the deep successive ditches. It was night when they emerged on the ramparted summit, a grassy pasturage, rock-strewn with the midden of a thousand years of building and destroying. Then, as the parade of queens crossed the great enclosure, a castle built itself on the southern point, rose course by course to battlements, and towers sprouted from the corners. As it was completed, lights shone from slitted windows and sentries mushroomed between the castellations. When they came to the place where a moat should be, there was a moat with stars reflected in its waters and the dim white hulls of slow-moving swans. And at the entrance a drawbridge grew suddenly and then crashed down, the iron cage of the portcullis clanked slowly up, and the brass-studded leaves of the gates creaked open, and when the pageantry had entered, the drawbridge raised, the portcullis rattled down, gates closed, and then the castle became insubstantial and then transparent like a thin cloud, and the wind dispersed the shreds, leaving a rock-strewn plateau with sheep grazing under the stars.

Sir Lancelot crawled painfully awake out of unconsciousness compounded of drugs and enchantment. In the darkness his head throbbed with flashing light and he was cold with dampness creeping into his marrow. His searching hand discovered that he was disarmed and dressed only in the light jacket and pants he wore under his mail. Exploring further, his fingers found a cut stone floor coated with cold greasy moisture, while his nose made out the smells of old suffering and fear and hopelessness and filthy death, the sour odours that penetrate the walls of dungeons.

He sat up painfully and embraced his knees, trying to penetrate the fusty darkness. He put out his hand and then drew it back, fearing to know what his fingers might find. For a long time he sat drawn into himself, trying to make as small a target as possible for the fear that waited in the darkness around him. Then he heard light footsteps approaching and he closed his eyes tightly and made a passionate child's prayer for protection, and when he looked again he was blinded by the flame of a single candle. It was a moment before he could make out the damsel holding it, who said to him, 'What cheer, Sir Knight?'

He considered this question carefully – studied stone walls without windows and the thick oaken door with a small iron grille and a lock as big as a shield, and then he glanced back at the maiden. 'What cheer indeed!' he said.

'It was only a manner of speaking, sir. My father says it is proper to ask what cheer of a knight.'

'Would it be proper for a knight to ask where he is and how he got here and why in the name of the four Evangelists your father holds me here?'

'It's not my father, sir. He is not here. You see, I myself am a kind of prisoner. I was sitting in my father's manor hall, combing lambs' wool to make yarn and wondering how I could help my father at next Tuesday's tournament, because, you see, last Tuesday he had a fall and he is hard to live with when he is defeated – I guess any knight is.'

Lancelot broke in, 'Fair damsel – for the love of God's body, tell the last first. Who holds me here?'

'I've forgotten your supper,' said the girl. 'It's just outside.'

'Wait, damsel – who——?'

She was gone and the light with her, but in a moment she returned with a wooden bowl piled with bones and soaked bread, like a dog's dinner. 'It isn't very good,' she said, 'but they told me to bring it.'

'Who?'

'The queens.'

'What queens?'

She put the bowl on the stone floor beside him and stood the candle beside it to free her fingers for counting. 'The Queen of Gore', she ticked her on her little finger, 'the Queen of the Isles, the Queen of North Galys, and – let's see – Gore, Isles, Galys. Oh, yes, the Queen of Eastland. That's four, isn't it?'

'And what a four!' said Lancelot. 'I know them all – witches, enchantresses, devils' daughters. Did they bring me here?'

'They are beautiful', said the damsel. 'And their gowns and jewels – you would have to see them to believe them—'

'Listen to me.'

'Yes, they brought you here, sir, and me also, for I was sitting in my father's hall, combing lambs' wool.'

'I know, and suddenly you were here. I went to sleep under an apple tree in the sun and I am here. What do these wicked queens want with me?'

'I don't know sir. You see, I only got here and they said to bring your supper and lock up after. I'll look around, sir. Maybe I can tell you more in the morning. I must go. They told me not to speak and to hurry back, as you might eat me.'

'Can you leave the candle?'

'I'm afraid not, sir. I couldn't find my way out of here without it.'

When she had gone and the darkness closed down, the knight clawed in his bowl and gnawed his supper from the bones while he thought about the strange and frightening creatures who had made him prisoner.

He had two reasons for fear. In his long and relentless struggle with himself and with the world to become the perfect knight, few women had crossed his attention. Thus, in his ignorance he found a fear of unknown things. And second, he was a straightforward, simple man; the sword, not the mind, was the tool of his greatness. The purposes and means of necromancy, demons, and secrets he found foreign and fearful. His few failures and fewer defeats had been accomplished through enchantment and now he was taken prisoner by that same black and midnight art. His heart quaked in the darkness and he felt the stone walls press in on him. His heart pounded and his stomach pressed against his chest and shortened his breath. But this was no alien sensation, for Lancelot, like all great practitioners of any art, was a sensitive and a nervous man. An opponent in the field meeting the cold perfection of his command of weapons would have thought him nerveless, little knowing his sick wretchedness before the fight began. And while he quaked at the barrier, waiting for the trumpets, his quick eye nevertheless automatically observed, tabulated, and stored away every move and gesture and tendency of his opponent. So even now when he was near to panic, his second mind probed his opponents, for although they were ladies and queens, they were also his enemies, and enemies must have purpose and means and direction.

They could not hate him, he thought, for he had not injured them. Therefore, revenge was not their end. Robbing was out of the question, for they were bloated with possessions and he had nothing but his armour and his fame. What, then, could be their purpose? They must want something of him, something perhaps he did not know he had, a service, a secret. It was beyond him and he gave up, but his fighting mind out of habit went on with its analysis. If a man flinched under a certain stroke, or cut short on the near side, there was usually a reason – an old wound, or even an old sorrow. A man took the profession of arms for clear and definable reasons, but why did man or woman study the despicable arts of necromancy?

Lancelot was lost again, and he reined and spurred his mind to a new course when a picture came to him, but a living picture in the round and clear and brilliant as cathedral glass. He saw a young, determined Lancelot, only then called Galahad, go sprawling to the hoof-mauled tourney ground under the blunt lance of a fourteen-year-old. Again Galahad tried, and again flew through the air. His short chin set and his lips were blue with determination. And the third time the blunt lance tore him from his saddle, and when he struck the earth a scream of pain went up his spine. The tough chevroned dwarf, wide as a barrel, carried the boy to his mother, bubbling with pain. 'The other boy was too big my lady,' the squire explained. 'But he's outclassed his age and there's no holding Galahad here.' There was holding him easily for a long time, for he couldn't move. They put bags of sand against his back to keep him still. And as he lay wedged while his wrenched spine mended, his opponent grew treetop tall in the boy's mind. Waking and asleep the blunt spear wiped him from his horse until he found a poultice for his pride. Under his left arm there was a tiny knob so small that only he knew it was there. Three turns to the right and half a turn back with the fingers of his left hand, and in mid-course he grew to a black cloud and overwhelmed the fourteen-year-old. But the secret knob could do more than that. Two turns right and two left, and he could fly and hover and dart. Sometimes in the joust he left his horse and flew ahead and struck the giant bay down – and last – a straight push in and he became invisible. He would wait anxiously to be alone in his sandbags to bring out his dream. It was odd that he had forgotten all about it when his real ability began to grow. And suddenly Lancelot, in the darkness of his prison, knew about magic and necromancy and those who practised it. 'So that's it,' he thought. 'Poor things – poor unhappy things.'

It is not true as is romantically presumed that people frightened or injured or persecuted are wakeful. More often than not they retire to sleep to be free of trouble for a time. A man like Lancelot, tempered in soldiery, seasoned and tanned by perils, lays up supplies of sleep as he does food or water, knowing its lack will reduce his strength and dull his mind. And although he had slept away part of the day, the knight retired from cold and darkness and the unknown morrow and entered a dreamless rest and remained in it until a soft light began to grow in his cell of naked stone. Then he awakened and wrung his muscles free of cold cramp and again embraced his knees for warmth. He could see no source of light. It came equally from everywhere as dawn does before the rise of the sun. He saw the mortared stones of his cell stencilled with patches of dark slime. And as he looked, designs formed on the walls; formal rounded trees covered with golden fruit and curling vines with flowers as frankly invented as are those of an illuminated book, a benign sheltering tree, and under it a unicorn glowing white, with horn and neck lowered in salute to a maiden of bright needlework who embraced the unicorn, thus proving her maidenhood. Then a broad soft bed shivered and grew substantial in the corner of the cell, a bed with a cover of purple velvet on which great cushions like soft bright jewels were piled. The air grew warmer from a heraldic sun in glory which formed itself with wavy rays on the ceiling sky.

Sir Lancelot was a simple knight who had not learned to trust his eyes at one moment and deny them the next. He stood up and saw and felt the long rich ochre robe which fell to his ankles. He went to the bed and lay on its shrinking softness and crossed his wrists behind his head in time to see four rich and cushioned thrones take semblance and then form and then stabilize on the far side of the cell while a rich carpet grew like quick grass on the stone floor.

An odour like a potpourri of rose leaves and cinnamon, lavender and frankincense, spikenard and cloves, filled the room, and the tapestries moved under a little summer wind which came from nowhere.

'What will be, will be in comfort,' Lancelot told himself.

For a few moments there was a waiting silence like a stage all decked and furnished before the play begins, and then a rank of lutes from bass to treble struck a slow, soft, rhythmic pace that informed the mind of the pace of princesses in stately procession to a sovereign's coronation. Only the prison door remained – an ugly reminder of studded oak and rusty iron.

And now it opened of itself and the four lovely queens flowed in to rhythm, pausing to touch a little foot between each step. They took their places on the thrones and they were perfect in beauty like waxen flowers. Their white jewelled hands lay quietly on the arms of their thrones and their mouths smiled serenely as they looked at the knight lying on the bed. The music fell away and there came a silence such as a seashell gives to the ear.

Then Lancelot stood and saluted them. 'Greetings, my ladies, and good welcome.'

They answered in unison of a litany. 'Greetings, Sir Lancelot of the Lake, son of King Ban of Benwick, first and best knight of Christendom. Welcome and good cheer.'

'Shall I repeat your titles, my queens?' he asked. 'I know them well. You are Queen Morgan le Fay of the land of Gore, half-sister of great Arthur the King, daughter of the Duke of Cornwall and of that fair Igraine who became Uther Pendragon's queen. And you are Queen of the Outer Isles—'

Morgan said, 'No need to repeat them all if you know them.'

For a moment he studied their perfect brows, their brilliant, shining eyes, their smooth and lovely cheeks.

'My ladies,' he said at last, 'if time in darkness has not confused me, it was yesterday that I went to sleep under an apple tree on a sunny plain with my nephew Sir Lyonel beside me. I awakened in a cold and bitter cell, stripped of my arms, a prisoner: am I your prisoner?'

'A prisoner of love,' said Morgan. And when the others tried to break in she said coldly, 'Silence, my sisters. Let me speak. Afterwards you may have your chance.' She turned back to Lancelot. 'Sit, my lord,' she said. 'And you are right. We took you prisoner.'

'Where is Sir Lyonel?'

'You were alone. No one was with you.'

Lancelot sat on the edge of the velvet bed. 'What can you want with me?' he asked, puzzled.

Three queens laughed in little shrieks and Morgan smiled.

'A willing prisoner is easier to handle,' she said. 'Therefore, I will explain. We four have everything we can wish for: lands, wealth, power, and pretty things beyond belief. Besides these, through our arts we have access to things beyond the world and under it, but, more than this, if something we wish does not exist, we have the power to create it. You must then understand that to us new playthings are very rare. And when we saw the best knight in the world sleeping, we thought that you are that rarity, a thing we do not have. And so we took you. But there is one thing we do not do, because it is not in our natures. We do not share. And so we must contend for you. But in the past when we have contended, it has happened that the prize was so ripped and torn that the winner did not want it. You must agree that even the best knight in the world, if he were a dismembered bloody pulp, would not be worth possessing. Wait, sisters, I am almost finished. We have decided to let you make your choice of one of us, and all have sworn to be bound by it. I hope it will be so. These queens have not always felt the bind of oaths.'

Lancelot said, 'If I chose none of you, what then?'

'Why, then I am afraid the darkness and cold stone will close around you. Even the best of knights would not live long, but if he lived too long I think food and water would be removed. But forget that grimness. Each one of us will plead her case. It will be amusing for us to plead, a new experience. I will be last. Will you begin, my lady of North Galys?'

'Gladly, sister.' She tossed her head and her hair leaped like red flame. She dropped her lids, partly covering her emerald eyes.

She moved towards Lancelot like a great lovely cat, and when she stood near to him he smelled the nerve-disturbing odour of her body, and it was musk. His senses stirred in a small agony, and his tongue felt the salt taste of rut. Her voice purred low and deep as though it vibrated her whole body.

'I think you know what I can promise you – sensations you are only dimly aware of – ecstasy mounting, growing, swelling, bursting – endless and no satiety, no end until you know the crucifixion of love, and scream for the cross, and help to drive the nails while every nerve, every white writhing nerve, joins the demonic and whips itself to rage of exulting and raging passion. You lick your lips. You think you know. What you know is only a whisper beside the pandemonium I promise you.'

He was breathing in heaving bursts when she went back to her chair and sat with a small cat smile of triumph watching him. And Morgan said, 'You devil. That was not fair. Don't answer, perfect knight, before you've heard the others.'

'Is it fair to let him cool off?' said the green-eyed queen.

'The Queen of the Outer Isles,' said Morgan le Fay.

The golden-haired sea queen sat quietly on her throne and her eyes were dancing, laughter-soaked.

'It was a brilliant performance, sir,' she said. 'I am the first to admit it. The place still reeks of it. I do not want to criticize my dear opponent, but it seems to me that after a while one might tire even of her versatility in a rather simple activity at which goats are better versed than men and rabbits superior to all others. You might one morning wish for coarse bread to take away the taste of spices. And those whipped nerves might conceivably thicken and grow dull. This – art – has been known to change from lovely to loathsome in a flick of time.'

The roan-haired bared sharp teeth. 'Get to your own business,' she snarled. 'Let mine alone.'

'Sweetly, sister – gently. Sir Best Knight, I think you will agree that no state, climate, activity, pleasure, pain, joy, sorrow, defeat, or victory does not with surfeit become tiresome. My gift to you is change. One day will echo with laughter like a rippled blue pool smiling in the sun while wavelets chuckle among mossy stones; the next will mother storm, fierce, wild crashing violence – mind-torn – wonderful. I promise that every joy will be emphasized with a little pain, rest will follow riot, heat alternate with cold. Lusts of the flesh and mind will bring cool ascetic healing and sharpenings. I promise that no experience will blunt itself upon itself. In a word, I will extend your feelings, senses, thoughts, to the outmost limit, so that never will you feel the universal blight of waste, of curiosity unsatisfied, possibilities unexplored. I offer life. You will be king one day and work-ruined serf the next, to give your kingship value. Where others offer one thing, I offer everything set in layers of contrast.' Her eyes were slaty grey now, sombre, and with a glint of coming tempest. 'Finally, I offer you a proper death, a high and shining death as the final ornament of a proper high and shining life.' She glanced in triumph at the contending queens.

Morgan said, 'She brought out all of her treasures, didn't she? That promise would keep her busy. It would take some doing.'

Sir Lancelot rested his elbows on his knees and his chin in his cupped hands. The scars of old wounds on his face stood out white and his eyes were slitted, shining between half-closed lids. The questing queen could not read his thoughts.

The Queen of Eastland sighed. Ashes of roses she was, soft and sweet and clothed in lavender, and in her hazel eyes there seemed to live pity, haven, and understanding linked with forgiveness.

'Poor, weary knight,' she said quietly. 'My friends here have seen you as they themselves are – all lust and restlessness – these are their specialities. I know that every man has these two hungers, some more and others less. I have an advantage over my competitors, Sir Lancelot; you see, I know your mother, little Galahad.'

Morgan laughed and the other two cried 'Shame!'

Lancelot's head jerked up and his eyes glinted dangerously. But the Lady of Eastland continued softly, 'Queen Elaine of Benwick across the sea, a wife to great King Ban, Elaine the precious queen, and beautiful so that ambassadors from all the world forgot their missions when they looked at her. But she did not forget a snub-nosed urchin with a dirty face named Galahad. After the formal brilliant theatre of the court in which she played her part, she never forgot or was too tired to climb the circling turret stairs to carry a little cake to a child who had forgotten to wash his hands. No embassy ever kept her from a tearful child in trouble. And wars and butchery about the walls did not dull the passionate tragedy of a grubby finger cut with a new knife, weeping little tears of blood. And when the fever came she dissolved the world and did not return until one small freckled forehead cooled and restored the world again.'

Lancelot sprang up, crying, 'Stop it! Oh! Foul, oh! Rottenness. Look! Fingers of both hands crossed. And here's a paternoster across your face.'

Queen Morgan muttered, 'Are you offering to be a mother to him, dear?'

'I offer the peace he never found anywhere else, the safety and warmth he still seeks, praise for his virtues, and a gentle and compassionate conscience for his faults. Sit down, fair knight. I meant no disrespect. I know that Guinevere resembles Queen Elaine in looks – but that is all. Think what I offer you.'

'I will not listen.'

'Think of it.'

'I do not hear.'

'But you will remember. Think of it.'

'Ladies, I have had enough,' he said. 'I am your prisoner. Send for men. Do what you want with me, but be sure I will go down fighting. You have failed.'

Queen Morgan's voice cut like a scimitar. 'I have not failed,' she said. 'My clever little coven sisters have offered you bright-coloured shreds of a whole garment, broken pieces of a holy figure. I offer you the whole of which all else is part – I offer power. If you want harlotry in fancy dress, power will get it for you. Admiration? – a whole world aches to kiss its backside with slobbering lips. A crown? Power and a little knife will place it on your head. Change? With power you can try on cities like hats, or smash them when you tire of them. Power attracts loyalty and requires none. The will to power keeps a baby suckling grimly long after he is fed, counsels a child to take his brother's toy, reaps a gaggling harvest of concupiscent girls. What drives a knight through tortures to his prize or death? The power of fame. Why does a man heap up property he cannot use? Why does a conqueror take countries he will never see? What makes the hermit grovel in the black filth of a cell but the promise of power, or at least influence in heaven? And do the humble mad saints reject the power of intercession? What crime is there that does not become a virtue in the hands of power? And is not virtue itself a kind of power? Philanthropy, good deeds, charity, are they not mortgages on the currency of future power? It is the one possession that does not flag or become tedious, for there is never enough of it and an old man in whom the juices of all other desires are dried up will crawl on his tottering knees towards his grave still grabbing with frantic hands for power.

'My sisters have laid out cheese for the mice of small desires. They courted sensations, restlessness, and memory. I do not offer you a gift, but the ability, the right, and the duty to take all gifts, anything you can conceive, and when you weary of it, to smash it like a pot and throw it on the midden heap. Best of all, I offer you power over men and women, over their bodies, their fears, their loyalties, and their sins. This is the sweetest power of all. For you can let them run a little and stop them short of heaven with a casual claw. And when your contempt for this nastiness finally sickens you, you can shrivel them in writhing clots the way you'd put salt on a regiment of slugs and see them melt down in their own slime.

'My sisters spoke to your senses. I speak to your mind. My gift – a ladder to climb to the stars, who are your brothers and your peers, and from there to look down and for amusement stir up the anthill of the world.'

Morgan le Fay was not playing gifted tricks. Her words were armed with passionate honesty and they rang like a battle axe on a bronze shield.

Sir Lancelot stared at her, unbelieving, for her face had become a catapult firing red-hot words against his defence.

'What is this? What *is* power?' he asked.

'What is it? Power is itself – whole – self-contained, self-sufficient, self-sustaining and unassailable, except by power. A sense of power makes all other gifts and attributes seem puny. That is my gift.' She leaned back in her throne, panting and sweating, and the other three queens had melted under the heat of her. Then all four returned their eyes to Lancelot, bright flat eyes of active but casual curiosity. So might they watch a stallion for his response to the iridescent shells of cantharides or a rival's forehead for the first antimony sweat.

Lancelot with his finger traced figures against the nap of his ochre robe, a square and a triangle. He erased them and made a circle and a cross side by side, then circled the cross and crossed the circle. His face was puzzled and sad. At length he looked up at Morgan. He said gently, 'And that is why you twice tried to murder your brother the king.'

She spat at him. 'Half-brother and half-king. A weak king. What does he know about power? I tell you, in the world of power, weakness is a sin – the only sin – and it is punished with death. This is very interesting, of course. But we did not come here to discuss sin. Come, Sir Best Knight. We have made our offer. It remains for you to make your choice.'

'Choice?' he asked blankly.

'Don't pretend you don't remember. You are to choose among us.'

He shook his head slowly. 'I have no choice,' he said. 'I am a prisoner.'

'Nonsense, we've given you a choice. Are we not beautiful?'

'I don't know, my lady.'

'That is ridiculous. Of course you know. There are no more beautiful women in the world or any half so beautiful, we've seen to that.'

'I guess that's what I mean. You chose your faces and your bodies, didn't you, and by your arts created them.'

'What of that? They are perfect.'

'I don't know what you started with. I don't know what you are. You can change appearance, I believe.'

'Of course we can. What difference does that make? Surely you aren't such a fool as to think Guinevere as beautiful as we?'

'But you see, ladies, Guinevere has the face and body and soul of Guinevere. It's all there and always has been. Guinevere is Guinevere. One can love Guinevere knowing what he loves.'

'Or hate her,' Morgan said.

'Or hate her, my lady. But your faces are not you. They are only pictures you have drawn of what you would like to be. A face, a body, grows and suffers with its possessor. It has the scars and ravages of pain and defeat, but also it has the shining of courage and love. And to me, at least, beauty is a continuation of all of those.'

'Why do we listen to his chattering?' Eastland cried angrily.

'Because we may learn, sister. We have, it seems, made an error. It is a matter for experiment. Go on, sir,' Morgan said, and her eyes were surfaced and expressionless like the eyes of a snake.

Lancelot said, 'Once on a night I stood in an open window looking out. I saw red eyes and into the torchlight came a great she-wolf who raised her head and looked into my eyes, and she opened her grinning mouth, and the great fangs and tongue were gouted with new blood. "Hand me a spear," I called, and the wise man beside me at the window said, "It will do no good. That is Morgan le Fay giving service to the moon." '

'Who was he? He was a liar.'

'No, my lady. He was not a liar and he was very wise.'

'Do you mention this to insult me?'

'No – I don't think so. I mention it because I wonder which is you – the lovely woman or the wolf, or something in between.'

'I don't want him now,' said she of the Outer Isles. 'He is a fool. He thinks too much.'

Lancelot smiled ruefully. 'Men have always been puzzled by wizards and enchantresses,' he said. 'Yes, and afraid – terribly afraid.

'This morning in the cold and dark, waiting on the pleasure of your ladyships, a memory came to me of a time when as a child with an injured back I became for a little while a magician, and suddenly I thought I understood – but understanding does not remove the fear. It increases it.'

'Are we to listen to this discussion, ladies? Children! He is insulting. I will turn his legs to snakes.' North Galys giggled. 'What a good idea. And the snakes would crawl in different directions and—'

'Listen!' said Morgan. 'Go on, son of a pig. Tell us why your great discovery makes you afraid. I am always glad to hear such things. It stimulates the imagination.'

Lancelot stood up and then sat down again. 'I am hungry,' he said. 'There was not much meat on the bones you sent.'

'Why should there have been? The dogs had them first.

Nevertheless, remember them. They may be your last food. Go on about fear.'

'Maybe it's too simple, madame. But you know how children, when they are forbidden something they want, sometimes scream and storm and sometimes even hurt themselves in rage. Then they grow quiet and vengeful. But they are not strong enough to revenge themselves on the one they consider their oppressor. Such a one sometimes stamps on an ant, saying, "That's for you, Nursie", or kicks a dog and calls him brother, or pulls the wings from a fly and destroys his father. And then, because his world has disappointed him, he builds his own world where he is king, where he rules not only men and women and animals but clouds and stars and sky. He is invisible, he flies. No authority can keep him in or out. In his dream he builds not only a world but remakes himself as he would wish to be. I guess that's all. Usually he makes peace with the world and works out compromises so that the two will not hurt each other badly. There it is, you see.'

'What you say is true, but what then ?'

'Well, some few do not make peace. And some of these are locked away as hopelessly insane and full of fantasy. But there are others more clever who, through black arts, learn to make the dream substantial. This is enchantment and necromancy. Not being wise enough or kind enough, the magic manufactured world does not function and many are injured and many killed by its ill design. And then rage comes as to the child, destructive rage, vindictive hate. There lies the fear, for wizards and witches are children, living in a world they made without the leavening of pity or the mathematics of organization. And what could be more frightening than a child with total power ? A spear and sword are terrible, God knows. That is why the knight who carries them is first taught pity, justice, mercy, and only last – force.

'I am afraid, my ladies, for you are crippled, vengeful children with power. And I am your prisoner.'

'Let him burn with the fires of hell,' Eastland cried, and her face was white and bloated.

The red-haired witch of North Galys threw herself on the floor, her hooked fingers clawing the stones. She arched her back and beat her forehead on the floor and screamed until

Morgan raised both arms, palms forward. Sir Lancelot crossed his fingers tightly under his robe. He heard the magic words – and the darkness closed like a fist, and the air chilled, and he lay naked on the stones.

For a castle which was a figment of magic the dungeon where Sir Lancelot lay was remarkably strong and well built, with all of the discomforts and damp unpleasantness of age and permanence. The knight did not long remain stretched on the stone floor, for his knighthood too was well built and permanent, its foundations fixed in the best and bravest materials of the human spirit. He stood and felt his way through the fetid darkness to the wall and along the wall to the iron-bound oaken door. It was locked, of course, but through the grille he could smell the chill wind in the corridor.

Perhaps he must die, but if he must the code required that he approach his death as though it were a part of life, and if any chink appeared in the inevitable, he must seize it instantly and with all of his strength, for if there were flaws in the knightly law, humble acceptance of injustice and force were not among them. A man could accept death with a good heart and gaily if he had exhausted every honourable means to avoid it, but no man worth his spurs crawled to his fate or bowed his neck to the stroke. He knew it was no good feeling for a weapon in his cell. There was no loose stone, no balk of wood, no nail, to arm his nakedness. His only cutting tools were teeth and fingernails, his club a fist, his ropes the muscles of his arms and legs. He might be left as Merlin was left, alone and helpless, to die of dark and hunger and cold. But if he were right and his captors were violent and vengeful children, they would not be able to forbear watching the suffering of their victim and gloating over his struggle to live. He thought again of Merlin, whom he remembered prophesying about him as a little boy standing braced against his lady mother's knee. What of that prophecy he might have forgotten Queen Elaine had kept alive for him. He would become the best knight in the world, Merlin had said. Well, now the world agreed that it was so – the prophecy had come true – more reason to trust the latter part. After a long and lusty life, he would die of love, or grief of love – but love. There was as little love as there was light in this grim place, and save for his formal knightly love for Guinevere, there was no love in Lancelot to break his heart. Therefore, this was not his death time. It was his duty under chivalry to accept whatever God might send, but also even God expected him to use what endowments he had.

His pondering made the dark less black and the cold less freezing. If this was not his death time, then he must take advantage of any opportunity that might offer, even anticipate it. When the dark and evil queens came to luxuriate in his pain, their weapons and armour lay in magic arts. And Lancelot knew, as did everyone, that necromantic tactics required certain invariable ingredients. The hands must engage in formulary gestures and the voice must utter ritual syllables. Robbed of either of these, an enchanter was helpless as a sheep. If these enemies thought they could bring about his death, they differed with Merlin and Merlin was the greater, and this meant that for all their powers they could not see the future, or penetrate his thinking. If he stood silently behind the door then, they would not know he was there. And if he pinned the arms of the first in to prevent gestures and with his free hand covered the mouth to stifle spells, and meanwhile protected his rear from counterattack with shouted paternosters, he might succeed. At least it was worth a try, and a try – a headlong try – was all the rules of chivalry required.

His fingers searched the edges of the door and confirmed that it opened inwards, as it must. If it were otherwise a prison door might be torn from its hinges by the might of frantic prisoners, but seated against heavy lintel and stone frames, it was secure. Thus he would have the shelter of the opening door. But if they came, when would they come? Sometimes a man was left until darkness and hunger and despair ground down his spirit to a craven babbling pulp. But these were women with the petulance of children, and patience was not in their nervous natures. Also, they were arrogant and angry. They would not let their fury cool. But long soldiering had instructed Lancelot. For flurry and clash of arms there were a hundred hours of waiting, and a good soldier learned waiting.

Sir Lancelot leaned against the wall and called up another campaigner's trick, that of sleeping lightly while standing up.

At intervals he awakened and rubbed his hands together to supple them against the cold.

He did not know what time had passed when a sound aroused his sentry ear – soft footsteps distant in the corridor. His heart leapt, for only one person was approaching, and lightly, almost secretly it seemed. No guard with iron-shod feet and clashing sword. Then a little light was visible through the grille and Lancelot stepped back to take advantage of the opening door.

The huge lock turned very slowly and as quietly as its rusty mechanism permitted. The hinges puled, and a ribbon and then a streak of light came through, and as a figure entered Lancelot leaped. His right arm imprisoned the arms and sent the candle flying and brought back the dark. His left hand jammed against a soft mouth and he cried loudly, 'Our Father Who art in Heaven, hallowed be Thy Name. Thy kingdom come—' He paused, for there was no resistance from the soft small body of his prisoner. 'Who are you ?' he whispered hoarsely, and a gurgle came from behind his restraining palm. He released it a little, ready to clamp it back.

'Let me go. I am the damsel who brought your dinner.'

His arms fell to his sides and he shook with the great chill of tension long-held and suddenly released.

'Now we have no light,' the small voice said.

'Never mind that. Where are the queens ?'

'In the great kitchen. I saw them through the door. They've a pot on the fire big enough to scale a pig. And they are putting things in it I wouldn't care to mention, and some of them alive. They look like ancient white-haired hags and they are cooking up a brew potent enough to rip the gates from Camelot.'

'Did they send you here ?'

'Oh no, my lord. They would put me in the pot if they knew.'

'Do you know where my armour is – my sword ?'

'In the gatehouse. I put them there myself.'

'My horse ?'

'I stabled him and fed him too.'

'Good. We will go now.'

'Wait, sir. Is it true you are Sir Lancelot ?'

'I am.'

'There are twelve doors and twelve locks before you are free.'

'Well?'

'I can unlock them, sir.'

'Then do it.'

'Or not, Sir Lancelot.'

'Damsel, we must hurry. What are you talking about?'

'Next Tuesday, sir, my father fights in tournament against those who defeated him.'

'What of that?'

'If you will give me your word to help him win, I will unlock the doors.'

'By my Saviour's Blessed Heart,' he cried, exasperated. 'The gates of hell are yawning and you bargain.'

'He is impossible to live with when he loses, sir. Will you give me your word?'

'Yes, yes, of course. Now let us go.'

'We can't until you know what you are to do.'

'Then tell me – quickly. The hellish four may come.'

'Oh! I don't think so soon, sir. They are deep in cooking and they are sipping that dark magic simple that comes from Hind or Cipango or some outlandish place. A holy hermit told my father it is the evil blood of white poppies—'

'Damsel—' he said. 'What do I care whose blood it be?'

'Well, only that after a little time it causes sleep. I think the queens will sleep.'

He sighed – defeated. 'It is as practical to hurry an acorn towards treeness as to urge a damsel when her mind is set. Very well, my dear – in your own good snail-paced time. What is your father's name?'

'Sir Knight, he is Sir Bagdemagus, and he was foul rebuked at the last tournament.'

'I know your father well,' said Lancelot, 'a good and noble knight, and by the faith of my body he shall have my services and you also.'

'Thank you, sir. Now you must know that ten miles to the west there is an abbey of white sisters. Go there and wait, and I will bring my father to you.'

'I promise as I am a true knight,' said Lancelot. 'Now let us go. Tell me, is it day or night?'

'It is night, sir. Now we must feel our way along the corridor and up the stairs. Take my hand, for if we lose ourselves in this hive, we are lost.'

Twelve locks she turned and opened, twelve protesting doors, and in the gatehouse she helped to arm him as a knight's daughter should. She brought his horse and gentled him while he saddled. Then he mounted and said, 'Damsel, I shall not fail by the Grace of God.'

He rode out of the castle gate and across the echoing draw-bridge and turned to wave farewell, but no castle was there – only the star-girt sky and the east wind bowing the grasses on the embattled hill, and the shuddering cry of a long-eared owl hunting moles in the meadowland. Then Lancelot sought the entrance of the walled plateau and his eyes, grown accustomed to the lightless cell, found the night brilliant under the stars. He crossed the ditches and descended to the plain, but finding no road or path, he took a direction he thought was westward.

He rode for many hours until his head reeled with the weariness of safety after tense and deadly danger, and at length he saw a pavilion pitched under a tree and turned his horse towards it. He called out courteously to warn its owner, and when no answer came, he dismounted and looked inside and saw a sweet soft bed and no one there.

'I will sleep here,' he decided. 'No one could refuse me a little rest.' He tethered his horse nearby to feed. Then he removed his armour and placed his sword handy and laid himself down in the bed and almost instantly he fell asleep. And for a time the way took him into the dark and trackless caverns of rest, but then he emerged and ranged in the forests and pastures of his memories and his desires. And then it seemed a lovely woman lay with him, embracing and kissing him, voluptuous and eager, and in his sleep the knight happily repaid kiss with kiss and embrace with searching caress until his anticipation floated him to the surface of sleep and he felt a bearded cheek against his ear and a hard-muscled arm about his waist. Then with a war cry he leaped from the bed, reaching for his sword, and his companion bounded after him, and they two embraced again in combat, gouging and biting, rolling, kicking, dancing like cats. They rolled fighting and scratching out of the tent as the dawn was spilling from the east. Then Lancelot took a bulldog's grip on his opponent's throat and pressed with all his might to squeeze his life away, until bulging eyes and thick protruding tongue and hands raised helplessly in the air proclaimed surrender.

Sir Lancelot rolled away and sat up panting. 'What kind of monster are you,' he demanded, 'to give foul caresses to a sleeping knight? Speak up – what are you doing here?'

'I can't,' the other said, painfully massaging his throat with his hands. And then he croaked, 'I am here because it is my pavilion. I thought to find my love awaiting me. What were you doing in my bed?'

'I found it empty and took my rest.'

'Why then, since you were not expecting a lady, did you return my embraces?'

'I had a dream,' said Lancelot.

'That I can understand,' said his late opponent, 'but why then, on awakening from your dream, did you attack me?'

Lancelot said, 'It is not usual for the victor in a fight to offer explanations to the loser. Nevertheless, I am sorry I have hurt you. But you must know that I have lately been the victim of enchantments strange and terrible. And such things warp the mind towards usual events. When I awakened to find a bearded reptile kissing me, I thought it a new vile enchantment, and fought to free myself. How does your throat feel now?'

'Like a goose's neck wrung for Christmas feast.'

'Do you believe me?'

'About the enchantments? I have no choice. I may not say nay until I am well enough to fight again.'

'Come,' said Lancelot, 'let me dip a scarf in cold water and wrap your throat. My mother did that for me when my neck was stiff and it removed the pain.'

And in the tent, while Lancelot wound the cool poultice about the throat of his erstwhile enemy, the door curtain parted and a dear and lovely lady entered, who, seeing them, cried out, 'What is this? What have you done to my lord, Sir Bellias?'

Lancelot looked helpless but Sir Bellias said, 'I suppose you must tell her. I can't.'

Then Lancelot, with many stammerings and pauses, reported what happened.

'It is a shameful thing,' the lady said, 'if it were not so funny.'

Bellias croaked, 'Do not blame him, my love. See, he has tried to make amends with a cold poultice.'

The lady had been staring at the knight, and now she said, 'Are you not Sir Lancelot?'

'I am, my lady.'

'I thought I recognized you, sir, for I have seen you many times at King Arthur's court. We are honoured, sir.'

'I wish the circumstances could have been different, madame.'

She tapped her teeth thoughtfully. 'I have only one worry, noble sir, and that is for your honour.'

'How is that involved?'

'It isn't really, but we must take great care that this tale does not get out, for if it did, laughter would peal through the world like bells and Lancelot's knightly deeds would fall before Lancelot's misfortune in bed. The queen particularly must be protected.'

Lancelot paled. 'I can trust you two, and no one else knows.'

'Yes, that is true,' she said, and then, after a while, 'Let us change the subject and forget the past. Will you be in court, sir, at the next high feast?'

'God willing, madame.'

'We also, sir. And do you know, Sir Bellias has long wished to be of the fellowship of the Round Table. You have weight at court. Do you suppose you could speak to the king in my lord's favour?'

Sir Lancelot looked at her and surrendered gracefully. 'I can promise nothing, but if he proves himself worthy in the tournament I will be glad to speak for him.'

'That is a good and knightly promise,' she said.

And Lancelot said, 'Whenever I hold speech with a lady, I find I have a promise in her hands. Do you know of an abbey nearby?'

'Surely, sir. The road to it is only a mile eastward towards the sun. Why do you ask?'

'Another promise,' said Lancelot disconsolately. And slowly he armed himself, and when he was about to depart he said to the lady, 'Please do not forget your promise.'

'Mine? What promise?'

'About – about – the—'

'Oh! Of course,' she cried. 'I won't forget. I mean, I don't remember. And Sir Bellias will swear by his honour as a knight of the Round Table. No one ever violates that oath.'

Sir Lancelot found the road easily enough, a remarkable road paved with stone and higher in the middle than at the sides. And there were ditches on either side to carry rain water away. The way stretched straight as a spear across upland and lowland, turning aside for nothing, and as he went the country changed. The fields were neat and cultivated, bordered with clipped hedges. It was the time of haysel. Lines of ragged men with swinging scythes moved across the grassland, and behind them an overseer strode back and forth, keeping the line straight, encouraging stragglers with his long thin stave, which whistled like a wild dove's wings. And soon he came to rabbit warrens, pigeon cotes, sheep pens, then little houses on wheels with hens feeding about them, and grazing cows. Ahead he saw the walls of the abbey, new whitewashed and shining in the morning sun, and near it fish ponds seething with carp and all manner of coarse fish, and a swannery enclosed with woven withes. Near the abbey walls were fruit trees laid out in perfect rows, and lines of bee-hives of bound grass from which came the muffled small roar of the labouring legions. A small, swift river washed the walls and on a dam there stood a mill whose slow, majestic wheel turned in the race, and in the doorway were piled tow sacks of grain. And everywhere bees, rabbits, pigeons, fish, trees, river races, and men worked steadily to produce food and more food for the great abbey barns, whose huge doors were guarded by sacred symbols set over them like traps to arrest theft. It was a thriving, humming factory, and the storehouses bulged with plenty.

When he rode near to the wall the knight saw a great double gate in which there was a small gate, in which there was a slat, and all of them closed, but overhead hung a bell with a rope dangling. He leaned from his saddle and clanged the bell. The slat snapped open and a small slab of bread sailed out and struck his shield and fell to the ground. He looked down on the grey and dusty bread, and perhaps because he had not eaten or rested, his temper flared and he reversed his spear and beat the gate with the butt until it roared with oaken protest.

The slat opened again and then the door opened and a small

nun with a turtle's face stepped out, crying, 'Pardon, my lord. I didn't know. I thought it were one of them thieving pilgrims that bedevil the hens and warrens so that we must set man-traps, God save us all, save them. Here, I'll open the gate to you, noble sir.' She scrabbled the latches and swung open the gates, and Lancelot rode through without striking her or even laying a flat curse on her shoulders. And it wasn't long until he sat in a pleasant chamber with the abbess, a huge woman, cheeks bursting with tiny veins, a mouth like a split strawberry, and quiet, watchful eyes. She sent a covey of young nuns scurrying like fledgling grouse.

'Your damsel has not come,' she said. 'Or her father. But they will be welcome, and you can wait here for them. I'll have an apartment readied for you.'

Lancelot's quiet servant reported to him that although she smiled she was not friendly.

'I owe my service to that damsel and to her father,' he said. 'She set me free from four evil enchantresses.'

'Very good,' she said. 'Of course it would have been more suitable if you had applied to the Church.'

'I would still be there, madame. The Church was not available.'

'Still,' she said, 'it would have been proper. The Church is organized to do these things, to do many things. But of late we have seen things done and attempted which might well be left in our more practised hands. It is not my habit to be obscure, sir. I refer to the knights errant presently swarming over the country-side claiming the king's warrant. No good will come of this. I hope you will report my words.' She caressed her huge hands, each finger armed like a weapon with a stone-studded ring.

'I know about this,' Lancelot said. 'It serves several purposes. Keeps the young knights fit for war, teaches them justice, self-control, and the ways of government, stops petty rebellion, and what is crime but small rebellion? And last and perhaps most important, not only keeps the king's authority alive in far places, but informs the king himself of the health of the kingdom.'

'So it may, sir,' she said. 'But it also interferes with those who have handled these matters for a long time. We are quite capable of hanging our own people. But when the collection of tithes, dues, and privileges is upset on grounds of justice, it not only upsets the balance but inspires unrest and even open rebellion. The king's government should not encourage changes unwanted by the people on whom they fall. There will be trouble, mind you. And you may tell the king I said so.'

'But if the evils remain uncorrected, madame?'

'Understand,' she said explosively, 'I do not say the impulse is bad – only misguided. The knights are dealing with forces they do not understand. The best intentions in the world may have a hellish end. I could give you examples.'

'But I must insist, madame, if the abuses are not corrected by the authorities in whose hands—'

'Now stop there, Sir Knight,' she said, and her cold eyes closed their surfaces to him. 'I do not think even the most irresponsible of the errant knights will deny that the world was created by God the Father.'

'Certainly not, madame. Why, they even—'

'And all the things in it, sir?'

'Of course.'

'Then can it not be that the removal of created things might be displeasing to God? You are going at it from the wrong direction. The evils of the world so called may well be put here to educate and chastise.'

'My lady Abbess,' he protested, 'you must not think I would presume to argue with you on holy matters. That is unthinkable.'

'Well,' she said, 'at last a little humility.' She breathed heavily and her cheeks, which had grown fiery red, seemed to bubble and subside like a disturbed omelet.

'You would not object, my lady, if the questing knights limited themselves to dragons and giants and enchanters?'

She waved her hand in a sad gesture. 'Life is hard and ugly enough as it is,' she said. 'Why must they search out unpleasant, ugly, evil things to shock and sadden us? What is wrong with good old-fashioned tournaments and jousts? They served our fathers very well.'

A cloud of eager messengers buzzed in Lancelot's ears, and he heeded them and held his peace, knowing that he could arouse nothing but opposition in this well-defended mind. 'Quite true,' he said. 'I see it now. I am sorry, madame.'

At last she smiled at him with her strawberry mouth. 'No

harm done,' she said. 'No breakage of God's pots that can't be glued with a little penance.'

Sir Lancelot felt only a sad sick sorrow, and he wished he were not ignorant. 'I should go to rest, my lady,' he said. 'I fight on Tuesday next.'

She clapped her hands. 'I shall be there to see it,' she cried. 'Such a goodly company and proper military bearing. Last Tuesday fifty knights were slain. With your world-renowned arm in it, the next should be even better.'

He went to his rest in the room prepared for him, confused and weary. He could not fight with anger against men he loved, and he loved too many. But when the trumpet blew, he could kill anyone or anything. He did not wish to wonder about that. For a short time a noise of pounding kept him wakeful, for they were replacing worn timbers on the gibbet by the chapel, for the abbey had manorial rights and duties as well as spiritual. But soon he drifted off and dreamed of Guinevere, cool-fingered queen, and in his dream he confirmed his service to her while he should live. And he dreamed she leaned over him, saying, 'You can't remake the world. There's little enough you can do to remake yourself.'

Then in his dream he saw himself with a scaffold about him. And he was taking out bricks from his neck and shoulders and replacing them with others, neatly mortared but new-looking. Even he knew this was funny and he laughed in his sleep.

Sir Bagdemagus came to the abbey followed by a cloud of mail-clad knights, surrounded with a butterfly swarm of lovely ladies. And when Sir Lancelot had been greeted and embraced and kissed, and after the tree of compliments had been stripped bare and the damsel's rescue told and retold while she stood blushing by, disparaging the celebration with little throwing gestures, then her father and Sir Lancelot went apart and Bagdemagus said, 'I find no words to thank you for helping me next Tuesday.'

'Your daughter told me, sir, that you were evil used.'

'They banged me up,' the knight said honestly. 'I couldn't seem to get a spear point fastened. And now I have to meet the same champions and my bones are still sore from the beating they gave me.'

258

'Is it true that some of King Arthur's knights turned the tournament against you?'

'That's true enough. They are fighting fiends. My heart quakes like a boy's when I think of meeting them again.'

'What knights are they, sir?'

'Well, the leader is the King of North Galys.'

'I know his wife,' said Lancelot.

'She is not here. Gone on a pilgrimage to Our Lady of Walsingham. Then I suppose the most formidable were Sir Mador de la Porte, Sir Mordred, and Sir Galatine.'

'Good men,' said Lancelot. 'But there is a difficulty. They won't fight me.'

'Why not?'

'I beat them several times and they refused the lists with me. That's why I am on quest. I couldn't find opponents.'

'That is bad news,' Sir Bagdemagus said. 'But if you come to the lists on my side and they refuse to close, they will lose by default. I'd rather have that kind of victory than none.'

'Oh, they won't refuse,' said Lancelot. 'They never do. They'll be away on affairs or sick, or some oath will keep them out. I know how they do it. I'm sorry, sir. I'd like to have a do with Mordred again. Never liked him. He's a sneaky one.'

'Is it true he's the king's son?'

'That's the talk. You know what talk is in a court. If the king had as many sons as king's sons say, he'd have no time for ruling. You know the saw, "If claiming princes rightly claim the sinister bar, then midwives were more busy than they are."'

'How would it be if you wore a new device? Too many people know Sir Lancelot's shield.'

'They're too smart for that. They'd watch an unknown knight behind the barrier and know me by the way I sit a horse. They are no fools.' He tapped his temple with the little knife he wore to cut his meat. 'Is there any cover near the lists, a copse or undergrowth?'

'Why yes – a grove of beech trees. Why?'

'Well, I thought if there were more than one strange knight it might confuse them and if, let us say, four of us should hide ourselves until after the trumpets, they could not withdraw. When the lists are blown, they are committed.'

'That is true,' Sir Bagdemagus said. 'How many knights do you want?'

'Send me four of your best. I will make the fifth. And let there be five suits of white armour and white shields, with no device at all. They may think at first we are new men out to win a shield of arms.'

'I will do it.'

'And let me have them soon. I must instruct my knights and drill them so we may fight as a unit.'

So it was done and quickly told.

On Tuesday, with ladies clustered in the stands like coloured flies on a currant cake, Sir Mordred and his fellows led the van, fighting hard and dumping riders right and left, when suddenly from out of the little wood five white knights issued and struck like white lightning, and wheeled as a unit and struck again, and wheeled and struck. Then Lancelot joyfully engaged his special enemies. Sir Mador took the first fall and broke his hip. Then Sir Mordred, and he and saddle flew, and when he struck the earth his helmet buried itself to his shoulders. Then Galatine got such a head stroke that blood burst from his ears and nose and eyes, and his horse ran away with him over the horizon because he could not wipe his eyes to see which way to turn. Meanwhile, Lancelot toppled twelve knights with one spear, and took another spear, and accounted for twelve more, while his white companions, wild with triumph, fought better than they ever had before. There was no need to sound the trumpet of peace. Before it could be blown North Galys's men had departed and Sir Bagdemagus held both field and prize. And he laughed and shouted happily to find his honour mended and his fame increased.

He led Sir Lancelot to his own castle, talking the while and banging with his hand on his champion's back plate so that the clatter drowned his words. And at the castle gifts were given – horses, hounds, robes, jewels – and Bagdemagus raided the lexicon of compliments and encouraged his daughter to speak likewise. They begged Sir Lancelot to bide with them, to stay with them, to live with them all his life, and Lancelot, smiling, had to wait for hoarseness and exhaustion to make a pause in which he could insert his need to search for Lyonel, his nephew.

Then Bagdemagus offered to go himself, to send his daughter, his sons, the body of his retainers. He ordered Sir Lancelot's health drunk in metheglin and in those horns which must be drained because they will not stand. No one in the hall dared refuse, except only Lancelot, who said it made him sick.

And in the morning he rode away from a silent castle ruled by sleep and headache, commandeered by metheglin.

Lancelot did not believe he had come far from the apple tree where the adventures had begun. Wishing to search for Lyonel, he sought to return to the place where he had lost him. He found the Roman road and followed it, and on the way he came upon a damsel riding a white palfry covered with a net and dangling red tassels to ward the flies in the manner of Andaluz.

'What cheer?' she asked in the accepted way.

'It will be better when I find my nephew, Sir Lyonel. He slipped away whilst I slept and he is lost.'

'If he is your nephew, then you must be Sir Lancelot.'

'Damsel, I am. Can you give me news of any fighting hereabouts?'

'Perhaps I can help you, sir,' she said, and she observed him shrewdly. 'There is a castle held by Sir Tarquin, the hardiest knight in all these parts. He wages a particular personal war 'gainst King Arthur's knights, and it is said he has killed some and taken over threescore prisoners with his own hands.'

'He must be a good man with a spear.'

'He is. And on his castle gate he has nailed up the shields of those he has taken.'

'Ha!' cried Lancelot. 'Is there a shield deviced with a rooster?'

'It seems to me I have seen it, sir, but there are many birds, animals, snakes, monsters not seen or heard of this side of Africa. I think a rooster.'

'With spread wings – crowing?'

'I dare believe it, sir.'

'Fair damsel, take me there of your gentle courtesy.'

She valued him with her eyes and chose her words with care. 'Were you other than you are I would not conduct you to your death,' she said. 'Nor would I ask a boon knowing you might survive. But you are Lancelot and I dare do both. When you have had your do with Sir Tarquin, will you promise me a service on your knightly word?'

'If I would not – would you conduct me?'

'I must search for a knight to help me, sir.'

'I see. It appears that there is no damsel in the world without a problem whose solution requires the jeopardy of my life.'

'Have you not sworn service to damsels and gentlewomen?'

'I have indeed. But sometimes I wish I did not have to honour my oath so often.'

'We are helpless creatures,' she said primly, 'relying on men's strong arms.'

'I wish I were so helpless,' said Lancelot. 'Very well, my dear, I promise on my honour. Lead the way.'

In an hour's time she brought him to a walled and gated manor house beside a stream. And on the closed gate he found Lyonel's shield. A large brass basin hung by a chain from a tree to serve as an alarm. Then Sir Lancelot beat the basin to clamour with his spear, but the gates remained closed and the house silent. He watered his horse at the stream and returned and struck the brass again, and he rode back and forth before the gate, growing more angry.

'Perhaps he is away,' the damsel said. 'He sometimes lies in wait beside the great road.'

'You appear to know him well.'

'I do, sir. Everyone does. He does no harm to ladies, only to Arthur's knights.'

Lancelot said crossly, 'Why not ask him to undertake your quest?'

'He does no service to ladies either,' she said.

'He is perhaps wiser than I am,' said Lancelot furiously, and he went to the basin and struck it with such force that the bottom flew out of it.

'No need to lose your temper, sir,' the damsel said. 'He will return and he has never refused a fight. I think I see him coming yonder.'

Sir Tarquin came riding fast, driving before him a war horse on which a wounded knight lay bound. And on the shield hanging from the saddle bow, Lancelot made out the device of Sir Gaheris, Gawain's brother.

Tarquin drew up, seeing an armed man before his house, and his ruined basin swinging in the wind.

'Fair knight,' said Lancelot, 'put that wounded man to the earth to rest a while. I am told that you have a slight distaste for knights of the Round Table.'

'If you are of that cursed fellowship you are well met,' Sir Tarquin cried.

'It is pleasant to be welcomed,' Lancelot said, and he took his place, and the two met with such equal force and precision that both horses were forced to the earth.

Then on foot they fought with swords and equally giving and taking wounds until their breath was gone and by silent accord they rested, leaning on their swords. And when he could speak, Sir Tarquin said, 'You are the best knight, the strongest and best winded I ever met, and my admiration goes out to you. I would rather you were friend than enemy. There is only one man in the world I cannot forgive.'

'It is pleasant to have a friend. Who is the knight you hate?'

'Sir Lancelot. He killed my brother Carados at the tower. And in honour of my hatred I fight and capture and imprison any knight of Arthur's fellowship I find. But when I meet Lancelot, I will kill him or I will die.'

'It seems a sad and silly thing to use war against associates. Why do you not seek out Lancelot? I don't think he would refuse you satisfaction.'

Tarquin said, 'Sooner or later he will come to me, and I would rather fight him on home ground and hang his shield on my gate above all the others. But forget all that. Let us make peace and dine as brothers.'

Lancelot said, 'It is an attractive offer to a weary man. But, sir, if you had as much heraldry as hate, you would have observed my shield.'

Then Tarquin gasped. 'You are Lancelot?'

'It is recorded in the church at Benwick, my erstwhile brother, Lancelot of the Lake, son of King Ban and Queen Elaine. I can elaborate the family tree if you wish.'

Tarquin said thickly, 'Welcome you are,' and he raised his sword and rushed to combat. There was no resting now, for this man was dedicated to the death of his opponent and he did not cease but charged and struck and crowded in, seeking an opening.

Sir Lancelot knew the danger in such concentrated hate, the superhuman strength, imperviousness to hurt, but he knew the weaknesses also of abandoned tactics. He offered openings to draw great strokes and only warded at the last moment. He fought defensively with little movement, trying to weaken with exhaustion his panting, hate-driven enemy, and gradually he saw the feet drag and heard the whistling breath, and in a small pause observed that Tarquin swayed dizzily. But Lancelot liked the greatness of his enemy and he thought, 'If he did not hate me so much, he would have more chance of killing me.'

He dropped his shield and drew a charge, then stepped aside and threw his shield under the dragging feet. Tarquin fell face downwards, and Lancelot trod on his wrist, forced up the neck guard of the helm, and drove his point into the spine. Sir Tarquin quivered once and died instantly under the stroke of mercy.

The damsel ran to him with little excited cheers, and Lancelot regarded her gravely and wondered why onlookers were so much more warlike than were fighting men.

'Now you can keep your promise,' the damsel cried. 'You will come with me, won't you?'

'I have no horse,' said Lancelot. 'There he lies with his neck broken.'

'Take the horse of the wounded knight, sir.'

Sir Lancelot strode to Gaheris and cut his bonds and greeted him. 'Will you lend me your horse?' he asked.

'Of course,' said Gaheris. 'You have saved my life.'

'Can you walk?'

'I think so, sir.'

'Go then into that manor house. You will find many prisoners there, my friends and yours. Release them and greet them for me. Tell them to take everything they need and want. I will meet them in the king's court at Pentecost. And tell them to give my greetings and my service to Queen Guinevere. They are to tell her that they are free in her honour.'

'Why must you go?' said Gaheris.

'The damsel there. I made a promise. Damsels I find the

sharpest bargainers. Now farewell. And tell Sir Lyonel that we will go on another quest one day.' And Lancelot mounted and followed the damsel on her way.

The damsel said, 'That was a very pretty piece of knightly business, sir. It is rightly said that you are the best knight in the world.'

'I am growing to be the weariest in the world,' he replied. 'Maybe that is why I make promises without asking what I have promised to do. Whether you know it or not, Sir Tarquin was a strong knight, and although he lost he left his mark on me. Tell me what you wish of me. It might be that I should rest a little and take care of my bruises and cuts.'

'Sir,' she said, 'Tarquin spent his days fighting and killing knights. But there is one nearby who molests damsels and gentle-women. He lies in wait and rushes out on unprotected ladies.'

'What does he do to them?' Lancelot inquired.

'He robs them.' The maiden blushed. 'On the young and fair he forces his foul lust.'

'Is he a knight?'

'He is sir.'

'Well, he should not do such things then. He is bound by oath to protect ladies. Has he distressed you? You are very pretty.'

'Thank you, sir. I have escaped him so far, but I must use this path, and if you will teach him to obey his oath – or kill him – you will give joy to many ladies. He lies in wait not far from here, hidden in a forest by the way.'

Lancelot considered, and then he said, 'You will ride ahead of me. I must see what occurs.'

'Do you mistrust me, sir?'

'No. But I have known ladies to discover rape in an un-solicited kiss, and others who issued an invitation perhaps unknowing and cried havoc when it was accepted.'

'Such a thought is unworthy of you, sir.'

'I think that is so. I do seem to distil unworthy thoughts when I am weary and my bones ache. But my plan is more than that. If the ambushed knight should see you attended by an armoured man, he might hesitate to attack you.'

'Then you could range the forest and drive him out and cut off his head.'

'How bloodthirsty you are, my dear. But then, you see, I would be executing a man for hearsay crimes and I'm afraid my heart would not be in it. But if he molested you with force I would then bring anger and indignation to ally themselves behind justice.'

'Well, if you put it that way.'

'It does make a difference, doesn't it?' he said. 'Ride on ahead. I will keep you in sight, but he will not see me or suspect that he is being trapped.'

'I don't like that word,' the damsel said. But she picked up her palfrey, and as she rode she took ribbons from the saddle bag and wove them in her hair, and a silken cloak to cover her with shimmering green and hang richly over the horse's rump. And as she neared the forest beside the way she sang sweetly in a high and penetrating voice.

'Well baited,' Lancelot muttered to himself. He saw the damsel ride near to the groping branches of the forest, singing gaily, and then an armed man galloped out and with precision grasped her from her saddle to his own, and her song turned to a soaring scream.

Sir Lancelot thundered near and cried out, 'Hold; caitiff knight!'

The ravisher looked up from his prey and saw the mailed eagle bearing down on him, and he dumped the lady on the ground to struggle with her enveloping cloak. He drew his sword and dressed his shield, which seeing, Lancelot threw his spear from him and drew his blade. One parry and one cut and the unfortunate lover dropped from his horse, cloven through the neck to his throat.

The damsel came near, brushing the dust and bits of twigs from her cloak, and she looked down on the slaughtered man. 'Now have you the payment you deserve,' she cried.

With one great shudder his life ran out, and the damsel said, 'As Tarquin studied to destroy good knights, so did this fellow spend his days distressing ladies, damsels, and gentlewomen. His name was Sir Perys de Foreste Savage.'

'You knew him then,' Lancelot observed.

'I knew his name,' she said.

'Is my promise kept?' he asked. 'Am I free to go?'

'With all my thanks,' she said. 'And with the thanks of ladies everywhere who celebrate your name. For you are renowned to all gently born as the goodliest and most courteous knight living. Wherever ladies speak together they agree on this, and they agree that you have one sad and mysterious lack – one flaw which troubles ladies.'

'What is that?' he asked.

'No one has ever heard that you loved anyone, my lord,' she said. 'And ladies hold that this is a great pity.'

'I love the queen.'

'Yes, that is noised about, and also that you love her as though she were carved in ice. And many say that she has enchanted you so that you may not love anyone else, rejoice no damsel, warm no lady with your love because of the cold enchantment. Wherefore the ladies blame the queen for holding captive what she does not use herself.'

He smiled at her, a grey-eyed kindly smile. 'It is the habit of women to put the blame on women,' he said. 'I cannot teach the world what it must say of me. Whispers are selfborn. But I can tell you, and if you wish, you may tell the others. I am a fighting man. You cannot think a spear is made for anything but war. Think so of me. You were thinking of a wife for me, perhaps children. I have fears enough without the added calamity of worry to spoil my aim. I am away at my profession of war most of the time. My wife then, though married, would be husbandless, my children fatherless, and our only joy would be the sorrow of being parted. No. I could not have it. A warlike husband must be always in two places at the same time. In bed he is at war, at war in bed, and thus split he is half a man in either field. I am not brave enough to slice myself in two pieces.'

'But there is other love—' she said softly. 'Surely at court you have seen—'

'Yes, I have, and it has not beckoned me. Intrigues and plans and jealousy, one or the other always injured. A month of anger for a moment's joy, and always jealousy and doubt, corroding, leprosy. I am a religious man – at least in so far as I am aware of sin and subscribe to the ten laws. But if adultery, habits, lechery, were not sternly ill spoke by God, my fighting arm would find them sinful because weakening. And if that were not enough, consider this: have you ever known a happy paramour? And should I of my own free will search out and help to build unhappiness? That would be stupid as well as cruel.'

The damsel said, 'Most strong and lusty men cannot help themselves. Love reaches out and their reluctance disappears like smoke.'

'Their strength then becomes their weakness,' Lancelot said. 'Their very manhood makes them helpless. Should I choose that if I have choice?'

'I think you do not love ladies – something prevents—'

'I knew you would. I've been wasteful of words. You will whisper that I am – not a man – because I have so far overcome man's chief weakness and perplexity.'

'I think the queen's enchantment must be very strong. Everyone said it was, and now I see it is—' And the promise went out of her eyes and her mouth grew bitter like the down-pouting lips of a little girl robbed of her sweet.

'Farewell,' he said. 'And ask this question when I am gone. If I do not love ladies, why do I serve up my life to them?'

'Enchantment.'

'Goodbye,' he said, and rode on and caught her palfrey and tethered it to a tree for her. But in a moment he untied the reins and led the horse back to her.

She did not look at him. 'Thank you,' she said.

'Is there any other service I may offer you?'

She looked at the ground. 'None that I think of, sir.'

'Then – well – then farewell!' He turned his horse and put it to trot, and the damsel watched him go and she was troubled for him.

Now Lancelot rode alone through forests damp and black where escaped slaves of the soil hid themselves in hollow trees and shallow caves, but these faded like shadows at his approach and did not respond to his calls. Then he crossed a fenny land where the reeds grew as tall as his horse and open water dangerous with quicksand where great colonies of ducks and wild swans lived in peace and rose into the air in thundering dances at his approach.

Far out in the water he saw round reed huts with conical roofs, each on its little island, each with its dugout boat. When Lancelot hailed the huts, short dark men with slings rained baked clay bullets on him with such force that his shield was dented and his horse lamed. It was a wild, unfriendly land where men were lessoned to ferocity by fear of men. The unsubstantial fata morgana and the restless ignis fatuus, rolling fairy lights of the fen, were less terrible than strangers of their own kind, for in this impoverished land the only property men knew was other men. The chill of suspicious rage cut like an icy wind, so that the knight turned inland to higher ground. In a semi-ruinous castle he killed two giants and released their prisoners and sent them to Queen Guinevere, and then for many days he sought adventure, but word of his coming travelled ahead of him, so that recreant and evil knights who usually were posted at river fords and narrow passages deserted their plunder spots and hid themselves until Lancelot had passed, for no one dared break a spear with him, so that his very greatness made him lonely and uncared for. He slept in shelters deserted by their owners and fed on what scraps and berries and husks he could find along the way.

> *Now turn we back to yonge Syr Gaherys who rode into the manor of Syr Tarquin slayne by Lancelot. And there he found a yoman porter kepyng many keyes. Than sir Gaherys threw the porter unto the grounde and toke the keyes frome hym; and hastely he opynde the preson dore, and there he lette all the presoners oute, and every man lowsed other of their bondys.*

Gaheris discovered many friends there and knights of the Round Table. He told them how Sir Lancelot had killed Tarquin and rescued them and ordered them to await him at King Arthur's court. In the stables they found their horses, while in the armoury every man sorted out his own armour, and then they feasted on venison in Tarquin's kitchen. But Sir Lyonel and Sir Ector de Marys and Sir Kay the Seneschal determined to ride after Sir Lancelot to join him on his quest, and when they had eaten and rested they set out, inquiring about him as they went.

Now return we to Sir Lancelot, who came at last to a pleasant courtelage, and there he found an old gentlewoman who made him welcome. She gave him roasted meat and blood pudding and fat pork pasty gleaming with spices. The ancient chatelaine remembered King Uther's court when she had been young and fair. She brought wine to Lancelot and begged him to tell her how it was at Arthur's court, what ladies were admired and what they wore, and how the queen looked and what she said, and she would have kept the knight talking until dawn but he begged to rest. At last she let him go to a pleasant chamber in her defensive wall over the castle gate. And he piled his armour on an oaken chest and sank into a deep soft bed of clean white woolly sheep skins, the first bed he had slept in for many a day. He had just entered his first dreamless sleep when there sounded a loud and frantic beating on the gate below his chamber. He leaped from the bed and looked out of the window and saw a knight attacked by three others. And even while defending himself the lone knight beat the gate and cried for help. Sir Lancelot armed himself and then he leaped from the window to the ground and went lashing in against the three attacking knights, and he cut them down one after the other and would have killed them if they had not begged for mercy.

'You are shamed men,' said Lancelot. 'It is unknightly for three to fight one. Therefore, you will not yield to me but to this lone knight and you will go to Arthur's court in his name and yield to the queen.'

The lone knight cried out, 'You are Lancelot,' and he raised his visor and it was Sir Kay. Then the two embraced and kissed each other for joy.

Then one of the beaten knights said, 'Sir, we do not want to yield to Sir Kay when we had already beaten him. It is an honour to yield to Lancelot, but to admit that Sir Kay overcame us would cause laughter.'

Lancelot unsheathed his sword. 'You have a choice,' he said. 'Yield to Sir Kay or make ready to die.'

'Well, in that case, sir—'

'On Whitsun next,' said Lancelot, 'you will yield to Guinevere and tell her that Sir Kay has sent you to be his prisoners.'

Then Lancelot beat on the gate with the pommel of his sword until it was opened. And the ancient lady was astonished

to see him. 'I thought you went to bed. How did you get here?'
she asked.

'So I did, but I jumped from the window to help this old friend
of mine. And I will take him to rest with me.'

In the chamber over the gate Kay thanked his friend for saving
his life. 'Since I set out to find you, sir, I have had one battle
after another.'

'That's strange,' said Lancelot. 'I have found no one to meet
me for many days.'

'Well, it might be that men who would break their necks to
engage with me would break their necks to avoid having a do
with Lancelot. That device on your shield would make a man
think twice.'

'I hadn't thought of that,' said Lancelot.

Sir Kay said, 'Old friend, there is a matter I would like to
speak about if you would promise not to be angry.'

'How could I be angry with you?' said Lancelot. 'Say on.'

'It is a matter that concerns me deeply, sir. From the moment
you left the king, a line of defeated knights have filed in to yield
themselves to the queen's grace. Now all the prisoners from
Tarquin's cells will be arriving at the king's court.'

'It is my custom,' said Lancelot. 'The queen takes pleasure in
it when noble knights submit to her pleasure. What have you to
say of that?'

'Noble they may be, sir, but famished they are. They arrive
in swarms like locusts and strip the king's larders bare. A
defeated knight is, if anything, hungrier than a victor.'

'It is the king's pleasure to be hospitable, sir.'

'I know that. He loves to provide bounty – but I am seneschal.
I am the one who must provide the bounty and make a record of
what is consumed.'

'The king is not niggardly.'

'That I know. He never thinks of it until the cupboard is swept
clean of every crumb. Then he says to me, "Kay, I don't know
where these things go. It's only last week we slaughtered ten
beeves and salted six wagonloads of herrings. Are you sure you
keep account? Can the kitchen boys be stealing?" Then I tell
him how many noble knights are eating at his table and he says,
"Yes, yes—" and he doesn't listen but he says, "I must look at

your accounts one day." You see, sir, if you stay much longer on quest, we shall be stripped to the bone by your noble captives. After they have yielded to the queen, they settle down and stay for weeks.'

Lancelot laughed. 'Poor Kay,' he said. 'Troubles follow you. Should I ask a knight if he is well provided before I fight with him?'

'Don't laugh at me,' said Kay. 'Everyone laughs at me. I tell you, it is a serious matter. One of your captives can eat half a sheep at a sitting – and the beer – the beer runs like water. But please don't tell the king I spoke of this. It would make him angry. He takes no note of money or supplies until he has none, and then I am blamed. Kay must be mean so the king can be generous.'

'I hadn't thought of it,' said Lancelot. 'But I don't know what I can do.'

'It's not only the knights,' Sir Kay said bitterly. 'Everyone has squires and dwarfs and damsels and all ravenous, particularly the damsels. They may be lovely things, all spirit and grace to you, but to me they are devouring monsters.'

'Well, go to sleep,' said Lancelot. 'I promise to fight only well-fed bachelors.'

'Now you are making fun again,' said Kay. 'You don't know how I have to cut corners. You think the roasted meat grows on trees. No one gives the seneschal a thought. I tell you, before a good Whitsun or a Pentecost gathering I get no rest. There's never any reward, but if anything is wrong— Oh, they remember me then. Sometimes I wish I were a kitchen boy.'

'Well, you aren't, my friend. You are my dear, kind, thoughtful Sir Kay, the most wonderful seneschal who ever lived. Your name is earned for all posterity on the happy bellies of the court. The world would get along nicely without me, but not a single day could pass without you, Sir Kay.'

'You are just saying that to please me, sir,' said the seneschal. 'But, you know – there is a grain of truth in what you say.'

Now Lancelot sat quietly and his eyes were puzzled.

'Why are you sad, sir?' his friend asked.

'Not sad – well, perhaps sad. It is a question. You might find it insulting.'

Kay said, 'I know my friend well enough to be sure he would not insult me. What is the question?'

'You are foster brother of the king.'

Kay smiled. 'I am. We suckled at one breast, swaddled together, played cock-a-hoop, hunted and learned arms together. I thought he was my brother until the revelation came that he was Uther's son.'

'Yes, I know. And in the first troubled years you were a very lion at his side. Your name lighted terror in the king's enemies. When the five kings of the north made war against Arthur, you with your own hands killed two of them, and the king himself said your name would live forever.'

Kay's eyes were shining. 'It is true,' he said softly.

'What happened, Kay? What happened to you? Why are you mocked? What crippled your heart and made you timid? Can you tell me – do you know?'

Kay's eyes still shone, but with tears, not pride. 'I think I know,' he said, 'but I wonder whether you could understand it.'

'Tell me, my friend.'

'Granite so hard that it will smash a hammer can be worn away by little grains of moving sand. And a heart that will not break under the great blows of fate can be eroded by the nibbling of numbers, the creeping of days, the numbing treachery of littleness, of important littleness. I could fight men but I was defeated by marching numbers on a page. Think of fourteen *xiii*'s – a little dragon with a stinging tail – or one hundred and eight *cviii*'s – a tiny battering ram. If only I had never been seneschal! To you a feast is festive – to me it is a book of biting ants. So many sheep, so much bread, so many skins of wine, and has the salt been forgotten? Where is the unicorn's horn to test the king's wine? Two swans are missing. Who stole them? To you war is fighting. To me it is so many ashen poles for spears, so many strips of steel – counting of tents, of knives, of leather straps – counting – counting of pieces of bread. They say the pagan has invented a number which is nothing – nought – written like an O, a hole, an oblivion. I could clutch that nothing to my breast. Look, sir, did you ever know a man of numbers who did not become small and mean and frightened – all greatness eaten away by little numbers as marching ants nibble a dragon and leave picked bones? Men can be great and fallible – but numbers never fail. I suppose it is their terribly puny rightness, their infallible smug, nasty rightness that destroys – mocking, nibbling, gnawing with tiny teeth until there's no man left in a man but only a pie of minced terrors, chopped very fine and spiced with nausea. The mortal wound of a numbers man is a bellyache without honour.'

'Then burn your books, man! Rip your accounts and let them take the wind from the highest tower. Nothing can justify the destruction of a man.'

'Eh! Then there would be no feast; in war no spears or food to make the battle possible.'

'Why do men mock you, then?'

'Because I am afraid. We call it caution, intelligence, far-sightedness, having a level head, good conservative business sense – but it is only fear organized and undefeatable. Starting with little things, I have become afraid of everything. To a good man of business, venture is a sin against the holy logic of numbers. There is no hope for me – ever. I am Sir Kay the Seneschal and my old glory is gobbled up.'

'My poor friend. I don't understand it,' Lancelot said.

'I knew you wouldn't. How could you? The death-watch beetle is not gnawing at your guts. Now let me sleep. That is my nought, my zero, my nothing.'

Sir Lancelot sat by the window smiling at his sleeping friend, and when the snoring rattled the gate he arose from his seat and quietly removed his armour and put on Kay's, and took Kay's shield, and descending to the courtyard, he found and saddled Sir Kay's horse. Then quietly he opened the gate and passed through and rode away in the darkness.

And in the morning when the seneschal awakened and missed his armour he was perturbed for a moment – but then he laughed. 'There will be some sad knights this day,' he thought. 'They tumble out like mice to fight Sir Kay. But with the armour of Sir Lancelot I will ride in peace, and men informed by fear will give me courtesy.'

Sir Lancelot rode into a fair meadowed land splashed with yellow flowers and woven throughout with pleasant streams where brown trout jumped for flies and others cruised silently stalking trout.

Beside a clear pool maidens were washing linens and spreading them on the meadow to whiten between sun and grass. They watched the knight go by and waved to him with the clean wet garments in their hands, and one bold maid of twelve brought him a cup of wine made from corinth berries and stroked his horse's shoulder, waiting for the cup.

'They say you are Sir Kay,' she chattered.

'That is so, little maid.'

'They say Sir Lancelot is hereabouts.'

'Perhaps.'

'Oh! Do you know him, sir?'

'Yes, I do.'

'Is it true, sir, that he is tall as a pine tree and fire flashes from his eyes?'

'No, that is not true. He is only a man. In some ways a very ordinary man.'

'Is he your friend?'

'Yes, you might say so.'

'Then I think you have no right to say what you said.'

'What did I say?'

'You said he is not as tall as a pine tree and his eyes do not flash fire. You said he was an ordinary man.'

'In some ways.'

'If you were his friend you would not insult him when he is not here to defend himself. But you are only Kay. Perhaps you know no better. Give me the cup!'

'Thank you, little maid.'

'If I see him I'll shout up to him what you said. And he will ram his spear down your throat. Everyone knows he is tall as a pine tree.'

'Are those pavilions I see there yonder, little maid?'

'They are. And if you are wise you will not go near them. Some knights are there and they will give you a tumble. You had better creep away before they see you.'

'You think that would be wise? Are they such good knights?'

'Well, they aren't Lancelots, but they might spread Sir Kay like linen on the grass.'

'What are their names?'

'Sir Gawter, Sir Gilmere, and Sir Raynold. They are well known here.'

'Perhaps if I do not anger them they will let me pass.'

'Oh, it isn't anger, sir. They wait there looking for a do with some passing knight.'

'What if Sir Lancelot passed?'

'Why, then I think they might have business elsewhere.'

'Well, I suppose I must take my chance. If they should overthrow me, will you succour me, little maid?'

'I owe service to all true knights as they owe service to me, sir. And you have spoken courteous and fair to me. I had been told Sir Kay is vain and full of pomp and boasting. But you are a gentle humble knight and these are false tales. When you have fallen I will help to unarm you and ease your pain as a true damsel should.'

'Gramercy,' he said. 'You are a courteous young lady.'

'No matter how badly you may fare with arms, if I hear ill spoken of you, sir, I will correct it, for you seem a well-spoke gentleman.' The little lady watched him go.

Lancelot looked back to wave to her and he saw a curiosity. The little fingers of each hand were hooked in the corners of her mouth, pulling it to a wide white band; her middle fingers pushed up her nose against her face, while her forefingers pulled down the corners of her eyes, which were crossed against the bridge of her nose. And from her drawn mouth her tongue projected and wagged up and down at him. His hand paused, half raised to wave.

The maiden dropped her arms and unconcernedly went back to her washing by the pool.

Sir Lancelot moved on, thinking, 'There must be something I don't understand about little maidens.'

And there was. At the pool she turned her back, because she liked this knight and did not want to see him hurt.

Meanwhile, Sir Lancelot rode near three silken pavilions set up beside a wooden bridge over a small deep stream. Three white shields hung on three spears at their entrances and three knights lolled drowsily on the meadow grass until the sound of an approaching horse aroused them.

'Oh, God is bountiful,' Sir Gawter said. 'Look who comes – the great Sir Kay. The noble, brave Sir Kay. Brothers, I tremble and my heart grows weak, but I must meet him though I quake with fear.'

'No – wait,' the others said. 'You can't swallow all the sweets.'

Sir Raynold cried, 'I cannot let you face this dragon. Poor thing that I am, I will fight him though I die.'

'Wait a moment,' said Sir Gilmere. 'I can't let you venture such valuable lives. I will fight him.'

'He will be gone before we can decide which one must sacrifice himself,' said Sir Gawter. 'Here – I have three straws. The shortest wins him.'

And as Lancelot passed without speaking, their heads were together as they drew straws for him. He crossed the bridge and continued on his way, but in a moment, with a clatter, Sir Gawter – the winner – galloped after him, shouting, 'Hold, false knight!'

Sir Lancelot drew up and waited for him. Sir Gawter forced his horse to dance sideways with a spur in his near side. He said, 'If I did not know the shield of proud Sir Kay, I would know him by the smell of kitchen grease. How did you dare to creep over our bridge?'

'Is it your bridge, young sir?'

'Do you imply that I am a liar, sir? You'll pay for that.'

'I only asked. I did not take your bridge – I only crossed it.'

'Ho, now you turn threatening. I have heard of your pompousness, sir. I shall remove it.'

'I do not threaten you.'

'Why did you pass without greeting? Are you too proud to hail ordinary knights?'

'I sought to avoid a quarrel.'

'Are you a coward then?'

'No. But I had no quarrel with you. Please let me pass, young sir.'

'Then I will give you a quarrel. You are a liar, a cheat, a fool, a coward, and a dishonour to the order of knighthood. Now do you have a quarrel?'

Sir Lancelot said, 'An ill-mannered pup is to be whipped, not quarrelled with.'

277

'You have just now spoken your life away, you grease-stained kitchen knight.'

Sir Lancelot sighed. 'I have done my best to let you escape with honour, sir. I am a temperate man, but there is a limit to my patience.'

'Let us hope that at last you have reached it,' Sir Gawter cried. 'Defend yourself, if you can.' He waved gaily to his brother knights watching from the bridge, positioned himself, and charged. His spear shattered on Lancelot's shield and Sir Gawter was lifted clear, carried on spear point for a time, and cast headlong into a muddy ditch. Then Lancelot passed on his way without a word.

Sir Raynold and Sir Gilmere, watching from the bridge, were wonder-filled. 'What has come to Sir Kay?' they asked. 'This knight does not fight like him.'

'Perhaps a strange knight has killed Sir Kay and taken his harness,' Gilmere said. 'In any case, we are for it. We've made our challenge and there's no retreat.'

Then each one engaged Lancelot and both were unhorsed, and all three found themselves swearing to go to court and submit to the queen as Sir Kay's prizes.

Now as the 'Frensshe' books say and Malory also, as well as Caxton and Southey, Sommer and Coneybear, Tennyson, Vinaver, and many others, Sir Lancelot continued on his way, overturning knights one after another, and the way to Arthur's court was thronged with defeated men paroled in Sir Kay's name to Guinevere. Sir Lancelot went gaily, pleased with his joke, but also hoping that this new fame might help Sir Kay out of his hopelessness. And on the way he came on fair knights of the Round Table who had been prisoners of Sir Tarquin – Sir Sagramor le Desyrus, Sir Ector de Marys, Sir Ewain, and Sir Gawain. Each one he fought and each one overthrew, and as he passed on his way, Sir Gawain sat bruised and battered on the ground and spoke to the others.

'We are fools,' he said. 'I must have lost my mind. Look how that knight sits his horse! Remember how he rode low and easily! Think of that unwavering spearhead, and particularly recall

the way he saluted the fallen with his hand. Now – who is it?
We are fools!'

And the other three cried, 'Lancelot and no one else.'

'Of course,' cried Gawain. 'If we had used our eyes we would
have saved our bruises. Now if we find a knight with Lancelot's
device we may lay on with confidence, and I for one will joy to
bring Sir Kay to his knees.'

Sir Ewain said, 'But meanwhile our word is given to take our
battered repentance to the queen in Sir Kay's name.'

Lancelot, continuing on his way, was made aware of a change
in those he met. No longer did knights come tumbling out to
fight with him. Some gave him peaceful courtesy, dripping with
respect, and others found urgent need to be absent from their
posts. Pavilions set up beside the path he found deserted, bridges
unguarded, the roads unplagued with careless errantry. And
peaceful men greeted him by his name. Moreover, damsels,
ladies, and gentlewomen appeared from nowhere to beseech his
aid in strange, incomprehensible affairs, of wounded husbands,
lands unlawfully taken. Distressed and pillaged maidens sprouted
beside the road and with blushes and lowered eyes sought
wordlessly to call his heart to them. And Lancelot was puzzled
that with his visor down and Kay's shield at his shoulder he was
recognized. He did not know, nor had he ever had need to know,
how word can fly on swallows' wings deep into desert places.

Perhaps a squire heard Gawain's words and spoke them to a
passing friar, who gave them, along with forgiveness, to a con-
fessing maid, who told her father in the hearing of a jongleur
hurrying to a wedding. Wayward men, escaping bondsmen,
outlawed bowmen creeping in the greenwood, lord abbots with
their trains of well-mounted monks heard and spread the news in
ever-growing circles. Even the birds and butterflies, the yellow
wasps, sang and fluttered the news until the very voices of the
sparkling brooks told how Sir Lancelot was venturing with Sir
Kay's shield. Dwarfs and countrymen, charcoal burners greeted
him. And tinkers leading frippery-laden mules, collectors of the
staple with their great tow bags of wool, lordly traders with
purple cloth from golden Tuscany spoke his name in passing. It
is a marvel and a mystery how words grow wings and range the

countryside, and no one understands the limitless penetration of a whisper.

The nature of adventures changed. No longer did he fight gaily and openly. Only dark and secret matters came to Lancelot's attention – things incomprehensible.

A lady beside a wounded knight required blood of an enemy for the saving of her lover's life. Strange trickeries opened up to him.

He heard a little bell and, looking up, saw a hawk flying overhead, and when it settled high in a great elm tree, lures trailing from its feet became entangled in the branches. Then a lady came running from the road and cried out to him, 'Please, my lord Lancelot, get my hawk for me.'

'I am not good at climbing, lady,' he replied. 'Find some small urchin to go up the tree.'

'I cannot,' she cried in panic. 'My husband is a violent and vengeful man and he loves this hawk. If he finds that I have lost it he will slay me.' And she broke into wails and little screams of fear until Sir Lancelot dismounted to quiet her.

'Very well,' he said unhappily. 'Help me to unarm. I cannot climb in armour.' He tied his horse to the elm and laid his weapons by, and clad only in light breeches and a shirt, he struggled clumsily up the tree, and high up in the branches he caught the hawk, attached the lures to a rotten branch, and threw the struggling bird down to the lady.

Then from a hiding place in the bushes an armed knight strode out, holding a naked sword, and he cried, 'Now, Sir Lancelot, I have you as I want you, unprotected and unarmed. Your time has come and I have planned it so.'

Lancelot said reproachfully, 'Lady – why have you betrayed me?'

'She has done only what I commanded,' said the knight. 'Now will you come down to your death, or must I put fire to the tree and smoke you down like an animal?'

'What a shameful thing,' said Lancelot. 'An armed man against a naked one.'

'I will recover from my shame before you grow a new head, my friend. Now – will you come down, or must I build the fire?'

Now Lancelot tried to bargain with him. 'I can see that you

are a man of passion,' he said. 'I will come down. Take my armour to one side, but hang my sword on the tree. Then I will fight you, naked as I am. Then, when you have slain me, you can tell how it was done in a fight.'

The knight laughed. 'Do you take me for a fool? Don't you think I know what you can do with a sword?' And he moved both sword and armour away from the tree.

Lancelot looked desperately about, and he saw a short dead limb of the tree and broke it off, and came slowly down the tree, and in the lower branches he saw that his enemy had forgotten to move his horse away, and suddenly Lancelot leaped over his horse and lighted on the other side.

The knight slashed at him, but Lancelot, using his horse for a shield, defended himself with his elmwood club. He caught the sword blade deep in the wood and yanked it away, and clubbed his enemy to the ground and battered his life away.

'Alas,' the lady cried, 'why have you slain my husband?'

Lancelot paused in putting on his armour. 'I don't think I will answer that, my lady. If I were not a knight I would use my stick on you, and not on your head.' And he mounted and rode away, and thanked God for his deliverance.

As he went along his way he thought in saddened wonder about the man he had killed. Why was his hatred so great against Lancelot, who had done him no harm? He was innocent of those passions of jealousy which cause a small man to destroy what others admire, nor had he so far in his life felt the self-loathing that makes a man revenge himself on a world he blames for his own inadequacies.

Like most great fighting men, Lancelot was generous and kindly. When it was necessary to kill men he did it quickly, without anger and without fear. And since cruelty, unless it be a disease, grows only out of fear, he was not cruel. Only one thing could make him blindly cruel. He did not understand treachery, having none in himself. Thus, when he was confronted with this mysterious impulse, Lancelot grew frightened, and only then could he be cruel. And since knightly quests and the accounts of them are only illustrations of virtues as well as knightly vices, it came about that as he proceeded on his way he heard a woman screaming with fear, and moving towards the sound, he saw a lady running and a knight following her with a drawn sword in his hand. Sir Lancelot pushed his horse in the way of the pursuing man, who cried out to him, 'What is your right to come betwixt a man and his wife? I am going to kill her as is my right.'

'No, you are not,' said Lancelot. 'You are going to fight me.'

'I know you, Lancelot,' said the man. 'This woman, my wife, has betrayed me. She is unfaithful. It is my lawful right to slay her.'

'Not so,' the lady said. 'He is a jealous man. He eats and sleeps in jealousy and sees wrong in everything. I have a young cousin, young enough to be my son, and my husband is jealous of this child. He imagines foul things. Save me, Sir Lancelot, for my husband is without mercy.'

'I will protect you,' he said.

Then the husband said, 'Sir, I respect you, and I will do whatever you say.'

The wife cried, 'Oh, be careful, sir! I know him. He is treacherous.'

'You are under my protection, lady. He cannot hurt you. Now let us go along.'

When they had gone on for a time, the husband shouted, 'Look behind you. Here come armed men.'

Lancelot swung about, and at that moment the man leaped at his wife and slashed her head from her body, and he bent down, spitting and cursing over her headless trunk.

Then, because this was foreign and frightening to him, rage overcame Lancelot, who was ordinarily a cool, calm man. He drew his sword and his face was black with ferocity and his eyes vindictive as the eyes of a snake.

The husband fell to the earth and clasped Lancelot's knees, crying and praying for mercy, while the knight tried to push him back to get a cut at him. But he buried his head against Lancelot's legs and sobbed like a great baby.

'Stand and fight,' Lancelot raged.

'I will not – I plead mercy on your knighthood.'

'Listen. I will disarm. I will fight you in my shirt.'

'No— Mercy.'

'I will tie one arm.'

'Never— I plead mercy. You have sworn to give mercy.'

Then Lancelot, sick with disgust and sickened by his own rage, broke free and leaned against a tree, trembling and feverish. The lady's head, dirty and blood-splashed, grinned at him from the road where it had fallen.

'Tell me my punishment. I will do anything,' the husband cried. 'Only leave me my life.'

Then Lancelot's cruelty became cold. 'I will tell you,' he said. 'You will take this body on your back and the head in your hand. You will never leave it, day or night. When you come to court, take it to Queen Guinevere. No matter how it may disgust her, tell her what you have done. She will tell you your punishment.'

'I promise on my faith.'

'Your faith! It was a shameful hour when you were born. You will obey, because if you do not I will hunt you down and tear you to pieces. Now pick it up. No, do not lay it on the horse. Take it on your back.'

He watched the man ride heavily away with the swaying corpse embracing him from behind. And Lancelot breathed deeply with his mouth open to keep from vomiting, for his rage and his cruelty had sickened him. He sat on the ground under a tree while evening came – too weak to move, too ill to find a better resting place.

Evening ground-walking birds thronged the path, turning over leaves for bugs, quarrelling and chattering. They paid no heed to the sitting knight. One, a chief bird with a cockade and an air of command, marched belligerently to his ironclad foot and picked at it sharply and looked up sharply as though daring him. And Lancelot smiled because he remembered doing the same thing and possibly for the same reasons.

As though the unanswered challenge of the chief bird had cleared the air of suspicion, the small and quiet emerged from the wood, but their smallness did not mean that they were meek – only cautious. Each one had war against others and endless difficulties with his fellows: matters of property, treasure trove, violations of respect for size and age and strength – mice and moles, ferrets, weasels, and small snakes, hurrying to some shelter now the night was coming. Government among a single kind was hard enough. Among many kinds it was impossible, and always had been, for the small creatures were not peaceful or kindly or cooperative. They were as quarrelsome and as selfish, as greedy and vainglorious, as sneaky and pompous and unpredictable as humans, wherefore it is hard to understand how they get their eating and breeding done at all, let alone increasing, building nests and burrows, preening fur and feathers, sharpening beak and claw, storing food and guarding it, and still having time to quarrel and snap and curse one another, and only occasionally taking time to love and to die.

With the coming darkness one kind crept away and other kinds emerged, changing workers in the structure of the world. With the darkling, dimpsy dusk, the night-eyed took possession; lean quiet hunters and furtive catchers and nibblers and coasting murderers chuckling and hooting according to their kind. Among the trees the bats flitted in restless pendulum flight, their voices thin and high and brittle, penetrating teeth. They brought a night chill with them and pinned the darkness up so that the stars could show. So many lives were about, and all with friends and enemies, that Sir Lancelot felt alone and lonely in his heart, darkened and chilled also, and no stars shone in him. It was a new, strange feeling to him, for he had not ever been lonely since the rupture of the earth when Queen Elaine died and he had to put it together again without love. He shivered all over at once with that chill everyone knows as the signal that a witch is walking with waves of spells going out ahead. Sir Lancelot crossed the fingers of both hands and wet his lips for a paternoster should one be needed. And he knew the witch was near because the night people disappeared or froze into motionless invisibility, and then he heard human footsteps approaching and a warm voice that sang:

> '*Awaken not, my love,*
> *It is not day.*
> *This night will never end,*
> *This night, my love,*
> *Will never end,*
> *Will never, never end.*'

The song ceased. A damsel approached in the dim evening. 'My lord,' she said, 'I heard you call.'

'I did not call, lady.'

'I heard a loneliness.'

'I did not call,' he said.

She seated herself beside him.

'I felt enchantment like a mivvering of the mind,' he said. 'Are you an enchantress?'

'I am what Sir Lancelot wants of me.'

'You know my name?'

'Better than any other name of all the names. Better than the name of Guinevere the queen.'

He started like a fly-plagued horse. His arms felt cold against him.

'What power has she over you?' she asked.

'The power of a queen to whom my knighthood is dedicated.'

'And your heart? Is it dedicated?'

'My heart is only a small pumping engine, lady,' he said sullenly. 'My heart stays in its place and does its work. I have heard of hearts that left their posts and wandered wailing like truant ghosts, of hearts that have broken, of yearning, laughing, playful hearts, of wishful and of lonely hearts. Perhaps there are such hearts. My own is a slow, steady pump. In combat it speeds to give me what I need. It never speaks, never shirks. My heart is dedicated only to its work.'

'Perhaps you do not listen,' the damsel said. 'I heard it from a distance saying your quest was finished and your way was opened back to Guinevere.'

'Then I must lesson it. I do not wish even my little toe to speak behind my back, let alone my heart. Lady, what are you up to, gossiping with my heart like servants at a well? Who are you? What do you want of me? If you are an enchantress, your art will have told you that my fingers are crossed.'

'Have you ever seen me?'

He leaned near and gazed at her in the thickening night. 'No – I don't remember you.'

'Do you find me fair?'

'Yes, you are fair, very fair, but that may be enchantment. Tell me what you wish.' His voice was impatient.

She leaned close – so close that her dark eyes were large and he saw the night sky and the stars reflected in them. Then the surfaces trembled with the tears of her effort and the stars lost their sharpness and he saw the shapes of little monsters moving in the double sky he looked into. He saw a crab crawling sideways, its claws outstretched, and a scorpion with whipping tail, a lion and a goat and fishes that swam from constellation to constellation. He knew he was growing drowsy.

'What do you see?' she asked softly.

'Those signs enchanters use to tell fortunes.'

'Good. Now see your fortune.'

Her eyes became one turbulent pool of dark water and then, below, a face was formed and it moved towards the surface and grew clear – a clean, chiselled face, deeply cut chin, and cool eyes, careful eyes, and a mouth strong and full-lipped but twitching at the corners with amusement. Then one eyelid dipped for a moment, the mouth parted, and lips moved as though whispering – then the face grew rigid, a painted face, a representation of a face. The cool eyes were sculptured eyes, the brows minute chisel cuts.

'You see a face,' the soft voice said.

'I see a face.'

'Do you recognize it?'

'Yes.'

'Is it clear?'

'Very.'

She panted with effort. 'Look closely, sir. There is your fate, for all your life – your love, your only love.'

'It cannot be.'

'It is. And I offer thanks to the things of air and fire and water, the good helpers. Now you may come from the vision. It is fixed for all time and it cannot change. You have become mine – husband, lover, slave. Come from the spell, my darling dear.'

'I don't think I was ever in a spell, my lady.'

'That's the way it seems when it is over. Perhaps you won't remember what you saw, but I know you saw my face, and you are mine.'

Now Lancelot looked sharply at her and he was deeply troubled, for he saw a poor demented girl trying to move the world with a straw. He wondered if it would not be kind to agree with her, to get her to a priest to exorcize the demons of insanity. And then he thought of that broad-backed dwarf who had taught him arms and other things.

'A lie is a good and valuable thing,' he said. 'A wonderful precious thing to hold in reserve. But never use this jewel until you have exhausted every truth. Truth is common stuff, ready to your hand, but lies you have to make yourself, and you can't be sure they are any good until you have used them – and then it's too late.'

Lancelot said gently to the girl, 'Damsel, I could agree with what you have said, but a moment of peace is not worth anything. Sometime you may learn to make great enchantments, but now – well – a little necromancy is a dangerous thing.'

She started to her feet. 'You are lying,' she cried. 'You saw my face. You are caught.'

'No, damsel. I did not see your face. I saw Guinevere the queen. And that is foolish because it is impossible that I could ever love the queen dishonourably and bring dishonour and shame to my friend and liege king and befoul my knighthood.'

'You saw my face,' the damsel cried. 'My spell was the strongest there is.'

'Your spell was weak and staggering like a newborn colt,' said Lancelot. 'It is true that you have learned to make pictures in your eyes, but silly pictures, foolish things. They will only get you laughed at. You made me see Queen Guinevere at the stake with faggots piled about her for treason against the king. What foolishness is that? And if that were not nonsense enough, I saw myself in full armour riding in a cart pulled by oxen through a swamp. That would be funny if it were not insulting. I think you had better go home and learn to do magic with thread on a torn shirt. Maybe someday you can go on quest with some young, well-thought-of knight.'

She was strangely silent, and after a while Sir Lancelot said, 'I am sorry to hurt your feelings, my dear. And I must go. I have an agreement to be in Arthur's court at Whitsuntide and the time is near. Is there anything I can do for you before I go? Some little favour?'

She came close to him and spoke in a whispering voice, and the whites of her eyes showed in the starlight and made her seem blind. 'There is, my lord,' she said. 'One little service only you can do for me.'

'Tell me. I will do it.'

'Nearby there is a noble chapel called Perilous and in it a dead knight lies wrapped in a shroud and beside him a sword. It is guarded by giants and fearful monsters. Bring me that sword if you can.'

'How will I find it in the dark?'

'It is not far. Go along the path until you see a light. I will wait here for you.'

He stumbled away in the darkness and he was sad for her. He found the light, a candle burning in a little hut, but with a rude cross set over the door. Inside, there was a figure covered with white cloth, while on the whitened walls grotesque faces were painted by a childish hand. Beside the shrouded figure lay a wooden sword. Sir Lancelot stooped to pick it up and raised the shroud enough to see that it was a rag dummy dressed in a man's clothing. And his heart was heavy when he went back to the damsel.

She had moved to a clearing and her face was wild and child-like under the stars. 'Did you get the sword?' she called.

'Yes, my lady.'

'Give it to me.'

'It is not seemly for a damsel to carry a sword.'

'Ha! You have escaped. Had you given me the sword you would never have seen Guinevere more.'

He dropped the stick with its tied-on cross guard to the ground.

'Give me a token, my lord,' she said.

'What token do you wish?'

'A kiss – I will treasure it.' She moved to him as though she walked in sleep, her face upturned, her lips parted, and he could hear her pounding heart.

Then some movement, some instinct deep in the fighting man, caused him to seize her wrist and shake the long slender knife from her fingers.

She put her face in her hands and wept.

'Why did you want to kill me? I had not harmed you.'

'I am lost,' she said. 'You would have been mine and no one else could have you.'

'*And, Sir Lancelot, now I telle the: I have loved the this seven yere, but there may no woman have thy love but quene Gwenyver; and sytthen I myght nat rejoyse the nother thy body on lyve, I had*

kepte no more joy in this worlde but to have thy body dede. Than
wolde I have bawmed hit and sered hit, and so have kepte hit my
lyve dayes; and dayly I sholde have clypped the, kyssed the to my
heart's content dispyte of quene Gwenyvere.'

King Arthur held Whitsun court at Winchester, that ancient
royal town favoured by God and His clergy as well as the seat
and tomb of many kings. The roads were clogged with eager
people, knights returning to stamp in court the record of their
deeds, of bishops, clergy, monks, of the defeated fettered to
their paroles, the prisoners of honour. And on Itchen water,
pathway from Solent and the sea, the little ships brought
succulents, lampreys, eels and oysters, plaice and sea trout,
while barges loaded with casks of whale oil and casks of wine
came tide borne. Bellowing oxen walked to the spits on their
own four hoofs, while geese and swans, sheep and swine, waited
their turn in hurdle pens. Every householder with a strip of
coloured cloth, a ribbon, any textile gaiety, hung it from a window
to flap its small festival, and those in lack tied boughs of pine and
laurel over their doors.

In the great hall of the castle on the hill the king sat high, and
next below the fair élite company of the Round Table, noble
and decorous as kings themselves, while at the long trestle boards
the people were as fitted as toes in a tight shoe.

Then while the glistening meat dripped down the tables it
was the custom for the defeated to celebrate the deeds of those
who had overcome them, while the victor dipped his head in
disparagement of his greatness and fended off the compliments
with small defensive gestures of his hands. And as at public
penitence sins are given stature they do not deserve, little sins
grow up and baby sins are born, so those knights who lately
claimed mercy perchance might raise the exploits of the brave
and merciful beyond reasonable gratitude for their lives and in
anticipation of some small notice of value.

This no one said of Lancelot, sitting with bowed head in his
golden-lettered seat at the Round Table. Some said he nodded
and perhaps dozed, for the testimony to his greatness was long
and the monotony of his victories continued for many hours.

Lancelot's immaculate fame had grown so great that men took pride in being unhorsed by him – even this notice was an honour. And since he had won many victories, it is possible that knights he had never seen claimed to have been overthrown by him. It was a way to claim attention for a moment. And as he dozed and wished to be otherwhere, he heard his deeds exalted beyond his recognition, and some mighty exploits once attributed to other men were brought bright-painted out and laid on the shining pile of his achievements. There is a seat of worth beyond the reach of envy whose occupant ceases to be a man and becomes the receptacle of the wishful longings of the world, a seat most often reserved for the dead, from whom neither reprisal nor reward may be expected, but at this time Sir Lancelot was its unchallenged tenant. And he vaguely heard his strength favourably compared with elephants, his ferocity with lions, his agility with deer, his cleverness with foxes, his beauty with the stars, his justice with Solon, his stern probity with St Michael, his humility with newborn lambs; his military niche would have caused the Archangel Gabriel to raise his head. Sometimes the guests paused in their chewing the better to hear, and a man who slopped his metheglin drew frowns.

Arthur on his dais sat very still and did not fiddle with his bread, and beside him sat lovely Guinevere, still as a painted statue of herself. Only her inward eyes confessed her vagrant thoughts. And Lancelot studied the open pages of his hands – not large hands, but delicate where they were not knobby and scarred with old wounds. His hands were fine-textured – soft of skin and very white, protected by the pliant leather lining of his gauntlets.

The great hall was not still, not all upturned listening. Everywhere was movement as people came and went, some serving huge planks of meat and baskets of bread, round and flat like a plate. And there were restless ones who could not sit still, while everyone under burden of half-chewed meat and the floods and freshets of mead and beer found necessity for repeated departures and returns.

Lancelot exhausted the theme of his hands and squinted down the long hall and watched the movement with eyes so nearly closed that he could not see faces. And he thought how he knew everyone by carriage. The knights in long full floor-brushing robes walked lightly or thought their feet barely touched the ground because their bodies were released from their crushing boxes of iron. Their feet were long and slender because, being horsemen, they had never widened and flattened their feet with walking. The ladies, full-skirted, moved like water, but this was schooled and designed, taught to little girls with the help of whips on raw ankles, while their shoulders were bound back with nail-studded harnesses and their heads held high and rigid by painful collars of woven willow or, for the forgetful, by supports of painted wire, for to learn the high proud head on a swan's neck, to learn to flow like water, is not easy for a little girl as she becomes a gentlewoman. But knights and ladies both matched their movements to their garments; the sweep and rhythm of a long gown informs the manner of its moving. It is not necessary to inspect a serf or a slave, his shoulder wide and sloping from burdens, legs short and thick and crooked, feet splayed and widespread, the whole frame slowly crushed by weights. In the great hall the serving people walked under burdens with the slow weight of oxen and scuttled like crabs, crooked and nervous when the weight was gone.

A pause in the recital of his virtues drew Lancelot's attention. The knight who had tried to kill him in a tree had finished, and among the benches Sir Kay was rising to his feet. Lancelot could hear his voice before he spoke, reciting deeds like leaves and bags and barrels. Before his friend could reach the centre of the hall, Sir Lancelot wriggled to his feet and approached the dais. 'My lord king,' he said, 'forgive me if I ask leave to go. An old wound has broken open.'

Arthur smiled down on him. 'I have the same old wound,' he said. 'We'll go together. Perhaps you will come to the tower room when we have attended to our wounds.' And he signed the trumpets to end the gathering, and the bodyguards to clear the hall.

The stone stairway to the king's room was in the thickness of the wall of the round tower of the keep. At short intervals a deep embrasure and a long, bevelled arrow slit commanded some aspect of the town below.

No armed men guarded this stairway. They were below and had passed Sir Lancelot in. The king's room was round, a horizontal slice of the tower, windowless save for the arrow slits, entered by a narrow arched door. It was a sparsely furnished room, carpeted with rushes. A wide bed, and at its foot a carved oaken chest, a bench before the fireplace, and several stools completed the furnishings. But the raw stone of the tower was plastered over and painted with solemn figures of men and angels walking hand in hand. Two candles and the reeky fire gave the only light.

When Lancelot entered, the queen stood up from the bench before the fire, saying, 'I will retire, my lords.'

'No, stay,' said Arthur.

'Stay,' said Lancelot.

The king was stretched comfortably in the bed. His bare feet projecting from his long saffron robe caressed each other, the toes curled downwards.

The queen was lovely in the firelight, all lean, down-flowing lines of green samite. She wore her little mouth-corner smile of concealed amusement, and her bold golden eyes were the same colour as her hair, and odd it was that her lashes and slender brows were dark, an oddity contrived with kohl brought in a small enamelled pot from an outland by a far-wandering knight.

'How are you holding up?' Arthur asked.

'Not well, my lord. It's harder than the quest.'

'Did you really do all the things they said you did?'

Lancelot chuckled. 'Truthfully, I don't know. It sounds different when they tell about it. And most of them feel it necessary to add a little. When I remember leaping eight feet, they tell it at fifty, and frankly I don't recall several of those giants at all.'

The queen made room for him on the fire bench and he took his seat, back to the fire.

Guinevere said, 'The damsel – what's her name – talked about fair queen enchantresses, but she was so excited that her words tumbled over each other. I couldn't make out what happened.'

Lancelot looked nervously away. 'You know how excitable young girls are,' he said. 'A little back-country necromancy in a pasture.'

'But she spoke particularly of queens.'

'My lady, I think everyone is a queen to her. It's like the giants – makes the story richer.'

'Then they were not queens?'

'Well, for that matter, when you get into the field of enchantment, everyone is a queen, or thinks she is. Next time she tells it, the little damsel will be a queen. I do think, my lord, there's too much of that kind of thing going on. It's a bad sign, a kind of restlessness, when people go in for fortune-telling and all such things. Maybe there should be a law about it.'

'There is,' said Arthur. 'But it's not in secular hands. The Church is supposed to take care of that.'

'Yes, but some of the nunneries are going in for it.'

'Well, I'll put a bug in the archbishop's ear.'

The queen observed, 'I gather you rescued damsels by the dozen.' She put her fingers on his arm and a searing shock ran through his body, and his mouth opened in amazement at a hollow ache that pressed upwards against his ribs and shortened his breath.

After a moment she said, 'How many damsels did you rescue?'

His mouth was dry. 'Of course there were a few, madame. There always are.'

'And all of them made love to you?'

'That they did not, madame. There you protect me.'

'I?'

'Yes. Since with my lord's permission I swore to serve you all my life and gave my knightly courtly love to you, I am sheltered from damsels by your name.'

'And do you want to be sheltered?'

'Yes, my lady. I am a fighting man. I have neither time nor inclination for any other kind of love. I hope this pleases you, my lady. I sent many prisoners to ask your mercy.'

'I never saw such a crop of them,' Arthur said. 'You must have swept some counties clean.'

Guinevere touched him on the arm again and with side-glancing golden eyes saw the spasm that shook him. 'While we are on this subject I want to mention one lady you did not save. When I saw her she was a headless corpse and not in good condition, and the man who brought her in was half crazed.'

'I am ashamed of that,' said Lancelot. 'She was under my protection and I failed her. I suppose it was my shame that made me force the man to do it. I'm sorry. I hope you released him from the burden.'

'Not at all,' she said. 'I wanted him away before the feast reeked up to the heavens. I sent him with his burden to the Pope. His friend will not improve on the way. And if his loss of interest in ladies continues, he may turn out to be a very holy man, a hermit or something of that nature, if he isn't a maniac first.'

The king rose on his elbow. 'We will have to work out some system,' he said. 'The rules of errantry are too loose and the quests overlap. Besides, I wonder how long we can leave justice in the hands of men who are themselves unstable. I don't mean you, my friend. But there may come a time when order and organization from the crown will be necessary.'

The queen stood up. 'My lords, will you grant me permission to leave you now? I know you will wish to speak of great things foreign and perhaps tiresome to a lady's ears.'

The king said, 'Surely, my lady. Go to your rest.'

'No, sire – not rest. If I do not lay out the designs for the needlepoint, my ladies will have no work tomorrow.'

'But these are feast days, my dear.'

'I like to give them something every day, my lord. They're lazy things and some of them so woolly in the mind that they forget how to thread a needle from day to day. Forgive me, my lords.'

She swept from the room with proud and powerful steps, and the little breeze she made in the still air carried a strange scent to Lancelot, a perfume which sent a shivering excitement coursing through his body. It was an odour he did not, could not, know, for it was the smell of Guinevere distilled by her own skin. And as she passed through the door and descended the steps, he saw himself leap up and follow her, although he did not move. And when she was gone the room was bleak and the glory was gone from it, and Sir Lancelot was dog-weary, tired almost to weeping.

'What a queen she is,' said King Arthur softly. 'And what a woman equally. Merlin was with me when I chose her. He tried to dissuade me with his usual doomful prophecies. That was one of the few times I differed with him. Well, my choice has proved him fallible. She has shown the world what a queen should be. All other women lose their sheen when she is present.'

Lancelot said, 'Yes, my lord,' and for no reason he knew, except perhaps the intemperate dullness of the feast, he felt lost and a cold knife of loneliness pressed against his heart.

The king was chuckling. 'It is the device of ladies that their lords have great matters to discuss, when if the truth were told, we bore them. And I hope the truth is never told. Why, you look haggard, my friend. Are you feverish? Did you mean that about an old wound opening?'

'No. The wound was what you thought it was, my lord. But it is true that I can fight, travel, live on berries, fight again, go without sleeping, and come out fresh and fierce, but sitting still at Whitsun feast has wearied me to death.'

Arthur said, 'I can see it. We'll discuss the realm's health another time. Go to your bed now. Have you your old quarters?'

'No – better ones. Sir Kay has cleared five knights from the lovely lordly rooms over the north gate. He did it in memory of an adventure which we, God help us, will have to listen to tomorrow. I accept your dismissal, my lord.'

And Lancelot knelt down and took the king's beloved hand in both of his and kissed it. 'Good night, my liege lord, my liege friend,' he said, and then stumbled blindly from the room and felt his way down the curving stone steps past the arrow slits.

As he came to the level of the next landing Guinevere issued silently from a darkened entrance. He could see her in the thin light from the arrow slit. She took his arm and led him to her dark chamber and closed the oaken door.

'A strange thing happened,' she said softly. 'When I left you I thought you followed me. I was so sure of it I did not even look around to verify it. You were there behind me. And when I came to my own door, I said good night to you, so certain I was that you were there.'

He could see her outline in the dark and smell the scent which was herself. 'My lady,' he said, 'when you left the room, I saw myself follow you as though I were another person looking on.'

Their bodies locked together as though a trap had sprung. Their mouths met and each devoured the other. Each frantic heartbeat at the walls of ribs trying to get to the other until their held breaths burst out and Lancelot, dizzied, found the door and blundered down the stairs. And he was weeping bitterly.

And so at that tyme sir Lancelot had
the grettyste name of ony knyght of the worlde,
and moste he was honoured of hyghe and lowe.

EXPLICIT A NOBLE TALE OF
SIR LANCELOT DU LAKE

John Steinbeck wrote *The Acts of King Arthur and His Noble Knights* from the Winchester Manuscript of Malory's tales. His work is more than redaction, since John added to the original stories. It was written in Somerset, England, in 1958–9 and it is unfinished; it was not edited or corrected by John.

The excerpts from his letters, which follow, show that he wrote two drafts of parts of the book. These letters were written to Elizabeth Otis, his literary agent from 1931 to his death in 1968, and to me (the former indicated by ERO, and the latter by CHASE). They describe some of his thoughts, show how he worked, and give some of his ideas about writing. John did not finish *King Arthur*, and did not say why or how he felt blocked, if indeed he was, when he stopped work on it.

What is evident is his great and genuine interest in the subject. In these letters a novelist describes his hopes, some of his plans, and how he proceeded in this portion of his work as a writer.

CHASE HORTON

appendix

To Ero – New York, 11 November 1956

I am going to start the *Morte* immediately. Let it be private between us until I get it done. It has all the old magic.

To Ero – New York, 19 November 1956

I have been dipping into the Malory. And with delight. As long as I don't know what is going on in the world, I would like to have a try with this. I'm going to try anyway.

Now as to method. I am in some wonder about this. When I first read it, at about Louis' age, I must have been already enamoured of words because the old and obsolete words delighted me. However, I wonder whether children now would be so attracted. They are more trained by picture than by sound. I'm going to make a trial run – not removing all of the old forms, nor all the Malory sentence structure, but substituting known simple words and reversing sentences which even now are puzzling.

There are several things I will *not* do. I will not clean it up. Pendragon did take the wife of Cornwall, and that is the way it was. I think children not only understand these things but accept them until they are confused by moralities which try by silence to eliminate reality. These men had *women* and I'm going to keep them. On the other hand, I am going to keep the book and chapter heads and in these I shall keep the Malory-Caxton language intact. I think it is going to be fun to do.

When I have some of it done, I shall with an opening essay tell of my own interest in the cycle, when it started and where it went – into scholarship and out again on the other side. In this essay I shall also try to put down what I think has been the impact of this book on our language, our attitudes, and morals, and our ethics.

I have a feeling that this will go very fast – if there aren't too many interruptions. Also, I think that in this I can weather interruptions. I find I know it very well, after all these years.

One other thing I do not want to do. There are many places in this book which are not clear, as poetry is not clear. They are not literal. I don't intend to make them clear or literal. I remember too well my own delight in conjecture.

Now as for title – I don't know what was on Caxton's cover but on his title page it was:

The Birth, Life and Acts of King Arthur, of his Noble Knights of the Round Table, their marvellous enquests and adventures, the achieving of the San Greal and in the end Le Morte Darthur with the Dolorous Death and Departing out of this World of them All.

I should perhaps like to take an earlier part of this and call the book *The Acts of King Arthur*. Of course I would explain this in the introduction – quoting the Caxton title page. But the Book is much more Acts than Morte.

Anyway – that can all be discussed. The main thing is to see whether or not I can do it at all— And the best way to find out is to do it.

Do you have a Caxton edition ? I should like you – as you read my version – to compare it, so that recommendations can be made.

Next, what would you think of Chase as a kind of Managing Editor ? His knowledge and interest seem to be great and he could be of help to me when I come a cropper. It would be good to have someone to consult with. And he might have an opening essay to precede mine. Let me know about this.

To Ero – New York, 3 December 1956

The work on the stories of Arthur goes well and happily. This is by way of being a progress report and prospectus. In the matter of the Arthurian book I find myself singularly well prepared. I have had some Anglo-Saxon and of course, like everyone else, have read a good deal of Old and Middle English. Why I say 'everyone else', I don't know because I find that very few people have.

There are, however, in the Winchester manuscript a large number of words which, while I can pick out the general meaning, may have special meanings too. It is difficult to find lexicons or dictionaries of the older languages. However, I have the library and Fannie working on this and I hope to have some material this week.

My enthusiasm for the work grows. I am comparing Caxton with the Winchester and I find that Caxton is quite different. He not only edited but put the text in a different manner in many cases. Although he brought out his edition within a few years of Malory's death, his language is quite different from the Winchester. I am inclined to believe that there are two reasons for this. First, Caxton was printer and editor and city man, whereas Malory was very, very much country – and also in jail quite a bit. Also the Winchester manuscript was monkish copyists' work and is probably much more nearly like Malory. I find myself using the Winchester more than the Caxton. If anyone is going to edit, I prefer doing it myself. Besides, there are lovely nuances in the Winchester which have been removed by Caxton.

In a fairly short time – as soon, in fact, as I finish the Merlin, we will get together on the method I am using and come to a decision.

To Ero – New York, 2 January 1957

Your letter came this afternoon and bless you for the admonition to slow down. I don't know where I get this race against time, part of a starvation or bankruptcy fixation I guess. I have known for some time that this is not a job to whip out. There's a lot of reading but a lot of thinking to do also and I don't think quickly.

Arthur is not a character. You are right. And here it might be well to consider that Jesus isn't either, nor is Buddha. Perhaps the large symbol figures can't be characters, for if they were, we wouldn't identify with them by substituting our own. Such a thing is worth thinking about surely. As for ability as either a fighter or as a ruler, it is quite possible that Malory didn't find these necessary. It was the blood that was important and second the anointing. With these two ability wasn't necessary, while without them ability had little or no chance of operating. You will notice too that no moral law obtains. As a man King Harry was a murderer, but as a king, he couldn't be. This is a state of mind very difficult for us to follow but it was real just the same.

I'm going to go in to town next Monday. I want to go to the Morgan Library and meet the people there. And it is time to come up for air too.

To Ero – New York, 3 January 1957

Just reading and reading and reading and it's like hearing remembered music.

Remarkable things in the books. Little meanings that peek out for a moment, and a few scholars who make observations and then almost in fright withdraw or qualify what they have said. When I finish this job, if I ever do, I should like to make some observations about the Legend. Somewhere there's a piece missing in the jigsaw and it is a piece which ties the whole thing together. So many scholars have spent so much time trying to establish whether Arthur existed at all that they have lost track of the single truth that he exists over and over. Collingwood establishes that there was an Ursus or the Bear which in Celtic is Artur which he quotes Nennius as translating into

Latin as Ursus horribilis. But Ursus horribilis is the grizzly bear and as far as I know has never been found outside of North America. But you see what you get into. I can see how a man, if he wanted to, could get bogged down here and spend many happy years fighting with the other specialists about the word bear and its Celtic Artur.

Twelve was the normal number for any group of followers of a man or a principle. The symbolism was inevitable. And whether the Grail was the cup from Golgotha or the Gaelic cauldron later used by Shakespeare doesn't in the least matter since the principle of both was everlasting or rather ever-renewed life. All such things fall into place inevitably but it is the connective – the continuing line with the piece missing in the middle – that fascinates me.

Another beautiful thing is how Malory learned to write as he went along. The straggling sentences, the confused characters and events of the early parts smooth out as he goes along so that his sentences become more fluid and his dialogue gets a sting of truth and his characters become more human than symbolic even though he tries hard to keep the symbol, and this I am sure is because he was learning to write as he went along. He became a master and you can see it happening. And in any work I do on this thing I am not going to try to change that. I'll go along with his growing perfection and who knows, I may learn myself. It's a lovely job if I can only lose the sense of hurry that has been growing in me for so long. That's the real curse, and why and for whom? Maybe I've written too many books instead of one. But Malory had one great advantage over me. He was so very often in jail and there wasn't any hurry there, except now and then when he wished he could get out.

To Chase – Sag Harbor, 9 January 1957

Reading on and on and I am so slow. I literally move my lips. Elaine can read four books while I mumble through one. But I guess this isn't going to change. Anyway, I'm having fun and there is nothing to interrupt.

Going into New York next Monday. I'm going to have lunch with Adams of the PM Library next week. I have suggested Thursday if he is free then or Wednesday or Friday if he is not. He is going to bring Dr Buhler along whose name you will know from his Medieval and Renaissance work. Of Buhler, Adams says: 'He has some of the lustiness of his subject.' Anyway they are being very cooperative in every way. I hope you will also be free for lunch. I have suggested the Colony Bar, 12:30 next Thursday, the 17th I think. Can you come ? If they are not free that day I will call you and let you know, but I would love it if you could join us.

I'm getting many glimmerings but I'm going to leave them that way. Nothing is so dangerous as the theories of a half-assed or half-informed scholar. I'm pretty sure that a lot of it was only glimmerings to Malory also. Can't thank you enough for sending the books but it is going to take me a long time to catch up. I'll call you in town.

To Chase – New York, 18 February 1957

The idea of thanks from you to me is ridiculous. The enormous amount of work and thought you are putting into this would be hard to repay. And the future is loaded with more work. Thank heaven it is work we both like to do –

In so far as I am able – which isn't far – I am trying to exclude everything right now until I have put down the base pattern to see what is there for me.

To Chase – New York, 14 March 1957

Now Malory was a pretty exact man with words. He does never mention Frensshe books – but only Frensshe *book*. In other words, he did not need a library, and there is little evidence that he used one. He never once refers to the alliterative poem in English nor to Geoffrey of Monmouth. He was not a scholar. He was a novelist. Just as Shakespeare was a playwright. We know where Shakespeare must have got his English history, since the parallels are too close, but where did he get his Verona, his Venice, his Padua, his Rome, his Athens ? For some reason it is the fashion to believe that these great men, Malory and Shakespeare, did not read and did not listen. They are supposed to have absorbed by osmosis. I read the Mabinogion thirty years ago and yet in *Sweet Thursday* I repeat the story of the poor knight who made a wife out of flowers. And in something else I retold the story of the man who hanged a mouse for theft. And I am not in a recall class with Malory or Shakespeare.

And I want to elaborate a little on the egg of an hypothesis that the *Morte d'Arthur* might have been a political protest of sorts.

When Shakespeare wanted to inveigh against the throne – because he was no fool – he did not attack the Tudor throne but the older lines – ones of which Elizabeth may have been a little jealous since she was descended from a Welsh upstart. A frontal attack on the crown was the surest suicide, known in both Malory's and Shakespeare's times. But let's see what you would feel if you were for Neville, duke of Warwick – and Edward IV were king. Such a king could do no right.

Let me tell you a story. When *The Grapes of Wrath* got loose, a lot of people were pretty mad at me. The undersheriff of Santa Clara County was a friend of mine and he told me as follows: 'Don't you go into any hotel room alone. Keep records of every minute and when you are off the ranch travel with one or two friends but particularly, don't stay in a hotel alone.' 'Why?' I asked. He said, 'Maybe I'm sticking my neck out but the boys got a rape case set up for you. You get alone in a hotel and a dame will come in, tear off her clothes, scratch her face and scream and you try to talk yourself out of that one. They won't touch your book but there's easier ways.'

It's a horrible feeling, Chase, particularly because it works. No one would ever have believed my book again. And until the heat was off I never went any place alone. And we didn't invent it.

The knight prisoner was unfortunate but not guilt-ridden. And that makes one suspect all the stories of knights taken prisoner by sorcery. Until recently we could destroy a man by simply naming him a communist and he could be charged by a known liar and still be destroyed. How easy then must it have been in the fifteenth century.

We know why Cervantes was in jail. Do we really know why Malory was?

You know, Chase, I never worked with anyone who was more fun to work with. You catch fire the way I do. If we do our work well, we will have built a tiny rush fire in the anteroom to the faculty club. But it's real fun, isn't it? And the parallels with our own time are crowding me.

To Chase – Florence, Italy, 9 April 1957

People ask me when I will have the *Morte* thing ready and I choose a conservative figure and say ten years. The size of the job, however, makes me feel that this might be a conservative estimate.

I think I wrote to Elizabeth that Dr Vinaver has been greatly impressed with the rough translation of the early part that was sent to him and has offered any help possible. And that was a very rough translation indeed. I can do better than that.

To Ero – Florence, Italy, 19 April 1957

Later I am meeting and conferring with Professor Sapori, who is the great authority of Medieval economics and a fascinating man. I am also going to see Berenson at his earliest convenience. He knows where everything is and sees the sparrow fall.

But you can see that I have not been without activities here. I am in a state of wonder at the enormous amount of effort on the part of Chase. He is doing fantastic work. Please tell him how much I appreciate it and also that I will forward to him anything I can turn up here. If he is interested in the suit for recovery, there might be some references in the Morgan Library, but I will soon have assembled all of the sources consulted here and in Rome for the bibliography which will be an astonishing structure by the time we are through. I am getting more and more a sense of the time. If he has not read *The Merchant of Prato* by Iris Origo, Jonathan Cape, London, 1957, tell him that he will be interested. It is the Paston letters of Tuscany gleaned from one hundred and fifty thousand letters of one business firm in Prato in fourteenth and early fifteenth century and a beautiful job. I have a copy and will send it if he has difficulty finding it. As a matter of fact I think I would do well to send the books I am accumulating home to Chase as I finish them. We are going to have a rather formidable library before we are finished and I couldn't be happier about this.

To Ero and Chase – Rome, Italy, 26 April 1957

I had letters from the American Embassy and from Count Bernardo Rucelai of Florence, who is an old friend of the keeper. So I was very well received. The archives are the goddamndest things you ever saw, acres and acres of just pure information. I had a hard time tearing myself away. I have certain things to look for and the US Information Agency is going to get me someone to see if the material I want is in existence. Incidentally, Chase, the bibliography is leaping what with Florence and now here. Maybe I can't find what I want but there is no harm in trying and apparently no one has ever looked in this direction or in Florence before.

I have been reading all of the scholarly appraisals of the *Morte* and the discussions of Malory's reasons for his various attitudes, and all the time there has been a bothersome thought in my brain knocking about just out of reach, something I knew that was wrong in all of the inspection and yet I couldn't put my finger on it. Why did Lancelot fail in his quest and why did Galahad succeed? What is the feeling about sin, or the feeling about Guinevere? How about the rescue from the stake? How about the relationship between Arthur and Lancelot. It has all been turned over so often and like the Alger Hiss case there has seemed something missing. Then this morning I awakened about five o'clock fully awake but with the feeling that some tremendous task had been completed. I got up and looked out at the sun coming up over Rome and tried to reconstruct what the task had been and how if at all it had been solved, and suddenly it came back whole and in one piece. And I think it answers my nagging doubt. It can't be a theory because it won't subject itself to proof. I'm afraid it has to be completely intuitive and because of this it will never be very seriously considered by scholars.

Malory has been studied as a translator, as a soldier, as a rebel, as a religious, as an expert in courtesy, as nearly everything you think of except one, and that is what he was – a novelist. The *Morte* is the first and one of the greatest of novels in the English language. I will try to put this down as purely and simply as I can. And only a novelist could think it. A novelist not only puts down a story but he is the story. He is each one of the characters in a greater or a less degree. And because he is usually a moral man in intention and honest in his approach, he sets things down as truly as he can. He is limited by his experience, his knowledge, his observation and his feelings.

A novel may be said to be the man who writes it. Now it is nearly always true that a novelist, perhaps unconsciously, identifies himself with one chief or central character in his novel. Into this character he puts not only what he thinks he is but what he hopes to be. We can call this spokesman the self-character. You will find one in every one of my books and in the novels of everyone I can remember. It is most simple and near the surface in Hemingway's novels. The soldier, romantic, always maimed in some sense, hand – testicles. These are the symbols of his limitations. I suppose my own symbol character has my dream wish of wisdom and acceptance. Now it seems to me that Malory's self-character would be Lancelot. All of the perfections he knew went into this character, all of the things of which he thought himself capable. But, being an honest man he found faults in himself, faults of vanity, faults of violence, faults even of disloyalty, and these would naturally find their way into his dream character. Oh, don't forget that the novelist may arrange or rearrange events so that they are more nearly what he hoped they might have been.

And now we come to the Grail, the Quest. I think it is true that any man, novelist or not, when he comes to maturity has a very deep sense that he will not win the Quest. He knows his failings, his shortcomings and particularly his memories of sins, sins of cruelty, of thoughtlessness, of disloyalty, of adultery, and these will not permit him to win the Grail. And so his self-character must suffer the same terrible sense of failure as his author. Lancelot could not see the

Grail because of the faults and sins of Malory himself. He knows he has fallen short and all his excellences, his courage, his courtesy, in his own mind cannot balance his vices and errors, his stupidities.

I think this happens to every man who has ever lived, but it is set down largely by novelists. But there is an answer ready to hand for every man and for novelists. The self-character cannot win the Quest, but his son can, his spotless son, the son of his seed and his blood who has his virtues but has not his faults. And so Galahad is able to win the Quest, the dear son, the unsoiled son, and because he is the seed of Lancelot and the seed of Malory, Malory-Lancelot has in a sense won the Quest and in his issue broken through to the glory which his own faults have forbidden him.

Now this is so. I know it as surely as I can know anything. God knows I have done it myself often enough. And this can for me wipe out all the inconsistencies and obscurities scholars have found in the story. And if the *Morte* is uneven and changeable it is because the author was changeable. Sometimes there is a flash of fire, sometimes a moody dream, sometimes an anger. For a novelist is a rearranger of nature so that it makes an understandable pattern, and a novelist is also a teacher, but a novelist is primarily a man and subject to all of a man's faults and virtues, fears and braveries. And I have seen no treatise which has ever considered that the story of the *Morte* is the story of Sir Thomas Malory and his times and the story of his dreams of goodness and his wish that the story may come out well and only moulded by the essential honesty which will not allow him to lie.

Well, that was the problem and that was the settlement and it came sweetly out with the morning sun on the brown walls of Rome. And I should like to know whether you two find it valid at all. In my heart and in my mind I find it true and I do not know how in the world I can prove it except by saying it as clearly as I can so that a reader may say: 'Of course, that's how it had to be. Whatever else could be the explanation?'

Please let me know what you think of this dizzying inductive leap. Does it possibly seem as deeply true to you as it does to me?

I shall dearly like to know what you think.

From Ero to J. S. – New York, 3 May 1957

Your letter about Malory this week is one of the most impressive letters that you or anyone else has ever written. Now you are back home. The creative process has started. I never saw it so accurately described. Time, place, feel. Enter novelist.

Wonderful that you are coming to consider my friend Guinevere, she has been so neglected. You may not want to do much with her, but she really must have been an important part of the picture.

To Ero and Chase – Florence, Italy, 9 May 1957

I continue to write in covers like this because it is nearly impossible for me to write separately. I am going every day to the craft shops and at the same time doing my scrimy little newspaper pieces (which nevertheless take time) and also going over the material developed by my girl who is working in archives.

I can't tell you how pleased and glad and relieved I am that you approve of my Malory approach. It has given me a whole new drive and a perceivable end, which I never had before. And your backing makes me feel that I am on some kind of firm footing. Chase, your letters are a very great help to me and are filed for much rereading. And Elizabeth, I too have felt this lack about Guinevere. She has always been the symbol when in fact she must have been a dame. I have been reading a great deal about women in the Middle Ages and I think I know now why modern scholars can't think of her as anything but a symbol. There was just a different way of looking at them. It shows up in every phase of women's life as described by contemporaries. Baldini particularly sets it down clearly. I believe that Malory also set it down. I know what you mean, Chase, about the impossibility of ever getting scholars to agree. I might put in a chapter just listing their disagreements with one another down through the centuries. Hell, I might put in a chapter about anything. I don't know where this is going now but I do have a taste for it and a tone of it and that is the only true beginning. And I don't think I am wrong in developing as much material as I can. With a little time and some instinct, something of my own will emerge. At least it always has. And all kinds of feelings are beginning to squirm up into the thinking level. But I don't want them up there for some time. I would like it to boil around for quite a while.

To Chase – Florence, Italy, 17 May 1957

Last evening I spent with Professor Armando Sapori. He is quite old and has been ill but he asked me to come, and often during the evening when I asked to go for fear of tiring him he demanded that I stay. He speaks no English, but one of his students, Julio Fossi, translated for us in so far as we needed translation. He is a man so learned and so simple that I understood him mostly very well. As he spoke the Middle Ages came back – the Amalfi League, beginning of the Renaissance, the entrance of Greek thought and conception of the commune or city, not from Greece but from the Arabs and incised as it was in Rome by Saracen slaves after the Crusades.

The other day I came across Strachey's volumes of Southey's translation of the *Morte*. It was cleaned up, so that it might safely be put in the hands of Boys. Could you get that for us ? The translation is good but I'll have no part of the cleaning up for boys. Let boys beware – and boys won't thank God.

**To Chase and Ero – Grand Hotel,
Stockholm, Sweden, 4 July 1957**

I started a letter and now we have finally got some kind of order in our planning. In the first part of this letter I got us as far as London. If we start northwards on the fifteenth of July, that will give us ten days, we would go up through Warwickshire and to the wall and then when we had made our bows to Hadrian move gradually down the western country to see some of Wales and also Glastonbury and Tintagel, etc.

I shall take along the books you sent and besides the book of maps I have got the large-scale maps of some of the country, particularly of Warwickshire.

To Ero and Chase – London, 13 July 1957

Well, on Monday we're off with a driver named Jack in a Humber Hawk. We are armed with books, papers, your letters, cameras and sketching pads. The last is for show because we can't draw. We are both looking forward to this a great deal. Of course there are lots of things we won't see but there are lots of things we will. From the enclosed list you will see what we intend.

Itinerary

From this base will cruise the area of interest in Warwickshire.

Thursday	Grand Hotel, Manchester (Vinaver)
Friday	Lord Crew Armes, Blanchland
Saturday	Rothbury and the Wall
Sunday	Wall and down into Wales, possibly to Malvern
Monday	Tresanton St Mawes near Falmouth
Tuesday	Winchester (Mss.)

Rolling and tossing about last night, I had an idea which seemed to have some validity to me and I want to ask you what you think of it. The trouble with such ideas is in my ignorance. I mean that this may have occured to many people and the field be thoroughly covered. Anyway, I am going to put down the thinking just as it developed and pretend that it has never been considered before. Unfortunately I do not have my *Morte* with me. It has been sent to the ship, so I will have to rely a little on memory which in me is not so hot. OK then, it goes like this.

In considering a man about whom there are few and sparse records, there are three directions one may take to build up some kind of reality about him – His work (the most important). His times (important because he grew out of them) and finally his associates or people with whom he may have associated. In the case of Malory a great deal has been made of his association with Beauchamp, the learned parfait knight, the worldly, the romantic, the brave and the experienced. And this preoccupation seems to me to be extremely valid. But there is another man whom I have not met in my reading and this is a man about which a great deal must be known, his publisher Caxton. If I remember correctly, in his preface Caxton never indicates that he knew Malory. In fact it does seem from his words that he did not. We know that there were two, probably three and perhaps a number of other copies of the *Morte*. But the book was finished a very few years before Caxton printed it. I do not think that it could have been issued in sections as it was completed, therefore we must believe that the first appearance of the *Morte* could hardly have been before 1469. Between that time and Caxton's printing of it, a very short time elapsed, not enough time for the mss. to be widely copied, distributed, memorized and read or recited. Why then did Caxton pick up and print this book ? If he had wanted to print the Arthurian story as something which might be popular, he could have chosen the alliterative poem which was very much better known, or he could have had the classic tales translated, the Romaunt, the Lancelot, etc. But he took the work of an unknown writer with no background in learning or scholarship, a felon. I cannot believe that Malory's *Morte* was well known at the time Caxton printed it. Why then did he print it ? I think the only way to approach this is to inquire into his other choices. Did he print other unknown works by unknown men ? I don't know, but it's easy to find out. I don't have a library to consult. What were Caxton's business habits and practices, his editorial habits and practices ? It is my feeling

that he was not a man to go out on a limb except in bucking the copyists' organizations with his movable type. Could a pattern of his activities be arrived at ? Did the new work of an unknown writer so sparkle with Genius that Caxton, the editor, was drawn to it on a critical basis ? It was not a time when novelists were commonly undertaken. Malory would have had no backing of school, college or church. His book was not revolutionary as Wyckliff's translation of the Bible was, nor did it have the fascination of the Lollard heresies. It was a traditional book, dealing with traditional stories. Caxton could easily have got translations made by well-known and respected men. Malory had no noble backing, no sponsor and I believe that this was a pretty good thing to have if you wanted your book to be well received. Was Caxton an inspired editor with a great sense of literary values as opposed to traditional and business values ?
I don't know these things but I would like to. For what seems to emerge is this. The first printer chose for one of his early but not his earliest efforts the works of an unknown writer, or if he were known at all it was as a robber, a rapist and a felon who had died in prison. That his book was immediately successful there is no doubt, but how in the world could Caxton have known that ? These are all questions but they are questions I would like to have resolved. How much is known about Caxton ? My own knowledge is abysmally nonexistent. But have these considerations ever been entertained in connection with the *Morte* ?

I have a feeling that if Chase has not already considered and resolved these questions, that he will react to them like a dog whose tail is soaked in kerosene and then lighted. I have not in my reading come on these questions. Damn it, it is hard not having a library available. And tomorrow we will be on the road. I'm sorry to throw this polecat to you, but let us not fail to discuss it as soon as I get home and perhaps to try to resolve some of it. I don't know but I do have a feeling that Caxton is well documented. If it weren't Sunday I would go out and try to find a book on Caxton. But London is shut tighter than a drum.

To Ero – Sag Harbor, 7 August 1957

I went also to the Rylands Library in Manchester to inspect one of two existing Caxton first printings in the world. Dr Vinaver was of great help to me and offered any help he could give and opened his files and his bibliography to me. He was very much excited by my approach to the subject, saying it was the first new approach in many years. I went also to Winchester College to see the manuscript of the

Morte which was only discovered in 1936, having been lost since it was written by priestly scribes in the fifteenth century.

Since my work in this field requires that I know the countryside in which Malory lived and operated, I rented a car and driver and went to Malory's birthplace in Warwickshire, to the place where he was imprisoned. I then found it necessary to visit Alnwick Castle, Wales, Glastonbury, Tintagel and all of those places associated with King Arthur. This journey took ten days of very rapid travelling since I had to go from one end of England to the other to get a sense of topography, colour of soil, marsh, moor, forest and particularly relationships of one place to another. Elaine made an extensive photographic record of all the places visited on this major effort. This is destined to be the largest and I hope the most important work I have ever undertaken. Throughout the trip I have filled in my library with books, records, photographs, and even microfilms of documents which cannot be removed from their repositories. I am very much excited by this work and am highly gratified by the respect and encouragement of the authorities in the field. Far from resenting my intrusion, they have all gone out of their way to give me every possible help.

To Chase – New York, 4 October 1957

It does seem to me that there is no problem about how Malory got books. If he didn't get them he would have been a fool and he was no fool.

Damn it – the subject is endless, isn't it ? I'm looking forward to seeing you on Tuesday. And I'm going to stay in all week so we can repeat. Also my energy seems to be beginning to come back. Thank heaven for that. I had reached a point of despair.

Malory is uneasy in the Knight of the Cart probably because it didn't mean anything to him. The earlier fact that carts were used solely for condemned prisoners was not enough for him even if he knew it. There are many places in the *Morte* where he is uneasy because he doesn't know the reason, nor the background, but when he is sure – when he is dealing with people and countryside – he is not a bit confused.

To Chase – New York, 25 October 1957

Of course I am very much excited about the microreader. Sure it weighs seventeen pounds, but you can carry a large library in a shoe box. We're going to have lots of fun with that. When Archie

MacLeish was Librarian of Congress, he was microfilming lots of things that couldn't be moved. I'm sure some of the Universities and probably the NY Public Library are doing the same. Is there any way to find out what the various repositories have filmed and whether it is obtainable?

I hope the machine you got has a reverse. Quite often one wants to turn back. Won't it be fun to track down the things we want and can't take out. Very exciting. I've just finished the second volume of *Henry V*. I believe Wylie died after proofing the first volume. At least that's what the introduction to Volume II says. His detail is marvellous. And did you notice one thing? He was so immersed that he was writing in the old words and even the old constructions. It's a great history and it is just possible that Henry may have been Malory's Arthur symbol.

Right now I'm staying away from Malory. But when I go back to him I think it will be with a new dimension and that, my friend, is completely your doing. This work is collaboration, and don't think it isn't. The fact that I will do the final writing does not make the work less collaboration. Meanwhile I'm having a hell of a fine time with the books. And I'm going to take all the time I need – or rather, want. And I want a lot. I have even stopped writing letters except to you and Elizabeth. I want to forget how to write and learn all over again with the writing growing out of the material. And I'm going to be real mean about that.

To Chase – New York, 1 March 1958

Yesterday I wrote the very first lines of the book, either for first printed page or endpaper, which I here enclose.*

I guess this is the first time I have ever written a first part first. It is also probably the only passage in the whole thing which will be written in fifteenth-century spelling. (Save possibly a footnote or caboose material.)

To Ero – New York, 4 March 1958

I think the time has come for a progress report in the matter of the Malory work. I also want to make a kind of declaration of immediate intention in regard to this work. As you know, the research and reading

---

*John's opening words, dedicated to his sister, Mary, are reproduced on the dedication pages.

and accumulation of knowledge has gone on over a long, long period now, and must continue to go on at least until the autumn. You will understand that I am pumped full of information, some of it possibly ill assimilated and perhaps being slowly digested. As usual it is the texture rather than the exact information which has the most profound impact on me, but even so a remarkable amount of factual material seems to be getting through to me. I have read literally hundreds of books on the Middle Ages and have literally a few hundred more to dip into before I shall be ready to start writing. The enormous accumulation of notes which Chase and I have made are necessary, even though they may not come to the surface of the work to be done. To proceed without the information would be to proceed without foundation. Last year I spent some time in England, as you well know, going to a number of places which will be referred to in the work, to absorb the physical feeling of the places. I thought that I had covered the field fairly well. It is only with continued reading that I find that there are gaps in my information. I shall find it necessary to return to England to pick up, or rather to fill up the holes in my visual background. I think the best time to go would be the first of June. I must go to spend some time at Glastonbury, at Colchester and at parts of Cornwall in the neighbourhood of Tintagel and then north again to spend a little more time at Alnwick, and at Bamborough Castle in Northumberland. These last two are very important since one may well have been the Maiden's Castle referred to by Malory, and the other might be Joyous Garde. And I must have the feel and look of all of these places, which are not only referred to but are parts of Malory's experience in the fifteenth century. Pictures do not do any good. There is a great charge to be gained from going there. I shall be very glad if Chase can accompany me to these places, since our research has been done in conjunction.

I plan to spend the month of June in England picking up final topographical information and also consulting with certain authorities, such as Professor Vinaver of the University of Manchester, and others who are preeminent in the field of the fifteenth century. I shall return to America about the first of July and will continue the reading in the light of what I have found in this next trip into October. And if I can judge at all by my own state of information and mind, I should be able to start writing on this book this fall. And of course, once started, I shall continue with it until a great part of it is completed.

Building a background for this book has been a long and arduous job but highly rewarding. I doubt very much whether I could have done it at all without the help of Chase Horton. Surely it might have been done but not with the exactness and the range and the universality that he has brought to the association.

I come now to something a little more exact. First, title of first proposed work, and this I shall want to discuss with you further, but I think I can put a preliminary discussion of this matter in this letter. When Caxton printed the first edition of a book by Sir Thomas Malory in the fifteenth century, he gave it a title and we do not know whether this was the title used by Malory or not. It may have been supplied by Caxton. The full title gradually was reduced to MORTE D'ARTHUR, but this was only three words in the title and did not describe the book at all. The full title in Caxton, you will remember, is: THE BIRTH, LIFE AND ACTS OF KING ARTHUR, OF HIS NOBLE KNIGHTS OF THE ROUND TABLE, THEIR MARVELLOUS ENQUESTS AND ADVENTURES, THE ACHIEVING OF THE SAN GREAL, AND IN THE END LE MORTE D'ARTHUR WITH THE DOLOROUS DEATH AND DEPARTING OUT OF THIS WORLD OF THEM ALL. Now this is the title that was used by Caxton and why this whole body of work should come to be known as MORTE D'ARTHUR, which is just one little part, I will never know. I propose, therefore, to give it a title which is a little more descriptive of what the body of the work is about. A title such as THE ACTS OF KING ARTHUR, which is sufficient, or if necessary, THE ACTS OF KING ARTHUR AND HIS NOBLE KNIGHTS. Now this would describe much more completely what the body of the work is about. It also would be a kind of a new approach, a living approach rather than a deathly approach to the whole subject. We will discuss this later, but I think that I am ready to leave the word 'Morte' out of this because it is such a *small* part of the whole body of the work. And if the followers of Caxton could abstract a few words from the whole title, I don't know why I can't abstract a few more, particularly if they're more descriptive. This is not essentially the story of the death of Arthur but of the life of Arthur. I think it's very important to put that in the title. We will never know, of course, what Malory himself called the work. It may well be that Caxton used the title that Malory himself used, which is the full title.

As to the exact method I shall use, it is beginning to take form in my head, but I don't think that it is complete enough to discuss it now but there must be much discussion before I go to active work in the fall. It seems to me that in addition to the daydreaming and nightdreaming that I do about the book that my first job is to complete my research on the Middle Ages and to pick up the material in England, which I failed to do on my last trip.

I am going to talk to Chase about the possibility of his joining me in England because I think that two sets of eyes would be more valuable than one, and two sets of information could be compounded into one thing.

My purpose will be to put it into a language which is understandable and acceptable to a modern-day reader. I think this is not only an important thing to do, but also a highly practical thing to do, since these stories form, with the New Testament, the basis of most modern English literature. And it can be shown and will be shown that the myth of King Arthur continues even into the present day and is an inherent part of the so-called 'Western' with which television is filled at the present time – same characters, same methods, same stories, only slightly different weapons and certainly a different topography. But if you change Indians or outlaws for Saxons and Picts and Danes, you have exactly the same story. You have the cult of the horse, the cult of the knight. The application with the present is very close, and also the present day with its uncertainties very closely parallels the uncertainties of the fifteenth century.

It is actually a kind of nostalgic return to the good old days. I think Malory did it, and I think our writers for television are doing it – exactly the same thing and, oddly enough, finding exactly the same symbols and methods.

Thus we find that the work I propose is not a period piece necessarily, and certainly not a specialized piece of work, but one with applications in the present day and definite roots in our living literature.

To Ero and Chase – New York, 14 March 1958

There seems to be something necessary about pressures. The other night I was lying awake wishing I could get to Malory with a rolling barrage of sling-stones and arrows – which isn't likely to happen – and suddenly it came back to me that I have always worked better under pressure of one kind or another – poverty, death, emotional confusion, divorces – always something. In fact the only really unproductive times I can remember were those when there were no pressures. If my record has any meaning at all, it is that pressures are necessary to my creative survival – an inelegant, even a nauseating thought, but there it is. So maybe I had better pray not for surcease but for famine, plague, catastrophe, and bankruptcy. Then I would probably work like a son-of-a-bitch. I'm comparatively serious about this.

A curious state of suspension has set in, kind of a floaty feeling like the drifting in a canoe on a misty lake while ghosts and winkies, figures of fog, go past – half recognized, and only partly visible. It would be reasonable to resist this vagueness, but for some reasons which I will set down later, I do not.

It is all very well to look back at the Middle Ages from a position of vantage. The story, or part of it, is finished. We know – to a certain extent – what happened and why and who and what were the causes. This knowledge of course is strained through minds which have no likeness of experience with the mind of the Middle Ages. But the writer of the *Morte* did not know what had happened, what was happening, nor what was going to happen. He was caught as we are now. In forlornness – he didn't know finally whether York or Lancaster would win, nor did he know that this was the least important of problems. He must have felt that the economic world was out of tune since the authority of the manors was slipping away. The revolts of the subhuman serfs must have caused consternation in his mind. The whisperings of religious schism were all around him so that the unthinkable chaos of ecclesiastical uncertainty must have haunted him. Surely he could only look forward to those changes, which we find healthy, with horrified misgiving.

And out of this devilish welter of change – so like the one today – he tried to create a world of order, a world of virtue governed by forces familiar to him. And what material had he to build with ? Not the shelves of well-ordered source books, not even the public records of his time, not a single chronological certainty, since such a system did not exist. He did not even have a dictionary in any language. Perhaps he had a few manuscripts, a missal, maybe the Alliterative Poems. Beyond this, he had only his memory and his hopes and his intuitions. If he could not remember a word, he had to use another or make one up.

And what were his memories like ? I'll tell you what they were like. He remembered bits and pieces of what he had read. He remembered the deep and terrible forest and the slime of the swamps. He remembered without recalling, or recalled without remembering, stories told by the fire in the manorial hall by trouvères from Brittany; but also in his mind were the tellings in the sheep byre in the night – by a shepherd whose father had been to Wales and had heard Cymric tales of wonder and mysticism. In his mind were perhaps some of the triads and also some of the lines from the poems of hidden meaning which survived in him because the words and figures were compelling and spoke to his unconscious mind, although the exact meaning was lost. The writer had also a sky full of cloud-like history, not arranged in time but with people and events all co-existing simultaneously. Among them were friends, relatives, kings, old gods and heroes, ghosts and angels, and devils of feeling and of traditions lost and rediscovered.

And finally he had himself as literary material – his vices and failures, his hopes and angers and alarms, his insecurities for the future and his puzzlement about the past. Everyone and every event he had ever known was in him. And his illnesses were there too, always the stomachache, since the food of his time was inadequate for health, perhaps bad teeth – a universal difficulty – maybe arrested syphilis or the grandchildren of the pox carried in distorted genes. He had the strong uninspected fabric of the church, memory of music heard, unconscious observation of nature, since designed observation is a recent faculty. He had all of the accumulated folklore of his time – magic and soothsaying, forecast and prophecy – witchcraft and its brother medicine. All these are not only in the writer of the *Morte* – they are the writer.

Let us now consider me – who am the writer who must write the writer as well as the *Morte*. Why has it been necessary to read so much – most of which will probably not be used ? I think it necessary for me to know everything I can about what Malory knew and how he might have felt, but it is also necessary for me to be aware of what he did not know, could not have known, and could not feel. For example – if I did not know something about contemporary conditions and attitudes toward medieval villeins and serfs, I could not understand Malory's complete lack of feeling for them. One of the greatest errors in the reconstruction of another era lies in our tendency to think of them as being like ourselves in feeling and attitudes. Actually, without considerable study on the part of a present-day man – if he were confronted by a fifteenth-century man – there would be no possible communication. I think it is possible through knowledge and discipline for a modern man to understand, and, to a certain extent, live into a fifteenth-century mind, but the reverse would be completely impossible.

I don't think any of the research on this project has been wasted, because while I may not be able to understand all of Malory's mind, at least I know what he could *not* have thought or felt.

With all of the preceding in mind, it must be clear that the opposite is going to be a definite difficulty. In translating, I cannot communicate all of the *Morte* because the modern mind, without great knowledge and intra-era empathy, is quite incapable of taking on a great part of it. Where this is so, the only recourse will lie in parallels. Perhaps I will be able to evoke a *similar* emotion or image although it cannot be an identical one.

The difficulties are now apparent to me in relation to this work. But the credit side must not be discounted. There is a continuing folklore which has never been lost, down from generation to generation. This body of myth has changed very little in its essence, although its clothing may vary from period to period and from place to place. And within the legend there is the safety of identification, almost a set of responses to mental stimuli.

Also the drives and desires of people have not changed. A man's true wish is to be rich and comfortable and noticed and loved. To these ends he devotes all of his wishes and most of his energies. Only when he is frustrated in these does his direction change. Within this pattern the writer of the *Morte* and I and those who may read my work are able to communicate freely.

To Chase – London, May 1958

Welcome to fifteenth-century London! We've just come in from two and a half days wandering with Vinaver. We couldn't get reservations in Winchester for tonight because of an agricultural fair, so we are driving there early in the morning so Vinaver can show John the manuscript himself. We will have lunch there with the librarian, see the mss. and drive back to London. We will call you *the instant* we get in, probably around 6:30 or so.

We have planned an All-Malory – Welcome to Chase Horton – Memorial Dinner Party for tomorrow night (Wednesday) – the Watsons, the Vinavers, us and you. Hope you aren't too tired; the Vinavers must return to Manchester early Thursday morning and this is their only opportunity to meet you. We'll have a drink here in our rooms, and dine downstairs in the Grill.

Can't wait to see you!

XXX from us both,

Elaine

Wed. morning
Just received cable. Will expect you join us no matter how late.

E.

To Ero – New York, 7 July 1958

I think this is a kind of a milestone letter, more so than a progress report, although it will be that also. As nearly as I can see, the long and arduous and expensive research towards my new work on the *Morte d'Arthur* is just about complete. That is, it can never be complete but the time has come to go to work on the actual writing.

I know you are aware of the hundreds of books bought, rented and consulted, of the microfilms of manuscripts unavailable for study, of the endless correspondence with scholars in the field, and finally the two trips to England and one to Italy to turn up new sources of information and to become familiar with the actual scenes which must have influenced Malory. Some of the places are unchanged since he knew them in the fifteenth century and of the others it was necessary to know the soil and the atmosphere, the quality of the grass and the kind of light both day and night. A writer is deeply influenced by his surroundings and I did not feel that I could know the man Malory until I knew the places he had seen and the scenes which must have influenced his life and his writing.

From scholars in the field all over the world I have received welcome and encouragement, particularly from Dr Buhler of the Morgan Library and from Professor Vinaver of the University of Manchester. All of the people who have given me of their learning and made their books and manuscripts available to me will be thanked in a special preface, of course, but I want to make mention now of the enormous job that Chase Horton has done towards this project. He has not only found and bought and inspected hundreds of books and manuscripts but his genius for research has pointed directions and sources which I doubt very much I should have found without him. On the trip to England just concluded, his work and planning and insight have been invaluable. Let me repeat, I do not think I could have done the work or achieved the understanding of the subject which I hope I have without his help.

Now that I come to doing the actual writing I must admit to an uneasiness approaching fright. It is one thing to gather information and quite another to set it down finally. But the time has come for that. I plan to start now, and barring accidents and the normal interruptions due to health and family duties, to carry it through as rapidly as my knowledge and ability can contrive.

I have given a great deal of thought to method and have come finally to the conclusion that the following will be my best method. There is only one complete *Morte d'Arthur* in existence and that is the Caxton first edition which is in the Morgan Library in New York. There is of course the earlier manuscript at Winchester College in England, which differs in certain things with the Caxton, and but for the misfortune of lacking eight sheets at the end, might be the one unimpeachable source. As it is, all work on Malory must come from a combination of these two copies. I have not only seen and examined both of these originals but I have also microfilm of both, and these two sources must be my basis for translation. I have the Caxton microfilm by courtesy of the Morgan Library and the Winchester mss.

from the Library of Congress. This then is my basic material for translation.

I intend to translate into a modern English, keeping, or rather trying to re-create a rhythm and tone which to the modern ear will have the same effect as the Middle English did on the fifteenth-century ear. I shall do a specified number of pages of this translation every working day, that is five days a week, and six to eight pages, of translation a day. In addition, I shall every day set down in the form of a working diary, the interpretations, observations and background material drawn from our great body of reading. By doing these two things simultaneously I hope to keep the interpretive notes an integral part of the stories being translated. When the translation is finished I should then have a great body of interpretation which is an integral part of the spirit of the stories and their meanings. The introduction, which should be a very important part of the work, I shall leave for the last since it must be an overall picture of the complete work, both translation and interpretation.

I think that is all for now. I am aching to get to work after the years of preparation. And I'm scared also, but I think that is healthy. I have spent a great deal of money and even more time on this project. It is perfectly natural that I should have a freezing humility considering the size of the job to do and the fact that I have to do it all alone. There is no one to help me from now on. This is the writing job, the loneliest work in the world. If I fail there is only one person in the world to blame, but I could do with a small prayer from you and from any others who feel that this should be the best work of my life and the most satisfying. Prayer is about the only help I can hope for now. Yours. And I am now going into the darkness of my own mind.

To Ero – New York, 9 July 1958

Yesterday I started the translating, starting from scratch, and continued today. By the end of the week I may not like what I've done but so far I do. It is absolutely fascinating – the process I mean. And I've thrown out so many ideas which I found at the time.

You remember when I started talking about it, I wanted to keep the rhythms and tones of Malory. But since then I have learned a lot and thought a lot. And perhaps my thought parallels Malory's. When he started, he tried to keep intact the Frensshe books – largely Chrétien de Troyes. But as he went along he changed. He began to write for the fifteenth-century ear and the *English* mind and feeling. And only then did it become great. His prose was understandable and acceptable to the people of his time. The stories and the relationships are immortal. But tone, and method, change. The twentieth-century ear cannot take in the fifteenth-century form whether in tone, sentence structure or phraseology. A shorter and more concise statement is the natural vehicle now. And oddly enough, this is just what Malory had to do to his source material. As he became confident, he shortened and tightened for his period. And he also clarified some obscure matters. Well, that is what I am trying to do – to make the material not a period-piece in form, to keep the content and the details but to cast them into a form for our time.

An amazing thing happens once you drop the restrictions of the fifteenth-century language. Immediately the stories open up and come out of their entombment. The small scholars are not going to approve of this method but I think Vinaver and Buhler will love it for it is Malory, not as he wrote, but as he would have written now. I can give you many examples in the way of word use. Let us take the word worship in the Malorian sense. It is an old English word *worth-ship* and it meant eminence gained by one's personal qualities of courage or honour. You could not inherit worshipfulness. It was solely due to your own nature and actions. Beginning in the thirteenth century, the word moved into a religious connotation which it did not have originally. And now it has lost its original meaning and has become solely a religious word. Perhaps the word honour has taken its place or even better, renown. Once renown meant to be renamed became of one's own personal qualities, and now it means to be celebrated but still for personal matters. You can't inherit renown. I'm just trying to give you an idea of my experiment. And so far it seems good. I am so familiar with the work now that I am no longer frightened of it. The work must also be a little expounded. For example – Malory says, '—Uther sent for this duke charging him to bring his wife with him for she was called a fair lady and passing wise and her name was called Igraine.' Now your fifteenth-century listener to the story knew immediately that Uther was on the make for Igraine even before he saw her – and if the listener didn't know it, the teller of the story could inform his audience with a raised eyebrow or a wink or a tone of voice. But our readers, having only the printed page, must be informed by the word. And I am no longer afraid to use the word. Many of the seeming gaps were doubtless filled in with pantomime by the raconteur but I must fill those gaps. And where once I would have been reluctant to add anything, I no longer am. You, Chase and Vinaver have removed that fear from me.

Anyway, I am started and I feel pretty fine and free. I am working in the garage until my new workroom is completed and it is good. Thank God for the big Oxford dictionary. A glossary is a very unsatisfactory thing but that big Oxford is the greatest book in the world. I find myself running to it constantly. And where Malory uses often two adjectives meaning the same thing I am using one. For on the one hand I must increase the writing – on the other I must draw it in for our present-day eye and ear. It may be charming to read: 'to bring his wyf with him for she was called a fayre lady and passing wyse and her name was called Igraine.' But in our time it is more communicating to say: 'to bring his wife, Igraine, with him for she was reputed to be not only beautiful but clever.'

I do hope this doesn't sound like vandalism to you. I think the content is just as good and true and applicable now as it ever was but I believe now that it can only be released from the fifteenth-century tomb by this method. If it or rather they (the stories) had been invented in the fifteenth century, it would be another matter – but they weren't. If Malory could rewrite Chrétien for his time, I can rewrite Malory for mine. Tennyson rewrote him for his soft Victorian audience and pulled the toughness out. But our readers can take the toughness. Malory removed some of the repetition from the Frenssche books. I find it necessary to remove most of the repetition from Malory.

It is my intention to write to you regularly in this vein. It is better than a day book because it is addressed to someone. Will you keep the letters? They will be the basis for my introduction.

To Ero and Chase – New York, 11 July 1958

You know in the new little house I can have my dictionaries instead of having to run into the house to look up a word. But it's not really bad. I just feel mean. I'll go to work and drain some of the meanness out.

And I did pretty well considering and a most difficult part too. When Malory tries to throw everything into one basket – action and genealogy, past and future, personality and customs, I have to kind of sort it out in so far as I am able. I am going very slowly and trying not to make too many mistakes which will have to be untwisted later. This going back and forth in time may have to be worked on. It was all very well when people knew that the first Elaine, sister of Igraine, was Gawain's mother, to put that fact in even before Gawain was born, but it might be a little confusing to a modern reader – to whom genealogy is not terribly interesting unless it is their own.

Elaine just came in with letters from both of you and I can't tell you how pleased I am that you approve of the method. It was like holding one's nose and jumping feet first into cold water. And it is contrary to all standard, scholarly Arthurian methods but, by golly, I'll bet Vinaver will approve of it.

Now as to character and personality. It is my belief that they are there and were understood in their time. It is for me to understand the shorthand and bring them out. Consider this little lost bit. Igraine has been laid by someone she thought was her husband and later discovers that at the time her husband was dead. Now in the first mention of her, Malory says she was a fair lady and passing wise. When she hears that her husband is dead and in some way she cannot understand she was tricked – Malory says, 'Thenne she marvelled who that knight that lay with her in the likeness of her lord. *So she mourned pryvely and held her pees.*'

My God! There's all the character you need if you only point it with a repetition. I have translated as follows: 'When news came to Igraine that the duke her husband was slain the night before, she was troubled and she wondered who it was that lay with her in the image of her husband. *But she was a wise woman and she mourned privately and did not speak of it.*'

It's all there, you see. A whole character – a woman alone in a hostile and mysterious world. She did the only safe thing. 'She held her pees.' The book is loaded with such things. They only need bringing into our focus. Malory's listeners knew exactly the situation she was in but a modern reader has no conception of a woman's life in the fifteenth century. She had to be very wise to survive at all.

Now the jokes are there too – sometimes they take the form of little ironies and other times of satire. Merlin loves to play jokes with a childlike joy in his magic. It only requires a word to show that Merlin loved what he was doing. It is a child's joy in being able to astonish people. Then of course there is the end of Merlin – a cruel and horrifying situation and funny as hell. An old man enamoured of a young woman who worms his magic out of him and then uses it on him. It's the story of my life and a lot of other people's lives – a broad and heartless joke – the powerful and learned man who gets his comeuppance from a stupid, clever little girl. Oh, there is plenty here. And I am becoming less shy with it all the time. I don't think I dare be shy or respectful as I will lose what he has. And he has plenty. But I do want to work very slowly and carefully at first and to be very careful that I do not miss the things he is saying. It will probably go faster as I go along.

Let me now discuss for a moment Arthur as a hero. There is no doubt in my mind that Malory considered him a hero but he was also a king anointed. This second quality tended to make him remote to Malory. In the fifteenth century the principle that the king could do no wrong was in full force. His faults were the balance of his counsellors. This wasn't just an idea – it was so. If he could do no wrong the factor of pity is removed. But in spite of this Malory has him sin with his half-sister and draw his own fate down on him. I know that in some of the later stories Arthur is to us only a kind of Scheherazade, but he was also the heart of the brotherhood. I think I can work on that. Naturally, Malory would be more interested in fallible people – who could make mistakes and even commit crimes. We are still more interested in crimes than in virtues. But what is lost to the modern reader is that Malory never lost track of the importance of the king. Here, Elizabeth's thought of the circle has particular emphasis. The circle couldn't exist without Arthur. In fact it disappeared when he was gone. Now these are simple things – but why has nobody read this man? Increasingly I come to believe that the scholars have not read him at all – at least not with the intention of understanding what Malory meant and what he conveyed to his listeners. I could go on with this indefinitely and probably will because it clarifies things for me to try to explain them. Also, the deeper I go the more worth doing it seems to me. Far from growing less – it billows greater all of the time. It is the problem of simple things, some of them not understood in our time and perhaps some of them not understandable in our time. The preciousness of blood line – that is going to be one to do. The conception that common people were actually another species – as different from gentle people as cows were. There is no snobbishness here. This is just the way it was. I'll put this aside now for a little.

To Chase – New York, 14 July 1958

Thanks for your good letter and also for the books that are coming along. I guess there are never enough books.

I think I'll continue to send the work letters to you and Elizabeth. It is very good to do them as I am working, don't you think?

To Chase – New York, 28 July 1958

I have been pretty inattentive but not unappreciative. The books you have sent are wonderful. Things have been so confusing here that I have got more and more mixed up, that's all. They're supposed to start on my house today. I think that will make all the difference. At least I will be able to get away from the confusion. It has all been built separately so it will take only about three days to set up.

To Ero and Chase – New York, 11 August 1958

Joyous Garde is now finished. At least it is finished enough so I can work in it. After work of course there are a hundred little refinements which I will make and install. I have never had a place like this.

I shall be in it every day from morning until I feel that this day's work is done. The fact that I can see in every direction is not at all deflecting. Quite the opposite. The fact that I *can* see in all directions makes it unnecessary for me to look. That may seem a contradiction, but it is not. It is just the plain truth. Now the fooling around, the excuses and the complaints are finished. Now I am insisting that I go to work and I can find absolutely no excuse for not going to work . . . No one ever had a better place for it.

For myself, I now have just about everything I can think of that anyone, particularly me, could want. A boat, a house, Joyous Garde, friends and work. Also I have some time left for all of them. Recently I have brooded about the closing down of time, I think this grew out of the frustration of not being able to work because of a kind of creeping clutter. Now that is all wiped out, at least of this morning. I have been a terribly persistent complainer. This is nothing new with me. I think I have always been. But now I am going to go out of my way to stop it. At least that is my resolution this morning. And I do hope it lasts.

To Chase – New York, 21 October 1958

I realize that after all of our months of work together, for me to cut myself off as I have must seem on the prima donna side. And I haven't been able to explain it simply, not even to myself. Kind of like an engine that is missing fire in several cylinders and I don't know quite what is causing it although, knowing something about engines, I am aware that the causes must be limited, that somewhere in a range of four or five will be the cause or perhaps several things may contribute to the difficulty. But this is my problem. The only thing that will be applicable to you is that the engine doesn't run. The whole thing must be a little insulting to you and I don't want it to be. It grows out of my own uncertainties.

You will remember that, being dissatisfied with my own work because it had become glib, I stopped working for over a year in an attempt to allow the glibness to die out, hoping then to start fresh with what might feel to me like a new language. Well, when I started in again it wasn't a new language at all. It was a pale imitation of the old language only it wasn't as good because I had grown rusty and the writing muscles were atrophied. So I picked at it and worried at it because I wanted desperately for this work to be the best I had ever done. My own ineptness and sluggishness set me back on my heels. Finally I decided to back off and to try to get the muscles strong on something else – a short thing, perhaps even a slight thing, although I know there are no slight things. And that didn't work either. I wrote seventy-five pages on the new thing, read them and threw them away. Then I wrote fifty pages and threw them away. And then it came to me in a quick flash what that language was. It had been lying around all the time ready at hand and nobody had ever used it as literature. My 'slight thing' was about present-day America. Why not write it in American. This is a highly complicated and hugely communicative language. It has been used in dialogues, in cuteness and perhaps by a few sports writers. It has also been used by a first person telling a story but I don't think it has been used as a legitimate literary language. As I thought about it I could hear it in my ears. And then I tried it and it seemed right to me and it started to flow along. It isn't easy but I think it is good. For me. And suddenly I felt as Chaucer must have felt when he found he could write the language he had all around him and nobody would put him in jail – or Dante when he raised to poetic dignity the Florentine that people spoke but wouldn't dare to write. I admit I am getting a little beyond my peers in those two samples but a cat may surely look at a Chaucer.

Now I seem to be flowing and I find I can't go to sleep at night because the myths keep flowing past my audio complex and the figures jump like chiefs over my visual complex. I am not speaking of the language of illiteracy although to classicists it will be so considered just as Chaucer was. The American language is a new thing under the sun. It can combine all the erudition of which I am capable with the communication of our own time. It is not cute nor is it regional. The frames have grown out of ourselves but have used everything that was there before. But most of all it has an ease and a flow and a tone and a rhythm which is unique in the world. There is no question where it comes from, its references, its inventions, its overtones grew out of this continent and out of our twenty generations here. It is English basically but manured and seeded with Negro, Indian, Italian, Spanish, Yiddish, German, but so mixed and fermented that something whole has emerged.

And that is what I am working with and that is why I have times of great happiness as well as times of struggle and despair. But it is a creative despair. It is a vulgar language as all living languages are. Its figures grew out of ourselves. Well, that's about it. I don't know that I will do it well but if I do it only ten per cent as well as I wish, it will be better than I can hope for.

We will be in next week to set up residence. And if I seem vague, you now know why. I am happy and perplexed as a cat in a clam bucket.

To Ero – New York, 3 January 1959

Since work is going very badly, I mull over things with the kind of repetitiousness that is making the work go badly. The sense of having done all this before is pretty constant. I am depending on Somerset to give me the something new which I need.

It is my profound hope that at Avalon I can make contact with the very old, the older than knowledge, and that this may be a springboard into the newer than knowledge. It is a brazen hope I guess, but all I can come by right now. And I guess I am grabbing at hopes. I can hope, for example, that I will come by a feeling not watered down and attenuated. Perhaps what I am fighting is simple age and a low-burning fire but I don't think that is so. I think it is confusion, or you might call it conflict of interests, each one cancelling another out to a certain extent. And this would be nobody's fault but my own. I can enforce a demand if I have one strong enough. And if anything, I have more respect for the craft than I ever had, much more because I know its hugeness and to some extent my own limitation. The angry young men and the Beats are simply trying to add velocity to the other three dimensions as they should. Because now it has finally seeped down from pure abstract mathematics that the fourth dimension is duration. But that doesn't need to mean fast. It may as well mean slow so long as duration is the dimension. It requires a language which has not been made yet but the Beats are working on it and they may create it. The measurement of time beyond sun, moon and year is a very recent thing. When Julius Caesar claimed descent from Venus, he did not think of his ancestry as remote. Factors of light speed and concepts of the so far non-conceptual are all gumming the works, mine as well as theirs. I know that what I am going looking for in Somerset I can find right here. I am not such a fool as not to know that. What I am wishing for is a trigger rather than an explosion. The explosion is here. But in the haunted fields of Cornwall and the mines with the tin and lead pits, in the dunes and the living ghosts of things, I do wish to find a path or a symbol or an approach. An old man on St Michael's Mount told us he put the brackets on conys in the moonlight and zo got's dinner. It's somewhere there so common that those born there know it but can't see it. Maybe that's my trigger. I don't know. But it might be. I do hope that if it is not so I will know it soon and not go knocking at the shapes of doors that are no entrances. And please do know that in turning over the lumber of the past I'm looking for the future. This is no nostalgia for the finished and safe. My looking is not for a dead Arthur but for one sleeping. And if sleeping, he is sleeping everywhere, not alone in a cave in Cornwall. Now there, that's said and done and I've been trying to say it for a long time.

If this does seem to be taking a trip to Southernmost England very seriously it is so because it is much more than that to me. Not only is the time or continuum important, but I am taking note that there are two ends to a voyage – what you go away from as well as what you go towards.

To Chase – New York, 28 January 1959

The only glory that had come to England in memory was when history was accomplished with the long bow at Crecy and later at Agincourt. Laws of the Edwards made practice with the bow compulsory. When Malory attacked Monks Kirby, he did so with picks, jacks and bows and arrows. He was charged with lying in wait for Buckingham with bows and arrows.

In his raids he was accompanied by yeomen. The weapon of the yeoman was the longbow. He fancies himself somewhat of a tactician as some of the battle plans of the *Morte* indicate. Yet in the *Morte* there is no mention of the bow, no use of the yeoman as a soldier. Commoners are mentioned but not yeomen. And yet in his living history there was no English success which did not involve the bow. Isn't it interesting that some reference to the bow did not creep in ?

I am by no means content with this thing. The Winchester ms. may have been before or may not. It is on paper with a water mark like those dated 1475. A vellum patch to repair a tear is gummed down indulgence of Innocent VIII 1489 and printed by Caxton. Copying did not cease entirely with Caxton for many years afterwards. The Winchester therefore may conceivably be *after* Caxton. It is largely in Chancery hand or script which is the model of Caxton's early type. There may well have been diehards who just can't believe in the printing press. Just as there are people who still don't like paperbacks or the linotype. A great number of books are printed with handset type. Print may well have seemed cheap and worthless to book lovers. This is only a question. I mean to ask a lot of them.

Why does every commentator become convinced that a man had to have read everything he knew ? In a time of recitation the memory must have been much better trained than it is now. For instance, a common man below the salt, on hearing a respected performer, must have in many cases memorized it as he went and when he met others probably repeated what he remembered of it.

In 1450 a rich man like John Fastolf had only eighteen books besides missals and a psalter. And that was a considerable library. He had incidentally Liber de Ray Aethaur. Is it possible that Malory departed from the Frensshe books not because he wanted to but because his memory failed? And his invention took over? Just a question. I have lots of them.

The memory was the only recording instrument of the great part of the population. Deeds and transfers were made permanent by beating young retainers so they would remember. The training of the Welsh poets was not practice but memorizing. On knowing 10,000 poems, one took a position. This has always been true. Written words have destroyed what must have been a remarkable instrument. The Pastons speak of having the messenger read the letter so that he could repeat it verbatim if it was stolen or lost. And some of these letters were complicated. If Malory were in prison, it is probably true that he didn't need books. He knew them. If I had only twelve books in my library I would know them by heart. And how many men had no memory in the fifteenth century? No – the book owned must have been supplemented by the book borrowed and thus by the book *heard*. The tremendous history of the Persian Wars of Herodotus was known by all Athenians and it was not read by them, it was read to them.

The reason I am beating this point is that I think not enough care has been given to this memory thing. In such memories – everything heard was catalogued until the library was enormous – and all in the mind. In Shakespeare's time a good man could memorize a whole scene from a play and write it down afterwards. That was the only way to steal it.

I don't want you to think that I am becoming overconcerned with who Malory was. I don't think that is very important. But I do want to know what he was and how he got there that way. If the Malory of the *Morte* is the Malory of the inquisitions and charges and escapes, he was no ivory tower boy lonely on a peak of nobility. His associates were husbandmen, yeomen, tailors, and how about Richard Irysheman? And the names – Smyth, Row, David, Wale, Walman, Breston, Thorpe, Hellorus, Hande, Tidman, Gibb, Sharpe? These are not noble names. They are farmers or guildmen. They were also tough men and thoroughly used to the harshness of the times.

I know it can be said that the form required certain conventions of chivalry. But particularly in the later parts, Malory slipped into things he knew, trees, plants, water, soil, habits of speech and clothing. Why then did he not slip into the weapons he knew – bows and arrows. Under Beauchamp he served with a lance and two archers. This is about the usual mixture. At Agincourt of an estimated six thousand English there were about four thousand archers. Now wouldn't you think that a man who served in France later but with much the same tactics, when he came to write of war, would have slipped in a little of what he knew ? He did in many other directions. His knowledge of men and animals pushed out the conventions of the romanceurs and put in what for the time was tremendous realism.

Now it is several days later. And I can't stress enough the lack of consideration among scholars of the word of mouth. Being used to books as mechanisms of communications, they fail to realize that until very recently, book and writing were the rarest form. Consider the million rules for living, spinning, farming, fasting, brewing, building, hunting, together with the arts and crafts. None written down and yet all communicated. I want to make a strong point of this, particularly in my own mind.

Second point. The conception that the Cycle was the property of the few, the literate, the erudite. That was not so. Chaucer himself has given us the answer. He didn't invent the form nor did Boccaccio. The stories were told, remembered, repeated. And only at the very last were they written. And the amazing thing is how purely they came down and with how little change. A careless scrivener could cause more havoc than a hundred tellers.

This time it's finished—

To Chase – Somerset, 24 March 1959

The countryside is turning as lush as a plum. Everything is popping. The oaks are getting that red colour of swollen buds before they turn grey and then green. Apple blossoms are not out yet, but it won't be very long. We had an east wind right out of Finland and the White Sea and it was cold. Then it switched to the West as if the Ode to a— and immediately the warmth of the Gulf Stream moved in. I'm ready to work now and naturally that frightens me. Must hold my nose with my fingers and jump in feet first. There's a kind of point-of-no-return feeling about it. I suppose I will get over it.

The micro projector works well. It sits in the deep embrasure of my window and projects on my work table. All in all, this is an ancient place. Elaine loves it too. There's a quality here that I haven't known for very long. The twentieth century seems very remote. And I would like to keep it that way for a while. Moon shots indeed! I'm wondering how long Edward IV can hold on.

To Chase – Somerset, 27 March 1959

It was a fortunate accident which drew me to this place. I thought, as you know, that it would be some time before I would settle in and go to work. But it is not. The work is coming as it should. I wonder why it has taken me so long to find my path. In a Somerset meadow it came to me and this I tell you truly. And you have probably known it all along. Thus went my thinking—

'Malory wrote the stories for and to his time. Any man hearing him knew every word and every reference. There was nothing obscure, he wrote the clear and common speech of his time and country. But that has changed – the words and the references are no longer common property, for a new language has come into being. Malory did not write the stories. He simply wrote them for his time and his time understood them.' And so you know, Chase, suddenly in this home ground, I was not afraid of Malory any more nor ever will be again. This does not lessen my admiration but it does not inhibit me either. Only I can write this for my time. And as for place – the place has become not a little island set in a silver sea, but the world.

And with that, almost by enchantment the words began to flow, a close-reined, taut, economical English, unaccented and unlocalized. I put down no word that has not been judged for general understanding. Where my time cannot fill in, I build up, and where my time would be impatient with repetition, I cut. So did Malory for his time. It is just as simple as that and I think it is the best prose I have ever written. I hope this is so and I believe it. Where there is obscurity or paradox I let intuition, my own judgement and the receptivity of our times govern me.

I'm trying to hold the production down. I don't want it to race but to come sweetly out so that every word is necessary and the sentences fall musically on the ear. What Joy. I have no doubts any more. I goddam well can write it. Just wanted you to know. In fact I *am* writing it.

'ludly sing cucu'

To Ero – Somerset, 30 March 1959

I have forgotten how long it is since I have written you. Time loses all its meaning. The peace I have dreamed about is here, a real thing, thick as a stone and feelable and something for your hands. World goes on with a slow, steady pace like that of laden camels. And I have so much joy in the work. Maybe the long day off is responsible or perhaps it is only Somerset but the tricks are gone, and the cleanness and the techniques and style that I can only think of as a kind of literary couture, changeable as the seasons. Instead, the words that gather to my pen are honest sturdy words, needing no adjectival crutches. There are many more than I will ever need. And they arrange themselves in sentences that seem to me to have a rhythm as honest and unshaken as a heart beat. The sound of them is sweet in my ears so that they seem to me to have the strength and sureness of untroubled children or fulfilled old men.

I move along with my translation of the *Morte* but it is no more a translation than Malory's was. I am keeping it all but it is mine as much as his was his. I told you I think that I am not afraid of Malory any more for I know that I can write better for my time than he could have, just as he wrote better for his time than anyone else.

Meanwhile, I can't describe the joy. In the mornings I get up early to have a time to listen to the birds. It's a busy time for them. Sometimes for over an hour I do nothing but look and listen and out of this comes a luxury of rest and peace and something I can only describe as in-ness. And then when the birds have finished and the countryside goes about its business, I come up to my little room to work. And the interval between sitting and writing grows shorter every day.

To Ero – Somerset, 5 April 1959

Another week gone and how did that happen ? With daily work and mail and spring coming, and gardening and going to Morlands at Glastonbury to see the processing of sheepskins as they have been done since prehistory. I don't know first how the week went so fast and second how so much was accomplished in that week.

The work continues a joy and a trial to me. End of last week and into the next, the Battle of Bedgrayne a terrible mess, even to Malory. I have to straighten out not only what happened but why, and cut deeply. Present-day people can read unlimited baseball scores in which the narration isn't very great and fifteenth-century people could listen to innumerable single combats with little variation. I have to bridge that so that the battle remains important, exciting, and doesn't get lost in a hundred running together of individual knights and still keep the sense that war was a series of man-to-man fights. Is a problem. This is the most terrible mess in the whole first part.

Malory can take six pages for the fighting, but when the most important two things in the first part happen – the conception of Mordred and the meeting with Guinevere – he devotes two lines to each. I can't spend much time on them but I have to give them dreadful importance. Never a dull moment, you see.

Now a question for Chase to mull over. When the battle is over and Merlin hotfoots it to Northumberland and reports all the details and names to hys mayster Blayse. And Blayse wrote the batayle word for word as Merlin told him— And all the battles fought in Arthur's time and all the worthy deeds of Arthur's court, Merlin told to Blayse and Blayse wrote them down. Now – who the hell was Blayse or who did Malory think he was ? Does he occur in the Frensshe books ? Did Malory make him up ? I would be very glad to know what Chase has to say about this.

To Chase – Somerset, 9 April 1959

I must be careful to avoid repeating what I have already written to Elizabeth and what you have doubtless seen. This morning a letter from Jackson. They have the dictionaries and I have ordered them. They have no lexicon of Cornish Celtic but suggest I try hereabouts which I will. Also no Middle English and I did not bring mine. They say it has been taken over from Oxford and is now handled by Michigan University Press. I think mine is Oxford and I left it at home. And darn it, I need one. Could you please either send me mine or another. I think that is all I will need. It's mostly words and their meanings. The rest I will find in Malory and in myself. I am getting an entirely new look at Arthur in the Merlin part and, I suppose it follows, a new look at Malory and myself. Enormous profundities here for one who wants to look. From the dream (serpents – throughout the questing beast to the recognition of the mother) is all one piece. But you will see what I have done with it when I send it. I will record it on tape in case of loss and probably will send the handwritten ms. on to you. Mary Morgan can type it, several copies on thin paper, and then maybe I can have a copy back, but I will have the tape recording just in case anything should happen. It never does happen if you are protected. I would like it if you would begin to work on a standardization of the names of people and places and also identification with names and places used today, at least where possible the places Malory was thinking of when he was writing. As for the proper names, they should be reduced to their greatest simplicity and made easy to pronounce. And all of the uncommon ones standardized. That in itself is a big job but I know you have done a lot with it already so you are well prepared. The Merlin has been a bitch with all of its confusions but I think you will be pleased with my handling of the Battle of Bedgrayne – a very difficult passage to bring out I can assure you. Also I can't tell you often enough what a good move this was to come here. If there were nothing else, the peace and the pace make it worth doing.

Three days in London next week. A kind of clearing of the palate for the Knight with the Two Swords. This is a profound piece and entirely different. It has the Greek sense of tragedy – man against fate, beyond his control and wish, and I must get everything I can from it. The form is all here in the *Morte* but sometimes it is out of perspective for the modern reader. It is that bringing it into focus that is my job. And I shall be really anxious to know what you think of what I am doing. No one seems even to have attempted it. I wonder why. As Vinaver says, no one thinks to go back to Malory. Well, I am and I find it very rewarding and I hope to make it rewarding.

This is the great changeable month for showers and for times of brilliant sun in the last hours. The gas stove went out last night and I had to build it back and in the process I learned.

In the ancient back of Mr Windmill's ironmongery there is a forge and tools from the Middle Ages. Mr Arthur Strand still uses them and he can make anything. He has become my pal. I may ask him to make me an axe or at least to adapt one. Maybe he will let me do it myself at his forge. I want an axe like the ones the Norse and Saxon warriors carried for war and work. All modern axes have a straight blade like this. ⊏⊐ This makes the force of the blow distributed along the whole length of the blade. But the old one was like this ⌒ so that the impact was on a small area and gave it much better penetration. With the old axe you can practically carve wood because of the small area of impact. I must speak to Mr Arthur about that. He can probably find me some old adzes too. In the evenings I am back to my wood carving— It lets me go on thinking and still have my hands busy. I'm making spoons for the kitchen now – out of pieces of old oak.

I think I'll go on a little on thin paper. I'm not quite warmed up for work yet.

To Chase – Somerset, 11 April 1959

(*continuing letter of 9 April* 1959)

Now it is Saturday, I don't know how it got to be. I shall finish the Merlin either today or tomorrow, and I really think it is good. But looking back through the pages I see many little things I want to change. Therefore I think I am wrong in the interest of hurry to send the ms. to you. I shall have it typed here, correct the typescript before I send it on. Then it will be much more nearly right. This will have had several treatments so that what you will receive will amount to a corrected third draft and when Mary Morgan types in the changes, it will be much more nearly finished. It will be longer before you receive it, but I think worth the time.

Well, the Merlin is nearly done and it is a far more profound and warming thing than I had thought. I do hope I am making the most of it. I have a wonderful sense of joy in what I have done. I don't know whether that will be sustained in re-reading. But it is worth it to have it at all.

I have made some quite good spoons for cooking and I have done so well that I have designed some salad forks which I hope I can execute for Elaine. The bowl of one will be the Tudor Rose and the bowl for the other the Triple Cross of Rome. And when they clash in tossing lettuce there will be a little bit of history in the salad bowl. I hope I can do them nicely. It is a nice thought, it seems to me.

Time now to go back to work. I shall finish this later. But I have a curious fight and then the sword – the sword of swords.

And I did – and I like it. And now I will finish this letter and send it on. Today came books we had ordered. Two volumes, 1832, a history of Somerset with all the details of Dugdale. What a joy!

I'm going down now to the joys of the Somerset books. Graham Watson found them for us and they are very rare.

To Ero – Somerset, 10 April 1959

Another week going fast. I shall finish the Merlin this week and I think it is the hardest of all. I also think it was the hardest for Malory because into this must be crowded all of the background and confusion of Arthur's birth and his assumption of power, of the rebellion and mystery of his birth. It amounts to a long and dissonant chronicle. But I think it is sorting out into something that flows in modern prose, but of course it can never have the rounded or elliptical form of some of the later tales which do not require throwback and where the cast of characters is not so huge. The Battle of Bedgrayne gave me hell but I think it comes through. I had to keep it mounting and moving and I tried to communicate some of the excitement as well as the sadness that is in it. The end of the book is a kind of magic dream full of mood and foreboding, a psychiatrist's dream of heaven if he cared to look. Between the serpent dream and the revelation to Arthur of his true right to the throne, it is all of a piece.

I feel that Arthur did not want to know because he was afraid of what he might find. He even goes looking for trouble and action to avoid thinking. This is not unlike experiences in our time, even the dress symbols are still with us unchanged. I'm dealing with all of it as the fringes of a dream. Anyway it is moving along and after this terrible first story nothing else can be as hard.

To Chase – Somerset, 11 April 1959

(*from Elaine S.*)

Jackson sent the two-volume *History and Antiquities of Somerset* by Phelps this morning, and we had to hide them for a day in order to get any work done. They will make fine fireside reading for us.
– John is working on 'The Lady of the Lake' sequence today, and only comes up for air every two or three hours to get a cup of coffee. He is beginning to live and breathe the book. In the evening he carves wooden spoons for our kitchen and talks about Arthur and Merlin.

A letter from Eugène Vinaver today tells how homesick he is for France, but he adds: 'It is better while I am busy with an English book to be here. English words come more naturally to one's mind when the flowers and the trees around one have English names.' He is talking about himself, but I think it applies to John as well, don't you ? Arthur seems to be *here*.

Vinaver also quotes what John once wrote: 'I tell these old stories, but they are not what I want to tell. I only know how I want people to feel when I tell them.' Isn't that a wonderful thing ? Eugène says it is the truest and most significant sentence he has found in all the innumerable books about books.

To Ero – Somerset, 12 April 1959

These long and ponderous chronicles will continue, I suppose. Another week gone or rather past and now it is one month today that we have been in this house.

One month in this house and it seems like ours. I had thought it would take at least a month and maybe more to get squirmed down in my writing chair, and today I am finishing the Merlin, the hardest and most complex tale of all. Malory wasn't comfortable in it either. He was troubled and unsure how to start and he doubled back and raced ahead and sometimes refuted what he had said a page ago. But I think I have it straightened out now, at least to my satisfaction. Nothing else will be as hard. I can feel this man's mind. He put things down he did not know he was writing and there is the richness, but hidden sometimes very deep. Well, we will see whether it is good or not. I have a feeling that it is.

Three days in London and then back and to the strange and fated story of the Knight with the Two Swords. I think I understand it – a kind of tragedy of designed errors, one growing out of the last and so building until there is no return. It is the only story of its kind in the whole cycle. When I have finished it, the season will be broad spring and then I shall take one or two days a week to look about me. The pattern will then be set and I will not be afraid of a break. But until then I want not to break my rhythm.

My joy in the work continues and increases. I think I have pulled an understandable character out of Arthur. And he has always been the weakest and coldest to our modern eyes. And if I can do that, the rich ones, Lancelot and Gawain, will be pure dreams to work with. And I have a curtain line for Merlin. This trick or method was not known in the fifteenth century but readers need it now. And they have it.

To Chase – Somerset, 20 April 1959

About the books. I'm going to ask you to try and get the lexicons you mentioned. It isn't such a rush now that I have the Anglo-Saxon, the Middle English and the two-volume Oxford. The big Oxford I presented to Bob Bolt, who found us this house. He is going to be a very important playwright and no better present could be given a writer. He was practically in tears.

I am half through the revising of the Merlin and I have changed my mind again. The wife of one of the masters of King's School is a good typist. I would like to see this in type before I send it on to you. I'll ask her to make four copies. This is not final of course but it will be much better if it is typed. It will give you something tangible to play with. I have a little tape recorder for playback now. It gives me a much better sense of words to hear it back. I catch errors I didn't know were there. Good Lord! how this thing grows in me. There is no way of making a tight short story form of the Merlin. It is, to a certain extent, episodic. But I am trying to give it continuity, believability, mood and emotional content, together with a kind of plan for its being. It is actually the formation of a kingdom. Do you remember that I always said that Malory was uneasy in this part? Well, so was I. But as he learned, so am I learning. And I have a sense of freedom in this material I never had before. I do hope you will like it. I think it is good writing – as good in its way as Malory's was in its way. I am awfully excited about it.

To Ero and Chase – Somerset, 20 April 1959

I wrote the beginning of the Merlin. The whole thing should be gone
over maybe and redone. I've learned so much about my own method
that the early parts are kind of outmoded already, I guess that always
happens. Anyway, I'll see what I want to do with it before I send it.
I still like what I'm doing. In London I ordered a table-top architect's
board that tilts. My back and neck get too tired.

To Ero and Chase – Somerset, 20 April 195

What is in a writer's mind – novelist or critic ? Doesn't a writer set
down what has impressed him most, usually at a very early age ? If
heroism impressed him, that's what he writes about, and if frustration
and a sense of degradation – that is it. And if jealousy is the deepest
feeling, then he must attack anything which seems to be the
longed-for success.

  Maybe somewhere in here is my interest and joy in what I am
doing. Malory lived in as rough and ruthless and corrupt an age as
the world has ever produced. In the *Morte* he in no way minimizes
these things, the cruelty and lust, and murder and childlike
self-interest. They are all here. But he does not let them put out the
sun. Side by side with them are generosity and courage and greatness
and the huge sadness of tragedy rather than the little meanness of
frustration. And this is probably why he is a great writer and Williams
is not. For no matter how brilliantly one part of life is painted, if
the sun goes out, that man has not seen the whole world. Day and
night both exist. To ignore the one or the other is to split time in two
and to choose one like the short stick in a match game. I like Williams
and admire his work but as he is half a man, so is he half a writer.
Malory was whole. There is nothing in literature nastier than Arthur's
murder of children because one of them may grow up to kill him.
Williams and many others of this day would stop there, saying,
'That's the way it is.' And they would never get to the heartbreaking
glory when Arthur meets his fate and fights against it and accepts
it all in one. How can we have forgotten so much ? We produce
talented pygmies like court dwarfs who are amusing because they
mime greatness and they – I should say we – are still dwarfs.
Something happens now to children. An artist should be open on all
sides to every kind of light and darkness. But our age almost purposely
closes all windows, draws all shades and then later screams to a
psychiatrist for light.

  Well – there were men once and there may be again. I have a friend, nameless of course, who bases his trouble on having been rejected by a woman. And he completely forgets the literally hundreds of women who accepted him. I told him that in a letter recently and I don't know how it will go down with him.

I'm serious today, perhaps because I have had a tussle with a section of Merlin in rewriting. I knew what I wanted to say and couldn't find the words for it. But I will, because I have time.

Jumping back a paragraph – I've been rejected by some, but my God some wonderful ones have accepted me. To forget that would be foolish and to brood on the others would be like brooding because everyone didn't like my looks. I'm grateful that some people do.

To Chase – Somerset, 25 April 1959

The Cornish Dictionary is not necessary for this work but for future work, so by all means send it by boat. If we had known about it in time, Mary could have brought it. Any lexicons of this area will be valued by me. I hate to get into the Welsh because I can't pronounce it.

I had an excellent day yesterday and got well into the Knight with the Two Swords – a strange and fated story. Hope I can bring something to the surface – the Invisible Knight etc. and the utter savagery coupled with sweetness. Also I cut down a local hatchet to the shape of a Saxon axe for wood shaping and dug a garbage pit.

My table-top tilt board came. Makes a draftsman's table of a card table. My neck and shoulders don't get so damned tired.

To Ero and Chase – Somerset, 1 May 1959

Yesterday something wonderful. It was a golden day and the apple blossoms are out and for the first time I climbed up to Cadbury – Camelot. I don't think I remember an impact like that. Could see from the Bristol Channel to the tops of the Mendip Hills and all the little villages. Glastonbury tor and King Alfred's towers on the other side. I shall go back over and over but what a day to see it first. I walked all around the upper wall. And I don't know what I felt but it was a lot – like those slow hot bubbles of molten rock in a volcano, a gentle rumbling earthquake of the Spirit. I was ready for it too. I'll go back at night and in the rain, but this was noble gold even to use Tennyson's phrase – mystic – wonderful. Made the hairs prickle on the back of the neck. Mary is here and she went with us – and she was very moved. Tomorrow after work I'm going back to Glastonbury to the Abbey. I'm ready for that now too.

I hope to finish the Knight with the Two Swords today. I do hope I've done it well. Merlin is out being typed. I don't know when it will be finished but I'll send it as soon as I check it over. I think Balin is good but I'll have to listen to it on tape before I'll really know. What a magic and fatal story it is.

Now – there's something I want to ask. We are supposed to leave the country on or before 11 June and re-enter. I was going to ask the Home Office for an extension rather than waste time and money for a rubber stamp in a passport. But if there was a reason, it would be different. Lying in bed last night a very definite reason visited me. I know the lay of the land of nearly all the work now save one – Brittany. And with the war against Rome coming up, and the whole complex of the Celtic migrations back and forth, I could well use a few days looking at Brittany. That would be the best reason for leaving England for a few days. —From Calais to Mont St Michel. What do you think, Chase ? And can you get me some geographical and historical material on the area with reference both to the myth and to the Brittany of Malory's time which will be what he himself has seen. This makes much sense to me, however, killing two birds.

Time for me to go to work. I'll finish this letter later. I have finished Balin and I am pooped. But I do think I got something in it. I dearly hope so.

Now I must set out my lettuces in flats so that they can get bigger before I set them in the garden. I start the seeds in my window sill.

To Chase – Somerset, 4 May 1959

Another week starting. Elaine and Mary off to Wells which gives me a fine long day for work. Start Torre and Pellinore, marriage of Guinevere etc. Half the typed Merlin came back, The rest early this week and I will get a carbon off to you and Elizabeth with strong hope that you will like it. After you have read it I suggest that you go back to Malory and see what I have done. You will instantly know why. I put the Balin on tape yesterday and listened to it back and it sounds pretty good. There will have to be lots of refinements of course in all of it but the essence is there and I can't find that I have missed much from the original. It is most painstaking work. You will notice that I have removed all of Merlin's prophecies having to do with future stories. They simply blow the point. Also Malory never could lead to a climax. He gave it away three times before he came to it. The hardest work was the battle. Nothing will be that hard again – am removing the tiresome detail and at the same time keeping action and plan of battle. But there are such profundities in Malory sometimes hidden in a phrase. I have to be very careful not to miss them and sometimes to blow them up a little to make them apparent.

To Ero – Somerset, 5 May 1959

The last part of the Merlin should be in type today and I will get a carbon off to you right away by air mail. I shall be on needles to know what you think of it. Meanwhile I am well into Torre and Pellinore, the first of the questing stories and the beginning of the Round Table. From this point on Arthur becomes a hero and almost without character. But this is the nature of all heroes and to make him human might be a revolution. God knows he is surrounded by humans and maybe that is necessary – the contrast. Actually Arthur becomes a little like the Caliph in the Arabian Nights – a kind of referee of adventures and one who devotes himself to a kind of mild commentary. I don't know what I am going to do about that. But every day is a challenge of major proportions. Every day something.

Now it is afternoon and the Merlin typescript has come back. I think I will go to Bruton a little later and mail it to you because I fervently want you to see it. Am I off on the wrong foot? It seems right to me but I can be very wrong. There must be some reason why no one has done this properly. Maybe it is because it can't be done – but I don't really believe that. I think the reason is that they tried to make it costume instead of universal. Well, anyway, you will know. And good or bad, I have a feeling that the prose is good. Incidentally, I am sending no copy to anyone but you. I have an original and two carbons here. Does Chase want or need one? It needs lots of work I know but this is just a draft.

The Post Office is going to go mad when I send it air mail. They think we are terribly extravagant anyway and this is going to make them think I am nuts. We give them more business than the whole town of Bruton.

Oh well – here we go. And I am well into Torre and Pellinore today.

Love to all there. I'm sorry I'm so nervous about this but after all, I've been at it a long time and this is the first and acid test – the hardest story and the first.

To Chase – Somerset, 7 May 1959

A small warm-up before my day's work. I finished Gawain's quest in Torre and Pellinore yesterday and continue with the second quest today. I hope to finish the whole thing sometime during the weekend.

I now have an architect's board that sits on a table and what a difference it makes. I don't get so tired leaning over – I shall not finish this today, because as surely as I write to you, I get a letter by return mail. Please do let me know of your reaction to the work I have sent when you get a chance. Maybe I'd better send two copies from now on. I am having an original and three carbons made.

Now it is Sunday and I have just finished the Three Quests. Tomorrow the Death of Merlin and if I am lucky next week Morgan le Fay, which is short. But it does more and I think I discovered some gold in the Quests. Of course the real things are to come.

Now Monday again. These weeks run by and disappear like rabbits in a shooting gallery. We've been here two months. Can you imagine that ? I can't. It seems such a short time that I feel I haven't got enough work done and I know that isn't true. I have done a lot. This flimsy paper is very unsatisfactory to write on. I love the foolscap, even the white British foolscap.

I got some typescript on Wednesday and will send it along— It will be much more of Malory than the Merlin, where I have always felt that he was floundering with his material. Today I start the Death of Merlin, a ghastly job, the ridiculous defeat of a great man, adored in all ages. I'll have to see what I can do with it. It's the banana-peel treatment, the great leveller. And it is time I got to it because there may be some false starts.

To Chase – Somerset, 11 May 1959

The fact of the matter is that there isn't enough time in a day to do what I want to do. I finished the Death of Merlin and the Five Kings yesterday. And today go on with Morgan le Fay. I like my version of the end of Merlin. It's a sad and a general story. Perhaps that is why it has lasted. It and the Marriage will go to be typed on Wednesday.

Planted three dozen lettuce plants yesterday and among the grasses in the back garden I found a number of strawberry plants all in blossom and cleared the rack away from them. I find all sorts of things back there.

My spelling – never very sure and fixed – has become completely infected by Malory. Batayle seems much more normal than battle – more warlike somehow even if it doesn't mean the same thing as battle.

What a way to live! I worked very hard yesterday what with writing and cutting grass with a scythe. Went to bed at nine o'clock before it was dark and instantly to sleep. A mist on the meadows this morning with the sun burning through. Everyone agrees that this is the most beautiful spring in many years. And some who have been burned by the last few seasons say we will pay for it later. Well, we shall see.

I may want to get out but I hate to. Also, I resent anything that interrupts the slow, steady flow of this translation. I feel that it is getting a flow and a good tone now.

Time's up now. A-working we must go.

I'll get this off.

To Ero and Chase – Somerset, 13 May 1959

Then your comments and Chase's almost lack of comment on the section sent to you. I must think very carefully and not fall into obscurity in my answer. To indicate that I was not shocked would be untrue. I was. I wonder if the three thousand miles makes any difference. It is apparent that I did not communicate my intention but I wonder whether I could have if I had been there. It is natural to look for arguments in my defence or in defence of the work as I am doing it. Let me say first that I hope I am too professional to be shocked into paralysis. The answer seems to be that you expected one kind of thing and you didn't get it. Therefore you have every right to be confused as you say and disappointed. I had never told you what my plan was, perhaps because I was feeling my way. I can say that this is uncorrected first draft, designed to establish style and method, and that the slips and errors will be removed, but that isn't good enough. Perhaps I thought I had told you that I am presently trying – not to bring up the whole cycle with its thousand ramifications, but to stick tight to Malory, who wrote in the fifteenth century. And all the reading and research is not wasted, because I see and I think understand things in Malory I could not have seen before. Finally, I have had no intention of putting it in twentieth-century vernacular any more than T.M. put it in fifteenth-century vernacular. People didn't talk that way then either. For that matter, people didn't talk as Shakespeare makes them talk except in the bumpkin speeches. These are all negatives, I know.

I know you have read T. H. White's *Once and Future King*. It is a marvellously wrought book. All the things you wished to find in my revision are superlatively in that. But that is not what I had wanted and I think still do not want to do.

Where does the myth – the legend – start ? Back of the Celtic version it stretches back to India and probably before. It splits on the migration – part going to Greece, part to Semitic exits, part coming up through Georgia and Russia and Germany to Scandinavia and crammed with the Norse and part in Iberia and Celtic Gaul flooding up to Britain, Ireland, Scotland, where it incubates and there moves out again all over the world. Where do you stop it or limit it ? I chose to start with Malory who was the best writer, better than the French, better than the parts of the Mabinogion and closer to our general understanding. White brilliantly puts the story in the dialects of present-day England. I did not want to do that. I wanted an English that was out of time and place as the legend is. The people of legend are not people as we know them. They are figures. Christ is not a person, he is a figure. Buddha is a squatting symbol. As a person Malory's Arthur is a fool. As a legend he is timeless. You can't explain him in human terms any more than you can explain Jesus. As a person Jesus is a fool. At any time in the story he could have stopped the process or changed the direction. He has only one human incident in the whole sequence – the lama sabach-thani on the cross when the pain was too great. It is the nature of the hero to be a fool. The Western sheriff, the present literary prototype as exemplified by Gary Cooper, is invariably a fool. He would be small and mean if he were clever. Cleverness, even wisdom, is the property of the villain in all myths. I am not writing this to titillate the ear of the twentieth century. Perhaps I am overambitious, but I am trying to make it available, not desirable. I want the remote feeling of the myth not the intimate feeling of today's man who in his daily thought may change tomorrow but who in his deeper perceptions, I am convinced, does not change at all. In a word I have not been trying to write a popular book but a permanent book. I should have told you all of this.

It has been my intention in all of this and still is, to follow each story with an – what can I call it ? – essay, elucidation, addendum. In this I propose to put the reality, the speculative, the explanative, even perhaps the characterization, but I wanted to keep it separate. I do not know that Merlin was a Druid or the memory of a Druid and certainly Malory never suspected it. In the studies I can speculate that this may have been so, although I suspect that the Merlin conception is far older than Druidism. His counterpart is in every great cycle – in Greece, in the Bible, and in the folk myths, back to the beginning. Chase says wisely that Saxon and Saracen are probably the same thing. Foreigners from far off. They always occur. To Malory the most recent mysterious and powerful strangers were Saracens. Saxons, unless he was a Celt, were part of himself, even though he probably thought of himself as of Norman descent – for social reasons.

Very well, you will say – if that is your intention, where are those comments which intend to illuminate ? Well, they aren't written for two reasons. First, I'm learning so much from the stories, and second, I don't want to break the rhythm. I found there was a rhythm, and I was pleased with it. Also, by their nature, these stories must be spare. In the additions I have made, I've tried to keep that spareness.

I know I seem to be defining my thesis and that's exactly what I am doing. But there are some things I don't understand. You say the killing of the babies is an unkingly retelling of the Herod story. But that is the theme of the whole legend. The Herod story is simply another version of the timeless principle that human planning cannot deflect fate. The whole legend is a retelling of human experience. It is a vision of 'Power corrupts'.

You will understand that what saddened me most was the tone of disappointment in your letter. If I had been sceptical of my work, I would simply have felt that you had caught me out. But I thought I was doing well, and within the limits I have set for myself, I still do.

The first story is by far the most shapeless, the most difficult and the most loaded.

The story of the Knight with the Two Swords is more direct but not less mysterious.

Finally, and I won't labour the point after this, I feel that I am reaching towards something valuable. It doesn't sound like me because I don't want it to. And it occurs to me to wonder whether you would prefer that I don't send the stories as they are done, but wait until the very end when the between chapters are in place. I had thought at the end of four or four hundred and fifty pages, to go back and complete that part, since it will be one volume, before going on. There may be two versions, one simply the translation and the other the translation plus the inner chapters. As for the translation I am sure of one thing – it is the best by far of any that has been done. But you must let me know about this. On this end— Mais, je marche!

To Ero – Somerset, 14 May 1959

Now I have thought a day and throbbed through a night since I rewrote the letter. Also I have corrected somewhat the copy enclosed. The first was uncorrected, and I still feel about the same. Maybe I am not doing it well enough. But if this is not worth doing as I am trying to do it, then I am totally wrong, not only about this but about many other things, and that is of course quite possible. Alan Lerner is making a musical about King Arthur and it will be lovely and will make a million-billion dollars – but that isn't what I want. There's something else. Maybe in my rush to defend myself I've missed what I wanted to say. Maybe I'm trying to say something that can't be said or do something beyond my ability. But there is something in Malory that is longer-lived than T. H. White and more permanent than Alan Lerner or Mark Twain. Maybe I don't know what it is – but I sense it. And as I have said – if I'm wrong then it's a real whopping wrongness.

But, can't you see – I must gamble on this feeling about it. I know it isn't the form the present-day ear accepts without listening but that ear is somewhat trained by Madison Avenue and radio and television and Mickey Spillane. The hero is almost bad form unless he is in a Western. Tragedy – true tragedy – is laughable unless it happens in a flat in Brooklyn. Kings, Gods and Heroes— Maybe their day is over, but I can't believe it. Maybe because I don't want to believe it. In this country I am surrounded by the works of heroes right back to man's first entrance. I don't know how the monoliths were set up in the circles without tools but there was something more involved than petty thievery and schoolboy laziness and the anguish of overfed ladies on the psycho couch. Someone moved a whole lot of earth around for something beyond 'making a buck'. And if all of this is gone, I've missed the boat somewhere. And that could easily be.

I feel sad today – not desperate but questioning. I know I'll have to go along with my impulse. Maybe it will get better as Malory got better – and he did. If when I've worked the summer away and the fall – if it still seems dull, then I will stop it all, but I've dreamed too many years – too many nights to change direction. I never thought this work would be intensely popular, but I did believe it would have a constant audience, not changed but made available. I changed myself because I was sick of myself, dropped my tricks because I didn't believe in them any more. A time was over, and maybe I was over. I might just possibly be wiggling like a snake cut in two which we used to believe could not die until the sun set. But if that's it, I'll have to go on wiggling until the sun sets.

Nuts! I believe in this thing. There's an unthinkable loneliness in it. There must be.

To Ero – Somerset, May 1959

I am moved by your letter with the implied trust in something you don't much like. Surely I did not intend to misinform you. It seems that we were not talking about the same things. One of the difficulties seems to lie in the great length of the work. I wish I could discuss this with Chase. I agree with him about the breaks for volumes. But I am more and more reluctant about the Roman episode. It has never seemed to belong. There isn't much of any story. The two great and continuing stories are those of Lancelot and Tristan. The Lancelot breaks in the middle, Tristan comes in and then Lancelot and the Grail sequence and the morte. I am going to think very carefully about leaving the Emperor business out. The first volume then would go to the beginning of Tristan. I think at this moment, subject to change, of course, to do the translation of all of that – leaving out the Emperor business perhaps – then going back – reworking the translations with even more freedom – then putting in my own work between the stories, which would embody a great deal of the knowledge Chase and *I* have accumulated. Now that would make a very deep and hefty first volume. Also we would then know what we have and whether the method stands up. It should also be complete enough to go towards publication as it stood. If it did not stand up, and I must believe that it might – *then* to continue with Tristan and finally to the Grail and the morte. I think this would be the test volume. If it turned out to be no good, we could either abandon or change the whole plan. Now that means from the beginning to the end of the first part of Lancelot leaving Claudius Emperor out. What do you *both* think of this as a method ? It is more than possible that I might finish this first volume in draft at least before I come home. If I do the whole thing and then find it no good – that's too much. Think about this please.

I know one of the problems concerning these things I am sending to you and again it arises out of my failure to explain. Or in explaining have not gone far enough. These are translations in which I have tried to extract the meaning in Malory as closely and as completely as I can. They are *not* the final form. Once done, they will be the working material and I shall not go back to Malory again but shall work from my own translation which by that time will have no relation to Middle English. I know this is a long way around but it is the only way I have of avoiding the compelling and infectious Malorian prose. So bear with me a little. I think I know what I want, and I'm trying to get it.

To Chase – Somerset, 22 May 1959

Thank you for your letter of confidence. One can go on in the face of opposition, but it is much easier not to. I am learning something new every day. In a matter this large it is impossible to carve out a bunch in advance. It is like the wood carving I do – the wood has its way too – and indicates the way it wants to go, and to violate its wishes is to make a bad carving.

Yesterday I finished the first part of Morgan – called Accolon. A fabulous character and quite a dish. I am going to have an essay about Malory's feeling about women.

I am a bad scholar and moreover have not many references at hand and beyond that find myself sceptical of many of the references that are *blandly accepted* just because they have been printed. Sometimes a truth lies deeper in a name or an appellation than anywhere else. Now here is a premise, a kind of inductive speculation that should delight your heart. It came to me in the night, dwelling on the fact of Cadbury. Look at the place names – Cadbury, Caddington, Cadely, Cadeleigh, Cadishead, Cadlands, Cadmore, Cadnaur, Cadney, Cadwell. According to Oxford 'Place Names' the first element refers to someone named Cada—

Then there are the Chad places – beginning with Chadacre and lots more ending with Chadwick. These are attributed to Ceadvalla – the Celtic counterpart. There are many other variations. Now look at the cad words in the dictionary and see where so many of them point, Caddy, cadet, caduceus, Cadi is Arabic and you come back to Cadmus, a Phoenician, founder of Thebes, bringer of the alphabet to Greece. Caduceus – symbol of the herald, later of knowledge, particularly medical, and the snake staff still used on licence plates. Cadmus sowed the dragon's teeth also, which may be another version of the tower of Babel, but the main thing is that the myth ascribes his origin to Phoenicia. Were the Trojans forerunners of the Phoenicians ? Geographically they should have been the same group and the Brut name is strongly entrenched here as well as the tradition of Troy.

But let's go back to the Cads. We know that in 1,500 to 2,000 years the only foreigners to come to these islands were Phoenicians, that they brought design, ideas, probably writing, and certainly ideas straight out of the Mediterranean. They also concealed these islands from the world so that their source of metals was not known – this to protect their monopoly of the tin which made all of the bronze in the then known world. And where did these Phoenicians come from ? Well, their last stopping place and probably their greatest outland port was Cadiz – a Phoenician word which has never changed.

Is it beyond reason to conjecture that the Cad names as well as the Cead words, the Cedric words, came from Cadiz, which came from Cadmus, who is the mythical bringer of culture from outside ? Such things have a very long life. Kadi is a judge to this day, Caddie a gentleman, Cadet a noble. Caduau a gift or a bribe. I know nothing of the Semitic languages. But I'll bet you will look to the Hebrew and other Semitic origins of the syllable Cad – or Kad right back to the Mesopotamians – Babylons, Tyres, etc. Why would not these rich and almost mythical people who came in ships and brought curious and beautiful things have names of their origin – the people from Cadiz, the people of Cadmus, the bringer of knowledge, the messengers of the gods. They must have been godlike to the Stone Age people. They would have brought their gods, their robes of Tyrrhenian purple; their designs are still *on* early British metal and jewellery. Their factors would have lived with the local kids and their memory seeped into the place names. There is little doubt that they brought Christianity to these islands before it even got a start in Rome.

In none of my reference books can I find even a hint of this thesis. It is supposed after fifteen hundred years of constant association with the West Country the one bright and civilized people disappeared, leaving no memory. I just don't believe it. I think the very earth shouts of them.

What do you think?

To Chase, Somerse, 25 May 1959
(*from Elaine S.*)

This is more or less in the nature of a P.S. to the letter I wrote to Elizabeth Saturday. Over the weekend John read the most recent ms. to me, and it is a *great deal* better. He also has been restudying Vinaver's notes on Malory, and points out to me, 'Malory cut and re-edited the French, so I can do the same with Malory.' I think the Steinbeck version is slowly coming to life, and I just am anxious for you to know. He says this first draft is just that, and he will make his version from it. I said, 'Why didn't you say so?' and he was indignant! You see, it is evolving slowly. I think both of you have given great help in the evaluation.

To Chase – Somerset, 8 June 1959

I have been thinking about E.O. You know in the many years of our association there has been hardly a moment without a personal crisis. There must be many times when she wishes to God we all were in hell with our backs broke. If we would just write our little pieces and send them in and take our money or our rejections as the case might be and keep our personal lives out of it. She must get very tired of us. And also this must be a weary pattern. We pile our woes on her and they must always be the same woes. If she should suddenly revolt, I wouldn't be a bit surprised. Instead of gloriously clean copy she gets excuses, and mimes and distress and former and future and bills. Writers are a sorry lot. The best you can say of them is that they are better than actors and that's not much. I wonder how long it is since one of her clients asked her how *she* felt – if ever. It's a thankless business. How sharper than a serpent's tooth to have a writer. The smallest activity of a writer it seems is writing. If his agonies, his concupiscence, his errors in judgement were publishable the world would be navel deep in books. One of the happier aspects of television is that it draws off some of these activities. Patience on a manuscript.

Now back to Malory or rather my interpretation of his interpretation to be followed, I hope, by my interpretation of my interpretation. As I go along, I am constantly jiggled by the arrant nonsense of a great deal of the material. A great deal of it makes no sense at all. Two thirds of it is the vain dreaming of children talking in the dark. And then when you are about to throw it out in disgust, you remember the Congressional Record or the Sacco and Vanzetti case or 'preventive war' or our national political platforms, or racial problems that can't be settled reasonably or domestic relations, or beatniks, and it is borne in on you that the world operates on nonsense – that it is a large part of the pattern and that knight errantry is no more crazy than our present-day group thinking, and activity. This is the way humans are. If you inspected them and their activities in the glass of reason, you would drown the whole lot. Then when I am properly satiric about the matter I think of my own life and how I have handled it and it isn't any different. I'm caught with the silly breed. I am brother to the nonsense and there's no escaping it. But even the nonsense is like the gas and drug revelations of the Pythoness at Delphi which only make sense after the fact.

I am working now on Gawain, Ewain, and Marhalt, having lost a little time over the issues of the boys. It's so full of loose ends, of details without purpose, of promises unkept. The white shield for instance – it is never mentioned again. I think I am breathing some life into it but maybe not enough. As I go along I do grow less afraid of it. But there must be some reverence for the material because if you reject these stories you reject humans.

There are two kinds of humans on the creative level. The great mass of the more creative do not think. They are deeply convinced that the good world is past. Status quo people, feeling they cannot go back to the perfect time, at least fight not to go too far from it. And then there is creative man who believes in perfectibility, in progression – he is rare, he is not very effective but he surely is different from the others. Laughter and tears – both muscular convulsions not unlike each other, both make the eyes water and the nose run and both afford relief after they are over. Marijuana stimulates induced laughter, and the secondary effect of alcohol false tears, and both a hangover. And these two physical expressions are expendable, developable. When a knight is so upset by emotion that he falls to the ground in a swound, I think it is literal truth. He did, it was expected, accepted. And he did it. So many things I do and feel are reflections of what is expected and accepted. I wonder how much of it is anything else.

Isn't it strange how parallels occur. About a month ago, while doodling in preparation for work, I wrote a short little piece and put it in my file where it still remains. I quote from it.

When I read of an expanding universe, of novas and red dwarfs, of violent activities, explosions, disappearances of suns and the birth of others, and then realize that the news of these events, carried by lights waves, are records of things that happened millions of years ago, I am inclined to wonder what is happening there now. How can we know that a process and an arrangement so long past has not changed radically or revised itself ? It is conceivable that what the great telescopes record presently does not exist at all, that those monstrous issues of the stars may have ceased to be before our world was formed, that the Milky Way is a memory carried in the arms of light.

To Ero – Somerset, June 1959 (Thursday)

Alas! I can only agree with you – Arthur is a dope. It gets so that you want to yell– Not that again! Look out – he's got a gun! the way we used to in the old movies when our beloved hero was blundering stupidly into the villain's lair. Just the same as Arthur. But it goes further and even gets into the smart ones. Consider Morgan – without checking whether her plan to murder Arthur had succeeded, she goes blithely ahead as though it had. But this is literature. Think if you will of Jehovah in the Old Testament. There's a God who couldn't get the job as apprentice in General Motors. He makes a mistake and then gets mad and breaks his toys. Think of Job. It almost seems that dopiness is required in literature. Only the bad guys can be smart. Could it be that there is a built-in hatred and fear of intelligence in the species so that the heroes must be stupid ? Cleverness equates with evil almost invariably. Is a puzzlement, but there it is.

I have a feeling that I am really rolling now in the stories of Ewain, Gawain, and Marhalt. In the first place it is a better story and in the second I am opening it out. Where Malory plants an incident and then forgets it, I pick it up. It's a long one and my version even longer in some parts, but it is also cut in parts. I am having fun with it.

I am constantly amazed at the feeling about women. Malory doesn't like them much unless they are sticks. And dwarfs – there is almost a virility fear here. Now in the fifteenth century people were not dopes. We know from the Paston Letters and from many other sources that they were demons and also very capable of taking care of themselves. The fifteenth-century man had no more likeness to the Arthurian man than the Old West had to the Western. But in both cases there is the yearning for the childlike simplicity of a time when the Great were not clever. Someone was clever enough to keep Malory in jail the last part of his life without ever bringing him to trial. No virtue is involved here. Some damn fine intelligence didn't want him around. The world was not young and innocent when Malory wrote. It was old and sinful and cynical. And it is not innocent now when the slick story and the Western flourish. Can it be that the true literature of the future will be Mickey Spillane ? It is at least conceivable.

Yesterday afternoon after work I went up on Cruch Hill where some schoolboys are excavating under the direction of good people from the British Museum. A neolithic fort and on top an Iron Age fort and on top of all a Roman temple. The neolithic people built a wonderful system of walls and defences. My God! the work they did and the earth and stone they moved. A fantastic amount of work. And all of Somerset is littered with these great works. There must have been a very large and highly organized population. You don't push mountains around without machinery unless you have lots of people. And the size and consistency of the design indicates not only a tight organization but a great continuity. The work – all in one pattern – must have gone on for generations. The lines are clean and straight and the intention did not change. It is remarkable.

To Ero – Somerset, June 1959 (Sunday)

Elaine is at church and I am in the middle of my day's work. She said this morning – 'You ask Elizabeth to take care of the damndest things. I'll bet she would like a client who just writes and sends in stories.'

And it is true, too. She is right. As a client I have always been a mess. Thank heaven there has been a little profit to justify it.

That being so, I think it would be good to write a letter to you telling you I know how much you do and always have done and second, a letter in which there are no pains, complaints, requests, explanations, or excuses. Wouldn't that be a relief ?

I can tell you one thing I have finally faced though – the Arthurian cycle and practically all lasting and deep-seated folklore is a mixture of profundity and childish nonsense. If you keep the profundity and throw out the nonsense, some essence is lost. These are dream stories,

353

fixed and universal dreams, and they have the inconsistency of dreams. Very well, says I – if they are dreams, I will put in some of my own, and I did.

Now much later, and I have had a wonderful work day, filled with excitements probably not justified but enjoyed just the same. It's a crazy story but it means something somewhere.

Now I've talked about myself steadily for months. How are you? Are you content? Will you take some vacation? Will you go out to Sag Harbor? More than anything I can think of I wish you could slip over here and settle into Byre, which is a very pleasant room. I wish you could feel this place, just let it seep into you. I haven't mentioned this but I have been trying to beam a thought in your direction hoping it would pick up force along the way so that one morning you would know you had to come here without even knowing why. I have sat sometimes arguing with you, even wrestling with your mind and trying to topple your arguments. 'Nonsense. It's expensive. I don't like the country. I have no reason to go.' 'Well, it isn't nonsense and it isn't even expensive. It isn't really country. It's the most inhabited place you ever felt and there's a goodness here after travail. There's something here that clears your eyes.' And you: 'My eyes are as clear as I want them to be. It's not sense.' Me: 'Well, there's something here that I think is related to you. I just want you to see it and feel it. It has meaning – I don't know what it means but I know how it feels.' And then you toss your head like a pony the way I've seen so often and you set your chin and change the subject. 'Then you won't consider it?' 'No.' 'I'll keep after you. There's a power here I'll put to work on you.' 'I wish you wouldn't. Let me alone.' 'It's more than meadows and hedges – it's much more than that. There are voices in the ground.' 'Go away.' 'Well, I won't. I'll wait until you are asleep and I'll send a squadron of Somerset fairies to zoom around you like mosquitoes – real tough fairies.' 'I'll bug-bomb them.'

To Ero – Somerset, July 1959 (Saturday)

The work comes sweetly and well. I am not going to send any until I have enough to show you the new departure, which I happen to love. Also I have a great plan for unity. But as I said – in a previous letter – I am not going to talk myself out of it. I do that too much. This much I can tell you though – if it continues this well I can go home in October with a free heart, knowing I can finish it anywhere. And it is beginning to take a whole roundness of form in my mind and millions of ideas are swarming and breeding and that's the best life possible to to me. It does take so long to get it though.

Now some words for Chase. It will be repetition for him since I am sure he has told me before. I should just like to have it all in one letter. About the first of the month I or rather we are going into Wales. I wish Chase would lay out an itinerary. I want to catalogue it in my mind so I can have access to it in memory wherever I go to finish it.

I'm glad Shirley likes the Triple Quest. That's its name by the way. I assure you the Lancelot is much better. Finally I have unlocked the door.

Now let me tell you about a miracle, of the kind that happens here. Day before yesterday I was writing about a raven, quite a character and a friend of Morgan le Fay. Yesterday morning at eight I was at my desk and there was a great croaking outside my door. I thought it was a giant frog. It awakened Elaine sleeping upstairs. She looked out the window and there was a huge raven pecking at my door and croaking – a monster bird. The first we have seen. Now how do you account for that ? I wouldn't even tell it if Elaine the Truthful hadn't seen it also.

To Chase – Somerset, 3 July 1959
(*from Elaine S.*)

Yesterday we drove through Plush Folly, a new addition to our place-name list. It is in Dorset. We had a lovely afternoon. John is taking one of his knights questing along the country and wanted some geographical details. Now that's the way to take advantage of being in England. We drove down to below Dorchester and climbed Maiden Castle, a vast hill-fortress which goes back to 2000 BC. It's a marvellous and enormous flat-topped hill with eight ditches, deep and steep-sided. You could sure defend one hell of a lot of people up there. From the top, we could look down on Dorchester and see clearly the form of the Roman city. The four Roman entrances to the town are now lined with trees and called The Walks.

We also went to Cerne Abbas to see the Dorset Giant, the several hundred feet high man carved out in the chalk hill. He is ferocious and swings a club over his head. He also is extremely phallic. John says some ancient people put him there as a symbol of fertility. I think they put him there to scare the tar out of passing ladies, who would then go home and say to their husbands, 'Don't stand there and tell me you are going to fight *them* ?'

I have your letter about Bodmin Moor and Caerleon on Usk, along with the map you marked, in the car with our other maps and guide books. John says he wants to go to both places soon.

We are up to our ears in Devonshire clotted cream, as this is the height of the strawberry and raspberry season. Our berries come from

Discove garden – and sometimes I make our own clotted cream. Whenever we are given cream by our friends, I stand it in a shallow pan on the warm part of the stove for six hours, then move it to the cool stone floor of the kitchen for several hours. When it becomes clotted, I skim it and chill it in the fridge and serve it with berries. Delicious! – I couldn't do without the *Constance Spry Cookery Book*; use it daily. I have learned to make a proper Indian curry. The ingredients are bought at the Bombay Emporium in London. We will have a curry dinner party in the fall.

I hope to have ms. tomorrow. I went by and jogged Mrs Webb about it Wednesday. She was typing a passage in which John has a maiden wash a knight's undergarments and hang them on a gooseberry bush to dry, before they spent the night in the forest. She wanted to know if I knew that in England babies come from under gooseberry bushes! He didn't and was delighted.

To Ero and Chase – Somerset, 13 July 1959

Of course, I did no writing while away. Always think I will but I don't. However, lots of thinking. I'm going to throw out my beginning of Lancelot and start again because I think I know it now. And after the Lancelot, I rather think I'll go back to the beginning and start over. Maybe I have my boy now. It does take time.

Chase, thanks for the Maiden Castle work. I am still drawn to my own suspicion. This is mainly because I know how it worked in Mexico. Spaniards came in, heard an Aztec word, and named the place the word sound in Spanish. There are hundreds of them. For instance Cuernavaca – cow horn. Aztec name was Cuanahuatl, which sounds a little like cuernavaca only it means the Place of the Eagles. *But* it was the sound that mattered, not the meaning. And I suspect that Maiden in Maiden Castle is a sound in a previous language and I'll bet it is the Indo-European root word mei meaning changed or heaped or not natural. And the great earthworks are 'heaps'.

But all of this is only interesting. I am trying to work on the 'people' of the stories. I'm glad the Triple Quest pleases you a little, Chase. At least it gives some reason for the three damsels. The Lancelot as I see the beginning now begins to make some sense to me and even in terms of the reason for the Grail quest, which comes later. It has always been considered that first comes the Grail and then the Quest. But suppose a quest was required and the Grail was placed as a target. But I am not going to do more trial runs. I'll send it when it is finished as a *fait accompli*. Perhaps I have done too many dry runs. But I feel better about it.

To Ero – Somerset, 25 July 1959

I sent the very first part of Lancelot to you yesterday after having received your wire. I think it is wise to send it. If it should happen to be lost in the mail I have a carbon, faint but quite readable as a safety factor. And I never had anything lost anyway. This ms. is beginning to be somewhat like what I want. You will see that little by little, while adhering to the story, I am putting my own construction on matters which are obscure and eliminatings things which either were meaningless or have become so. And if this work has some quality of a dream – why all life has that. Most people live in a half-dream all their lives and call it reality. Also, whenever by suggestion I can tie the story to the present by developing a situation which was true in both, I have done so. And since this is a curious decorative story I have tried to give it some quality of medieval painting, a little formal but not always. Mostly I have had to make the people come alive. In this first part and it is far from finished, Lancelot has not yet had to face his dual self. He is morally untested. That's why I love Lancelot I guess. He is tested, he fails the test and still remains noble.

You are worried about Vinaver's influence on the kind of work I am doing. I am not sure, of course, but I think really he will be the first to applaud it. He isn't the stodgy scholar you think. And he knows the changes others have made. I would almost bet he'd approve, and if he didn't I will be so well along by then that I don't think it would have much effect. I'm beginning really to love the work for itself and I am letting what mind I have go to its own sources. Back pathing – I think the analysis of witchcraft is rather brilliant, and so far as I know – new.

I agree with you about continuing from where I am and only at the last going back to the beginning. Also I am going to try to eliminate all of the side stories in this first draft and aim right down the main line. Tristan is another story completely. It can come later. But the story I want now is Lancelot, Arthur, Guinevere — Anyway, I am going to see what I can do with that main central and unified theme. And do you know, the title of that should not be Arthur but Lancelot. He's my boy. I can feel him. And I'm beginning to feel Guinevere and out of that I will get to feel Arthur.

To Ero – Somerset, 28 July 1959

Difficulty with work today – partly a mean decision about form and elimination. That damned Malory has got this quest in his teeth and is running mad with fighting. Also he gets so enthusiastic about curing crowds with a piece of bloody cloth that he gets all mixed up about who and why. Then he has Lancelot masquerading in Sir Kay's armour and suddenly forgets all about it. And I have to excavate these things and give them some point or else cut them out. About three out of eight adventures are really good, but they aren't the ones he likes at all. It is very difficult. I think I have maintained a fairish high level of interest so far in this story and I don't want to let it peter out in the usual Malory manner. Is a puzzlement. But if I just keep plugging away, I'll find a way out of it. I have to. The best way is the simplest but it takes an awful lot of thought to be simple.

I had a good letter from Shirley. I am terribly glad she likes the Triple Quest. As I know – one will choose the quest most like himself. I hope you will like the part of the Lancelot I sent. And I hope to finish this first part of the old boy's life this week and get it off to you. After this, his life grows more complicated. This first part might be called the childhood of a knight – full of wonders. But Lancelot has some pretty damned adult problems to face later, problems by no means gone from the world.

To Ero – Somerset, 28 July 1959

I should finish this piece today if all goes well, but it is early in the morning and I will start a note to you. You will find in this whole section a greater departure than the rest. It is above all a magical section, you might call it the innocence section of a life where dragons and giants dwell, the inside ones that come later. I have eliminated a number of the more obscure adventures in Malory, but others I have greatly expanded in a way that might deeply shock the master. I have the last scene of the section to do today and it is a hard one. Also, if it should grow as some of the others have, I might not get it finished. I hope I do, but it doesn't matter. As an exercise in images this has been very interesting to do. Throughout I have tried to needle the imagination to go further, but I have no idea whether it is successful. In this part I have tried it out to be a living wall painting, formal, a little florid and unreal, and yet having all the qualities of reality. What I want to be more than anything is believable. Now Lancelot, so far, is not a terribly complicated character, but I have one coming up today – Guinevere – who is a doodle. I think I have a line on her but we will see.

Later Sunday— Well there it is finished, dag nab it. Rough it is but it will have to stand on its own feet now. And tomorrow I'll get it off to you if the post office is open.

To Chase – Somerset, 1 August 1959

I've not written much lately because as you will see by the ms. being
sent on, I've been mazed in work. I finished the last episode in the
first book of Lancelot yesterday after a long and hard rough and
tumble, very satisfying, and I am quite able to say without vanity that
for the first time it makes sense, for that matter that the whole
necromantic climate makes sense. I feel that I am getting somewhere
at last. Today I have to tie the whole series of quests into one packet,
develop two characters, give reasons for the whole thing and finally
make a transition into the next Lancelot. But it feels good. The fury of
writing has come into it. You will find it very rough but that won't
matter. The essence is there and the fabric. And only you will be
aware of the mass of reading that went into it. It is crammed with the
medieval, I hope inserted so subtly that it does not protrude as
scholarship.

I keep asking you to do things for me and here's another. I use Cross
ballpoints now for writing. They are particularly good for carbons,
being thin, firm, and heavy in weight. I have three of them – one pretty
badly beat up. I think you know. I bought some refills and Mary
Morgan sent more and still I am running out. I love to switch pencils
because they seem to tire and need a rest before I do. Could you then
send me by air mail two pens and the following refills – eight with the
finest line they make, three with a medium line, and two with a heavy
line and all with the blackest ink they make ? I'm scared I will run out
and I become such a creature of habit when I am writing well that a
change irritates me.

Must get to work now. I would like to get the end of the first
Lancelot in the mail to Elizabeth before the weekend.

To Chase – Somerset, 9 August 1959

The Trip was pretty good, I saw most of the things I wanted – largely
having to do with waterways, topography colours, etc. Caerleon was
fine and Usk even better.

Also there was the typed first part of Lancelot. And a remarkable
good job of typing too. I haven't checked too closely but it seems very
accurate. And yes, I am going to follow the Lancelot now into the
second part. I see no reason to break it with the long Tristan. So – any
notes you may have will be welcome. I'll have to read for a few days
before I start because I will put Lancelot in no more long and
meaningless adventures unless they contribute to the development of
the fates of the three people.

I have been waiting for you to catch up with the anachronisms, Chase.
I knew all about them and put them in intentionally but that doesn't
mean they won't be eliminated. I have thought so much about that.
Indeed it is one of the greatest of the many problems, and perhaps this
must be dealt with in an opening essay. Where do you place Arthur?
Malory believed he lived in the fifth century since he had Galahad take
the Siege Perilous in 454 after the birth of Christ. He then proceeded to
put his knights in fifteenth-century armour and impose the twelfth-
thirteenth-century code of knighthood against a curious depopulated
and ruined countryside, which reminds us of England after the first
plague and ruined as the Wars of the Roses made it. His cities were
fairy-tale, even Walt Disney affairs. But how would you dress a fifth-
century dux bellorum, if you chose that time, particularly one who was
Roman by breed and background? I know what the late Roman heavy
cavalry wore and it had no relation to fifteenth-century cap-a-pie plate
armour. The jousting spear was unknown, chivalry had not been
invented.

One thing Malory did – he placed his time as BEFORE. Now there is a
curious time and one I have tried to adopt. Time interval in the past is
a very recent conception. Julius Caesar found no difficulty in being
descended from Venus and didn't feel the event very remote.
Herodotus makes his past a flat picture. Galahad is grandson eight
times removed of Joseph of Aramathea and Lancelot seventh degree
descended from Jesus Christ, although how that was accomplished I
do not know. I am not being didactic here. And I may change after
discussion. I have the following choices – I can choose a period and
stick with it, making this whole work a period piece, which I don't like
because these stories are universal; or I can, as did all the others, make
the past a large composite curtain called 'before'. Now that is actually
how most people see the past. In this pattern the lake village and the
Tuscany merchant can both operate because both belong to the
'before'. The only things that cannot enter are the things of the
'present', the 'now'. But on the other hand the human problems must
all be of the now. Malory put all of his fifteenth-century problems in
the 'before'. And I must put the problems of our time in the 'before'.
I want you to argue with me about this. Maybe I am wrong. I believe
these stories to be moral parables. Aesop put his wisdom and his
morals in the mouths of animals. I must put it or rather them in the
mouths of knights but it is the present I am writing about just as it was
with Malory. Oddly enough, if I make it a period piece, it becomes
their problem. But by setting it against a huge, timeless, almost formal

curtain of the 'before', I hope to make it doubly true of the 'now'. Do you see at all what I mean ? And is it valid ? I do feel that my introduction should deal with this problem, though. But we will discuss all of this long before we see print.

To Ero – Somerset, 22 August 1959

The work doesn't jell. You know that and so do I. It isn't one piece yet. There is a time when all the preparation is done when it has to take shape and no one can do that but I. It must become one thing and that it hasn't as yet. Then I got to thinking that I am here and a room here is like a room in New York. I can bite my nails anywhere. And so I am going to spend my last time seeing rather than writing, storing things up. We hope to sail home about 15 October on the *Flandre* if we can get a reservation. The last two weeks or ten days we will spend in London. Lots I want to see there too. Then I will have a storehouse to draw on. And I am much better when I have seen a place. We'll do the adjacent areas until September and when the traffic thins we'll go farther afield. And it will be just the two of us. I can't travel with anyone else. Then once home, I'll be on my own. And it is properly called the lonesomest profession in the world. Maybe then it will take form. Who knows ? But there is a point beyond which no one can help until it is done. Then of course it is different.

But I think I am right about the storing process. I want to know the whole coastline from the Bristol Channel to Land's End. I learned so much from seeing the lake and noting the tides. And tides were very important.

Gerald Wellesley called to say that Sir Philip Antrobus, who owns both Stonehenge and Amesbury Abbey (where Guinevere died), is one of his oldest friends and will be delighted to give us the run of the place, which we will do as soon as I have a reply to a note. Now there's a name, *Antrobus*. Oxford 'Place Names' has no original but says it is hardly English. I'll look up the family in Burke's as soon as I can get over to Alex Barclay's. Might it not be simply the Greek word *anthropos*, meaning a man ? It surely isn't like any other British name I ever heard. Anyway, we will spend time there probably next week. The whole Salisbury complex fascinates me. It is probably the oldest centre of population in all England. Maybe Sir Philip can get me access to Stonehenge to see closely the raising of the fallen stones now being done by the Ministry of Works. I want to see what was underneath. Might be more crossed axes. I will surely take my magnifying glasses so I can inspect closely. Also I want to take a long and critical look at Old Sarum. Sometimes when I squint my eyes I can see things truly. I spent most of the day Elaine was in London up on Cadbury hills wandering alone in the ditches. I know now why Caerleon is where it is but I have never read it. That's what I mean by tides. If in a boat, you catch an incoming tide at the mouth of the Usk, it will take you to Caerleon on one tide. And the same is true coming back. These things were very important. I know a lot about Camelot since wandering there by myself. It's a matter of sensing 'how it was'.

To Chase – Somerset, 27 August 1959

This morning I wrote my ninth letter to the Customs and Excise Office in London re ballpoint pens. I have had to get a licence to import, four letters, fill in forms, three letters. I have now told them if they cannot deliver the damn things to confiscate them and throw them in the ocean. Once you get involved with any government bureau, you are in trouble. I could probably sell my correspondence to *Punch*.

Yesterday to Amesbury and spent the day with the Antrobus who owns it and until recently owned Stonehenge. He took us all over the place. Nothing left of the early church except suggestions.

Their tradition (family) is that the name Amesbury or Almsbury comes from Ambrosius Aurelius and that this was the seat of that family and hence the property of Arthur, this being the reason Guinevere was sent back to it. In the church there is a carved head they presume to be that of Aurelius Ambrosius, but on looking closely I found a crown of fleur de lys. They are charming people. He is eighty-three and looks sixty. I asked about his odd name, Antrobus. It is a Cheshire family, quite an old baronetcy. He said they thought it might come from entre bais of French origin. He was astonished and interested when I suggested it might be the Greek word *anthropos*. If El Greco could live in Spain and Xeno in Greece, why not Antropos in England ? The idea delighted him.

Going to Glastonbury today to watch more digging. Next week we go south to cover the whole Cornwall complex. We may be gone a week or ten days. All storing up for the future. I am dissatisfied with my whole approach, completely dissatisfied. Maybe something will emerge. I don't know.

I'll write later and give you future plans. We plan to leave here 1 October, go to London for two weeks, and sail for home on the fifteenth on *Flandre* if we can get space.

Isn't it odd that Malory, who knew the route from Amesbury to Glastonbury, didn't mention Stonehenge although he had to pass it. I think I know why. But will tell you that when I see you.

To Ero – Somerset, 10 September 1959

It was a very good trip. We were out eight days and I now know the coast from the Thames to the Bristol Channel in great detail. Someday I will do the Welsh coast out around St David's Head and on up and some further day the east coast. Coasts seem to be very important to me. I don't quite know why.

As for my own work – I am completely dissatisfied with it. It just sounds like more of the same, a repetition of things I have written before. Maybe the flame has gone out. That has been known to happen and I don't know why it should not happen to me. I put things down with excitement and they turn out to be the same old stuff, nothing new or fresh, nothing that hasn't been said better. Maybe the future is clever little trick pieces with a semblance of originality and not any depth.

Anyway, we can discuss this when I get home. I have my arms full of material and I don't know what to do with it and I am too old to kid myself about it.

Please tell Chase that I finally got the pens after I had written the final letter telling them to throw them in the sea or anything else they wanted.

To Ero – London, 2 October 1959

Now about work. I have been thinking and thinking and thinking. It seems to me that I might have an answer but I would prefer to tell it to you if possible with some samples. Meanwhile I am inspecting the thought like a woman shopping in Klein's basement. It would, if I could do it, take care of most of the difficulties. Anyway, I'll keep going over it.

We are going to the river now. I'll write again soon.

To Ero – New York, (*undated*) 1959 (Wednesday)

I hope Chase doesn't feel that I cut him off short. I can't think of anything until I get this done. Also I stopped in and had long coffee with Pat. He sad-jokingly urges me to get to work on the Malory so he can 'live to see it'. And he isn't really joking, you know. I don't plan to write a single word on it until after 1 January. Too much yet to read and think about quietly. And Chase has such a mass of material for me.

[No correspondence on *Morte d'Arthur* from end of 1959 to below date.]

To Chase – Sag Harbor, 15 May 1965

I thoroughly agree with you that the list of ms., artifacts, and illuminations you have listed in the enclosed would be very valuable and interesting in relation to our work in showing the great distribution of the Arthurian theme as well as its almost universal acceptance, and that at a very early period. You will find these and many more evidences in Italy and I hope you will keep after it.

I have some other things I think it would be valuable for you to do, if it or rather they can be done in the course of your travels in Italy.

It would be good if you could find Professor Sapori and talk with him. He is a Florentine but he has held a history chair in the University of Pisa, and I think still does. As you know, he is the recognized authority in the economics of the Middle Ages, and since Florence was the node of the economic system of all Europe, he is well placed.

One of the Sapori's fields is the relations with the Arab traders of the period of the founding of the Amalfi League and on. As far as I know, it has never been asked whether the Arthurian cycle got a foothold in Islam and/or whether there was a parallel to be discovered. Also whether the legend can be traced to an Indo-European base. We know that the Legend of St George did come in from the East. One of the first references occurs in Egypt. It would be interesting to see whether there is any Hindi or Sanscritic name which sounds in any way like Arthur or Artu or any variations of this sound.

We know that Arthur was accepted as one of the nine worthies and sometimes of the Three Immortals, but when that came into being I for one do not know. The theme probably got into Sicily with its Norman rulers, but on the other hand it may there have run head on into the same thing coming west from the Arabs.

You should, if you possibly can, get into the Vatican Library. Permission can be got through the United States Information Service. There are very many other things to investigate and I will send them to you as they occur to me.

I hope all goes well with your plans.

To J. S. from Chase – New York, 18 June 1965

When we talked in April about the great spread of Arthurian material in all of Europe we mentioned Italy as a country where general knowledge of this material was known to the man in the street as early as 1100 AD. It was entertainment certainly, but much more.

In May I sent you a brief list of manuscripts and carvings that still survive in Italy. We both felt that if I could see and evaluate some of this material, it would prove to be helpful to you in planning your work on King Arthur. These talks resulted in a trip to Italy, just completed. The trip justifies our concept of a great interest in Arthurian material among the people of the streets as well as the people of the castles. For several centuries Arthurian stories, legends, readings were the number-one entertainment items.

In Rome the carved ivory mirror case is interesting. The best mirror case is in France at the Cluny.

At the Bargello in Florence they have a Sicilian quilt with many Arthurian scenes. This was made about 1395 AD.

In the Biblioteca Nationale in Florence there is a Venetian manuscript dated 1446, showing many of the Arthurian characters and scenes. This excellent library has more Arthurian material.

In Modena the cathedral has an archivolt over one doorway, showing Arthur, Gawain, and several other Arthurian characters; this doorway according to some scholars is dated as early as 1106. I learned in Italy that microfilm copies of any of this material you may need can be ordered. I have supplied pictures of some of these items and I will show you some additional pictures and notes.

As you have said, 'This is a never-ending search.'

To Chase – Sag Harbor, 22 June 1965

I have your letter of recent date together with your report of your findings of Arthurian material on your recent trip to Italy. Very interesting, and I think you are now convinced that the trip was necessary, as I suggested. It is true that most of the lists and pieces of puzzle are known, but as I have repeatedly pointed out, it is their position, where they are placed architecturally. For example, the placing of Arthur on an arched doorway must be evaluated through the relation to other figures on the same doorway, which is important. At various times, as you know, King Arthur was accepted as one of the 'Nine', the 'Seven', and the 'Three'. Relationships of these shifts in importance can only, because of the lack of literature, be understood by dating the buildings where they occur in relation to one another.

I would be glad if you would continue the study of the Sicilian bedspreads again, relating the figures one to another in importance. I have a strong feeling that, as in most symbolic folk art, these relationships hold a code or message which is only mysterious to us because we have not understood them.

All in all, Chase, I think your Italian investigation, while not complete, has opened a door on a new field of research and one which I hope you will want to pursue. As in most things, there are whole areas of interest and importance which have not been inspected with the new eye we are able to employ.

It is my hope that on your next trip you will find your way into the Vatican Library in Rome. As you know – fifteenth-century English gentry almost invariably appealed to the Pope in one controversy or another. I myself found some Malorian material in the Vatican, and I am sure there is more. See (Monks Kirby etc.). To the end that such future work on your part may be facilitated, I propose to write to the Monsignore who superintends the Vatican files to prepare for you permission for access and help in going through the records. I have always found these authorities extremely cooperative in any area except only the Holy Office, which is not in our pasture anyway.

And before I forget it, let me congratulate you on your recent findings. It was not only luck as you protest. It was also learning what to look for and how to see it once you found it.

I can now see light at the end of the passage of this long, long job. I hope we can soon get together and plan the clean-up operation.

Meanwhile, get some rest and prepare yourself for future effort. There's no rest for the curious.

To Ero – New York, 8 July 1965

I go struggling along with the matter of Arthur. I think I have something and am pretty excited about it but I am going to protect myself by not showing it to anybody so that after I get a stretch of it done, if it seems bad, I can simply destroy it. But right now I don't think it is bad. Strange and different, but not bad.

Daphne du Maurier
Myself When Young 95p

– the shaping of a writer

'A delightful book, full of amusing and charming stories, pinpointing the literary influences and the first stirrings of books to be written in later years, and with a happy and romantic ending' THE TIMES

'A world of famous names . . . Regent's Park and Hampstead . . . dinner parties, flirtations, grand winter holidays in Switzerland . . . Cornwall and the house by the river at Bodinnick' SUNDAY TIMES

Rebecca West
The Birds Fall Down £1.25

An engrossing recreation of the momentous events that led up to the Russian Revolution . . . seen through the eyes of Laura, eighteen-year-old daughter of an English MP and grandchild of an exiled Russian royalist – a vivid canvas, shot through with intrigue, conspiracy and murder, bringing to life the days of tumult that changed the world.

'One of the most fascinating true stories ever to have been used as a basis for fiction' BERNARD LEVIN

'An outstanding achievement' SUNDAY TELEGRAPH

W. Somerset Maugham
A Writer's Notebook 90p

Maugham kept a notebook throughout his long creative life. Here are collected fifteen manuscript volumes – omitting only the traveller's impressions of China, published separately, and some other material Maugham considered of no interest. A unique and remarkable exploration of the mind of one of this century's finest writers.

Ten Novels and their Authors 90p

When an American editor asked Maugham to list the ten best novels in the world's literature, the result was this unique and fascinating set of essays. Maugham relates each of his chosen masterpieces to the life of its author, underlining his own conviction that the novel exists in essence as 'a source of intelligent diversion'.

James Stephens
The Crock of Gold 70p

Part fantasy, part fairy tale, part polemic in the Irish war of the sexes, to explain the story of this remarkable book would be as difficult and pointless as to explain Lear's nonsense rhymes or Lewis Carrol's *Alice* stories. To read it for yourself is the only answer, the only way to discover whose was the crock of gold and where and why it was buried.

Alexandre Dumas
The Three Musketeers 80p

The first – and perhaps the greatest – of all the cloak and dagger adventures is this superb chronicle of the young Gascon D'Artagnan and the Three Inseparables, Athos, Porthos and Aramis, musketeers in the service of Louis XIII. Across the colourful canvas of France moves the crafty Cardinal Richelieu and his beautiful agent, Milady, plotting against Anne of Austria and the Duke of Buckingham, to win the favours of King Louis.

Frank Hardy
The Unlucky Australians £1.25

with an introduction by Gough Whitlam

A unique story of the Aboriginal Australian by one of Australia's foremost writers, who set out into his country's landscape in the tradition of Steinbeck's *Travels with Charley*. The outcome of his journey is this powerful evocation of the modern Aborigine and his world. To read it is to hear the voices – vivid and real – of those Australians who have been shouldered aside – The Unlucky Australians.

You can buy these and other Pan Books from booksellers and newsagents; or direct from the following address:
Pan Books, Sales Office, Cavaye Place, London SW10 9PG
Send purchase price plus 20p for the first book and 10p for each additional book, to allow for postage and packing
Prices quoted are applicable in the UK

While every effort is made to keep prices low, it is sometimes necessary to increase prices at short notice. Pan Books reserve the right to show on covers and charge new retail prices which may differ from those advertised in the text or elsewhere